ACCLAIM FOR ERIN HEALY

"Heart-pounding suspense and unrelenting hope that will steal your breath."

—TED DEKKER, *NEW YORK TIMES* BESTSELLING
AUTHOR, ON *NEVER LET YOU GO*

"*Motherless* by Erin Healy is a mesmerizing story about secrets and the lies we tell ourselves. If you loved *Gone Girl*, you will gobble this one up. Highly recommended!"

—COLLEEN COBLE, *USA TODAY* BESTSELLING AUTHOR OF
THE INN AT OCEAN'S EDGE AND THE HOPE BEACH SERIES

". . . an edgy, fast-paced spiritual thriller that will please Dekker fans."

—*LIBRARY JOURNAL* ON *STRANGER THINGS*

"Healy's fascinating plot is fast-paced and difficult to put down once started."

—*RT BOOK REVIEWS*, 4 1/2 STARS AND
TOP PICK! ON *THE BAKER'S WIFE*

"Healy's many fans will love this mesmerizing novel of supernatural suspense . . . readers who enjoyed Alice Sebold's *The Lovely Bones* might want to try this."

—*LIBRARY JOURNAL* ON *MOTHERLESS*

"*House of Mercy* is a . . . story of suspense with a bit of the supernatural. A story full of symbolism depicting the love of God. A great read that kept me turning the pages."

—LYNETTE EASON, BESTSELLING, AWARD-WINNING
AUTHOR OF THE WOMEN OF JUSTICE SERIES

"Erin Healy's *Motherless* is a complex and emotional web that drew me in and kept me spellbound. Mysterious, rich, and compelling. A masterfully told story."

"*Motherless* is part supernatural mystery, part romance from beyond the grave, and will keep you guessing until the very last minute. Erin Healy is an artist who paints magnificent images with her words."

"*Motherless* packs an incredible one-two punch as Healy delves into the darkness of our humanity and the enormity of our need for grace, redemption, and love. Her vivid imagery, compelling characters, and deft hand at suspense keep you turning the pages to the very end."

"*Motherless* is one of the most emotional novels I've read. Healy's characters are so rich and true, they pulled me into their story and wrapped me into their lives until I turned the last page. Highly recommend."

"[*Stranger Things*] is thought-provoking and engaging, and becomes even more so as the story progresses."

"A combination of suspense, mystery, religion, and even romance weaves this tale into a cohesive, compelling read."

"Fans of Ted Dekker will appreciate Healy's chilling story of the dangers on the road back to hope and faith."

—BOOKLIST ON NEVER LET YOU GO

"The adventure-filled main story and a heart-pounding supernatural spiritual element are woven together seamlessly to create a winning combination sure to appeal to readers."

—RT BOOK REVIEWS, 41/2 STARS ON NEVER LET YOU GO

HIDING PLACES

OTHER BOOKS BY ERIN HEALY

Motherless

Stranger Things

Afloat

House of Mercy

The Baker's Wife

The Promises She Keeps

Never Let You Go

WITH TED DEKKER

Kiss

Burn

HIDING PLACES

ERIN HEALY

THOMAS NELSON
Since 1798

NASHVILLE   MEXICO CITY   RIO DE JANEIRO

Published in Nashville, Tennessee, by Thomas Nelson. Thomas Nelson is a registered trademark of HarperCollins Christian Publishing, Inc.

Published in association with Creative Trust Literary Group, 5141 Virginia Way, Suite 320, Brentwood, TN, 37027.

Thomas Nelson titles may be purchased in bulk for educational, business, fund-raising, or sales promotional use. For information, please e-mail SpecialMarkets@ThomasNelson.com.

Unless otherwise noted, Scripture quotations are taken from the King James Version. Public domain. Scripture quotations marked NIV are taken from the Holy Bible, New International Version®, NIV®. Copyright © 1973, 1978, 1984, 2011 by Biblica, Inc.™ Used by permission of Zondervan. All rights reserved worldwide. www.zondervan.com. The "NIV" and "New International Version" are trademarks registered in the United States Patent and Trademark Office by Biblica, Inc.™

Publisher's Note: This novel is a work of fiction. Names, characters, places, and incidents are either products of the author's imagination or used fictitiously. All characters are fictional, and any similarity to people living or dead is purely coincidental.

Library of Congress Cataloging-in-Publication Data

Healy, Erin M.
 Hiding places / Erin Healy.
 pages ; cm
 ISBN 978-1-4016-8960-5 (softcover)
 I. Title.
 PS3608.E245H53 2015
 813'.6--dc23
 2015011118

Printed in the United States of America

15 16 17 18 19 20 RRD 6 5 4 3 2 1

For the Gleichmanns, who made legendary
hospitality a family tradition.

God sets the lonely in families.

Psalm 68:6 NIV

SATURDAY

CHAPTER 1

The Twix bar was for her grandfather. Kate sneaked into his workshop so she could tuck it into his toolbox, where he kept forbidden sweets from her grandmother's watchful eye. Grandy had diabetes, and Gran feared it. But Grandy said there was nothing to fear about occasional indulgences, and Kate believed him. Why else would two little candy bars make him so happy? Besides, if she stopped smuggling Twix into his toolbox, he might stop leaving her thank-you gifts—"old junk" that was far more interesting than anything she ever got for birthdays or Christmases. Last month, when Kate turned eleven, her mother gave her a red velvet dress weighed down with sparkling beads. Kate hoped she might outgrow it before she had any chance to wear it.

Long ago the workshop had been a garage. And before that a carriage house for buggies pulled by horses. Kate remembered the old photos that once hung in the lodge, even though Gran took them down a long time ago. Today wood dust coated the floor, and the air still smelled of stain, though Grandy had sanded and refinished the outdoor furniture way back in the spring. His domain was cozy and brightened by a line of windows and a view of pine trees.

Kate entered from the outside, where she was less likely to be spotted, and found his toolbox sitting atop a massive Masonite worktable almost as tall as she was and as wide as the queen-size beds in the lodge's guest rooms. Here Grandy repaired broken chairs and rewired old lamps and restrung the frayed cords of miniblinds and curtain trolleys. Usually he stood. The tall stool pushed under the tabletop was for her whenever she asked if she could watch.

When Kate lifted the toolbox lid to put the Twix bar inside, a bright flash made her flinch and drop the candy. After blinking the stars from her eyes she carefully raised the top again.

A contraption of springs and wires attached to the lid moved a tiny tack hammer. This was poised over an old camera with a flash cube, ready to strike the shutter release and take another picture. A sticky note bearing Grandy's neat block printing told her the rest of the story.

Can you believe this old beast still works? She's yours, Agent K. Don't let the film canister go to the bad guys.

The camera was a plastic but weighty box just bigger than a card deck. Kate put her eye to the viewfinder and framed a picture of Grandy's powerful radial arm saw, but when she pushed the shutter button nothing happened. She turned the camera over in her hands. Her thumb brushed a small lever and moved it slightly. Would it break if she pushed on it?

When Grandy's voice reached her from outside the shop, she was still trying to decide.

Though Kate was welcome here, being caught in the act of exchanging gifts ruined the fun. She ducked under the big table into the shadows of boxes and boards stacked against its legs just as he opened the door. Kate flinched when the door hit the stopper and bounced off.

"What do you mean it's gone?" Grandy demanded.

He slammed his desk chair into the nook under his computer,

then turned to a small window that overlooked the side yard, his cell phone to one ear, his fist on one hip.

"How did you lose it?"

At the answer, Grandy kicked over a small tower of five-gallon buckets. They separated and rattled around the concrete floor. With one arm he swept all of the paperwork off his desk. A paperweight hit the wall.

Kate clutched the camera and made herself as small as one of the buckets that wobble-rolled past the workbench. She knew better than to hold her breath but found it hard to breathe quietly. She'd never seen her grandfather do much more than slap a table when he was upset.

"You had no right, Gorman. It wasn't yours to risk."

Mr. Gorman was Grandy's best friend, owner of the Kwik Kash Pawnshop. Gran thought a pawnshop was a terrible place for a child to spend her time, so Grandy took Kate there at every opportunity, the easiest secret she ever had to keep. That and the one about Grandy's motorcycle, which he kept at Mr. Gorman's house. Grandy took her for rides in the summertime. Mr. Gorman, hairy as a yeti and nice as a teddy bear, always told her a knock-knock joke and then gave her a slug for the toy dispenser at the front of the store. It spit out plastic pods that held tattoo transfers, bouncy balls, and sticky men that could walk down the glass display cases that held the knives.

"No," Grandy said impatiently. "I don't know. Don't ask me to understand, 'cause I don't. I can't."

Grandy threw the phone down onto the clean surface of his desk and continued swearing, a loud rush like snow running off the mountain in spring. The desk chair rattled and squeaked as he pulled it back out and sank into it.

"I'm gonna kill him," he muttered.

Silence finally filled the workshop and lingered until Kate's tailbone ached. Her big toe began to tingle, and when it spread to her other toes and she couldn't stand it anymore, she wiggled her foot. Her shoe tapped the table leg and a nail rolled off the workbench, striking the floor like a gong.

Her grandfather sighed.

"You've been detected, Agent K." He swiveled in the chair as Kate crawled out on all fours, uneasy though he smiled. It wasn't his usual smile somehow.

"It's all right." He extended an arm to her and she stepped into a one-armed hug, nothing like his usual bear squeeze. "Even grown-up friends have fights now and then."

"I didn't mean to spy."

"I didn't mean for you to have to."

"What'd Mr. Gorman do?"

"Something stupid."

"Will it be okay?"

Grandy looked away.

"Long as you're here for hugs, girl, yes. Everything will be okay."

She showed him the camera. "It took my picture."

"Can't wait to see that one!"

"But now it won't work anymore."

"You have to advance the film first." The lever made a noise like a zipper as he pushed it farther than Kate had dared.

"Mr. Gorman should say he's sorry so you guys can make up." Kate took the camera back, and her grandfather rose to collect the scattered buckets. "That's what we have to do at school when someone does something stupid."

"Yes. Yes. I remember giving plenty of students advice like that in my day."

"Back when you were a teacher?"

"That's right."

"But grown-ups don't have to do what kids have to do," she said.

"Maybe that's true. But here's my experience: the older you get, the more you want. You think you're smarter; you think you can do what you want, get away with more." Air huffed out of the buckets as he nested them.

Kate's grandfather stared at the buckets. She lifted her camera to frame him once more but decided she didn't like this picture. Her mother often stared out the window with the same flat mouth, the same dull eyes. The expression made Kate feel unbearably lost, as if the people she loved had vanished to someplace she couldn't go and left her behind to fend for herself.

"You aren't really going to kill Mr. Gorman, are you, Grandy?"

"What?" He blinked and set the buckets on the floor. Dust floated through the faint morning light behind him. "No! Of course not. You know that's just a figure of speech. Tell you what: the truth is, I'm smarter when you're with me. So after I cool off—let's say lunchtime?—you come with me and we'll visit the Kwik Kash, and maybe you can talk some sense into me and Gorman both just by standing there and smiling. Would you do that for me?"

She nodded and kept her fears to herself. Because the Grandy who spoke to her looked like the man who put cameras in his toolbox for her to find, even sounded like him and wore his hair with the same crooked part down the left side of his head, but his eyes belonged to someone Kate didn't recognize at all.

CHAPTER 2

Charlie left his latest home with less than when he'd arrived: the clothes on his back, his favorite knit cap, and a harmonica in the cargo pocket of his outdated pants. And more: a split lip and a bruised cheek, both of which were swelling.

Home was a bridge that spanned the South Platte River and supported Interstate 25. Charlie slipped out of the cramped spaces framed by girders and plywood scraps, cushioned with sleeping bags and deteriorating foam rubber, thinking about how quiet a dozen people could be when one of their own was taking a beating. When Merridew gave Charlie the ultimatum and the fist across his face, Charlie's brothers and sisters had looked away.

Overhead, hundreds of cars hummed across the freeway slab, causing the steel arches to vibrate like a musical tone under his fingers when he played his harmonica. He half walked, half scooted down the gentle slope to the riverbank. The bridge supports framed a view of the Denver Broncos' Mile High Stadium. Tomorrow the traffic and the crowds would pour into the vast parking lot, and the bridge would hum with a different energy.

Charlie jumped the last six feet onto small round stones that shifted when he came down.

They weren't really his brothers and sisters, all those boys and girls sitting in awkward quiet up there at the top of the arches. They were just a ragtag bunch of homeless kids. It was time he moved on anyway. He was twenty-one and hadn't even needed a family—just a place to sleep and a little help pooling resources for food. That much he could find somewhere else.

"Charlie." The whisper belonged to a girl, the light-footed Eve, who was as pale as a ray of light. Her call floated down on his head.

He scooped up the South Platte in his palms and tried to hold the cold on his puffy lip. The water turned pink in his palms. Eve descended without a sound, and the rocks didn't even register her weight as she crossed them.

But Charlie didn't give her his attention until she moved away, upstream, and fished something out of the river. A gold and blue beer can. She brought it to him.

"Hold this on your cheek," she ordered.

It worked better than the water, which had already wet his shirt. The fact that the beer belonged to Merridew also helped.

"I know you don't want to rob that shop," she said. "But we can't do it without you."

Eve barely cleared five feet. She had fine gold hair, hummingbird bones, and translucent skin that combined to create a deceptively delicate package. But Charlie knew as well as anyone that she was entirely capable of taking care of herself.

He turned and walked away, pressing the numbing can to his face. The wobbling river rocks made swagger impossible, which was annoying.

"Please." Eve followed like a stray dog. "Merridew's going to make us do this whether you help or not. There's a million ways it could go wrong. I know you pretend not to care and we all hate Merridew, but we need your experience here. Tell me I'm wrong."

Charlie didn't have to tell her anything.

"We all know you have a record, breaking and entering. It's no secret."

He began the short climb from the river up to Walnut Street, which made a hairpin turn under the bridge. From here it was only a couple of miles to downtown Denver, where he could stake a corner with his harmonica and panhandle enough for a meal and time to come up with a plan.

"Charlie, don't be a jerk."

He stepped out onto the road. Eve caught up and jogged to match his long stride.

"Drogo's still just a baby," she said. "He and Ender have never done anything like this before. Who knows what might happen?"

"So convince Merridew to change his mind."

Eve reached out and took a fistful of Charlie's T-shirt, jerking him out of stride.

"The guy who gave you that right hook doesn't change his mind. Look at me."

Charlie twisted toward her but she didn't let go of his shirt. Stepping in close, she lifted her other hand to his eyes. It contained a wad of cash, wrinkled ones, maybe ten, twelve dollars. Pocket change.

"It's all I've got," she said. "Take it. Get something to eat and calm down. Then help us out. Do it for Ender. He's the closest thing you've got to a brother."

"Not a brother who'd step up when Merridew was going at me."

"Well, Merridew's the dad now."

"Not my dad."

"C'mon, Charlie. He earned the right and now's not the time to challenge him, is it?"

"You think there's such a thing as the right time? You don't even know what you've lost yet."

Until three days ago, the street family Charlie and Eve belonged to had always abided by a strict code of nonviolence. This was not the way of most street-family cultures. Charlie had seen, during long days of independence, the ways other Denver families enforced compliance and loyalty. Taxing a member's personal belongings or privileges was common. Punishment could be physical. Beating, starving, isolating, excluding. Street-family fathers with cultlike authority punished with ritual abuses. Branding, burning, cutting. Others created elaborate fantasy worlds in which members learned to play specific roles—worker, enforcer, ruler—until it became their reality. Violence was expected and necessary, both as punishment and, meted out to enemies, proof of allegiance. Violence was power.

But the man who had originally invited Charlie to join them operated differently. His approach to governing was at the same time passive and effective. In his family, no one was an enemy. Don't bother us and we won't bother you. Live and let live. Every man for himself.

It was a philosophy Charlie could subscribe to. A large enough group of people living together agreeably this way could, in theory, protect itself from the risks of living alone. Until Merridew forced his way into the ranks and proved it wasn't enough.

A drop of blood from his lip dripped onto Charlie's shirt. He touched his fingertips to the cut.

"Least Ender could've done was come ask me for himself."

"I'm asking for him," Eve said. "*I'm* asking you."

The chill of the beer can and the pure November air started to clear Charlie's head. In another time or another place he might have done it for Eve, because she had more guts than the rest of them put together, and it would be easy to care for someone like her. But she belonged to Ender. She was his to look after. What right did they have to ask him for anything?

He took the rumpled money. She used both hands to make sure he got it all.

"I'll think about it."

CHAPTER 3

Kate left Grandy's workshop by the other door, the one that led into the dim old hallways and updated slate floors of the Harrison Lodge.

Ages and ages ago the lodge had been a private mansion, a summer getaway for a rich businessman. Her great-great-grandfather. Or maybe it was three greats. No one talked much about him. Then, long before Kate was born, someone had turned the mansion into a hotel. There was an occasionally popular restaurant on the first floor, well-appointed guest rooms and a library on the second, and a third-story event center with full-circle views of peacefulness. These days the Harrisons worked like the servants they'd once employed.

The hall that Kate entered ran the full length of the lodge, front to back, and if she had gone all the way to the end she would have passed Gran and Grandy's private suite, and Great-Grandma Pearl's room opposite theirs. Here on the main floor the old people didn't have to climb stairs or venture outdoors when the weather got mean.

But instead of going that way Kate turned left and ducked under a velvet privacy rope and entered the lodge's public foyer. Light from two-story windows filled the entryway, making it the brightest space in the lodge. She looked out the window through the viewfinder of her new-old camera, wondering if this would be a good spot for snapping proof of the guests who said they had no pets and then smuggled them in anyway. She decided she could get better pictures from the library's balcony upstairs.

The hard gray floors were covered with thick area rugs to reduce noise and absorb tracked-in snow. Beyond the leaded-glass double doors was the reception desk: a shiny dark wood face, speckled granite counters, sleek new computers. An island of empty mailboxes stood in the center of the floor, and behind these, hidden from customers, a clutter of paperwork topped a second desk under the windows. Kate's mother sat here staring down the winding driveway, a paperback novel parted under her fingertips.

A red silk scarf hung from a hook just behind the counter, at the end of the old mail slots. The scarf was a recent gift to her mother from a guest who visited once a month and smelled like fish. Kate did not like him, and she was sure her mother had only accepted the gift to be polite. The horrible color gave her mother's skin the sick hue of Chef's hollandaise sauce.

Today Kate used her mother's preoccupation with her book to lift the lid on the wooden comment box attached to the wall by the front door. She pulled out two cards. As far as she could tell, the sloppy handwriting of the first card praised Chef's eggs Benedict, which was Kate's *least* favorite menu item. That oozing yellow sauce and yolk killed her appetite every time. But she put the card back in the box. It would make Gran happy for a while. The other card, written in tight, microscopic print, was a complaint about a draft in one of the rooms. Kate put this one in her jeans pocket and closed the lid just as Gran appeared from the opposite hall and crossed to the reception desk.

Kate stepped into the shadow of the potted tree standing next to the box, and when Gran called her mother's attention away from daydreams and over to a computer screen, Kate slipped away.

As she passed the desk she stretched her long arms over the hinged half door and pulled the long red scarf off its hook. She imagined herself a magician as the silk fluttered along behind her, then stuffed it up the sleeve of her turtleneck.

Beyond the reception desk was a staircase that made two right-angle turns up to the second floor. Across from this flight was the dining room, with its views of the silvery creek that cut the property in two and of the lodge's six private cottages lined up like a crescent moon. At the other end of the lodge were the kitchen, the family dining area, and a private keeping room where Kate often did her homework.

No one called after her as she passed the dining room, entered the kitchen, and paused to take deep breaths of sautéed onions and carrots. Then she turned into the keeping room, where the fireplace was cold and books and games were askew on their shelves and the mismatched afghans were piled in lumps on the sofa and chairs. Her older sister Olivia, dressed in the black slacks and white blouse of a waitress, stood before a wall mirror, trimming the ends of her false eyelashes with tiny thread scissors, one lash at a time.

"Still too long?" Kate asked.

"Gran doesn't know what she's talking about," Olivia muttered.

Kate walked through the room to the sliding glass door, pushed it open, and stepped out onto a small patio.

The cottages at the Harrison Lodge were more popular and more expensive than the rooms upstairs. They were duplexes, and each unit had a view of the creek and was tucked among evergreen trees and shrubs and vines that bloomed in summertime. The miniature houses had a pretend quality—always clean, always perfect, never as warm as a real home. Kate liked to imagine the guests as lifelike dolls.

The units were named from east to west for the order of the day: the Rising Sun, the Morning Glory, the High Noon, the Twilight, the Nocturne, and the Full Moon. Kate lived with her mother and two sisters in the Rising Sun. It was built before the others, the first and oldest cottage, which a housekeeper and a cook had shared in the prehotel days.

But Kate aimed for the neighboring building, the Morning Glory. Bear Creek bisected the property, ran all the way into Evergreen, filled the tiny lake, and then continued its downhill journey right out of town. Right now, in November, the creek ran low, so she decided to cross on the rocks rather than on the footbridge because it was more of a challenge. A successful crossing involved seven rocks and no slipping. That proved too much to ask this day, after she'd chosen a pair of slick-bottomed cowboy boots when she dressed that morning. The third stone was almost fully submerged, and she went into the water, lost her balance, and fell to one knee. The creek flooded both boots. But even that she considered a great save because she had thought to keep the camera out of the frigid water.

She slogged up the other side of the bank, smiling.

Behind the Morning Glory was an old pine tree, sticky with sap. Above the lowest branch was a forgotten birdhouse that no one tended anymore, not even Grandy, its wood warped and long stripped of its paint. It had a hinged lid like Grandy's toolbox, like Gran's comment box, and if Kate stood on the metal unit that supplied the Morning Glory with cool air in the summertime, she could just lift the lid and reach inside.

Her fingers seized a plastic bag and lifted it out. It was a clear sandwich bag with a zip top, and it was a third full of a dried green weed.

Kate jumped down with the herblike stuff in her fist, picked up the camera she'd set beneath the tree, wrapped both in the red scarf, and peeked out from behind the Morning Glory to make sure Olivia hadn't seen her. Olivia couldn't have known Kate had discovered her hiding spot or she would have picked a different place. After this, she probably would. But not long ago a little bag like this got Olivia into big trouble with the sheriff, and Grandy had to pick her up in town, and when Kate started asking questions, her grandfather said they should never mention it to the girls' mother. This was easy enough for Kate. She loved Olivia, who had pretty eyes and was nice. Much nicer than their older sister, Alyssa.

When the coast was clear Kate broke into a wet, squishy run. Her boots were made for riding, not walking, and they slipped around on the layer of fallen pine needles until she reached the pea gravel path that led to the Rising Sun. She clutched her red bundle with both hands, wishing she could do more. Wishing she could help Grandy the way she helped everyone else.

She had passed the front porch and was rounding the corner to the back of her cottage when the front door opened.

"Hey, Kat with a K!"

Kate pulled up. There was nothing nice about that voice, and the last thing Kate wanted was for Alyssa to follow her. Alyssa pulled the door closed and locked it.

"You've got your key with you, don't you, Killer Kat?"

Kate wished she were brave enough to snarl. In truth, Alyssa scared her with her sleek gray suit and pointy high heels and long fingernails turned into daggers of purple shellac.

"Is that Mom's scarf?" Alyssa accused, crossing the porch.

"Just bringing it back for her."

"I don't believe you."

Alyssa never did.

Kate felt half as tall as her sister, half as strong. Alyssa reached out and pinched the scarf, yanking it away from Kate's arms.

"Hey!"

The camera and Olivia's bag of weed tumbled to the ground. The bag bounced softly and came to rest under the edge of the porch. The camera fared worse. The flashbulb broke off and rolled in the opposite direction. The camera's door popped open, exposing the flimsy brown film beneath.

"You really should be more careful," Alyssa said. As Kate scrambled to pick up her things, Alyssa folded the scarf into a neat square and carried it off to the lodge, where she'd probably tell their mother a lie worse than Kate's.

Kate's throat tightened as she held the camera against her stomach and groped under the porch for the bag, then continued to the back of the cottage, where she had just enough room to walk between the house and a low wall of dry stacked rocks. She ran her fingers along the rustic board-and-batten siding, counting panels. She was so upset that she had to count twice. But at the right place she pushed against the wall and a narrow door sprang open, exposing a small storage room.

On the inside of the door a simple handle allowed her to pull it closed. The door worked on a kind of magnetic spring, which she could secure with a hook-and-eye latch.

The old supply closet wasn't wide enough for Kate to fully extend her arms. With a palm on each wall her bent elbows formed a W. But it was long enough to accommodate an old olive-green cot, and there was room for stacks of library books, and partly empty

Gatorade bottles, and boxes of graham crackers, and a rusty gas lamp that she used when the flashlight batteries wore out, though it hissed loudly and made the room stink.

Still clutching the broken camera with one hand, Kate turned on a small flashlight, put it between her teeth, and lifted the cot to rest it against the wall. Then she raised the trapdoor underneath, leaned it against the erect cot, and descended the iron rungs of a ladder that dropped down into an underground tunnel. It hurt to hold the flashlight between her teeth, and she hoped someone would get her the mini headlamp she'd put on her Christmas list.

The narrow tunnel that started here ran a long way off in the direction of the lodge as if hollowed out by a very big marmot. Kate knew, because she had explored it, that the cavern led to nowhere. It eventually terminated at a set of wood stairs that climbed to a blank wall. Still, though nothing but bugs and spiders could come or go down here, Kate paused to shine her light into the blackness until she was certain it held no surprises.

The lodge was full of such hiding places, where an eleven-year-old could spy out all the secrets that no one wanted her to know. And of all the things Kate knew, this fact rose above the rest: when you are eleven in a world where everyone else is twenty and up, way up, the grown-ups will try to keep you from knowing anything important at all.

Important things like these: She knew that her father was not Alyssa and Olivia's father, and that he had run off before she was born. So far she hadn't learned his name.

She also knew that Great-Grandma Pearl danced in her nightie beside the creek when she thought everyone else was asleep, even though the cottage guests would see her if they just lifted the curtains in their windows. At least one guest had complained about it on a card.

A battered army locker that had once belonged to Grandy sat at the base of the iron ladder, and it brimmed with all the things she'd hidden from her family for their own good. Kate opened the locker and set Olivia's bag on top of an old parking ticket she'd swiped when her mother fretted over the fee. This sat atop a stack of romance novels that she'd taken from her mother's bedside table because they always made her cry and then she was sad for days after. Why did grown-ups like stories with sad endings?

She pulled the stolen comment card out of her pocket and placed it on a stack of others, all finding some fault in the Harrison Lodge or in the Harrisons themselves. Next to these was a piggy bank that held Kate's savings, which had been nearly wiped out when Kate replaced the money Alyssa had stolen from the petty cash box before Gran could notice it was missing.

At the moment Kate regretted parting with her money. Maybe she should have let Alyssa get caught. Because Alyssa stole money from petty cash at least every other week, usually when she was in charge of the bank deposit.

She put the camera and its flashbulb on top of her favorite sweater, a gift from Gran that had snagged on a tree and quickly come unraveled. She didn't want Gran to see the damage, and now Grandy would be disappointed in her as well. Kate sighed.

Of all the secrets Kate hoarded, she had never shared any of them with anyone, not even her best friend, Reece. But today as she rearranged her stash, she wondered if she should tell her mother about the conversation between Grandy and Mr. Gorman. She knew what a figure of speech was, of course. Alyssa in particular was always threatening to kill someone. But Grandy's reaction worried Kate for reasons she couldn't name.

She had good instincts, Grandy always said. Kate hoped that this time they were bad. There was nothing she could collect for this locker that might spare Grandy the consequences of murder.

CHAPTER 4

The sliding panel was no bigger than a book and was hidden from view behind a potted plant with huge green leaves. Pearl had complained that the foliage belonged in the tropics, not in the Rocky Mountains of Colorado, but her daughter didn't care. And at moments like these, as Pearl stood in her large closet with her fingers on the silver knob, peeping out into the lodge's foyer without being spotted, she didn't care either.

An approaching storm announced itself in her stiff knuckles. Her knees and ankles ached. She was cold in her dressing gown and had thought to fetch her robe because she had no reason to dress before lunchtime. But her son-in-law's inappropriate tone had drawn her to the slim panel. He seemed to be shouting into his mobile phone. If she could hear him in the privacy of her own rooms, surely the guests in the neighboring dining room could too.

After he passed she waited to see if anyone approached the front desk to file a complaint with Janet. Could it be that no one minded that sort of thing these days?

When the child came out from the private hallway, Pearl quite forgot the question. The Harrison Lodge had never been the most hospitable place for children. Really, could any hotel be friendly, especially to a child forced to live in one? And so the girl's resilience fascinated Pearl, had always captivated her attention.

From a distance.

Young Katherine Whitby teetered on the brink between childhood and adolescence, neither skinny nor chubby, with limbs that seemed slightly too long for her body. Her long sleeves didn't quite cover her wrists and her jeans didn't quite reach the tops of her shoes. She had the Nagasawas' round face and coarse hair, black as Kenneth's, though the shine seemed to dull with each generation. Her eyes were like no one else's, ocean blue and big as quarters. Her father's eyes. The rascal.

Pearl watched Janet's daughter steal a comment card from Donna's box, the box Donna treated as if it were a holy oracle—and Donna not three feet away! Then, quiet as an approaching snowstorm, the little thief glided across the foyer, caught that hideous red silk scarf of Janet's right off its hook, and vanished out of Pearl's frame of view.

Whatever Janet and Donna were studying on that confounded computer couldn't possibly be as interesting as what Pearl had just witnessed.

In the closet, the old woman withdrew from her peephole and pushed the panel closed, curious about the motives of another human being for the first time in decades. And when she tried to remember why she'd come into the closet in the first place, she simply couldn't put her finger on it.

CHAPTER 5

Someday they'd have a bigger place in a better part of the city, a house, and he'd have a better-paying job so she wouldn't have to work so hard. The Fox said this at least once a week, usually when she was on her way out the door, her eyes puffy from not getting enough sleep between her housekeeping and bartending jobs.

"Keep Coz outta trouble," she'd say.

"We ain't never found trouble we couldn't get out of, baby."

Then he'd give her a kiss to carry with her on the bus and she'd leave, smiling.

This particular Saturday, after she was gone, the Fox roused their son from his blankets on the sofa. He yanked out the boy's earbuds and let them dangle. A distant heavy beat tapped the floor.

"Up now, son." He gave the boy a firm shoulder shake, then went to the window and lifted one slat in the brittle plastic blinds. In the parking lot two floors down, a few of his Heavies were wasting the day in a line of parked cars, tinkering and smoking, dealing and plotting. Three of them were gathered around an open trunk, ogling whatever it contained. Hot products, the Fox guessed, that they'd sell to the highest bidder. There was his closest brother Hector, the wild man Jones, and the linebacker Brick. Jones clapped Brick on the arm and threw his head back, laughing at the sky.

On the sofa, Coz groaned and pulled a blanket up over his head.

"We got work today," the Fox said.

"You work."

"I do. And your mama works harder 'n botha us. Work's your way outta these projects someday, so get a move on."

"Mama says school's my way out."

"She's right."

"So which is it?"

"There ain't no school today, is there? C'mon now, up. S'already afternoon."

Coz swung his adolescent legs off the couch but didn't lift his head. He was a marionette at this age, all skinny limbs and floppy head, waiting for some no-gooder to pull his strings.

"You got some moral dilemma goin' on inside that melon o' yours? Go pull your pants on. And put on some respect while you're at it."

The Fox had already poured himself a bowl of cereal and eaten it by the time Coz shuffled into the bathroom, where he'd dropped his jeans before crawling under the blankets last night. Sometime in just the past few months—the Fox wasn't sure exactly when it had happened—Coz went to sleep a child and woke up a man. His mother had tried to point it out. The Fox remembered that now. She saw it in the way his eyes registered the neighbor girls as they scuttled down the gray halls in whispering groups. Heard it in the smack she had, until then, successfully scolded off his lips. Smelled it in the laundry she carried down to the basement washers every Monday night. But the Fox didn't give her any credence until the day Hector called Coz *brother* rather than *boy*, changing everything with just a few letters of the alphabet.

The Fox had been with the Mile High Heavies for nearly twenty years, since he himself made the shift from boy to brother. He was an old man now by the gang's standards, a respected leader who'd paid his share of bills over the years with drugs and fenced goods as often as with hard-earned paychecks. Every so often one of the brothers would father a child and be reformed. More often they became lesser men than they were before, throwing off their women and the kids they'd made together. A few were like the Fox: decent brothers, loyal and responsible to their family circles, offended by claims that anything in their lives needed to be done differently.

So nothing changed in the Fox's life until that day when Hector called his son *brother* and took him without Fox's permission to be inked with the MHH insignia. When Coz came home with inflamed art on a neck skinny as a baseball bat, the Fox saw red. Coz was nobody's brother and only one man's son, and he would never be a Heavy just because some underling assumed it was his destiny. The boy deserved options, however limited they may be.

Since then the Fox had made subtle moves toward the margins of the Heavies' activities, surprised by the energy it took to keep one twelve-year-old child, not to mention himself, profitably occupied. He'd found unexpected help in the form of a detective from the Denver PD. In exchange for information about certain city gang activities—never the Heavies'; the Fox was no traitor or coward— the detective put in a good word for the Fox on odd jobs. Legal jobs.

Coz emerged from the bathroom still bleary-eyed.

"What is it today? Hauling? Framing?"

The Fox put his bowl in the sink. Coz poured himself a cup of red fruit punch and collapsed onto a counter stool.

"Security."

"Like for a club?"

"Weed dispensary."

"Security like where you get a uniform? A piece?"

"None o' that."

"Rent-a-cop without a gun. What kind of—"

"I got a gun. You don't." The Fox began depositing items in front of Coz: a bowl, a box of Cocoa Puffs, a jug of milk, a spoon.

"You done security before?" his son asked.

"All week long."

Coz snorted and poured. "How'd a guy like you pass the background checks?"

"It's under the table."

"What's that mean?"

"It means it's win-win. Now shut up and eat. We leave in five."

"Security is boring."

"Boring's a jail cell for thirty years. Boring's life in these projects."

"Might be interesting if they paid in product."

"Wouldn't you like that."

"What's my cut?" Coz grinned at his father and shoveled a spoonful of Cocoa Puffs into his mouth.

"Every time you speak, it gets smaller."

The boy tried not to laugh. The proof was in his shining eyes and concave chest and the line of milk that spurted out his nose. Which is how the Fox knew it was going to be an okay day.

CHAPTER 6

The electronic doorbell of the Kwik Kash announced their arrival. Grandy held the door for Kate as he always did. She sipped a chocolate-peanut-butter-banana smoothie that he'd bought for her at the café across the street. Mr. Gorman was standing behind a glass case, writing up papers on a toaster oven while its owner waited. He glanced up and gave Grandy a blank-faced nod.

"With you in a minute." As if he'd never seen them before in his life. No "Hey there, partner!" No knock-knock joke. No slug for the vending machine.

Kate held the smoothie cup close to her face. The nuttiness masked the scents of the shop. It smelled like something vaguely burning, with all those TVs sitting on those gray metal shelves, their screens turned on to prove they worked. Kate often believed she could detect the musty attics and damp garages where people unearthed the stuff they wanted to sell and the sweat that stuck to their clothes when they hauled it in.

A fishbowl full of lapel buttons—from political campaigns, from tourist attractions, from TV shows and fund-raisers and sporting events—sat on the counter. Normally Kate wasn't interested in these, but she spotted a large round purple pin with two men and the face of a white tiger on it. *Siegfried and Roy Beyond Belief*, it said. She fished it out and put four quarters on the counter to pay for it. Mr. Gorman nodded at her.

A boy stood between the fishbowl and the toaster-oven man,

his head bowed over the iPhones in the glass display case, hands plunged deep into the unipocket of his gray sweatshirt. With his shaggy red hair he looked like a long-armed orangutan escaped from the Denver Zoo. The boy was Austin Benson, her best friend Reece's brother.

Austin *was* an ape. At school Reece had told her all about his birthday. *Disaster*, Reece had said, as if the word was a pleasure to say. He had wanted Google Glass, but their parents gave him a Nintendo 3DS. Austin called the Nintendo *embarrassing* and threw it to Reece, who said she would have kept it *with gratitude* if their father hadn't made Austin take it back. Dumbhead Austin said his mom and dad didn't understand diddly. *Diddly* was Reece's word, and also *dumbhead*, because the word Austin really used had made their mother cry.

There were two phones on the counter where Austin stood, along with a Nintendo. Maybe his birthday gift.

Kate pocketed the pin and angled for the knives case. She wondered if Austin was going to pawn the Nintendo for money to buy a Google Glass. She would spy on him and report to Reece.

Kate studied the real-life blades through the glass. People reacted to eleven-year-olds looking at weapons. She liked to guess how a person would react. Toaster-oven man, she supposed, would watch her and silently disapprove but keep his thoughts to himself. Besides, she really did like the twin knives with the dragons on their hilts. The beasts were silver with black-glass eyes, and they breathed red leather flames down the length of their black sheaths.

"Dragon knives are still here, Grandy," she said, pointing.

"Mm-hmm."

"Maybe you'll get them for me for Christmas!"

"Maybe I will."

"Really?"

Toaster-oven man was watching Grandy, not her.

"What?" Their eyes met. Grandy looked at the display case as if it had appeared out of mist.

"The dragon knives? For Christmas?"

Grandy frowned but didn't say anything. Set his paper coffee cup down on top of the glass and had a long look at Mr. Gorman, who signed the papers and peeled off a copy for the toaster-oven man, every movement slow and measured. The customer thanked him and left the shop.

Austin's Nintendo was sitting atop a similar sheet of paper. "Sure I can't talk you into a trade?" Austin asked.

"I buy and I sell," Mr. Gorman said. "No trades."

"Okay. Gimme a minute to think about it."

Mr. Gorman put the phones away and looked at Grandy. "Happy to see you, Daniel," he finally said, not sounding happy at all. "Come on back." He picked up the toaster and Austin's Nintendo and passed through a privacy curtain, blue and dusty, hanging in a doorway behind the counter.

Kate moved to go too.

"Stay here, Agent K."

"But you said—"

"It'll just take a minute."

He followed, and when he lifted the curtain Kate caught a glimpse of a chaotic office, every inch of wall space covered with overflowing shelves, every inch of floor space stacked with boxes and teetering products, every inch of desk space piled with papers.

Kate wandered the aisles, pretending not to notice that Austin was pretending not to watch her. Reece's brother was creepy. She looked at wristwatches and old computers and game systems. He braced his arms on the glass-top case and stared at the phones. She turned a corner and lingered at a rack filled with games in clamshell cases, because from here she could see into a wall-mounted mirror that pointed right at Austin. One of Mr. Gorman's security cameras was pointed in the same direction.

In the office, the men's voices rose from hushed to audible. Upset but controlled.

"I don't care if you were in a corner," Grandy said. "All I care about now is how you're gonna fix it."

A knot formed in Kate's stomach.

Mr. Gorman shushed him. Grandy said something she couldn't hear.

Austin slipped around the counter, and Kate realized Mr. Gorman had forgotten to lock the cabinet after putting the phones away. Austin slid the panel open, snatched one of the iPhones, and scurried out the door, dropping the device into his unipocket on the way.

Reece was not going to believe this!

Kate wasted no time. She put her smoothie on the floor and reached the door before it closed all the way, slipping out before the electronic doorbell could chime a second time. Austin was already turning the corner at the end of the building. When he vanished between the store and the adjacent parking lot, Kate ran on light feet out between two parked cars, where Austin wouldn't see her.

He aimed for the creek that ran behind the Kwik Kash and the lot where Kate now stood. The same creek wove through the inn's property a mile or so upstream. Though the water was out of sight at the base of a sloping bank, Kate could hear the smooth flow bouncing over rocks.

She crouched and jogged to the next row of cars, then to the third, and then she straightened just enough to see. She had out-paced him. Austin was walking the way Kate did when she needed to slip past adults without being noticed. Not too fast or slow, too stealthy or urgent, too loud or quiet, too focused or bored. But much more aware of her surroundings than she seemed to be. Drawing attention to herself always resulted in unwanted questions about what she might or might not be doing.

The doorbell of the Kwik Kash sounded again and Austin flinched, then cast a look back over his shoulder. Even before he turned back around he had picked up his pace. Seconds later, Mr. Gorman appeared at the corner of the building. The pawnbroker sent up a "Hey!" like a warning shot, and both guys were sprinting toward the creek, the yeti chasing a rabbit.

Kate stood to her full height to see as much as possible.

Austin threw his head back and pumped his elbows. He was smaller and faster and would have outdashed Mr. Gorman if not for the steep bank at the back of the store. Here the sidewalk ended and the earth sloped away, and a slide of fine dirt and pebbles put Austin on his bottom and tumbled him all the way down to the creek. His right heel splashed into the water.

Mr. Gorman took the bank in three clumsy leaps and was on Austin's legs before he could get up.

"Let's have it back, you little punk."

Kate recoiled. His voice was mean and unfamiliar. She glanced at the shop. Where was Grandy?

Mr. Gorman started smacking at Austin's hip pockets, then his sweatshirt. Austin shouted and sat up, pushing at Mr. Gorman's chest, batting at his arms. Kate inched out from behind the car. With one hand, Mr. Gorman held Austin's shoulder and kept the boy's fists at a distance. Austin tried pounding on Mr. Gorman's hands, but the bigger man didn't even seem to notice. His weight on Austin's ankles kept the kid rooted.

"He's attacking me!" Austin shrieked.

Kate looked back toward the store to see if anyone heard. If it were two boys duking it out down by the creek—say, Austin and his nemesis, Jake Diller—she would have run for Grandy. But this was Mr. Gorman, and Austin had stolen something from him. Which meant there couldn't be anything wrong about this particular kind of fight.

Could there? She stepped to the top of the bank for a better look.

"Got it!" Mr. Gorman said, but he was having difficulty pulling the stolen merchandise from the soft sweatshirt pocket. "You think I wouldn't notice what you did?" The man was already breathless.

"I'll give it back," Austin whined.

"That you will." He released Austin's shoulder to get a better handle on the pocket, and Austin went for Mr. Gorman's face. He caught hold of the man's beard and yanked. Mr. Gorman's head jerked and Kate thought they crashed foreheads. But the only sound was a roar from Mr. Gorman, who stopped worrying the pocket and brought his fist straight up into Austin's nose.

Austin's head snapped back. Kate gasped. Blood poured out of the teenager's nostrils and ran down over his lips. He let go of Mr. Gorman's hair, groaned, fell back onto the rough bank, and went still.

"Austin!" she screamed.

Mr. Gorman twisted to look up at her, and she clapped her hand over her mouth, wanting to run and wanting to stay in equal parts. Where she stood, she already had a good head start on Mr. Gorman. If he made a move to chase her she'd sprint away.

But Mr. Gorman didn't try to chase Kate. When he looked at

her his eyes weren't crazy. He looked confused, surprised that something so bad could have happened. It was the way Reece looked the time she accidentally ruined their science fair project the day before it was due.

Austin groaned again and his hands went to his face. "You broke my nose!"

Was he crying? A broken nose was worth crying over, if you weren't a spy.

Mr. Gorman's expression changed, but Kate couldn't describe it this time. Calm now, he turned back to Austin's pocket, withdrew the shiny black phone, then patted the pocket closed again.

"If you don't want the cops hauling you off for stealing, you'll come up with a good story for what happened to your nose. Some story that doesn't involve me," Mr. Gorman said. His voice had a nervous wobble in it. "What you did—I got that on camera. No cameras out here, though."

"I want my Nintendo back," Austin demanded.

Mr. Gorman got off of Austin's legs carefully, stepping wide to stay clear of feet and knees.

"Then come get it, boy."

The pawnbroker started walking back up the bank. Austin rolled over onto his hands and knees, soaking his pant legs in the creek. Blood dripped off his chin. Kate thought he might throw up, and she felt sorry for him. He shouldn't have taken that phone, but Mr. Gorman shouldn't have hit him.

When he reached the sidewalk, Mr. Gorman stared at her like she was the one who'd robbed him. He'd changed the same way Grandy changed, before her very eyes and with no explanation. It was the first time Kate remembered feeling truly afraid, with everyone changing and her not knowing why.

"You'll keep quiet about this too. Telling tales will just make trouble for you. And your grandpa."

When Mr. Gorman went back into his shop, Kate stepped out from behind the cars and half walked, half slid down the loose slope toward Austin. He was stooping to wash his face in the creek.

"Is your nose okay?" she asked.

He turned on her. "Better than your nose is gonna be, you snitch!"

Kate took a step back.

"I didn't tell!"

"Right." The water running off Austin's face darkened his sweat-shirt. He pressed a finger to the soft spot beside his nose and winced.

"You might need stitches."

"*Snitches* get stitches, Kate Whitby."

"I never snitch!"

"Ever have stitches in your nose before?"

He lashed out with his fist, swinging within inches of Kate's head. She jerked back and landed on her seat on the bank. Then she scrambled back up and ran.

Austin's voice chased her. "Better watch out."

CHAPTER 7

"A re you and Mr. Gorman friends again?" Kate asked Grandy
as they returned home on Upper Bear Creek Road.

The tendons in his hands stood up like mountain ridges as he
clenched the steering wheel.

"Yes," he said, so clipped that Kate said nothing more for the
rest of the drive.

The Harrison Lodge was hidden from the road by thick stands
of Ponderosa pines and blue spruce and stood at the end of a long
curving driveway. The narrow lane passed under a fancy wrought-
iron arch before climbing the wrinkles of the Rocky Mountain
foothills.

The quiet destination stayed mostly empty during the month
of November, when only a handful of people came to this blink of
a town called Evergreen even for the inn's promotional packages.
It was too late for fall colors and too early for good snow; too cold
for water sports and too warm for ice; too close to Denver and too
far from the ski resorts. Each winter Grandy made the case that
they should just close the place until spring. Kate's sisters would
cheer, their mother would grow weepy, Gran would laugh without
humor, and Great-Grandma Pearl would glare until Grandy put his
argument away.

Even so, Chef's menus regularly drew locals to the restaurant,
which did a fine business even when the rooms and cottages were
nearly empty, especially on weekends. When Grandy pulled his

Explorer into the parking lot, it was cramped with lunch guests. Staying out of the bustle was a very important job, and Kate had become an expert long ago.

She sprang from Grandy's car and took her fears of Austin to her secret closet at the back of the Rising Sun. She had discovered the storage compartment when she was six, on one of the many days she was fleeing her sister Alyssa, who was threatening her on that occasion with a pile of scat she'd shoveled off of a footpath. *A little scat for Kat-with-a-K*, Alyssa chanted. *Kat the Killer.* As Kate hightailed it around the back of the cottage she tripped on a rock, hit the wall, and bounced off when the door sprang open.

It had never occurred to Kate that it might be a bad idea to go inside. All that mattered was escaping Alyssa, who was eleven years older and as powerful as any grown-up. Alyssa was so mystified by Kate's disappearance that her taunting soon turned to angry shouts when she dropped and then stepped in the very mess intended for her kid sister.

Kate spent a lot of time in the cubby with her homework and her thoughts, and often with her mother's laptop, because she could still access the lodge's network and browse as she liked without interruption. If she wanted to she could crawl into the cubby through a small door in the back of her bedroom closet, but she usually didn't. It was a hassle to rearrange shoes and dresses and boxes, and almost impossible to make it all look undisturbed. Also, she often forgot to leave the panel unlocked, and her library books were always in the way.

On this particular Saturday afternoon, books were not enough to occupy Kate's mind, which kept darting to upsetting images: Grandy kicking over buckets, Mr. Gorman throwing a punch, Austin bleeding into the creek. Everyone's knuckles, tense balls of frustration. So Kate set her books aside, closed her eyes, and called up her mental spy notebook.

Kate had a fine memory. Last year, for Kate's tenth birthday, Olivia gave her a copy of *Harriet the Spy*, which had taught her a thing or two about how to lurk in the shadows of the adult world. It was this story that set Kate on the path to a life of espionage. If anything, though, the book was a manual on how *not* to spy—that is, by keeping a written record of what she spied on. Harriet took notes in an actual notebook, which made a real mess when her friends found it. So Kate kept a virtual spy notebook, stored in her brain cells rather than on paper. Not foolproof, but good enough until computer people came up with something like a brain chip that couldn't get lost.

She plowed through her mental notes in search of an idea for how to prove to Austin that she hadn't tattled on him. Something someone had said, something she might have seen. Austin wouldn't change his mind without proof, and he was old enough to make her life difficult. Even now, that fist flashing toward her face made her flinch.

As she flipped through events of the past few days, she paused at a particularly memorable character, a guest who claimed to run a bed-and-breakfast in San Francisco. The woman had checked in at dinnertime, arriving in a sleek silver Jaguar convertible that everyone stared at after she went into the dining room, where she started complaining right away. The town of Evergreen was more hick than historic; the November landscape was disappointing compared to the spring and fall photos online; her dining room table was not private enough; the creek ran too low; the fire in the hearth was too hot. She had booked through the weekend but mused aloud about departing in the morning. She blamed Olivia for the mustard sauce that dripped off her fork onto her ruffled silk blouse. She refused to leave Olivia a tip.

Kate wondered if the lady was gone yet.

She went down into the chilly tunnel beneath the cot and opened her metal footlocker. Underneath the morning's loot she found a green plastic harmonica that she had won at her school's fall carnival. She also found a roll of duct tape and a pair of scissors, and she took the items back outside, down the gravel footpath and over the thin creek, which quietly applauded her plans, then around the inn to the main parking lot. There were several cars in the lot, but it was easy enough to spot the Jaguar with its silver wildcat leaping across the hood.

Quickly she hid herself behind the front fender and went to work. She cut a piece of tape longer than the harmonica and applied it to the length of its cover, leaving several inches hanging off each end. Then she cut two more pieces, shorter than the first, and stuck them to her wrist. Lying on her back, she slipped beneath the car and taped the instrument in front of the grille, leaving the harmonica holes exposed and facing forward. She applied the short pieces of tape to each end for extra strength. The whole effort took less than a minute, and the result, she hoped, would be an irritating noise that would take a long time for the snooty lady to locate.

Kate peeked around the car for anyone who might see her. And though she held her breath, a tiny, silly part of her wished to be caught. She waited extra seconds for her mother, who might or might not be staring down the lane from the reception desk window just then, to notice her little girl. Someone might appear at the entrance, looking for her. Olivia, Grandy, maybe even Gran. *Kate? Where are you? Come play a game of checkers with me. Let's go to the movies tonight. Want some ice cream?*

But there was only Alyssa, the sister to be avoided at all costs, coming out the double doors and down the three steps. Alyssa carried a bank bag and walked swiftly, her heels tapping an even rhythm on the blacktop all the way to her car.

It wasn't the first time Kate had seen Alyssa rush off with a few dollars from behind the front desk as if she were on official business, Saturday afternoon at three. Note for the mental manual, Kate thought: sometimes doing brazen things right out in the open draws less attention than sly sneakiness.

Lucky for Alyssa the lodge didn't use security cameras. Gran said their very presence would suggest that the lodge wasn't inherently safe.

What you did—I got that on camera.

In the end it was Mr. Gorman who provided Kate with the solution to her Austin problem. The sudden idea made her so excited that she stood up by the Jaguar, scissors in one hand and silver tape in the other, grinning wide and catching a startled look on Alyssa's face behind the windshield of her car.

"It'll be okay!" Kate said aloud.

Mr. Gorman's security cameras would prove that she never talked to him after Austin ran off with the phone. Austin would be able to see that she had only followed him out of the store. All she had to do was ask Mr. Gorman to show him.

Simple as that.

She read the reply on her sister's lips: *Scat, Kat.*

"Shoo, fly," Kate said with a smile.

Alyssa drove off quickly. Kate gave her an exaggerated wink and waved good-bye with the scissors.

CHAPTER 8

At five twenty Saturday evening Charlie squatted beside a Dumpster with Ender. It was almost comfortable, their spines pressed against a brick wall that was the back of a motorcycle showroom. An empty canvas laundry bag, the kind with a drawstring and a shoulder strap, was pooled between his feet. Charlie fiddled with his silver harmonica, tapping it against his knee, keeping the melody in his head. His name was engraved across the top. A long-ago present from the only person who might ever have cared about him.

In the end, Charlie had decided to do the job. For himself. For the money. Because Merridew was right about one thing: the 420 Green House would have cash for the taking. After it became legal to sell recreational marijuana in Colorado, most of the pot retailers were forced to operate on a cash basis. Colorado could do what it wanted, but the feds didn't have to like it. Until the DEA came to be on their side, it would be hard for the sellers to get banks and security firms to service the stores.

Across the alley from where Charlie and Ender squatted was the rear of the 420. In a former life, the 420 Green House had been a tire store. The showroom was now a dispensary, and the garage had been converted to a climate-controlled grow room with a ripe crop of cannabis plants. The old garage doors had been blacked out but not walled up. Two buildings down, a pretty black Camaro was parked beside a vacant loading dock behind an office-supply store.

Charlie thought the car was empty, but the tinted windows made it impossible to be sure. He and Ender stayed out of its sight just in case.

The evening temperatures fell with the sun. The store would be open until six. Drogo would arrive at five thirty.

Ender picked at a thread in a hole in his jeans. The kid claimed to be twenty but looked sixteen, was almost as blond as his girlfriend, Eve, and had proven himself an expert pickpocket. But he'd never crashed a store.

"Remind me again why we're doing this in broad daylight," Ender whispered.

"Sun's already set," Charlie said.

"During business hours. You know what I mean."

"Because they won't lock up their cash until after hours. Because the alarm system is disarmed. But once they lock down for the night . . ." He shrugged.

"How do you think Drogo is doing?"

"We're about to find out."

"It's potent stuff, what gets grown here," Ender said. "I mean in Colorado."

"I wouldn't know," Charlie said.

"Really? Everyone else seems to. The good stuff goes for four hundred an ounce out of state. They say it's even caught the eye of the Mexican cartels."

Charlie didn't care. They sat in silence, except for the harmonica knocking against Charlie's kneecap. Ender glanced at it. Charlie put it back in his pocket.

The rear exit at the back of the dispensary flew open on loose hinges and hit the side of the building, and Charlie twitched. But it was just a kid, a boy of maybe eleven or twelve in a muscle shirt and jeans too big for him, leaping over the threshold and jogging down the alley with a soda can in each fist. Shielded by the Dumpster, the brothers watched him run toward the Camaro, tuck one of the cans under his armpit, open the passenger-side door, and hop in.

Not empty after all.

"You think it's an employee on a break?" Ender asked.

With a kid? Charlie wasn't sure what to think. He looked at the shop door, which was very slowly falling shut. He looked at his watch. Five twenty-five.

"Let's go over it again," Charlie said.

"I got it. Drogo's got it. What are you worried about?"

"You. I'm worried about you messing this up. So tell me how you're not going to do that."

Ender tipped his head back against the brick wall and launched into a monotone recitation: "Drogo swipes the car, drives it into the grow-room doors. Everyone in the dispensary runs back to see what happened. Drogo plays drunk. I get him out while you swing around through the front door and take whatever you can get your hands on. We split before the cops get here. Eve picks us all up two blocks west. Piece of cake."

"Piece of cake," Charlie repeated. Until Ender figured out that Charlie wasn't going to meet them two blocks west. By that time he and the cash would be on a bus headed east. "You have your pepper spray?" he asked.

"Are you nervous? You sound nervous. Maybe you should let *me* go inside. You don't do weed. You wouldn't know a shwag from a headie."

"I'm not stealing the weed, Ender."

"Let me go."

"You're out here, got it? You get Drogo out, you take off. Don't wait for me, don't try to help me. I only need sixty seconds to fill this." He lifted the canvas laundry bag.

"Two of us would get twice as much."

Maybe Merridew would think of that next time, Charlie thought. After Charlie took whatever he could ransack and disappeared. Solitary again. Fatherless again. Free of the overlords.

"Just do what we agreed."

"All right, all right."

One more minute. Charlie hoped Drogo would be on time.

"Rumor has it Charlie's your real name."

"So?"

"I saw it on the harmonica. Charlie Fuse."

"Foo-*say*," Charlie corrected.

Ender chuckled.

"What? It's Japanese."

"It's a stick up your backside, man."

Charlie glared. "And Ender isn't? Who comes up with this stuff? Ender, Drogo, Eve? Merridew? Giggles and Scratch? You're all full of yourselves, picking names like that."

No one in the family used their real names. Charlie didn't know why, didn't care. Taking a new identity, especially a fantasy one, never changed anything about a person's real life.

"Doesn't matter how you pronounce it," Ender said, "so long as I can spell it. If Drogo and I go down we can tell the cops who to look for." He ribbed Charlie. "Wanna know my real name?"

"No."

They heard Drogo seconds later. First in the form of an idling engine, then a low birdlike call. Charlie scooted to the corner of the building and craned his neck to see into the lane that joined the alley.

With Scratch's help, the seventeen-year-old with the long black braid had stolen a very old Chevy Caprice from a cluttered auto body shop near their bridge. It was one of several old enough to hot-wire, and Drogo wanted it for the manual transmission. But the main reason for selecting this model was that the nose on the rusty gold body was as long as Pinocchio's, long enough to do serious damage to some old garage doors while offering the driver some protection.

Drogo saw Charlie. He gave Charlie a thumbs-up, and Charlie touched the small bill of his knit cap. Then Drogo crept forward, long nose poking into the alley.

The slow movement of the car triggered a motion-sensitive light that flooded the lane. Drogo hadn't been invisible before, but now he was in the spotlight. Charlie swore and withdrew into the shadows. "Go, go, go," he whispered. He shouldered the strap of his bag.

Down the alley, the Camaro's headlights flickered on at the same moment that Drogo stomped on the gas pedal, revved the engine, dropped the clutch, and peeled out into the alley. Smoke from the tires hit Charlie's eyes.

Drogo was less than halfway to the dispensary when the Camaro dropped into gear, and Charlie saw the truth in a heartbeat: the Camaro was the dispensary's freelance security, the reason why a twelve-year-old kid might come and go freely from a place where anyone under twenty-one wasn't legally allowed to enter.

The details didn't quite add up in Charlie's mind, but there was no time to process. He leaped across the alleyway, bag slapping his side. The Caprice hit one of the old garage doors and things began to crumple: the bumper, the metal garage door panels, the glass windows that had been painted black, and their piece-of-cake plans.

The Camaro was on top of the Caprice before Charlie made it across the alley. The driver nicked Drogo's bumper and screeched to a stop, trapping the sedan. Backing out of the scene had not been part of Charlie's strategy, but that didn't lessen the impact of this setback. The driver opened his door, used it as a shield, and propped his arms atop the doorframe. He leveled a pistol at the rear window. He fired into the car. Then he turned and fired at Charlie.

Charlie stumbled to his knees and felt chunks of brick strike his head. His heart hammered and his breaths came in short bursts.

The Caprice's horn sounded and didn't let up.

No legitimate freelancer would operate this way, shooting before warning, killing instead of apprehending. Drogo wasn't even armed!

From his position on his knees, Charlie saw the gunman come out from behind his door and jump up onto the trunk of the Caprice. He was a strange-looking dude with light brown skin, hair dyed the color of cinnamon, and an Abe Lincoln beard dyed white. By the light of the spot still flooding the alley, Charlie saw the gang tat on the side of the guy's neck. Three letters: *MHH*, large and loud and gothic. He knew the tag. The Mile High Heavies.

The Heavy walked over the car, weapon raised, kicking up glass in a crystal spray. Charlie moved. He scrambled along the side of the dispensary, stumbling over some wooden pallets leaning against the wall. He heard the gunman land heavily on the ground and did not look back, but plunged through the breezeway between the 420 and a Laundromat. He headed toward the parking lot at the front of the stores, fully aware that he might be running directly into more armed Heavies.

"You're gonna show your face 'fore I put a round in it," the gunman shouted.

Charlie did not doubt it.

The street family didn't carry guns. They had their smileys—long chains held together at the ends by a padlock—and they had knives. Violence was not beneath them, but guns and homes were the two things that separated most gangs from the families who knew to avoid them. Pepper spray and a harmonica were no match for that pistol.

Charlie broke out into an open parking lot and took a brazen risk, running straight for a busy Taco Bell on the corner of the block, where people getting off work were lined up in the drive-thru lane. He might reach the building before the gunman could take a shot. He hoped the guy would think twice before firing into a populated place.

He sprinted. He willed his arms to give him speed. His legs were pistons.

Behind him in the alley a child shrieked and a man yelled, unintelligible but clearly angry. Ender. His voice floated up over the buildings.

"You killed my brother," he screamed. "Now I've got yours!"

Ender had taken the kid? Charlie spun and nearly fell. *No, no, no.* Ender should have run as fast as Charlie was moving, fast and far in the other direction.

At Ender's announcement the gunman gave up Charlie and turned, his weapon now pointed back the way he'd come. He stalked back down the passageway between the dispensary and Laundromat, gun arm raised and locked. Two people inside the 420 were watching from the window. One of them had a cell phone at his ear.

"You let him go, I'll let you live," the gunman shouted.

All Charlie had to do was turn back to face that Taco Bell, put one foot in front of the other, and vanish. He didn't even have to run. Ender had bought Charlie's ticket to freedom and was about to pay a very high price for it.

Charlie hesitated, then swore and changed course. He veered away from the Taco Bell and went around the other side of the Laundromat, returning to the alley. He passed under a vent that blasted him with warm air and the scent of dryer sheets, smells of a normal life. At the rear corner of the building he peered around.

Ender had dragged the soda-can kid away from the open door of the Camaro. His smiley was wrapped around the throat of the boy, who was crying and gripping the chain, kicking out and wriggling, throwing his elbows. But Ender, though slim as a cigarette, had size and strength on him. He held the boy close and crouched as they backed away.

If anyone had come out into the alley to see the crash and the shot that followed, they'd fled it now. The scream of the Chevy's horn still filled the open air, held down by the weight of Drogo's body.

When Charlie arrived, Ender and the gunman were shouting at each other, swearing, talking over each other's words and jacking up the volume with strained lungs over the blaring car horn. Their demands were unintelligible. Drogo's killer was standing tall, his gun arm rigid and pointed straight ahead, the weapon turned sideways and locked onto its target. Ender flicked open a knife and put it to the boy's temple. They'd backed into the floodlight. Ender was quaking, and a trickle of blood ran down the kid's cheek, mixing with tears.

Charlie took off his cap and waved it, trying to catch Ender's eye. He caught the kid's instead.

The boy pointed and squawked against the smiley squeezing his throat, and the white-bearded gunman whirled and got off an unfocused shot. Again it hit bricks.

"Put it down!" Ender commanded, his voice ragged. "Gun down!" He pulled the chain tight enough to silence the kid's wails and bring on a fit of choking. "I mean it, man. Every second is one more breath he can't take."

The moment the Heavy put his weapon on the ground and kicked it away, Charlie broke into a sprint. He couldn't think of how he and Ender would make it out. A hostage was their best bet and their worst, a shield and a millstone.

The cops would be here in three minutes, Charlie thought, if this were a run-of-the-mill breaking and entering. Where were this man's gang brothers? Two minutes away? One?

He gave himself thirty seconds to get Ender out.

The gun slid across the asphalt and spun under the Camaro, and Charlie gave up any thought of retrieving it. He raced for Ender and the boy. The gunman made a break for them at the same time.

"Drop him," Charlie huffed.

"No." Ender's grip was white and his eyes wild.

Charlie's flight instincts were so revved up that he might have been able to toss the kid back into the Camaro from where they stood, but Ender would not let go. Charlie reached them first, crashed into the boy even as the Heavy's hands were reaching out to take him back. All three went down, Ender on his side. His knife sliced Charlie's shoulder. The smiley clattered. The gunman started pounding on Charlie's kidneys.

Charlie grappled for the pepper spray in Ender's back pocket and turned it on his attacker. In seconds, they were clear.

"Leave the kid!" Charlie ordered.

Ender's grip on the smiley was frozen. There was no time to debate.

So Charlie slipped his fingers under the boy's armpits and lifted. Together he and Ender shared his squirming weight, which might have been ninety pounds but seemed like one. The smiley chain finally slackened.

"Dad!" the kid shrieked.

"I'm comin' to get you." The man was still on his hands and knees, bold but blind. "You do what they say. I'm comin' to get you, son. We're all comin'."

Ender and Charlie plunged into the darkening streets. Behind them, the boy's father emitted a cry that raised the hairs on the back of Charlie's neck. It was no scream of defeat. It was a war cry, a howl, a primal call to battle that rose above the din of the Chevy's horn and the police sirens screaming down the boulevard. Charlie expected to be slaughtered by invisible warriors before they'd gone a hundred yards.

The two blocks to Eve's car were the longest he had ever traveled, second only to the long drive back to the bridge, with nothing but Eve's feathery voice—*What happened? What did you do?*—to blanket the boy's sobs.

CHAPTER 9

Kate ate most of her meals in the small private dining room adjacent to the lodge's huge kitchen. It was more truly a windowless alcove with a long rectangular table large enough for twelve, though Kate often ate alone. Even when she did not, it was rare that more than three or four of her relatives ever sat down to eat at the same time.

Dinner for those who wanted it could be had no sooner than five thirty, before the Saturday evening rush. At the midday and evening meals, Chef's staff put food in two old stainless buffet serving dishes at the end of the table and lit a burner underneath to keep them warm. The family ate as they had time.

The day's events had stirred up Kate's appetite. She showed up at five twenty-five, ravenous, to empty dishes and the scent of crab cakes frying in butter. She took her usual seat closest to the food, with her back to the corner and the widest view of the kitchen. She felt sheltered there, watching Chef, who was as large as her mother, grandmother, and Great-Grandma Pearl put together, move around the kitchen effortlessly. It was her domain.

Chef flipped the crab cakes and caught Kate looking at her. She lifted her hand, upturned, and hooked her finger. *Come here.*

Kate slid off her chair and went to the end of an ingredient table where one of Chef's assistants had filled bowls with sliced lemons and butter pickles and salty green capers and croutons. She didn't dare go near Chef's stove. Chef stuck a spoon into a glass bowl of aioli and tipped her head in the direction of the refrigerator and freezer.

"Dessert first today, eh? Since your supper's not out yet."

That was when Kate noticed the chocolate cake set out and already sliced. She grinned and quickly picked up a plate. The moist wedge fell on its side and broke in half. Kate mended this with a generous squirt of fudge sauce from a squeeze bottle and a snowfall of powdered sugar in a sieve. Chef came up behind her and crowned the cake with whipped cream.

"That'll make a day better," Chef said, as if she knew. Kate wondered. She returned to her corner.

Alyssa blew into the alcove with a huff. She was wearing earrings Kate had never seen before, pearly green glass in silver settings. The sounds of the dining room swelled when she entered, then hushed as the kitchen doors swung shut.

"You're sitting in my chair, Kat-with-a-K."

She wasn't, of course, but Kate didn't feel like challenging her oldest sister today. From her pocket she withdrew the purple Siegfried and Roy pin she had bought at Mr. Gorman's shop. Kate picked up her plate and left the pin in its place, then moved to the opposite corner, across from her sister.

Alyssa picked up the pin and turned it over in her hands. She looked at Kate, considered the old souvenir one last time, and tossed it into a nearby trash can.

Kate said, "Did you buy those earrings with what you stole from the cashbox?"

Alyssa matched Kate's stare, picked up a fork, and speared the widest side of Kate's cake. She put the bite of cake into her mouth and drew the fork out between her lips slowly.

"I'm not gonna tell," Kate said. "I just want to know what you do with it."

"It's none of your business." A crumb of Kate's cake popped out of Alyssa's mouth.

She said no more when Chef came over and filled the serving dishes with rice pilaf and crab cakes, then set a salad in the center of the table, casting a disapproving glare at Alyssa's telltale fork.

Gran came in next, escorting her mother. Great-Grandma Pearl wore a lavender-blue velour tracksuit that matched her eyes. Her hair too, in the right light.

Great-Grandma Pearl eyed Kate, her eyebrows lifted. Kate made sure to chew with her mouth closed.

"I'll have what she's having," her great-grandmother said.

"No, Mom. It's bad for your blood sugar. There's fish."

"Is it Friday? We should have fish on Friday."

"It's Saturday, Mom."

"Who eats fish on Saturday?" She sat opposite Kate and wagged a bony hand at the cake. "I'll have what she's having."

Gran dished up a child-size portion of rice, a crab cake, and a spoonful of salad, which looked like some kind of stringy slaw. She set it in front of her mother.

The old woman pushed the plate away while Gran plated her own meal.

The volume in the dining room rose once more, and Olivia blew in through the doors, fully dressed in her favorite cosplay costume, the Japanese anime heroine Asuna. Olivia, who was naturally raven-haired, wore a copper-colored wig that reached past her waist. The white dress was trimmed in red, accented with tiny daggers, and cinched at the waist with a sword belt. The long sleeves were cut away at the shoulders and lashed in red trim at the elbows, and the long skirt was cut away at the front to expose a red pleated miniskirt and white thigh-high leggings, also trimmed in red. Her ankle boots were white and soft. Olivia leaned into the alcove.

"Gran—"

"Why on *earth* are you dressed like that while you're on your shift, young lady?"

"You look great!" Kate shouted.

"Brian and I are going to a cosplay event in Denver right at eight thirty. I had to dress first. But, Gran—"

"Olivia, this is *not* the image we present to the public. Alyssa, you take over while your sister changes."

Alyssa pretended not to have heard.

Olivia pressed on. "Gran, table four is upset about their meal. They say the halibut is too bony."

"Chef can remake it."

"I remade it once already," Chef said, approaching the table with the bowl of aioli. Kate loved Chef's aioli. It was nothing like the hollandaise. "They found two bones. Fish have bones."

Great-Grandma Pearl was watching Kate eat her chocolate cake. "One should never eat fish on Saturday," she said. "Or Sunday, or Monday . . ."

Gran sighed. "Then they can order something else to their liking."

". . . or Tuesday, or Wednesday . . ."

Olivia said, "They want the meal comped."

"Oh they do, do they? Everybody wants everything for nothing these days. What was wrong with the rest of the meal?"

"I guess nothing."

"Or *Thursday*."

"Where's this plate of bony halibut? I'd like to see it."

"He ate it."

Kate thought that was funny. "He ate the plate?"

Great-Grandma Pearl smiled at her and whispered, "Also, one should never eat fish in a landlocked state. Not even on Friday."

Kate wasn't sure what a landlocked state was.

Gran said grimly, "As I suppose they ate everything else." She set her food down next to her aging mother. "Olivia, take a plate to your grandfather and then go get out of that ridiculous getup. He's in his workshop and would forget dinner entirely if not for us. Alyssa, see to her tables."

"I haven't eaten yet!"

"Nor have I," Gran said.

"Where's Mom?" Alyssa pouted.

"Working the front desk."

"Reading a romance novel probably. We don't have any hotel reservations tonight."

"But we have plenty of dinner reservations. I'll take the fish problem." Gran straightened her wool blazer before returning to the dining room.

"There's no time for me to change and change back before eight thirty," Olivia said to Alyssa, "so I'll just have Brian come get me now." She pointed at the corner of her sister's mouth. "You've got some chocolate . . ." Then she picked up a plate and began to heap it full for Grandy. Her sleek skirts brushed against the tabletop. "Table one needs water, and fifteen is waiting on their check already. Seven said they might get dessert. You can keep the tips."

Alyssa grabbed a napkin and stormed out the door.

Olivia ate a crab cake straight out of the pan with her fingers, then with both hands full backed out of the kitchen. "Chef, these are amazing!"

"Not as amazing as that dress! Take pictures."

"See ya!"

Three bites into her fudgy cake, Kate was wishing for a glass of milk but didn't want to get up to get one. She and Great-Grandma Pearl were alone now, and the old lady was looking to steal the dessert. Her knot of blue-white hair was slipping to the left, and Kate felt strangely aware of the silence.

"I like your outfit," Kate said.

"I like your sister's outfit."

"You mean Olivia's?"

"Certainly not that boring pantsuit the other one wears every day! What's her name?"

That made Kate giggle. "Alyssa."

"In my day, half a skirt was scandalous, and even then they only chopped it halfway up the leg. Whoever thought of cutting it in half top to bottom? I love it."

Kate's giggle rolled into a wide-open laugh, and Great-Grandma Pearl joined her, and the sound lingered inside of Kate even after they were quiet again, filling her belly with a feeling that was better than sweets. More than half of the chocolate cake slice remained. She stood and slowly pushed her plate across the table to Pearl, who was still smiling, then took the rejected plate of crab cake and rice in exchange.

"I like rice too," Kate said, cleaning the chocolate off her spoon with her tongue.

The pair ate without saying anything more. Alyssa came in and out of the kitchen twice, barking commands at Chef. Kate almost ate the crab cake, but when her great-grandmother lifted her own plate to lick up the last bits of chocolate frosting and powdered sugar, Kate decided to pick up the last five grains of rice with her fingers, hunting them down as if she were the crab.

Great-Grandma Pearl lowered the plate and watched her, and in a blink her eyes turned glassy. In another blink the sheen was gone. Kate placed the last sticky piece of rice on her tongue, worried that she shouldn't have eaten Pearl's supper.

"Did you want some rice?" she asked.

"Absolutely not."

Kate heard Gran's voice beyond the kitchen doors. Quickly, she stood and leaned across the table. She took back the cleaned dessert plate for herself and pushed the dinner plate, now bearing only a single crab cake, back toward Pearl. Gran entered just as Kate dropped to her seat.

"Some people are just not worth the trouble." Gran sighed. "Well, at least you ate your rice, Mom. That's something."

"Fish spoils after three days," she said loudly. "Don't eat the plate."

Kate pressed her lips together. Gran sat down next to her and picked at a cold crab cake.

Great-Grandma Pearl caught Kate's eye and winked.

CHAPTER 10

The Fox calmed himself. He drew long, steadying breaths until the approaching sirens were all but silent in his own ears, though they drew closer and closer. His eyes burned, but he centered himself by calling up a picture of his son in his mind. Coz was the reason he must not get angry right now. Time for that later.

When the boy was in focus, he found it easier to reconstruct his mental images of the dead men walking who had taken his child: the blond one, wild and cowardly, more frightened by his friend's death than by his own mortality; and the capped one, with emotionless Asian features, calmer in his urgency to get out, more dangerous. As he committed these faces to memory his heart rate slowed down and his own quivering muscles stilled.

He listened closely, weighing the time left. The sirens were less than half a mile away.

Now he moved, squinting as the pepper spray allowed. The cool air on his skin brought some relief. The hit had not been direct, had not got his nose or mouth. He could press through it. Beginning at the motion-sensor light where the night's events had begun and ended, the Fox scanned the ground for anything that might have been dropped, anything that might tell him where these men were from, where his son had gone. Time was short for both of them. He followed the Chevy's route to the dispensary doors, now impaled by the long hood with the bloody windshield. He squinted at the employees milling around the violated grow room as though stunned. One of them nodded back and approached him as he laid two fingers at the base of the driver's neck.

"What happened?" The man stared at the dead driver.

"Three guys," the Fox said. "This one drives in, number two makes a break for the front of the store, number three shoots number one. Wham bam."

"His own man did this? Why?"

The Fox restrained his urge to lash out. It was impossible not to hear the question as a challenge to his own choice. Why had he shot the driver without giving him a chance to stand down? Street instincts, that's why. Three against one—a man's got to level the playing field before the enemies realize it's tipped in their favor.

"I guess that's for the real cops to sort out."

"Your son okay?"

"Sent him out for a bite before it all went down."

The man shook his head. "Unbelievable. Your face—"

"Nothing. I got it."

"Let me get you some water."

"Your people okay?"

"Yeah. I think so. If anyone had been standing right here . . ." He wandered back toward the wreckage of his inventory.

The Chevy's cab was empty of any personal effects, empty of everything, which told him what he already suspected. The old car was hot. He'd find nothing here to connect him to his son. The driver would be of no help either. Still, the Fox checked his pockets and found a wallet that held two dollars, a driver's license bearing a Colorado address, and a bus pass. He stuffed the bundle into his own pockets.

The cops were a quarter mile away now. With watery eyes he moved swiftly, away from the car and alongside the rear wall. He went all the way to the far side of the Laundromat before turning back, finding nothing but an empty canvas bag.

The Fox loped back to his idling Camaro. He threw himself on his belly, retrieved his pistol, and put it under his seat, still warm from hours of afternoon surveillance. From the glove box he pulled out his backup gun, the one he would show the police when they asked to see the weapon he carried.

His cell phone was in his hip pocket. He had time enough to make one phone call before the first black-and-white came around the back of the alley.

The Fox punched in a number and pulled out the driver's wallet, flipping to the license.

"Hector," he said. "Need you to check out an address."

Merridew was waiting under the bridge when they returned. Dusk had morphed to dark, and the beams of Eve's headlights found him leaning against the seat of his vintage Honda motorcycle, ankles crossed, arms folded over his broad chest beside a concrete pile. The man's build was thick. If it had been up to Charlie to name him he would have said Viking without a thought. Norseman. Thor. Something like that. The guy even had a beard, everything but a horned helmet. He wore leather gloves, ready to ride.

The sight kicked Charlie's mind into the past, into the many nights he had come home late—after school, after work—to find his father standing exactly this way in front of the house, reeking of alcohol and leaning against the porch rail so that Charlie couldn't pass.

Charlie's shoulder throbbed where it had been nicked by

Ender's knife. He'd lost the canvas bag and worried that the police would know it was his.

Eve's dull gray Audi, having lost the clear coat that made it platinum years ago, glided up next to the bridge column where Merridew waited. He straightened and Eve rolled down her window. He brought his beefy hand down onto the car's roof, thunderous, then leaned in. Eve stared out over the dashboard while the self-appointed head of their ragtag family scanned the inside of the car. His eyes lingered on the boy, on the MHH tattoo screaming from the side of his neck. They'd taped the kid's mouth and wrists and wrapped a torn T-shirt around his eyes.

Right now, the boy's blindness might be his only salvation.

"Where's Drogo?" Merridew asked.

"Dead," Ender said.

"How?"

Charlie said, "Mile High Heavies."

Silence stretched.

"And then you come back here with one of theirs." Merridew said it softly. "You might as well have aimed a blinking neon arrow right at our front door."

"We needed the kid so we could get out," Ender defended.

Merridew exploded. "And then you should have dumped him in the gutter!" His voice bounced around under the bridge.

The kid's panic had long since given way to paralysis. His jeans were dark in the front where he'd wet himself. The stink of it filled the car.

"We'll go do that now," Charlie said. "I'll drive." Charlie pulled on the door handle and pushed it open. Merridew's boot lashed out and kicked it shut.

"Not here," Merridew said. "Don't make me think you messed

this up just to annoy me. You'll be lucky if I let you set foot under this bridge again." Then to Eve: "Follow me."

Merridew mounted his bike and led them away, leaning into the tight Walnut Street curve and navigating the knots formed by Colfax and I-25 and downtown Denver. They headed north, then east, shooting out over Interstate 70.

Charlie stared out the window, wishing he had just kept going across that parking lot. Wishing—just for one second—that he still had a home, four walls and a roof and food in a pantry that a real father had put there. But in this life fathers put their kids in harm's way and blamed someone else for their own failure. Fathers pointed fingers. Or drank away the guilt.

Eve drove with both hands tight on the wheel.

Ender twisted around in the front seat, reached over the car's headrest, and tore the tape off the boy's mouth. The kid recoiled and pressed his body into the door, making himself even smaller than he was.

"You know where you are?" Ender asked.

The boy shook his head vigorously.

"Know where we took you?"

More of the same.

Eve said, "You can't trust that."

Charlie considered taking off the boy's blindfold, but apart from the certain objections, he doubted he could hold the kid's eyes. Besides, this problem wasn't his fault. The boy wasn't his responsibility.

"What's your name?" Ender asked.

"Coz."

"How old are you, Coz?"

"T-Twelve."

"What's your daddy's name?"

"F-Fox. The Fox."

The old Heavy's look made a little more sense to Charlie then: the red hair and white beard, the wide eyes and tall lids and long nose.

"Why'd a smart fox drag his boy to a shootout?"

"Weren't supposed to be no shootout."

There wasn't, Charlie thought. There was supposed to be a canvas bag over his shoulder and a paved road falling away under his feet as he slouched toward a new life.

Charlie said to Eve, "Take the next exit. Just let him out."

"He's *twelve*," Eve objected.

"You think he'll be better off with Merridew?" Charlie asked.

Her angry eyes darted to his in the rearview mirror. She held her course. "He said we'll let him out. Just not so close to home. I'm not taking any heat for what you guys messed up."

Ahead of them, Merridew was a single red taillight cutting through the darkness.

An iPod in a red case lay on the seat beneath Coz's hip, where it had fallen out. A black skull and crossbones had been printed on the front, a stupid fashion statement that looked more like a bad omen. Charlie didn't want to look at it. He wrapped the earbuds around it and crammed the thing back into the kid's sweatshirt pocket.

"You didn't really need him," Charlie said to Ender. "We had a clean getaway."

Ender shrugged, and until they reached the outskirts of the circus-tent international airport, white tarps posted against the night sky, Charlie thought that would be his only answer.

Then Ender muttered, "Fox took Drogo. Wasn't gonna let him take you too."

Eve reached across the seat and offered Ender her upturned hand.

The Fox might have taken Charlie. He was right on his heels, until Coz's screams. The possibility that Ender was telling the truth both shamed and angered Charlie. He didn't owe anyone anything, didn't want to. He regretted that he'd turned back.

Beside Charlie, Coz was using his elbow to search for the door handle. Charlie reached across him and punched down the door lock, then hauled Coz up by his skinny arm into a seated position. Drew his seat belt across his chest and buckled it.

"Don't do that," Charlie said. "You'll fall out and smash your head open."

CHAPTER 11

On the second-story landing above the reception desk, Kate sat and threaded her skinny legs between the balusters, gripping the old wood spindles like jail bars. Beneath her, Janet Whitby sat behind the island of mailboxes, perched on a stool, reading a fat paperback.

Kate let her legs swing a little. A clod of dirt fell from the sole of her boots and made a tiny explosion on the carpet. Janet didn't notice.

A basket that sat atop the shiny granite counter usually held homemade cookies for guests checking in. Tonight there were no reservations and no cookies in that basket. Hoping for walk-ins, Janet had dropped in three from Chef's frozen stash, then ate them as they thawed.

Kate had perched here for almost thirty minutes, waiting for the right moment to call down to her mother, perhaps be invited behind the desk to share the last half of cookie that remained. She wanted to tell her about Grandy's argument with Mr. Gorman and about what Mr. Gorman had done to Austin. She wanted to know if it was okay. But this simple act required more courage—or good timing—than Kate had tonight. For one, there was no way to tell the story without disclosing Austin's theft, and would that make her a true snitch? Also, if her mother worried about Mr. Gorman hitting kids, Kate might never see him again—and then how would she get that video she needed?

Janet tended to a stream of people in for dinner and out again, including Lane Warren, who knew her mother from the grocery store and bent her ear for twenty minutes around the needs of other guests. And in the downtime there was her mother's engrossing novel, which seemed to muffle all of Kate's soft calls: *Mom? Mom?*

Although she wasn't really trying very hard.

Directly in front of her, a two-story window offered a view of the front entry and wiggly private driveway, which wormed its way from the lodge down to the distant mountain road. The wrought-iron lamp that swung under the high portico threw its yellow glow across the balusters and striped her lanky body with long shadows. Darkness would fall earlier and earlier between now and Christmas, the day Kate counted on to start bringing the light back.

From up here Kate could see the guests arrive before her mother could. She often saw things her mother never noticed, though they had identical views: whether the guests had heeded the no-parking signs along the driveway, whether they were balding, whether they were trying to keep a forbidden pet hidden in the car. She also watched them depart, lingering to chat before climbing into their vehicles.

Tonight Kate watched her grandfather drive down the hill in his big Ford. He disliked driving in the dark, and there was no apparent emergency to require it. When Kate saw him go she felt glad that she hadn't told him about Austin on the way back from town that afternoon. No need to make things worse between Grandy and Mr. Gorman.

In the wake of Grandy's taillights she saw a hunched form wrapped in a winter coat plodding up the driveway without any car at all. She guessed it was a man, though it was too dark to see for sure, and a hat pulled low hid the face. The longish hair could have gone either way.

The front door glided open, quiet as a trout cutting through the creek. The cool air lifted Janet's chin and prompted her to put down her book. She set it spread-eagled atop a stack of green folders next to a pile of yellow receipts. On the cover, a woman in a fancy dress was fainting in the arms of a man who didn't even have a shirt.

Janet smoothed her hair and glanced in a mirror hanging on the backside of the mailboxes. She touched up her lipstick with a finger, turned sideways, and pressed a hand over her flat stomach, then presented herself.

"May I help you?" she asked in her prettiest smiling voice.

A wild beard masked the old man's face. His coat was buttoned all the way up to his chin. He removed his hat and held it against his heart, then with his other hand pressed his oily bangs back from his forehead.

Her mother's model shoulders drooped.

"Don't suppose you have a vacancy?"

"We do." Polite, but no longer cheerful. She tapped on the computer keyboard to wake up the screen. Behind Kate, a door to one of the empty rooms opened and Gran emerged, carrying a stack of folded towels. Kate stopped swinging her feet and went as still as a rabbit who doesn't want to be seen.

"What are you looking for?" Janet asked.

His eyes were clear, pale, and maybe blue. Kate thought he might be shy, the way he avoided looking directly at her mother. He stuck his hat-free hand into one of his deep pockets and withdrew a crumpled pile of money. A small pile with a few coins that made music on the granite counter when they rolled out of his palm.

"Tonight I'm looking for a little charity."

Janet's fingers hesitated above the keyboard.

"I can work the difference," he said. "Grounds keeping, carpentry, maintenance, I've done it all. Just need a rest first."

"I'm sorry, but we're not hiring at present, and we do require a credit card," Janet said.

The man tapped the bills as if she were asking for what he'd already put in front of her. Just an arm's length away from Kate, Gran's sensible shoes toed the balustrade.

"Maybe you'd like something to eat," Kate's mother said. "I can have Alyssa find you a seat in the dining room?"

The man pursed his lips. Janet put her hand on the pile of money and gently pushed it back toward him. "On the house. The crab cakes were so good tonight. Let me ask Chef—"

"We're no charity here," Gran said.

The man looked up to the stern voice and swayed just a little. Gran was already stalking out of the shadows and toward the staircase that took two square turns down to the main floor. Kate withdrew her legs to the shadows. Her mother was shaking her head.

"You're welcome to eat if you have money to pay," Gran called out. A few awkward seconds later she joined Janet behind the desk. "It doesn't look like you can pay."

The man clutched at the bills, and a few fluttered to the slate floor.

"We have plenty of food," Janet said to her mother.

"It's our off-season. Business is lean." Gran always spoke in a loud voice, but Janet winced at it now. Gran stooped beneath the counter and fetched an empty white envelope. "If we started giving our rooms and food away just because the weather is turning we'd go under. If it's shelter you need, there are places in Denver."

The man spoke. "I wasn't meaning for you to give—"

"Have you been drinking, sir?"

The clear eyes blinked, then scowled.

"He's perfectly sober," Janet said.

"I'm afraid I must ask you to leave." Gran set the envelope atop the small mound of cash and gave the pile a short-tempered shove. Two or three pennies waterfalled onto the hard floor. A couple leaving the dining room late cast a curious glance at the trio.

"Mother," Janet pleaded under her breath. The man crouched to collect his scattered coins. From her perch, Kate saw him come unbalanced and take a knee.

"Where is your father?" Gran said to Janet, then moved toward the red velvet rope that separated their private residence from the rest of the lodge. "Daniel! We could use your assistance here. Daniel!"

The old man swept the ground with his palms. The paper envelope crackled as he tried to fill it quickly. Kate could see a quarter on the area rug behind him. When he stood, he cracked his shoulder on the overhanging counter.

"Oh my, oh no, are you okay?" Janet reached out but stopped shy of touching him. He waved her off and left the lodge, clutching his bruised arm. And then he did the strangest thing. As the doors eased shut behind him, he spit on the ground right in front of the door.

Janet looked away, her hand over her mouth. The man's quarter still lay on the carpet, glinting.

Sometimes a good spy has to think things through. Other times she has to jump at an opportunity before it's gone, and this was such a moment. Kate flew. She made it down the stairs in a fraction of the time it had taken Gran, but with a great deal more noise, a thundering of her clunky boots. She swooped for the quarter, snatched it up on the first pass, then backtracked into the hall that led to the kitchen.

"Kathy?" she heard her mother say.

The kitchen was clean and quiet. The stainless steel shone, the floors were still wet from mopping, and the brightest overhead lights had already been shut off. Chef was on the phone in her office.

Kate avoided Chef's office and followed the wall to the pantry, where she found a small cardboard crate that still held three huge pomegranates. Alongside these she placed what food she thought she could carry: a massive can of tuna, a bag half full of dinner rolls, a handful of red potatoes, a slab of baker's chocolate, and a wreath of dried figs.

Then she went to the freezer, yanked open the door, and pulled out four frozen cookies, their plastic wrap cloudy from the cold. She had no idea where the leftover crab cakes were and hoped the man wouldn't miss them too much. The box was nearly too heavy to haul out of the pantry and across the kitchen to the delivery door at the side, but she did it.

The blacktopped driveway for kitchen deliveries abutted the main parking lot, and Kate followed it to the front of the lodge, planning to turn downhill. The front entry was the last place she expected to find him. But there he was, still in front of the door, pacing and muttering, and he shook out his hands like a person who couldn't find any towels after washing up.

She adjusted her grip on the crate by bumping it with her knee.

He spun to the sound, startling her.

"Uh, I got this for you."

He came across the pebbled pavement until he was close enough to scan the contents of the box, but when he didn't take it she bent over and set it on the ground. She scooped his quarter out of her jeans pocket.

"And I think you dropped this."

She held it out to him.

The man glanced at the quarter, at the box, the quarter, the box. Then his gaze took in her boots, and he smiled.

"You were upstairs," he said. Then, staring straight into her eyes, he reached out and took the quarter. He took it the way the squirrels took peanuts from the wildlife dishes: swiftly, precisely, tails twitching the whole time.

His left eye drooped a little.

"Thank you, young lady."

"Welcome."

Kate shoved her hands into her pockets. He put the quarter in his.

They considered each other.

The old man lowered his voice: "You understand hospitality, child."

"Thank you," she said.

"Could be that you save this place after all."

Kate didn't know what to say. She hated when adults talked in zigzag lines.

He hefted the crate and a single potato rolled out onto the ground and into the beam of the floodlights. The man didn't notice. He uttered a happy groan.

"I *looove* pomegranates, don't you?"

They weren't worth the trouble, Kate thought. Too much messy work to get out all those tiny seeds. She'd rather spend that kind of time cracking a code. But she nodded.

"Don't lie to me, child."

Kate kept her smile glued to her face, and the old man chuckled. He shifted the crate to one hand and tousled her hair with the other.

"Yessir," he announced, "you've got what it takes." His palm was leathery and smelled of horses, but his skin was cold.

"Mister," she said, "I could sneak you into a room if you still need a place to sleep."

"Now that's a real nice thought, that is," he said. "But this here will keep me warm tonight."

Gran's loud voice reached out to them from inside the inn, her words muffled but her tone clear. She was still looking for Grandy.

"That'll be my cue to get going," the man said. "You tell the old witch I haven't had a drink in nine years."

"Nine years, bah!"

The outburst came from a ghost standing in the shadows. No, not a ghost, Kate quickly saw, but Great-Grandma Pearl, standing on the drive in her white nightgown. Her fine white hair was undone. It lay across her back like a paper-thin bridal veil and her feet were bare.

"You got nothin' on me," Pearl said to the drifter. Her white tresses quivered like her hands and arms, unstable limbs. "I've been a teetotaler eighty-seven years. Spit on that, why don't you? Eighty-seven years, Mr. Spit on My Welcome Mat!" She grunted and rolled one of her feet sideways, as if to see if she'd stepped in something.

The old man laughed at that, and Kate wondered if she'd made the right decision to give him food. It wasn't right for a man to go hungry if there was food to feed him, but she didn't like the way he laughed at Great-Grandma Pearl. She felt strangely like she had when she watched Mr. Gorman hit Austin in the face. But she couldn't say exactly what that feeling was. She watched the man saunter down the hill, his gait lopsided under the bulk of the crate.

Shame gnawed at Kate's stomach.

"I'm sorry, Grandma Pearl."

"Pooh. What for? He got what he needed. He's the one who should be apologizing. No one calls my girl an old witch. Even if she is one."

Gran's silhouette appeared in the doorway. Kate stepped back into the shadows.

"Daniel!" And then she saw Great-Grandma Pearl. "Mom! What on earth are you doing out here? Where are your shoes!" Worry soaked her strident voice, changing her tone completely.

Great-Grandma Pearl turned to Gran. "The British are coming," she announced.

"Is that so?" Gran gently took her pointy elbow and encircled her waist. She kissed her mother's temple.

"The British are coming," Pearl whispered again, then closed her eyes and sighed.

"If that's the case we'd better get you to bed. You'll want your beauty rest in time to welcome them."

Kate stayed put, shivering in the dark, until the women disappeared into the warm light of the lodge.

CHAPTER 12

T he end of the world lay east of the airport. By night, the plains
were black and their tall wild grasses dry and brittle. The gusty
air was far more clear than Charlie's thoughts, and when Merridew
opened his door and motioned him out of the car, understanding
blew across his mind. He spoke to Merridew, quick and low, before
Ender and Eve opened their doors.

"You do this and you'll bring every Denver gang down on
your head." They stood in the dark gap between the vehicle and
Merridew's motorcycle, their faces made of shadows.

"I'm not going to do anything," Merridew said. "You are."

He left Charlie rooted by the rear fender of the old car and
rounded the trunk to get Coz. He opened the door and tried to pull
the kid out. Swore when he had to stoop to undo the belt. Choice
words for Charlie's unnecessary precautions.

Coz stumbled out and Merridew pushed him forward, into the
beams of the headlights. The boy barely stood, crouching as if trying to stay out of harm's way. Ender got out of the car. Eve stayed in.

"I worry about your loyalty, Charlie," Merridew said. "You won't
take a family name, got trouble following directions. I haven't even
been on top three days now and one of our own is dead."

Wind flicked Charlie's ears and tugged at his cap.

With his gloved hand Merridew pushed down on the boy's
shoulder and Coz folded, kneeling on the ground. "Don't move."

Then he pointed to his bike. "Gun in the left saddlebag. Get it."

Charlie did not move.

Merridew lifted his stiff black boot and kicked Coz at the base of his spine. Coz wailed.

"Get it."

Charlie went.

The gun was old, a black Beretta 92 that might have once belonged to a cop. Charlie hefted it in his palm, feeling the textured grip against his thumb pad and the weight of the polymer pressing down on his conscience. He should have convinced Eve to drop the kid miles and miles ago. All the way back at the pickup location. All the way back at the Camaro. All the way back at whatever moment Ender had decided to believe that Charlie was a brother worth saving. Because he wasn't. He just wasn't.

In the distance cars flowed along the highway, painting sleek red and white lines against the night sky.

Merridew materialized at Charlie's ear, so close his beard tickled Charlie's skin.

"Kill him," Merridew whispered.

"I can't."

"You can."

"I won't. He's a *kid*."

"His people took your brother."

"But *he* didn't. They'll know you did it."

Merridew laughed. "If the Heavies show up at our bridge, it's because you led them there, dragging one of their boys back to our territory. You don't think I'd let this kid tell his daddy where we live."

"He doesn't know."

"You'll make sure of it."

"No."

"Then you'll never return to our bridge."

"Okay." Charlie held the gun out to Merridew, grip first.

"Because I'll kill you too. Boy dies both ways, and his blood's on your hands."

"How do you plan that?" Charlie asked. "Since I'm the one holding the gun?"

On his other side, Eve pressed the answer into his cut bicep: the teeth of a Taser. She applied her featherweight strength, and the hurt shot down his arm even without the electricity.

"Eve, c'mon."

Her eyes held an apology. "We've gotta make this work," she said. "If we don't stick together now none of us are gonna make it."

It would've been nice if she'd thought so before Merridew took over. But Charlie knew better than to say so. He held both hands up, the gun hooked around his thumb, and stepped away from the Taser.

"The range on this is fifteen feet." Eve said it like a threat.

Charlie heard it as a fantastic piece of information, such a gift that he wondered if she was on his side after all. Her face gave nothing away, but she adjusted her stance and shifted the Taser slightly left. He held eyes with her as he ejected the gun's magazine into the palm of his hand. The fifteen-round compartment held only one cartridge.

"Shouldn't take more than one," Merridew said. Between his thumb and forefinger he held another magazine, this one fully loaded.

In the car, Ender had taken the driver's seat. Ten feet away, on his knees in front of the car, the kid begged and blubbered.

"Please don't kill me. Please don't."

Charlie reinserted the magazine and aimed the weapon at Merridew. Eve held her position. He swiveled slowly and aimed the gun at her. Neither of his opponents moved.

Eve winked.

It was a test?

One bullet. A blank. One chance to prove that he could coexist with Merridew without actually having to do anything wrong.

He turned and walked to the front of the car, dry grasses bowing under his shoes and poking his bare ankles. He aimed the barrel at the knot that tied the T-shirt blindfold behind the kid's head. The gun wobbled, and he could not steady it any more than Coz could control his rattling sobs.

It was just a Heavy's head.

Charlie took a shaking breath.

A gangster's head. A killer's head. The last head who'd watched a bullet go through Drogo's head.

Coz's head.

When Charlie was twelve his uncle Jun told him a story of a god who told a man to prove his devotion by killing his son. The man didn't want to do it, but he was nothing if not loyal. So he raised a weapon against the boy—a knife? a spear? a hatchet?—and as the blade was poised to fall, the god changed his mind. It was enough for the man to kill a goat instead, he decided. Or was it some other creature? Tonight the variables didn't matter; what Charlie remembered most at this moment, as he aimed a pistol at a child's head, was the shock on Uncle Jun's face when Charlie asked if he knew any stories about a god telling a boy to kill his father.

Had there ever been such a thing as family loyalty, from the dawn of time until now?

Charlie swung his arm away and fired at the Audi's front

tire, only half surprised when the pistol bucked and the rubber exploded. Coz fainted. Eve launched the Taser.

The electrodes flew wide of him, their charged wires shimmering. That, then, explained the wink. The bullet was real enough, but her aim would be untrue. Charlie hoped Merridew didn't know her well enough to punish her for that miss.

He stumbled to the far side of the sedan, pushing the pistol down into his waistband against his backbone, barrel tangling in his T-shirt. Merridew was cursing and leaping toward the headlight beams where Charlie had just stood. Ender opened the driver's door and caught Merridew in the ribs. Lucky coincidence, or had Eve and Ender spent their sixty seconds alone in the car plotting a few bumbling moves?

Charlie vaulted the trunk while Merridew was still getting off the ground. He was three seconds out of Merridew's reach, all the time he needed to straddle the Honda, crank the engine, and spin out of the scene.

The rushing air roared in his ears, colder than he expected as he aimed for the road they'd left such a short time ago. He felt disoriented. He worried he was rocketing in the wrong direction, back toward Denver and the Fox and the bridge that could no longer be his home. East. He needed to find east.

His cap's bill flapped crazily on his brow. He yanked it off and made a clumsy move to cram it into his back pocket.

Which was when he noticed the gun was gone. Fallen, jarred, lost.

Five seconds later, he heard the second shot.

CHAPTER 13

Grandy's workshop was silent. The Explorer was still gone. The plate of food Olivia had prepared for him hours earlier sat untouched on his desk. Kate worried about where he had gone in the darkness.

She stepped out of the workshop into the lodge and Grandy's door shut hard behind her. At the other end of the long hall, Gran's head popped out of her private suite.

"Oh! Katherine. I thought it was Daniel."

"Grandy's not there."

"Clearly." Gran lowered her chin and studied Kate over the tops of her glasses. "Shouldn't you be in bed by now?"

"It's not a school night."

She hadn't meant to be sassy. She'd only wanted to make sure Gran could hear her. They regarded each other. Gran checked her watch.

"Go find something to do then. And if you see your grandpa, tell him I'm looking for him."

"Okay."

Gran went back into her suite and shut the door.

Kate wasn't someone who scared easily, but whenever the sun went down her worries went up, especially if she had to sleep in her empty cottage. Her mother would be on the desk until midnight, Olivia probably wouldn't come home until dawn, and sharing the cottage with Alyssa was worse than being there alone. If Kate slept at all she'd dream of Austin giving her stitches, and of Mr. Gorman punching Grandy in the nose.

The red velvet rope stretched across the entry between the hall and the lobby. Standing behind the little gold sign that said PRIVATE, Kate looked out toward her mother, who was telling a skinny lady and a fat man about all their different rooms. He wanted to see pictures because they couldn't very well get a good sense of the views at night, now, could they?

The click of a latch releasing and the gentle scrape of a door dragged open across carpet pulled Kate's attention back toward Gran's room. But it was the door on the other side of the hall that opened, and her white-haired great-grandmother leaning out into the passage this time, beckoning Kate with her bony finger.

Kate walked down to the threshold, having been barred from this room since she was old enough to walk. *Don't disturb Grandma Pearl. She needs her rest.*

"Is it okay with Gran?" Kate asked quietly so Gran wouldn't hear.

"So now I need permission from my daughter to invite a guest into my room?"

Kate stepped in and passed into another country. Opposite the door a low fire crackled in an old brick fireplace, and on each side built-in bookcases, loaded with disorganized books stacked upright and sideways and several titles deep, spanned the wall from floor to ceiling. Two green velvet reading chairs with cushions trimmed in piping sat before the hearth, on either side of a coffee table. To Kate's right, the window that overlooked the terrace was covered by a pretty screen instead of curtains, a dark-wood panel of tiny squares and rectangles and panes of rice paper.

On another wall, two simple wood tables flanked a double bed, which was topped with a gold satin bedspread quilted with cherry blossoms. Over the bed hung a pretty painting. A man walked up a mountain path toward a distant house. Beneath him was a white capped river; above him towering evergreens grew straight up out of the hillside. And above all this a great bird flew, a huge white bird larger than everything else, with long legs and broad wings that cast a shadow over the man and the house. A beautiful dresser almost as tall as Kate stood beside the closet, the shining grain of the wood seeming to ripple like water. Glass perfume bottles and small ceramic birds covered the dresser top.

"This room used to be my father's study." Great-Grandma Pearl gestured to the green seats. "The chairs are different but I've kept them in the same place. He and I would read together before the fire, after I was supposed to be abed."

Kate wondered if she could touch the books on the shelves.

"We don't know each other very well, do we?" Pearl said.

"No, ma'am."

"Why do you suppose that is?"

"I'm supposed to stay out of the way."

"We have that in common, then." Great-Grandma Pearl crossed the dim room. Her shoulders were stooped but her chin lifted her entire head, and she kept balance by reaching out to touch the two chairs as she passed.

"Gran says you're delicate."

"Delicate people make your gran feel strong."

"And Alyssa says you've gone crazy."

"Well, that much might be true."

Kate wasn't sure whether she should sit. She touched the shimmering bedspread. Great-Grandma Pearl paused in front of the closet and slid its wide panel door into a pocket.

"I wanted to talk to you about giving food to that man," she said.

Kate bit her lip. "Am I in trouble?"

"Not with me. But that child of mine, that Donna, your gran, you don't want her finding out about it. She forgets even more than I do."

"Forgets what?"

"Come here."

Kate approached the closet and was surprised to see that the inside reached all the way to the end of the wall behind the dresser and had space enough to walk into. Tidy rows of clothes hung on both sides. The whole closet smelled flowery.

"Go down there and look behind the dress with all the sequins. The one covered in plastic."

Kate wandered in and gently pushed the dress aside. In the wall, a tiny knob stuck out of a little rectangular panel no larger than a book. "What is it?" she asked.

"Open it."

The panel slid aside when she pushed it, sticking only once, and Kate found herself peering out into the reception hall. The leaves of a small potted tree offered some cover. Ahead of her were the red velvet rope and the pretty double doors, and off to the right were the reception desk and wide square staircase.

Kate looked back at her great-grandmother, grinning.

"My father liked to see the company before they saw him," she said, matching Kate's smile.

"Do you spy on people?"

"Maybe. This property is full of such spots. Haven't you found them yet, child?"

"Some."

Great-Grandma Pearl flipped off the light while Kate was still deep in the closet and went back into the main room. Kate dashed after her, half worried she would also close the door.

"Now Donna, she calls you Katherine. And your mother, she calls you Kathy. I've heard my son-in-law call you Katy, or Agent K, or something nonsensical like that, and that awful pantsuit child whom I must acknowledge is also of my blood, from what I hear she has turned your regal name into an animal's. Kat-with-a-K? How did you land something so banal?"

Kate was too overwhelmed to answer. She reminded herself to look up *banal*. And what was the other word? Oh yeah: *landlocked*.

"Fine then. What is it exactly that I should call you?"

"Kate, please."

"Very well, because you said please. How old are you these days, Kate? I can't keep track anymore."

"Eleven. How old are you?"

"Eighty-seven going on eight months. Got diapers and everything. Come here. I want to show you something else."

Pearl pulled open the drawer in the side table. She withdrew a large flat object, which Kate soon saw was another picture frame, larger than the ones on the dresser. Her great-grandmother touched her fingertips to the glass as she sank onto the gold silk.

"A long time ago, during the second war, a man came to Evergreen without enough money to buy food. My father overheard his story at the general store and invited him to take lunch with us. See?" Great-Grandma Pearl held the gilded frame out to Kate. It held a black-and-white photo, damaged by water spots, of a young Japanese man wearing a work shirt, sagging trousers that rumpled at his ankles, and a battered hat. He looked clean but oddly skinny, and kind: a full smile reduced his eyes to crinkling slits. A leather satchel hung from his fingertips.

"Father had traveled to Japan in his line of work and also in his leisure, and perhaps his familiarity put both men at ease. Kiyoshi Nagasawa. We called him Kenneth. Do you know this name?"

Kate shook her head.

"Of course not. No one teaches the children their family history anymore. Mr. Nagasawa was our guest for lunch that afternoon, which was when we discovered he knew a thing or two about gardening. This place wasn't a hotel then, you understand. We were just a rich family in a pretty house."

"So he was your gardener?"

"More than that, Kate Whitby. This man became your great-grandfather."

"That's Great-Grandpa Ken?" Kate leaned against the bed.

"Before he was even my husband, yes. I'm glad you at least know his family name."

"Great-Grandpa Ken was Japanese?"

"And as American as you or I, the third generation of his family born in this country. Though many Americans did not treat him as such when the war started."

"The war?"

"World War II."

Kate dug the toe of her shoe into the bald spot of carpet right beside the bed. Her great-grandmother smelled flowery like the closet. "Why not?"

"People had their own beliefs about him."

"There's this boy named Austin. He thinks I'm a snitch."

"Are you?"

"No!"

"Good then."

"But how do you make people believe the truth?"

"You don't. You have to decide what people think or say about you doesn't matter."

"Why?"

"Because if you don't, what they believe will *change* the truth."

Kate decided she would have to think about that.

"Did you ever hear the story of Joseph and Potiphar's wife?" Pearl asked.

Kate shook her head.

"Well, you might be a bit young for that one yet."

"Tell me!"

"It's a Bible story about someone who was falsely accused. You can look it up. Won't have your gran angry that you heard such a scandal from me."

"Did Great-Grandpa Ken die before I was born?"

"Before your mother was born, in fact. What few family pictures I had came down to make way for Donna's magazine-worthy hotel."

Kate's attention wandered back to the closet, and to the possibility of other spy spots with peepholes.

"Why am I showing this to you?" Pearl asked. She dropped her voice to a whisper. "Any guesses?"

Her great-grandmother's eyes were sharp and so penetrating that Kate thought she might be able to see every secret she had ever kept from anyone: Alyssa's theft and Mr. Gorman's violence and Janet's romance novels and Austin's revenge . . .

"So we can share a secret?" Kate whispered back, never more surprised than when her answer raised tears in Great-Grandma Pearl's eyes. What had she said wrong?

The old woman slipped the picture frame back into the drawer. "It was not always a secret that the Harrison Lodge got its start when my father first gave food and shelter to a man who could not pay for it."

A loud ding startled them both. Someone out at the reception desk hit the old bell several more times, and the sound was far too loud. The man who had demanded to see pictures of each room's view was calling out *hello, hello* as if Janet had left him to fend for himself.

"My dear Kate," Pearl scolded. "Did you leave the secret door open?"

"Sorry." Kate bounded off the bed.

"Don't you play hide-and-seek? Hiding places are only good for as long as they stay hidden."

"I know."

"We really ought to play sometime."

"But then you'd never see me again!"

Great-Grandma Pearl laughed like a little girl, and Kate plunged in among the musty clothes without needing to be told not to turn on the light.

CHAPTER 14

Charlie nearly lost control of the bike. The head-splitting noise of that shot ricocheted around in his ears long after the real sound died away, and then the denial set in.

Merridew was just angry, firing his fury into the empty fields.

Merridew had shot Eve for losing Charlie.

Merridew had taken out Ender for perceived disloyalty.

But not the boy. He had nothing to gain by killing a boy who wasn't even in the family.

What's your name? Coz. How old are you, Coz? T-Twelve.

Losing that gun had been no different from pulling the trigger himself, whomever it might have hit.

The front wheel took a pothole and the bike wiggled under Charlie's weak grip, his noodle arms. He wrangled it to the shoulder of the narrow county road.

The stars were brighter out here than they were in the city, but their light kept its distance. Even the white moon withdrew from the darkness. Charlie could see his own hands as silhouettes backlit by the bike's faint displays, but without these he might vanish even to his own eyes.

He looked back over his shoulder, seeking the Audi's headlights. Merridew must have shut them off. No need to hide from Charlie, every need to hide from faraway ears that might think they'd heard more than a car backfiring. Charlie turned off his own lights and cut the bike's engine.

The second bullet had found its target. Merridew wouldn't have stopped firing until it did. This thought sparked another, a stunner. What if Eve or Ender had found the gun first?

Charlie had to know where the second bullet had landed, who had stood in its way.

He dismounted the bike and kicked it into neutral, then guided it into a U-turn. To the northwest, the glowing airport was little more than a single white Christmas bulb. He tried to assess how far he had come and how long it would take him to walk the bike back, but the blanket of black sky made this difficult. Still, he had to know. All but blind, he angled away from the road to avoid headlights, willing his ears to detect what his eyes could not. He kept a slow pace to muffle his own noises. Brittle weeds scratched at his ankles and snapped under the rubber treads.

In a short time hushed voices came to him through the thin air and he paused. A tiny firefly light flickered some twenty-five yards away, and a dull clunking, metal on metal, joined the murmuring.

"Shine it here." Ender? Or Merridew? The voice was a distorted hiss, strained and afraid. Merridew wouldn't be afraid. "This nut."

They were trying to change the blown tire by penlight.

Careful not to make noise, Charlie laid the bike down on its side, then flattened himself on his stomach to avoid being seen should a brighter light flare up.

The lug wrench was cast to the ground and the weak light blinked. Someone swore. "Rust," the voice said. "It's stuck." Charlie strained to hear the sounds of Coz crying. Maybe the kid still hadn't come around after passing out. Maybe he was buckled into the backseat.

"Gimme the spare." Someone handed it over. A battering of tire on tire followed, until the rubbery noises gave way to a clatter and the old wheel came free. The rest of the job was finished swiftly, the spare tire crammed onto the hub, the lug nuts spinning onto the bolts, the wrench securing them.

"Put that wheel in the trunk. We go now. Lights off."

The car was already rolling away when the last person in threw the hubcap and the jack onto the floorboards, then climbed in and slammed the door. Still Charlie didn't know whether he eavesdropped on friends or foes. The Audi rolled by his position in blackout, moving down the road like a stalking black panther, all the way to the crossroads a quarter mile away. There, the headlights popped on and the car turned right, aiming for the interstate, and picked up speed.

Even after they were out of sight, Charlie waited long minutes before rising, stooping, lifting his bike, switching on the headlamp.

A cone of yellow parted the darkness and Charlie pushed forward, gaze sweeping the dry ground until he spotted scattered bits of rubber. Here he paused, then decided to walk the bike in a widening spiral. There would be blood even if there was no body, but Charlie didn't know which he'd rather find: mystery or certainty?

A shoe came into view. A bulky athletic shoe with the tongue lolling out to the side, just large enough to fit an adolescent boy's foot.

It was a mistake to let the bike fall, but all the blood had rushed out of Charlie's head and it wasn't a conscious choice. The beam of the lamp cut across the kid's blindfolded face and the puddle of sopping black earth under his cheek. Charlie fell to his knees.

In twenty-one years, he had seen his share of violence. Among relatives: abuse and abandonment. Among authorities: betrayal and hypocrisy. Among strangers: disregard and injury, every encounter a fight for respect, resources, and relief. And although his faith in people had been murdered again and again over the years since he was a boy, he'd never laid eyes on a dead child, let alone one brutally killed.

He could not stop the trembling in his body, not even when he reached out to touch Coz's shoe, proving the vision real.

My name is Coz and I'm twelve years old and I need some help.

Charlie couldn't have helped. This is what he told himself. There was nothing he could have done. There was no time, just as there had been no time to help Drogo.

Two boys, dead in one night.

Charlie's fault.

Not his fault.

His fault . . .

No, he didn't have to own this.

Charlie turned his face into the blackness and retched.

THE GUN WAS THE REASON MERRIDEW HAD KILLED THE BOY. The gun bore Charlie's fingerprints, and Charlie had a record, a face to go with the weapon that had killed the kid. Merridew would have left the weapon here, at the scene, where the cops could find it.

Charlie had to find the gun. He cleaned his face with the tail of his shirt and picked up the bike. By the light of the headlamp he made a search in a widening spiral, gradually moving away from Coz's body. But the cone of light wasn't bright enough to be useful in the scrub, and soon enough he couldn't see Coz anymore. He lost his center and sensed his search lines weren't clean. Merridew might have heaved the weapon thirty yards off. Way too far for Charlie to recover in the void of night, easy enough for law enforcement to catch sight of come the dawn.

How much time did he have before Merridew made a call to report his motorcycle stolen? How much more time after that before he stopped off at a pay phone and forced Eve to call in an anonymous tip to police? *There's a dead boy in the fields, east, a few miles past the airport . . .*

Even now, a set of slow-moving headlights traveled in his direction down the county road.

Charlie pushed the bike back to Coz, trying to decide what to do. He took off his button-front shirt and draped the light cotton over the boy's broken face.

"I'm sorry," he whispered.

The falling temperatures wicked all the warmth off Charlie's skin and sharpened his mind. He straddled the Honda and faced west, the direction a sane man wouldn't take. West was Denver, Merridew, the Fox, the informed authorities. But west was where he went.

Reason one: Everyone had seen him go east.

Two: He had a limited amount of fuel and no money to buy more.

Three: It would be easier to hide in the mountains than on the plains.

The headlights he had seen did not belong to a police cruiser, but the next set might. Charlie accelerated.

As he passed through Watkins he spied a motorcycle parked at a motel and pulled into the lot, keeping to the shadows of the building. With a screwdriver from a small tool kit he found in Merridew's saddlebags, he braved the neon exposure of the motel sign and removed the other motorcycle's tags. He also helped himself to the black helmet hanging from the bike handles. By the time he returned to his own ride he was dripping with sweat that chilled him to the bone. The helmet was too large, and this fact hurried him along. The last thing he needed was to be noticed by a biker twice his size. Charlie crammed the helmet down straight over his knit cap and still had wiggle room.

Merridew had left him only a quarter of a tank. Less than a hundred miles, Charlie guessed. And where could he go within that limited radius?

Only one possibility came to his mind, and he didn't like it. But he had to keep moving.

Charlie stayed west on Interstate 70 and made it through Denver without drawing any attention to himself, insofar as no one seemed to notice the fool wearing little more than a T-shirt doing sixty-five in the brisk November air. The scent was icy and slick, the kind of clear sky that warned of snow. By Commerce City he was a shivering mass of goose bumps and dread, his coarse sweaty hair plastered to his brow under the helmet and cap. He plowed past Arvada and Wheat Ridge, veered around Lakewood, then began to climb the short foothills toward Genesee.

The turnoff to Evergreen finally appeared. He had to decide.

Evergreen might be a stroke of good luck. He could get there without running out of fuel. It did not sit on any high-trafficked interstates or highways. And there were several different ways in and out of town.

Or it might be the worst decision he ever made. Uncle Jun lived there. Unless he'd moved away in the years since Charlie had seen him.

Would he be an ally or an enemy?

From Interstate 70 the road dropped south into a valley just as black and bleak as the fields east of the airport, though it was beautiful by daylight. Abutting the darkness, the north side of town was unexpectedly populated with bright homes dotting the foothills. He passed strip malls and gas stations and for a moment feared he had made a bad choice. It was more suburban than he remembered, too close to civilization with its face turned toward the Rocky Mountain peaks and its feet firmly planted in a forest of satellite dishes and mortgages.

Charlie dropped farther toward the tiny lake at the town's hub, second-guessing himself, desperate to get off the main drag. Could he even find his uncle's house after all this time?

First he needed a place to hide the bike. The national forest seemed his best bet for that. A mound of Ponderosa needles might hide the Honda through the winter. He would hide the stolen motorcycle, steal a jacket from a car or a campsite, and hitch a ride back into town. He'd find a bar, a directory, a phone number.

The parking lot of an Evergreen bar was the last place he'd seen Uncle Jun, almost five years ago now. His drunk father was passed out on the blacktop. The drinking had grown worse since Charlie's Aunt Makiko had died. His father's sister. His uncle's wife. Jun's small four-wheel-drive idled beside his brother-in-law, exhaust blooming in the cold night. *We must help each other out now that Makiko is gone*, Uncle Jun had said to Charlie. *You come home with me tonight. Your father can sober up in jail.*

He'll never be sober, Charlie said. He kept his arms crossed over his bruised stomach. He imagined internal bleeding, invisible wounds opened up by his father's intoxicated punches.

Then he will be a stranger to us both, and you and I will find our way together.

Instead Charlie took the car keys and forty-three dollars from his father's rumpled jacket, left the suffocating small town where everyone would openly stare at his brokenness, and drove back to

Denver. The next morning he dropped out of school and hit the streets. But he kept his name, not recognizing until now his hope that his father or uncle might track him down and forbid him from being so headstrong and stupid.

Now he was twenty-one, too old to ask Uncle Jun if he could change his mind. His visit to Evergreen would have to be brief.

The road that would take Charlie to the forest sprouted off Evergreen's central lake—he remembered that much, but nothing more specific. He steered the bike around a curve and was suddenly there, the lake a blacker black hole in front of him, the roads veering left and right. He reacted instinctively and went right, catching a quick glimpse of a sign. Upper Bear Creek Road.

Within a mile it became clear that this was not the road he needed. The lanes were narrow and the curves were tight, but the similarities ended there. He saw none of the one-room cottages or cracker-box homes sitting on top of the street as he had expected, no shelters built by the gold miners and lumberjacks who'd rushed to Evergreen a century and a half earlier and then decided to stay. Charlie was climbing past mansions, palaces, estates with storybook names posted on illuminated signs. The enormous homes withdrew into the trees at the end of carefully landscaped driveways, their warm gold lights winking behind foliage like hidden wealth. One after the other, after the other.

If his father had ever come this way, shame would have turned him around. But Charlie was not his father. The Rockies' national forests were sprawling places with multiple accesses. He decided to see what lay ahead.

Another mile later he broke out of the trees under a clear sky, where the homes became fewer and more scattered but no less affluent, and less than a mile after that he understood that he was becoming more and more exposed and less sheltered. The needle on his gas meter tipped toward empty. Charlie swore and pulled off the road, then turned and pointed his bike back downhill. Numbness had spread from his hands to the center of his chest, and he breathed the thin air through shrunken lungs.

Less than an hour had passed since he covered Coz's face, but he was angry to lose time. More, he was mad at the cold, and at the sound of Coz's plaintive sobbing in his head, which the rushing wind couldn't muffle. As he returned to the encroaching evergreens and mansions, Charlie pushed the bike a little harder to drown out the noise.

The engine's roar was not enough to warn away the animal that crouched in the lane just beyond the next tight curve. The massive cougar was at least a hundred pounds, its tail as thick as Charlie's arm. The creature froze on the center line and Charlie wrenched his handlebars and then the beast leaped away, neither of them fast enough. Charlie struck its hindquarters.

The world tilted, then tumbled. The right side of his body hit the ground first. The bike landed next, pinning him to the road and briefly dragging him before releasing his leg and somersaulting away, tapping his right ankle as it did—a swift strike that turned those small bones into broken twigs.

Pain swallowed him, and Charlie rolled until he was senseless. A swarm of dead leaves that had gathered in a natural drainage ditch accepted his body and, finally, blanketed him from the deepening cold.

SUNDAY

CHAPTER 15

Kate wasn't sure what woke her. The noise was a scraping sound from a nightmare. In it Austin dragged Mr. Gorman's dragon knife across a whetstone from Chef's kitchen. When she opened her eyes, Austin wasn't hovering over her, but Kate thought she heard the noise one more time.

Her mother breathed restlessly on the twin bed beside Kate's. By the light left on in the front room, Kate could see that Janet was still dressed in everything but her high-heeled shoes, kicked off in front of the door. Kate sat up. Janet stirred.

The clock on the nightstand said it was nearly one in the morning. Kate lay back down but couldn't return to sleep. Austin kept dragging that knife blade across her imagination, and though she knew the sound wasn't real, it frightened her just the same. She realized her mother had opened the window, and the room filled with all sorts of sounds that could inform a girl's dreams. Traffic down on the road. A splashing in the creek, a large lumbering animal stumbling through the current. Maybe an elk. Olivia's boyfriend's rattling old car creeping up the driveway.

A car door slammed, and a minute or so later Kate watched her middle sister come into the cottage as if breaking into a bank, stepping over the squeaky spot in the floor and opening the door just far enough to keep the hinges from squealing. A funny scent, mildly burned and stinky, rode into the cottage on Olivia's costume. She tried to close the door slowly, but the cross breeze from

Kate's open window yanked the doorknob out of her hands. Olivia barely caught it before it slammed.

She went into the other bedroom without turning off the lights, and eventually the tiny house stilled again.

Outside, a snarling yowl kept Kate's eyes wide open. In these foothills, it was impossible to tell whether a sound came from miles away or right next door.

A few minutes later—or had she dozed off?—a gust lifted the curtain at Kate's window, and then the front door blew open. Apparently Olivia had failed to secure the latch.

Kate rose from bed shivering and pulled down the sash. Her soft green blanket, which she wrapped herself in for TV time, was folded at the foot of her bed. She shook it out and draped the plush knit across her mother's shoulders, then after a moment's hesitation went out to close the front door and turn off the lights.

She moved decisively, thinking of Austin and that blade. Kate could cross the room in four long steps, and with each one she tamed her fear by mentally telling it to Alyssa, who would laugh and call her a Scaredy Kat. She imagined the door was Alyssa's big fat mouth. This got her to it easily enough. But when she arrived, one hand on the panel and one on the frame, she heard the mewling of kittens.

It was the oddest sound she'd ever heard in the middle of the night, outside, in November. But she heard it again.

The third time, she returned to her room, slipped into her lamb's-wool clogs and her black sweatshirt, took out the flashlight from under her pillow, and went outside to investigate, pulling the door shut behind her.

The thin cries seemed to come from all directions. They first drew her to look under the porch of the neighboring cottage, but when she knelt and shone her light under the wood slats, she thought the sounds came from behind her, out near the parking lot. She turned around and stayed on the lit path, then crossed over the footbridge that spanned the creek, her clogs sounding heavy on the boards. On the other side she paused and listened. Soft yellow lights brightened the inn's entrance.

A few seconds later the mewls resumed, this time luring her down the lazy driveway toward the main road. The blue spruce trees towered here, taller in the nighttime than they were in the day, bushier, meaner. A few oddball limber pines mingled with them, skeletal by moonlight.

At the bottom of the short hill the driveway turned one last time, and the inn fell out of view as the road widened just enough to allow slowing cars to turn under its arching iron entrance. She toed the two-lane road that ran along Beaver Creek and down to Evergreen Lake as the kittens' cries fell silent. She wondered where they might have come from. Few people here kept cats. Fewer still allowed them out of doors, where bears and coyotes might eat them for a snack. This thought, partnered with a sudden low growl and a rustling of leaves, nearly sent her running back to bed, which was by now hopelessly far away.

Kate spun with her light, looking for beady eyes. Instead her beam bounced off something shiny among leaves gathered on the ground just a few yards away. It shifted and growled again, and this time Kate heard not a wild animal, but the pained groan of a person. A man's broad hand and blunt fingertips lay turned upward beside his hip. She went to him, stirring up the leaves. His jeans were torn and bloody below the knees. The shiny thing that her light had caught was a helmet that hid his face and muffled his voice. He sounded like an animal and looked like an astronaut. She knelt beside him. It didn't seem right to touch him.

"Hello? Are you okay?"

His arms snapped outward, striking her flashlight and causing her to drop it. The light plunged into the leaf pile. She fished for it with fluttering hands but could not find it. All she had was moonlight, and by it she saw that his chest rose and fell in gasps. His fingers clutched the thin T-shirt stretched across his belly. Her anxiety fell away when she realized she'd scared him.

He said something that she couldn't understand over her rustling in the leaves.

She stilled and listened for him to say it again.

Instead his hands went to the helmet and he struggled with the strap, his arms trembling. Kate wondered if she should help him. When he finally freed his head, the helmet popped off and rolled away.

"Can you help me?" he said.

She didn't know how. But she didn't run away. She wished she could see his face. The mewling cats started up again, but now their sound came from a distant place.

He stretched out his hand, and she gave hers to him willingly. He searched it as a blind man might, sandwiching her palm in both of his and seeming to realize how tiny her fingers were. His plea took on a much more desperate sound.

"I'm sorry," he muttered, holding her hand against his heart. His words broke open in the cold air. "I'm sorry. I'm sorry. I'm so sorry."

THIS IS WHAT KATE WHITBY KNEW ABOUT HER FATHER: HE was not Alyssa and Olivia's. He had never seen Kate's face, nor Kate his. His name was not Whitby, which she had taken from her mother, who had taken it from her first husband, who died of a sudden illness when Alyssa was two. Kate didn't know her father's name at all, though she thought it might be Tom. Once she had found in her mother's drawer a small silver locket that bore the inscription *Janet & Tom* but no pictures. He was richer than rich, if Alyssa could be believed. She claimed to have remembered him from before Kate was born.

Whoever he was, she believed her mother looked for him every day, staring down the Harrison Lodge driveway for long minutes whenever she stood behind the reception counter with no guests to receive, as if he might one day surprise them all with a visit.

What are you looking for? Kate once asked.

Any man who will take us away from this town will do, Janet said.

The thought of being taken away from her grandparents and her friends and her home upset Kate so much that she didn't ask what her mother meant. But her mother's sadness occasionally made her waver. She tried to imagine living in an unfamiliar place without the people she loved most. She compared that to what it would be like to live at the inn without her mother. The result of this exercise was always the thought that it might be impossible for her and her mother to both be happy at the same time.

So when the man at the side of the road started apologizing to her, Kate couldn't help but wonder if he knew where he was, and who she was, and was sorry for abandoning her. She wasn't sure what she should do, so she waited for him to do something, but after several minutes of waiting she worried. What if he died with her hand in this deadlock?

She wriggled her wrist a little. He drew a long breath and swallowed.

"Are you dying?" she asked.

He coughed once. It might have been a laugh.

"Not lucky enough for that," he said. The shaking in his hands faded a little. He let hers go and pushed himself up on his elbows, wincing through his teeth.

"I'm Kate. What's your name?"

He didn't answer right away.

"Can you remember?" She started pawing the leaves for her lost flashlight.

"It's Charlie."

"What happened?"

This time when he replied he sounded more like a grown-up who knew what needed to be done. Like Gran usually did. This filled her with relief. "I think I broke my ankle."

A yellow glow finally emerged beneath some brown leaves. Kate retrieved her torch and swung it toward him. He threw a hand over his eyes, and she scrunched up her nose when she saw the red scrape that had torn the length of his bare arm. There was a larger cut on his shoulder.

"Does it hurt?"

He put his hands up against the light. "That hurts plenty."

"I meant your arm."

"Can I see that?"

Kate handed him her flashlight and he ran it down the length of his right leg. The light dimmed, then flickered bright again. Beneath his pant leg, which had been torn into wide flaps of denim that bunched around his knees, Kate could see his bloody skin and his ankle, which ballooned out over his shoe and forced his foot to point inward at a strange angle.

"I'll go get my grandpa." She hoped Grandy had returned by now. Kate reached for the flashlight. Charlie held it out of reach.

"No."

"It's okay." She stood up. "I know my way back in the dark."

"No." The word went straight to Kate's stomach, much like Austin's threat. There was anger in it. "I don't need anyone's help."

She did not point out that he had just asked her to help him only moments ago. Charlie lifted the beam of light onto the road and slowly swept it from side to side, looking for something. Kate saw nothing but asphalt and boulders.

"Did you fall off a motorcycle? You shouldn't ride at night."

"Sometimes we don't have a choice."

"Want me to go look?"

"Was just a skateboard," he said. "I'll get it later."

She thought he might be lying.

"But your ankle's broken. How are you going to get wherever you need to go?"

The light flickered again and Charlie turned it off. "We should save the batteries."

Now she knew he wasn't telling the truth.

"You're not even wearing a *jacket*." Kate tried to sound like Gran.

"Go home, Kate."

"My grandpa can drive you to the hospital."

"Town's just a mile down that hill."

"There's no hospital in Evergreen."

"I don't need a hospital, just an ACE bandage."

"Stores are closed."

"I'll go in when they open."

Kate crossed her arms and was deciding whether to leave when she remembered: "There's one in Chef's first-aid kit. A bandage."

"Chef?"

"I live at a hotel and we have a chef. Her food's really good. Are you hungry?"

Charlie sighed and lay back down. Leaves broke under his back.

"We have rooms where you could stay."

"Can't pay."

"So were you going to steal the bandage?"

Charlie's lack of money was a real blow to the possibility of his being her father. Or maybe he'd simply lost everything for a time, including his memory, like Sara Crewe's father from *The Little Princess*. Kate loved that story.

She stooped and groped for the flashlight, which she found on his chest. He gave it up, and she realized he thought she was going to leave him. Kate angled the light toward his face.

He turned away, but she could see that his chin was small and his jaw smooth. His cheekbones sat high on his wide face and his eyelashes were thin and short compared to the bushiness of his dark brows. Though he squinted and grimaced he had nowhere near the number of wrinkles her mother had, fewer even than her sister Alyssa, who was only twenty-two. Salt tracks led from the corners of Charlie's eyes into his hair, which was thick and wild and long in front of his ears, where the tracks stuck to his cheeks in a mat of dried sweat. So he was too young, too poor, and too stupid to be her dad.

"My gran doesn't like it when people can't pay," Kate said. "But she doesn't have to know you're here."

CHAPTER 16

The Fox sat at the kitchen counter where he and his son had eaten cereal less than twenty-four hours earlier. Hector, the brother who had taken Coz for his unauthorized tattoo, was chasing the address on the driver's license the Fox had taken from the dead man's pocket. He hoped Hector would come back with information. The Fox needed something to tell Coz's mother, who would wake soon and demand to know why their boy wasn't asleep on the old sofa.

In his right hand the Fox palmed a cell phone—his own thin tether to a world outside his hood. This was the phone Detective Warren called when he wanted to talk with the Fox. The Fox had never initiated a call to his contact at the Denver PD, though at the moment he was sorely tempted.

But it was impossible. The Fox was already connected to the break-in at the 420 Green House, and if Warren learned that Coz was abducted there, there would be no way to hide his role in the dispensary murder. And if the Fox was arrested for murder, he would have no further part to play in bringing back his son. The Fox put the phone aside.

But he was still staring at it when a heavy fist hit his front door.

"Deshawn," called a low voice on the other side, more startling than the knocking. No one called him by his first name.

The Fox strode to the door and threw it open before the visitor could make more noise.

Speak of the devil, the Fox thought.

Detective Warren stood in the hall in plain clothes, jeans and a worn leather jacket, square-faced and stoic, clean-shaven, so short the top of his head didn't even reach the Fox's chin. The Fox scanned the hall in both directions. Some ten feet away stood another officer in his blues—of course he did, because no law was dumb enough to enter the projects alone.

"Why you here?" the Fox muttered. "You want me dead?"

Across the hall, a door opened as far as the chain bolt would allow it. Warren's companion looked toward the interruption.

"Sir, are you Mr. Deshawn Johnson?" Warren asked as if they'd never laid eyes on each other before this moment.

"What the—"

"Mr. Johnson, may I come in?"

The Fox didn't know what to make of the act. Why go to the trouble when he could have called and arranged a meeting? "No, the lady's sleeping, man. It's a bad time. My boy—"

"It's about your boy." Warren held up his hand so the Fox could see it. Cradled in his palm was an iPod in a red case, the sheath stamped with a black skull and crossbones. Coz's iPod.

"Where—"

"I recognized the tattoo."

In a blink the Fox understood.

She would not stop screaming. The whole apartment filled with her wail, the whole complex, the whole of the Fox's lifeless heart and mind. The keening became such a part of the air he breathed that he no longer heard her grief as anything more than a background buzz. She could not be comforted and he had nothing to offer. His own fury had yet to take a shape.

The Johnsons' front door stood open to the whole world, which trickled in as the mother's pain woke them. The Fox and Detective Warren stood in the kitchen, the Fox sagging against the sink. On the wall under the fluorescent light fixture, a framed drawing of Jesus looked down on him. The companion cop, a silent sentry, stood watch at the front door, nodding at each person who entered as if taking a mental snapshot of all who came to witness the aftermath. Nod. Click. Nod. Click.

The women, many still in pajamas and robes and chunky slippers, filled the apartment's only bedroom. The men stood in the living room, staring at the empty couch with their arms crossed across their chests. Some glared at the officers as if bringing news of a boy's death was no different from doing the killing.

Hector was the only one who dared enter the conversation going on in the kitchen. He sat at the counter with both hands flat on the surface, fingers spread wide. He wore black gauges in his earlobes with a .500 Smith & Wesson bullet snugged through each one.

"Mr. Johnson," Warren was saying.

The Fox looked up slowly.

"Mr. Johnson, events at the dispensary tonight—I need to ask you some questions."

It was hard to interpret the detective's expression, cloaked as it was by the deception they had to keep up with so many of the Fox's friends in the room. *You pretend you don't know me; I'll pretend I don't know you. In all other aspects of this investigation, though, I expect you to tell me the truth.* The Fox wasn't sure he could remember the truth, or even the fiction he knew he must tell. Why hadn't they sent someone else to ask these questions? Was it sympathy or suspicion behind the cop's veneer?

Sympathy, the Fox decided. It was more dangerous for Warren to be here than it was for the Fox to have him here.

"You told responding officers that you sent Coz out for food just a few minutes before the incident occurred."

He nodded.

"About what time was that?"

The Fox blinked. Already he'd lost track of what day it was, let alone what hour. "A few minutes before it went down."

"What time on the clock?" Warren had no notebook for the Fox's answers, just attentive eyes that saw everything, recorded everything.

"Dunno. Five twenty? Five thirty? What time did it all happen?"

"Is it possible that whoever crashed the pot shop saw your boy leave?"

"What would they care about that?"

"Hard to say. But if we're dealing with a group that kills their own . . ."

Right. He'd forgotten his claim that the driver was killed by a partner.

"Where did you send Coz?"

"I told them. Taco Bell. The one across the corner."

"No one there remembers a boy matching your son's description. Is there any chance he might have gone somewhere else?"

"He's twelve. Boy gets distracted from time to time."

"Is it possible there were more than three perps at the attempted robbery, and that one of them followed Coz or lured him away?"

The Fox stared at Warren before managing, "Why'd they do that?"

"I'm just exploring every possibility."

"What other possibilities are there?"

"Unfortunate coincidences. But I don't much believe in those. Do you, Mr. Johnson?"

In the bedroom, the high-pitched wails had become hiccuping sobs that punctuated the men's silences.

Detective Warren said, "We found a weapon near Coz. With any luck it'll tell stories."

Fatigue weighed down the Fox's bones.

"We'll need you to come in and sit with a sketch artist, if you can describe the other two at the dispensary. The ones you chased off."

"Yeah. Sure."

"And when you're ready, I'm going to need you to identify your son."

The Fox turned around and faced the sink. He needed a dish to break. A knife to stab into the cutting board. A beer bottle to smash. But she'd cleaned up before going to work that morning, leaving nothing for him but coffee stains in the sink and Jesus on the wall, staring at him from that old Sunday school picture, apathetic. No judgment. No comfort. Deshawn Johnson aimed for his pretty blue eyes and smashed the glass with his knuckles.

THE DAWN HAD BROKEN BUT THE APARTMENT WAS COLD WHEN the Fox woke, arms still wrapped around her in their bed. Memory returned against his will. The face of his son on the cold steel table, the coroner dropping the sheet.

One of the neighbors had fetched something strong to help her sleep before he left to identify their son. She took the pills hungrily and sank into forgetfulness swiftly. He went, furious. He returned, nauseous. By the light of the morning the swelling around her eyes was still pronounced, and her brow was clamped down on bleak dreams. But when he slipped his warm arm out from under her neck and replaced it with her cool pillow, she didn't stir.

As soon as the Fox stepped out of the bedroom, Hector woke on the sofa, rubbing his long hands over stubbled cheeks. He seemed to understand he'd violated a sacred space, sleeping *there*, and stood before his whole body was fully awake. He caught his balance against the coffee table.

"Make coffee," Hector said, walking unsteadily into the kitchen while the Fox was still frozen in the doorframe.

Hector opened the cupboard doors that held the dishes and stared at the shelves for a very long time. He scratched the back of his neck. "Took me some time, but I got to that address you gave me from the license."

The Fox opened a different cabinet that held the coffee can and filters and handed both over to Hector. Waited.

"So the driver guy, Antonio something? They say he hasn't been living at home the last few months, say he's taken up with some group living at a bridge."

"Group?"

"Not sure. Don't think they knew."

"It was his family you talked to?"

"Could be. Lady I talked to's old enough to be his mama, all devil-may-care about where he's got to." Hector lined the coffee maker's basket and filled it with generous scoops.

"Which bridge?" the Fox asked.

"I-25 over the South Platte. Last they heard anyway."

"That's right here."

Hector nodded. "By the stadium."

The Fox had plenty of opinions about the Broncos' football field, sitting there in the middle of Sun Valley looking like millions of bucks while the housing projects limped along. He'd lost some of that lovin' feeling for Denver teams over the years the city spent pouring money into its sports venues. Might have brought the city plenty of money, but what good had it done him and his family?

"Antonio's family know he's dead?" he asked.

Hector shrugged. "Doubt it, if that cop don't even know his name yet. The old lady wasn't grievin' none."

Over the sink, Jesus' face contorted behind shards of red-tipped glass. The Fox saw the box of Cocoa Puffs Coz had eaten from so recently and picked it up.

"Drink some coffee," he ordered Hector. "Then go fetch Tanya. I need her to sit watch here. That detective says I gotta help draw some pictures; then you and I gonna visit whatever unlucky bastards we find at that bridge."

"Who cares about the cop? Just go to the bridge."

"So long's he's on our side, we do what he asks."

"Since when you all friendly with them?"

"Since I shot Antonio in the head."

Hector sighed and rubbed his eyes, swore under his breath.

"Hector?"

"What?" He punched the Start button on the coffeepot.

"It's one cop."

"Plus all the guys out at DIA, and everyone on the 420 hit—geez, Fox, it's a double homicide! You got all Denver PD on alert."

"And we're way ahead of them. How many Heavies also on our side?"

Hector finally resigned himself to the Fox's confidence. "Every single one."

"Somebody killed my boy. One of your brothers. What you gonna do about that?"

"Whatever it takes."

The Fox carried the box of cereal back into the bedroom. He set it on the floor next to the bed and lay down, back to his woman. He stared at the box hard, trying to remember his son's exact grin. It was only a matter of time before the grimace he'd seen on the coroner's table became the only memory of family that he had.

CHAPTER 17

The sky had lightened from slate to gray by the time the man named Charlie finally dragged himself up the needle-strewn hill that led to the back of the Rising Sun cottage. The route roughly followed the driveway, steeper than the road and harder to climb but sheltered. He hopped short distances with a hand on her shoulder, crawled longer ones, and occasionally paused on his knees and elbows and dropped his head into the dirt, grinding down the pain with his teeth. Underneath the ripped-up cuff of his jeans his ankle was oozing and puffy like a sausage.

Worse was his groaning. After Kate secreted him in the closet at the back of her cottage, she expected Alyssa to emerge in the nearby window with bedhead and a shotgun to demand what animal was making so much noise; she'd put it out of its misery.

But Alyssa slept through the wildlife.

Without words, Kate gave him her flashlight. Then she handed him a half-full bottle of Gatorade that she'd brought in a couple of days ago.

Do you have any pain-killers? he had asked much too loudly.

She had no idea. He rasped out a lot of big words that she struggled to remember, though she tried. A good spy would know the words.

The cot creaked when his weight settled on it.

Kate left him and tiptoed back around the house, and then inside. On her nightstand she found a piece of paper and tried to write down the names of the medicine he'd asked for, but the words were unfamiliar and she couldn't decide how to spell anything. Her mother's alarm clock squealed. Janet hit the Snooze button. Kate dived into bed, planning to feign sleep until her mother and sisters woke.

Pearl awakened as if from hibernation, knowing it was her great-granddaughter who had started the thaw. She had watched Kate feed a hungry man, and overnight became steeped in a warmth she hadn't known since 1950, before her husband and father both died that same year.

It might have been the last time she'd given any thought to the Bible as well. Joseph and Potiphar's wife! Whatever had made her think that would be an appropriate story to tell an eleven-year-old girl?

It had only taken her half an hour to dress, as she had donned nothing more complicated than feather-soft pants and cozy sweatshirts for years now. However far into slovenliness the world might have descended, she doubted such things were acceptable church attire even now. Pearl settled on a pair of camel-colored wool slacks, an angora sweater in winter white, and a string of Akoya pearls Kenneth had given her from his homeland for their first anniversary. She put them on with a tender sigh. Long ago, when her married girlfriends still used to come around with condolences and sad eyes, as if they suffered as much as she did, she used to say, "At least we weren't married long enough to start hating each other!"

Grief could be cruel. Most of those girls were dead now.

Pearl dusted her dated handbag with a bootie sock and decided it would have to do. Her hair needed setting, but what could she do about that on a Sunday morning?

With energy she didn't know she possessed, she marched across the hall and knocked on Donna and Daniel's door.

"Take an old lady to church, would you?" she asked her startled son-in-law, who, though clothed, looked haggard and perplexed.

"Church? What church?"

"Does it matter?"

He looked at his watch, as if that mattered either. It was barely nine o'clock. Early enough for anywhere. She could go to church in Denver if she wanted.

That was a little ambitious maybe.

"I'm not dressed," he said.

"In fact, you're wearing the same thing you had on yesterday."

"Am I?" He seemed ready to accuse her of lying, until his eyes went to his rumpled trousers.

If she'd had to guess, she would have accused him of sleeping in the saggy baggy things.

"It'll take me ten minutes to get to your car," Pearl said dryly. "That should be enough time for you."

THEY NEVER MADE IT TO CHURCH.

Pearl knew they wouldn't just as soon as they reached the end of the lodge's driveway, where they were delayed by a traffic backup on the two-lane road, which had been temporarily reduced to one. About thirty yards away, a sheriff's vehicle was parked on the opposite shoulder and an officer was directing traffic in turns, first eastbound, then west. There had been a recent accident, it appeared: motorcycle versus mountain lion, and the result was something of a draw. A pile of chrome and leather lay in a ditch on the far side of the road. The broken wildcat had yet to be removed.

"That's a grisly sight," said Pearl, averting her eyes. "Why doesn't he get it off the road?"

"I imagine there's procedures," said Daniel as they finally passed.

Instead of clearing up, the crawl of traffic slowed further as they approached Evergreen Lake, where a logjam of cars made it nearly impossible to pass through the intersection of narrow roads. She saw Daniel stiffen before she noted the spinning lights atop the sheriff's SUV. Just past the dam, at the signal, he swung his car left instead of right and parked himself in the middle of the road right in front of Bruce Gorman's Kwik Kash Pawnshop.

She recalled the days when a horse livery had stood in its place.

Today, skinny strands of yellow tape surrounded the ugly gray cinder-block structure. The barrier was all that separated the insiders from the outsiders. The knowers from the wish-they-were-knowers. The small gathering of officials from the expanding crowd, hungry for information. People hovered in front of the stores like fluttering moths at a lantern.

And though Pearl had been feeling a rising warmth in her heart and a kindling energy in her mind, the weather and the distraction conspired against her. The morning was chill and she'd forgotten her coat. Low clouds awaited the divine command to release their snow. She might have stayed home for coffee instead of this.

She stole a look at Daniel from the corner of her eye and decided it was best she was with him just now.

At the tape barrier a slim young deputy was making notes on an electronic tablet with a stylus. He had all the chiseled angles of youth, hard and confident. A thin white line of goose skin on his neck above the collar bordered a fresh haircut. *Sawyer,* the name tag said. He looked up at the Explorer when Daniel stopped the engine, then took a step toward it when Daniel got out, leaving the door open. Pearl folded her hands atop her purse and weighed the pros of being warm with the cons of not being able to hear what was said if she leaned over to pull the door shut. She opted to listen.

"Curtis," Daniel called out.

"Sir." The deputy put his hand up toward Daniel, a friendly request that he proceed no farther.

"Curtis, it's Daniel Torrance. We met at Arnie Simpson's kick-off party back in September."

Guarded recognition flashed across the young man's eyes. Pearl put Curtis Sawyer at less than half Daniel's age.

"What happened here?"

"Mr. Torrance, I need you to remove your car."

"Is Bruce okay?" Daniel reached for the yellow tape.

"Sir, do not cross this barrier."

The stern command was cold water on Daniel's boldness, a confirmation that everything was precisely as serious as it looked.

Gorman's storefront had been vandalized with spray paint, a sloppy scrawl of bubble letters sprayed across the windows. The black lines were crooked, novice. Ugly neon orange filled in less than half of the vulgar phrase. Apparently the artist had either insufficient supplies or insufficient time to finish the work.

Behind the yellow tape, two attendants were wheeling a gurney into the showroom. No white sheets, just black vinyl. The wheels rattled on the metal threshold.

"Who did this?" Daniel's voice quavered. He gestured to the windows. "Punk kids? Someone up from Denver?"

"We're working on that," said Sawyer, who relaxed a tad now that Daniel wasn't acting like a bull.

"Where are they taking him? Which hospital?"

"No hospital, Mr. Torrance."

Daniel's hands slowly fell to his sides.

"I'm very sorry. You and the—Mr. Gorman, you were friends?"

"I just saw him yesterday."

"Here?"

Daniel only nodded.

"What time was that?"

"Uh . . ." He shook his head as if to free the memory. "Noonish. One? After lunch."

"Why did you see him?"

"What?"

"What was the reason for your visit?"

"No reason." Defensiveness tinted his words. "Don't your friends ever drop in on you at work?"

The boy Curtis smiled. "Don't tell the boss."

But Daniel didn't relax.

"Did Mr. Gorman seem all right at the time?"

Daniel blinked. "Fine. Fine."

Sawyer tapped on the screen of his tablet.

"Who would *do* something like this?"

The deputy made some notes. Pearl's attention drifted to the moth people. She felt oddly the center of attention, sitting there in the middle of everything when she was usually the one doing the watching. The feeling intensified when she caught the stare of a young man loitering on the edge of the bustle, with the rubberneckers but apart. He slouched under a heavy gray hoodie that didn't hide his unkempt red hair or the purple butterfly bruise winging across his nose.

"What did the two of you talk about?" Sawyer asked.

"What?" Daniel's attention shifted from Gorman's store to focus fully on the young man. Pearl had to agree: the young deputy *was* acting a bit big for his britches. "I don't see what that has to do with anything. Am I a suspect now, is that it? Because I was his friend?"

"Mr. Torrance, I'm just getting information."

Daniel took a deep breath and held up his hand. "Of course you are. I apologize."

"The more we know, the faster we can figure out what happened to your friend."

"Yes, yes."

The deputy waited until the silence grew awkward.

"So, what did you talk about?"

"You know, I don't even remember."

The hooded boy with the ghostly eyes rubbed his arms to ward off the cold. As he did Pearl saw a bright smear on the elastic band that rimmed the bottom of his sweatshirt, a bright flash of unnatural color right at his sagging hips. It might have been orange.

But her eyes weren't quite as sharp as her ears. Someone stepped in front of him.

"Did you argue?"

"Of course not! What would we argue about?"

Sawyer nodded patiently. "It's okay, that's all right. It's just that a witness reported hearing Mr. Gorman arguing with someone yesterday afternoon. Any idea who that might be? Maybe he was having trouble with someone and mentioned it to you? A relative, maybe? A customer or employee who might have been upset about anything?"

"No. No one at all. Why? Was it . . . Do you mean this wasn't just a . . . ? Did they steal something?"

"If you can think of anything at all that might be useful, doesn't matter how small or insignificant it seems, promise to give me a call?"

Daniel backed away slowly. "Let me move the car for you."

"Appreciate your help, Mr. Torrance."

As Pearl's son-in-law returned, the kid at the edge of the crowd walked away. Daniel twisted the key in the ignition and closed the door. Comfort poured from the vents, warming Pearl's white hands. The boy vanished from her view.

"It's really too bad," Pearl said. "I imagine this will put a damper on your business venture."

Daniel stared at her, then put the SUV in reverse. "*What* venture?"

It was amazing what kinds of things an old lady could learn when everyone presumed she was addled and deaf.

"The one you were in with Bruce Gorman, of course. Do you plan to keep it up without him?"

He shook his head, disbelieving. "I don't know what you're talking about."

"Oh, I doubt that. Your wife is the one who's too busy to notice such things. But don't be mad at me. I have so much time on my hands that I simply can't help it."

"You're babbling again. And I'm sorry, but right now I just don't have the patience."

CHAPTER 18

When her eyes flicked open, the tiny cottage was silent. Ten o'clock—Janet, Alyssa, and Olivia would be occupied by the Sunday brunch rush. Kate went to the closet in her bedroom and parted her mother's many dresses and crawled over the scattered shoes. She pressed her ear against the small access panel in the back wall, knowing Charlie slept just on the other side and heard nothing, a prospect more frightful than Gran's wrath. What if he had died?

Kate dressed and raided the family's medicine cabinet. He'd asked to see anything in a prescription bottle, and Kate found three of them. In the little kitchenette she ate a bowl of Cocoa Puffs and left the box open on the counter. She pilfered a sleeve of graham crackers and put those with the pills in a plastic grocery sack, then aimed for Chef's first-aid kit, which was located in the big kitchen.

The possibility of being caught swelled in Kate's throat. Sundays were the easiest days for her comings and goings to remain unnoticed. Everyone was just too busy to be bothered with her. Still, after she left the bag on the front porch of their little cottage where the gold and russet mums were beginning to dry up, every step she took worried her. Chef was far less stern than Gran but would want to know what she was doing with a bandage.

When she reached the lodge, Kate entered through the private sliding glass door. She walked in a bold straight line through the keeping room, past the family dining area, through the crazy busy kitchen, all the way into Chef's office at the very back. She went straight to the first-aid kit that hung on the wall—which she was just tall enough to reach—retrieved the bandage, and shut the box. No one even said hello to her.

Feeling emboldened, she stepped into the walk-in freezer for a bag of frozen peas and walked back out.

A sous-chef sidestepped Kate on his way to the stove but said nothing.

She dared to call out "Morning, Chef" as she retraced her steps.

"Come back here and let me tie an apron on you, Kate! I need your hands."

Kate danced out the back door.

Some of her nervousness settled by the time she reached the back of the cottage. She stretched out her hand to touch it. The sight behind her little home brought her up short: there, beneath the broken branches of a scrub oak, was a spotty trail of blood. It wasn't quite as obvious as a painted line pointing the way to the little cottage. But anyone who paid attention might notice it.

The secret door bounced open under the pressure of her fingers.

"Charlie?" she whispered. What little light got in illuminated the bottoms of his shoes. He'd stacked a few of her library books under his swollen ankle.

The body on the cot did not move. She slipped in and closed the door, then latched it. The bag rustled as she stepped into the darkness. It swung into the wall, and pills rattled.

"Charlie."

He sprang up like a jack-in-the-box, and she jumped back.

"I brought you that bandage. And some medicine."

"Open the door." His voice was a dry whisper.

"Someone might see."

"Please. It's just . . . the air."

The little closet was cool, much more tolerable now than in the heat of summer. There was a vent no bigger than Kate's foot at the top of the door, under the eaves of the roof, but it let in hardly any light. Kate bit her lip, then opened the panel a few inches.

His ankle looked like a gnarly tree trunk, swollen and funny-shaped and not the right color for skin. The shoe was blood-sticky and torn up along the side. She started emptying the bag into his outstretched hands, trying not to bump him.

"It's late for ice," he said softly, draping the vegetables over his foot anyway. Pain screwed up his face. She took out the graham crackers and set them on the floor.

"You'll be more comfortable if you take your shoes off," she said.

He left them on and started sorting through the bottles. He held up each into the slice of light cutting across his body.

"Who's Janet?" He tapped several tablets into his palm.

"My mom."

"So what does she take pain pills for?"

Kate shrugged.

Charlie swallowed a few with the leftover Gatorade, then dumped a bunch of pills into a small pocket on the front of his T-shirt and handed the bag of bottles back to Kate.

"Better put those back before anyone misses them." He shifted his weight on the cot and leaned against the wall, his face falling into shadow. "What is this place?"

"An old storage closet, I guess."

"I meant your home. This is your house?"

"This is the Harrison Lodge. A hotel. We've got cottages."

"Lots of people, in other words."

"Not many right now."

"That's just great."

Now he sounded like Alyssa.

"So this is a storage room, but you can lock the door from the inside?"

Heat rose to Kate's cheeks. She felt stupid. Storage closets wouldn't lock from the inside and be invisible from the outside, but she'd never really thought about it.

"Maybe it was a spy hideout for some war a long time ago," she said.

"Yeah. Lots of wars here in Colorado."

Kate looked away. Maybe his broken ankle made him mean. Sometimes that happened with animals when they got hurt.

"Later I can bring you a plate of something hot. Something Chef made."

"What'd you say your name was again?"

"Kate."

She stole a peek at him. He was dirty and skinny, and his crazy hair mostly covered his eyes.

"Kate. Look, Kate. It's really important you don't tell anyone I'm here."

"I'm the world's best secret keeper."

"That so?"

"It is."

"Lucky me."

He didn't sound like he meant it.

"Why can't anyone know you're here?"

"How old are you?"

"Eleven."

He sighed at that news.

"Are you Japanese?" she asked.

"Yeah."

"My great-grandpa was Japanese."

"Go figure."

"Great-Grandma Pearl might like to meet you."

"When I said don't tell anyone I meant *anyone*."

"Why?"

"You don't want to find out."

He seemed a little different today than he had last night. Harder on the surface. Not so glad for her help.

"Okay. I promise."

"Look, you've already done a lot for me, Kate. But I have to ask you for just one more thing."

"What?"

"Well, first thing you need to know is I wasn't riding a skateboard."

Trapped in a shack with a busted ankle and an eleven-year-old girl who wanted to introduce him to her relatives—well, it didn't take a PhD to figure out how this one was going to end.

She was cute, with her round face and observant blue-gray eyes and tousled black hair, coarse like his but still all its own, not cut and gelled into some anxious adolescent style yet. But Charlie couldn't trust her any more than he could trust anyone else. He had to get out before she told. Before they found the bike. Before his so-called family or Coz's people came after him.

And where could he go on this bum ankle in these mountains where even the cougars would want their revenge?

He scooted to the end of the cot and put his foot on the ground.

The touch alone fired sharp hot pains up his calf and around his knee. He hadn't even put weight on it.

He needed time to heal, and he had no time.

If he silenced the girl, how much time would that buy? When she came back with his lost harmonica, engraved with his name and likely ripped from his pocket when the bike went sideways, it would be so easy to become what everyone already believed he was.

A broken body fell across the landscape of Charlie's mind, illuminated by the headlamp of a motorcycle, only this time it was Kate there in the empty field, body twisted on the dry blond dirt. He sank back onto the cot, but no amount of pounding on his forehead could make the image go away. He clutched the thin blanket in a fisted wad over his face and sobbed soundlessly until it was hard to breathe.

CHAPTER 19

The two kids the Fox had seen at the dispensary were blond and Asian. The dead kid in the stolen Chevy was perhaps Latino, or maybe Italian. But they could make their own judgments about him, couldn't they? As the Fox worked with the sketch artist to make portraits of the two who survived, Detective Warren had beaten the question of their ethnicity and ages into the ground.

You're sure the blond wasn't dyed, Mr. Johnson? Maybe the guy you think was Asian was really Latino? Gangs just don't usually cross ethnic lines unless they're prison gangs. But you think they were teenagers? Are you sure?

And then the question laid atop a thick slab of suspicion: *Mr. Johnson, you ever seen anyone like them hanging out with your boy?*

A uniformed woman at an adjacent desk suggested they might be dealing with a street family. Warren gave the woman his attention.

The sketch of the blond was good enough, but the Asian's eyes were too friendly, maybe because of how the artist had drawn the bill of his knit cap high on his forehead.

"Cap's all wrong. He has a cockier look than that," the Fox said. "Rougher around the edges. Hard."

The pencil hovered while the artist considered how to translate the emotional description into a physical one.

Another officer brought Detective Warren a report. "Prints on the Beretta yielded a name," he said. The Fox tried to see the papers but was too far away. "Breaking and entering a few years ago."

Warren examined the information and glanced at the sketch the Fox had coaxed to life. He frowned. Then he pushed the print-out of the mug shot toward the Fox. He kept his fingers over the placard the guy held, covering his name. "That him?"

To the Fox's surprise, it was. "Like that," he said to the sketch artist, pointing to the mug, though he was surprised to see the man younger than he remembered, just a kid, hair cropped close to his hairline, eyes stunned wide by the camera flash. "A little older."

"Only a couple of years," said Warren.

The artist shrugged and handed his sketch to the Fox. "Souvenir," he said. Then he excused himself. The woman at the next desk answered a call.

The cop and his snitch were alone. The Fox folded the sketch of Charlie into a small bulky cube and dropped his voice. "What's his name?"

"I'm not sending you out those doors with a name," Warren said gently, aligning the pages with a swift tap on the desk, then turning them over. "We're still waiting on ballistics."

"You need more proof this guy killed Coz?"

"Maybe you can tell me how this man who was at your robbery scene might have been the same one to pull the trigger that killed your son?"

The Fox had anticipated this question. "How can I tell you if I didn't see it? I sent Coz out. Could be the boy stuck around. Could be he took a bad route. In District 1 your fine citizens done always find themselves in the wrong place at the wrong time. Ain't it the truth?"

"Deshawn." Warren leaned forward, elbows on his knees. "Is there any chance Coz tipped these guys off to your job? They're all kids, teens—"

"Not a chance. Boy was straight up."

"You don't tell me the truth, some point I won't be able to help you."

The Fox cursed. "That day comes, I won't need your help, man."

Warren sighed. "Okay. So we wait on ballistics. The more careful we are now, the more easily we convict later."

"Patience ain't my strong suit. You got a gun, you got prints. How many suspects you got?"

"There was a shirt," Warren said. "When we found your son, there was a shirt draped across his face."

Anger and grief tangled in the Fox's throat. "What's a shirt got to do with nothin'?"

Warren shrugged. "A sign of respect. Someone with a conscience. Maybe even remorse."

"Not his killer's shirt, then."

"Do you remember what these two kids were wearing?"

For some reason all he could pull up in his mind was Antonio's blood-black T-shirt.

"Already told you I don't."

Warren leaned back in his chair. "You and I, we trust each other."

The Fox looked him in the eye, spun the tightly folded sketch around and around on his fingertips.

"I promise you'll know the guy's name before it shows up on the evening news."

"So you have a name," the Fox said, withdrawing a brown trifold wallet out of the pocket of his windbreaker. He set it on the desk. "You got an address?"

Warren glanced at it, then at him. "Not yet."

"Our killer's a man on the move?"

"If he's our killer."

Could be a man who lived with Antonio at his bridge, the Fox thought. Live together, break the law together.

"Then what problems am I gonna cause with nothin' but a name, Warren? What inside scoop I got on nomads that you don't?"

Warren folded his hands across his lean stomach and waited for the Fox to explain the wallet.

"This here belongs to Antonio Demarco."

"Who would be . . . ?"

"Huh. You don't know? Guess his prints didn't have no record attached to them. Not like our shooter here."

"Who's Antonio?" Warren repeated firmly.

"Dead kid in the Caprice that drove into the dispensary, shot by the same one who shot my boy." He nodded at the mug shot.

"I thought you said the blond one shot the guy in the Chevy."

"All for one and one for all."

Warren studied the Fox, his face unreadable.

"You stole a dead man's wallet from a crime scene?" Warren asked. "I should arrest you."

"Stole? What you think I am? Guy threw it into my open window as he drove by. Didn't even notice it until I was on my way over here."

The detective shook his head. "Your story has nothing in it for me to believe anymore."

The Fox lowered his voice. "C'mon, Warren. This is what you and I done three years now. Barter information. You give me a name. I give you an address." He held out the wallet for Warren to take. "What's any different here 'n' now?"

The detective did not answer that. But after a few moments he said, "Charlie Fuse."

"Fuse. Like the box in the basement?"

"Maybe the guy's dad was an electrician," Warren said dryly.

"Or maybe he's got a short one," the Fox said.

Neither man smiled. Warren took the wallet. It was nothing for the Fox to give up. By the time Warren found Antonio Demarco's home and then the bridge, the Fox would be long gone.

"Deshawn. I don't think Fuse is our killer."

"Why not?"

"A hunch."

"Hunches don't mean nothin'."

"You learn something about Fuse, don't wait until tomorrow morning to tell me about it," Warren said.

The Fox nodded. When he killed Charlie Fuse, Warren would be the first to know.

CHAPTER 20

Kate followed the trail back down the gentle slope, covering as much of Charlie's blood as she could by kicking dirt over it. If he didn't want anyone to know he was here, she'd make sure no one did. With her foot she shifted pine needles and loose dirt, turned over a few small rocks, and crushed the papery fallen leaves of the cottonwoods and aspens. The hillside looked different in the daylight, more exposed, even under the lid of these thick snow clouds. Kate reached out and caught a sinking snowflake in the palm of her hand.

She caught her first glimpse of the road when she was only halfway there. A fancy-looking blue sedan headed toward town approached with some speed and then, a few hundred yards past the Harrison Lodge driveway, slowed to take the sharp corner. The gust of its passing stirred the leaves on the shoulder, and Kate could see just how close the road was to where Charlie had fallen, and where she had knelt to help him. She noted the helmet, close to where he had pushed it off his head. Wind or the rush of passing cars, or maybe just the result of his own frantic movements, had tumbled it behind a rock and filled it half full of debris.

A bushy juniper sheltered her while she spied out the rest of the scene, squatting behind its thick greenery.

In the middle of the county road, black skid marks passed through a gruesome smear of blood and bits of fur before sliding right into a ditch. To one side of the skid marks was a big white truck with an animal control logo painted on the door. A man in a baggy suit and thick long gloves was slamming the rear doors closed. On the other side, lights were spinning atop a Jefferson County Sheriff's SUV. An officer in uniform stood over a shallow drainage ditch, where more leaves had collected through the autumn. A glint of chrome caught Kate's eye. Charlie's motorcycle. It lay on its side, the front wheel lifted into the air at an angle.

"The cougar got the worst end of that encounter," the wildlife man said to the officer while peeling off his gloves. "Any idea what happened to the rider?"

"Got someone knocking on doors. Maybe a local saw something."

"Think a Good Samaritan took him to the hospital?"

"Hard to say. Out here I'd expect a 911 call. But we don't have any on record for something like this."

"So maybe he wasn't hurt that bad." The wildlife man opened the driver's door, unzipping his big suit and peeling it off at the shoulders.

"If it was a DUI the guy might have just walked off."

Nearby footsteps on brittle leaves startled Kate. Not too far away—about a twenty-five-yard dash from Kate to the noise—a woman dressed like the wildlife man in an oversize cover-up and protective gloves came trekking out of the trees, her arms heavy with a load of spotted fur: two big cats, craning their necks to see where they were being taken.

"Told you I heard something!" she announced happily. "Found these boys rolling around by the creek."

Cougar cubs! One of them yowled. Kate almost stood up for a better look, then thought better of it. But it was pretty hard to resist them, though they were already bigger than full-grown house cats.

Even the sheriff's deputy was smiling. This would explain the crying she'd heard in the night.

"How old?" called her partner.

"Judging by their teeth and their spots, I'm guessing four months? Maybe a little less."

The quiet one tried to climb the lady's shoulder, then reached for her head while she still had hold of its hind legs. The man at the truck opened a small compartment in the side before helping her disentangle the cub from her cropped hair.

"You're a troublemaker," he said, carefully pushing the cub into the metal box.

The other kept crying. "Sorry, sweet pea," the woman said, prying him off her arms to join his sibling.

As they locked up, a flatbed truck pulled in behind the sheriff, and Kate stayed while the scene was transformed. The animal control truck left and another deputy returned, presumably the one who had been knocking on doors. The two law enforcement officers rearranged their cones to direct traffic around the crew hauling the bike out of the ditch. As they righted it, Kate could see the flaps of the saddlebags flopping around. They pushed the motorcycle up a ramp and onto the truck bed. They laid it on its side and secured the wreck to the truck with thick straps.

"Going to impound?" the driver asked the officer.

"Yessir."

A short time later nothing was left but the skid marks, the dried red blood catching the snowy flakes, and Kate, shivering, feeling sad for the baby cougars who no longer had a mother.

As soon as the official-looking people and trucks were gone, Kate sprang out of her shelter and slip-slided down the hill to the road. She ran to where she had sat beside Charlie the night before, kicking through the leaves for the silver harmonica he had described to her.

Her shoe tapped something hard; she fished for it with her hands and was rewarded with a shining instrument far more valuable than the plastic toy she had taped behind the grille of that rude lady's car. The chrome was smudged, and an ugly scuff clouded the engraving so that the first few letters of Charlie's name seemed to slide off the edge.

She put the harmonica to her mouth and blew, and a pretty hum that seemed to be made of six notes in one breath came down around her ears like autumn leaves. Kate grinned and tried a short, improvised melody.

Victorious, she hurried back up the hill.

HER PLAN TO TAKE THE HARMONICA DIRECTLY TO CHARLIE was derailed by an unexpected visitor.

"There you are!"

Kate jumped at the sound of Reece's voice.

"No one knew where you went."

Her best friend had come around the back of Kate's cottage and stood right there at the corner, between Charlie's invisible door and the dry stacked rock wall, which came up to her waist. Reece looked out over it toward Kate, making her way through the trees. Reece's smile was as shiny as her copper hair, so much prettier than her brother's orange locks. Kate hid the instrument behind her back.

"What are you doing here?" she asked Reece.

"It was Austin who wanted to come so bad."

"Austin?" A knot tied itself up in Kate's stomach. "Why?"

"You didn't hear?"

Kate's blank face was all the question Reece needed.

"That pawnshop man was *murdered*. Your grandpa's friend?" Reece put both hands up to the sides of her head. "Mom and Dad thought Austin had a good idea to see if your grandpa is doing okay. Trying to be all encouraging of him, you know?"

Kate blinked and found her head suddenly, awfully empty of everything but dread.

"I think I'll have nightmares about this," Reece said. "Mom said she can only think of one other murder in Evergreen. That was a few years ago. But this time it's someone we know, sort of, because he was your grandpa's friend. I don't know how I'm going to sleep."

Kate scrambled to think of something to say, anything that might not draw attention to her fear of Austin or her sudden worries about Grandy. "You could spend the night here." Kate tried to smile. "We might be haunted, but the ghosts won't murder anyone unless someone's trying to film them."

Reece shivered though she stood in a wedge of sunlight. "Very funny."

None of Kate's friends had ever spent the night at the Harrison Lodge. For one, Gran discouraged it. Also, someone had started a rumor that it was the same famous inn featured in an old horror movie. Of course they had it all wrong. Kate had watched the movie once when her mother worked late, and then when she learned the movie was based on a novel she read that too. Eventually she read an article that explained the author had been inspired by an old Colorado hotel a couple of hours away, up in Estes Park, and that one didn't even *look* like the Harrison Lodge. But she got a certain amount of respect for living in a haunted hotel, sleeping there night after night after night, so she let her friends believe what they wanted.

"Where is Austin anyway?" Kate asked.

"Eating, I guess. I just wanted to find you first."

Kate wasn't sure what to do with the harmonica. She couldn't give it to Charlie yet, and today's outfit didn't have any pockets, and it wouldn't do to have her mother or sisters find it in the cottage.

"There's cake on the dessert buffet," she said. "Want to get some?"

Kate was not at all excited for food, but the moment Reece nodded and turned away, Kate slipped the harmonica into a narrow cleft in the rock wall. Then she dashed to catch Reece's hand and tugged her toward the dining room. Anything to get her away from Charlie and find out why Austin *really* wanted to come here. She hoped he wasn't looking for her.

CHAPTER 21

Pearl Nagasawa was born Pearl Harrison in 1927, two years before her father, Dr. John Harrison, built the Harrison Lodge. The gold rush was long past and the heyday of Evergreen's lumber industry was already a matter of history, but the stunning beauty of these Rocky Mountain foothills would never fade. It was fashionable by then for the wealthy to build summer homes in Evergreen. Celebrity entertainers, Hollywood stars, businessmen, and even Chicago mobsters had been vacationing at Harry Sidles's luxury resort, Troutdale-in-the-Pines, for almost a decade by the time the Harrisons broke ground. At the time only five hundred people lived in Evergreen year-round, but come summer, the population swelled to five thousand.

In the beginning, a summer getaway from their New York City loft was all the Harrisons ever thought their lodge would be. The mansion was completed as the Great Depression got under way, but Pearl had no memory of that difficult time period in American history—not because of her age, but because this enclave seemed beyond reach of the disasters elsewhere in the world. However it happened, her parents emerged with their wealth intact. But they left their New York life behind, and by 1938 Colorado was their permanent home.

It was never Dr. Harrison's intention to make the family mansion a public hotel. That was his granddaughter Delilah's idea, come two generations later. But soon after the Second World War broke out, Pearl's parents thought the Harrison Lodge might be more socially useful. Having survived the Great War with injuries that made him ineligible to enlist again, Dr. Harrison was encouraged by his wife, Ethel, to open the gates to shell-shocked survivors of the fray. She had some nursing skills. Together they might give injured servicemen a place to peacefully recover.

But Dr. Harrison's heart was turned toward a different kind of survivor.

He argued that the trek into the mountains was too perilous for most of those wounded warriors, and Ethel's healing touch aside, he wasn't the kind of doctor they needed. He had entered school intending to be an anthropologist before the world governments interrupted his education. After his own stint as an American soldier, his education and his own search for a peaceful place to recover had taken him to Japan, where he found a culture steeped in tradition and beauty. The ritual of their culture revived him, and more: it was the Japanese, he believed, who taught him the principles of honor, excellence, and pride that ultimately made him a successful businessman.

The Japanese did not find the United States to be equally hospitable in 1941, or for a long time after. The state of Colorado was home to Amache, one of the ten internment camps established to ensure the population's loyalty would never be outwardly divided. Dr. Harrison never ceased to see a terrible irony in that move. Amache was the smallest camp, and it was built in one of the ugliest, driest regions of the state, where the smothering summer dust and the brutal winter winds choked crops and human spirits. The newsreel footage of families being driven from their homes as if they'd already committed treason stirred Dr. Harrison's grief—and resolve.

It helped that Colorado possessed something of a rebel spirit. The Harrisons found it catching. Then governor Ralph Carr, as if annoyed that a concentration camp would be parked in his backyard, all but spat in the face of anti-Japanese attitudes. He insisted publicly that the national Japanese American population, two-thirds of whom had been born on United States soil, was by and large "as loyal to American institutions as you and I." In 1942, during a brief period when President Roosevelt allowed Japanese Americans to "voluntarily" move away from the West Coast, many of them fled to the relative welcome of Governor Carr's territory.

Not everyone admired Carr for his stance or for his cooperation in helping to relocate displaced Japanese after the war was over. His political career was later truncated by those who considered him a "Jap lover."

So the circumstances of environment and experience came together in Evergreen, in the mind of John Harrison. And on the day he met American-born Kiyoshi Nagasawa at the Evergreen mercantile and brought him home for luncheon, John and Ethel decided to create an anti-Amache sort of camp, where a handful of Japanese might find warmth and shelter from the suspicious eyes of Americans who feared them.

Pearl was nearly fifteen when her father began to build the cottages on the other side of Bear Creek for this purpose. They began the work in April 1942, after the winter snow started to melt and before the wealthy returned to Upper Bear Creek Road, though fewer returned that year.

It was Pearl who eagerly mailed Kenneth Nagasawa's letters to his siblings and cousins and their friends, informing them of the Harrisons' endeavors and inviting them to come. She addressed the envelopes in her own hand and carried them down the mountain in her father's open motor car, breathless with the little white lie she planned to tell the postmistress—that she was helping her parents plan a summer party for her father's business acquaintances— and equally winded by the gratitude in Kenneth's eyes, which she thought were the very definition of exotic.

Their Japanese friends arrived by word of mouth and under cover of night. They came as laborers conscripted to help with the building project, while in reality they were erecting their own small homes, five duplexes that could house ten families. The Harrisons told the few neighbors who asked a half-truth: they planned to open a summer lodge when the war ended, because surely it would end someday. Their housekeeper and cook, sympathetic to the cause, vowed to keep the secret and did so loyally with a bright glint in their eyes.

IN HER BEDROOM-APARTMENT, THE PRECIOUS SPACE THAT had once been her father's study, Pearl scooted the rice-paper screen slightly away from the window so sunlight would fall on the bookcases. She needed the light to see into the cabinets beneath them. But there was more than sunshine out that window. At that precise moment she saw the wicked boy with the orange hair and bad posture, the same one who had been watching her and Daniel down in front of that horrifying murder scene. He went skulking by on the terrace, right in front of her, plain as day, looking for trouble. He was hiding something under that oversize sweatshirt of his and not doing a very good job of it. He approached the outer door labeled Private Residence as if it were his very own and marched inside.

People like him were the guests Pearl feared, the ones who saw others' personal space as an affront to their sense of entitlement. She had tried keeping that door locked, but Donna wouldn't allow it. Said the fire marshal forbade it. To which Pearl said maybe she would take up the matter with the sheriff. Upon the boy's invasion she resolved to make her own opportunity for this conversation as soon as possible. If men were being murdered in their own shops, families who lived in hotels should be granted a little latitude to protect themselves. Pearl was willing to bet there had been more murders than fires in Colorado in the past few years.

The best she could do in the present circumstances was lock her own door, which she did hastily. Then she placed her soft ear to the panel and listened until she was reasonably confident the boy had exited the hall. She couldn't be one hundred percent sure, but at least he hadn't tried to come into her own room.

She returned to her bookcase, thinking of her father and her husband and of how they might have confronted an interloping ape like that one. Well, her son-in-law could handle it today, if he wasn't too distracted by his friend's unexpected death.

What days they lived in! But this morning Pearl would focus on the past and on hope, neither of which she'd considered for a long, long time.

On the very bottom shelf—which was harder to get to than the very top one, she thought grimly as she forced her stiff knees to bend—she found the dusty volume she sought. The book was thick, heavy, an old family Bible first inscribed by her father's father in 1892. Colorado's dry climate had not been kind to the leather binding. A piece from the spine fluttered to the floor as she lifted it onto the table.

With the Bible removed, a sturdy leather tube that had been stashed behind it rolled off the shelf and onto the floor. She picked up the cylinder, not sure what it contained, but it was as coated with neglect as the old King James.

How did so much dust get into a cupboard she rarely opened? Time was to blame. Given enough time, everything neglected rotted. Even hearts.

It was not hard for Pearl to say where she had gone wrong. World War II had brought new life to her childhood home; the ensuing peace tried to kill it. Kenneth and Pearl married less than a year after the end of the war was declared. They needn't have waited. Their interracial marriage was scandalous enough that Pearl and he might as well have confessed to being traitors to the United States. The following summer most of Kenneth's friends and family left to reestablish their lives as Americans, and the Harrison Lodge cottages were put up for summer guests. The Nagasawas bore two girls, Delilah and Donna. Then, in 1950, Pearl's father died of pneumonia and a mountain lion took Kenneth as he hiked the creeks behind their land.

As the widowed mother of an infant and a four-year-old, Pearl spent that winter in declining shock, hardly aware that the people who had once shunned them now came out of the woodwork to console her. Even today she could recall nothing of it but a daze of sleepless nights and mounting anxiety.

Her daughters survived because Ethel Harrison postponed her own mourning to take care of them. The Harrison Lodge survived because those members of Kenneth's family who stayed after the war kept it going. Pearl didn't fully come back to consciousness for twenty years, when her daughters awoke her, and then it was really too late.

Delilah, who took after her father in appearance and her grandfather in generosity, took over the running of the lodge just as the Vietnam War was spitting out scores of broken American men scorned by their own people. *Father built this place precisely for this purpose*, she often said, actively inviting the marginalized, broken men to find refuge at the lodge. Donna was begrudging; their mother was simply disinterested.

In those days Donna resentfully called the house the Harrison Hospital, and Pearl didn't stop her. Donna married Daniel and moved to a home on the other side of Evergreen closer to the high school where he taught, and Pearl didn't stop her from doing that either.

Today Pearl wished she had intervened. Had taught her the values of the men she never had the chance to know. John Harrison and Kenneth Nagasawa were not perfect men, to be sure, but premature death and passing years had a way of stripping away flaws and preserving nobility. At least it was so in Pearl's mind, perhaps a symptom of her age. Her regrets.

Pearl carried the aging Bible to the table before the fireplace and blew the dust off the surface, then lifted the cover, where a family tree had been documented in her grandfather's precise handwriting as far as Donna's birth. Her father had inscribed Psalm 119:11 below his father's hand: "Thy word have I hid in mine heart, that I might not sin against thee."

"Wish I could say the same," Pearl whispered.

Pearl parted the pages roughly in the middle, which was where he had taught her to look for the Psalms. She was looking for a conversation between her father and Kenneth, yes, a conversation straight out of these pages the first time Dr. Harrison proposed his plan to the younger man—right here in this room, before this very fireplace, as she lurked outside the door. Pearl couldn't recall the citation, only the words, which took her a moment to find.

Why would you help me? Kenneth wanted to know. In those early days he smiled always but averted his eyes, keeping them downcast.

You are a man who needs shelter, of a people who have lost their place in this country, though I do hope that's a temporary circumstance. In the meantime, I have shelter. I have a place.

The onionskin pages crinkled under Pearl's wrinkled hand.

I have no means to repay you.

I am not the one to be repaid.

Ah, there was the passage. Her father had responded by quoting the psalmist: *"He that dwelleth in the secret place of the most High shall abide under the shadow of the Almighty. I will say of the Lord, He is my refuge and my fortress: my God; in him will I trust. Surely he shall deliver thee from the snare of the fowler, and from the noisome pestilence. He shall cover thee with his feathers, and under his wings shalt thou trust."*

Your God is a bird?

To this her father laughed. *The greatest bird, one who can outwit fowlers and protect the rest of us chickens.*

Then he is like the tsuru, who lives a thousand years and is forever loyal to his kind.

Your nation's stunning white crane. I don't think I've ever thought of him quite like that. But yes.

Pearl turned her head just far enough to see the painting hanging over her bed. The great white crane casting a shadow over the small man who scaled the mountain, aiming for a home on the peak. It was a gift from Kenneth to her parents on the occasion of their wedding. In the sheltered place that was the Harrison Lodge, Ken's artistic gifts had space to blossom. And in the lower-right corner, a column of Japanese characters represented another scripture

Ken came to know in the ensuing years: *Hide me under the shadow of thy wings.*

Both men had died so young, and it was fair to say that today Pearl knew more about shadows and far less about divine birds.

She reached for the old leather tube and unbuckled the cracked strap that held the cap in place. Stale air rose out of the cylinder. She reached inside, noting that her skin was nearly as papery and brittle as the contents she withdrew. When had she grown so old?

On the table she unrolled the aged blueprints that her father and Ken had used when they built the five cottages. She spread them flat with quivering fingers, the ends curling over her hands.

The five tiny homes—six, counting the slightly different one built with the lodge for the chef and housekeeper, where Janet and the girls now lived—were erected to serve many purposes: a living space, a guest suite, a hiding place. They were duplexes, two complete units in one building, separated by a secret compartment. Each unit shared a porch but had its own entrance, one bedroom, one bathroom, a kitchen, and a living room. And a four-foot space between bedroom closets where anyone who needed to could hide. A Japanese, say, from an American authority.

Dr. Harrison had come by the idea while reading about sympathetic Germans accused of sheltering Jews in their own homes.

To Pearl's knowledge, no one had ever actually used the little closets for their intended purpose during the war. Much in the same way no one ever truly needed the nuclear fallout shelters built in the following decade. Evergreen was remote and sparsely populated enough to be a hiding place unto itself. Nevertheless, the fact that they existed gave those who lived at the Harrison Lodge a reason not to be afraid.

Dr. Harrison had installed the little spy panel in his study so he could be forewarned of any undesirable visitors, and the nearby dumbwaiter, long ago boarded up, had been rigged to hold a man's weight and operated from the inside. It could rise all the way to the third floor, where he could gain a helpful view of the valley.

Pointless endeavors? For years now Pearl had thought that's all her long life was, an aimless extension of her father's grand but inconsequential ideals.

Until the night she saw little Kate Whitby, her youngest great-grandchild, give food to a man who couldn't pay for it. Delilah had done that once upon a time, Pearl recalled. She tended many men who couldn't pay—couldn't walk, couldn't think straight, couldn't even thank her—and Pearl didn't shield her from her baby sister's disgust over it. Those years were lean and not easily forgotten. Delilah had it right, Pearl finally decided—but not until after cancer took her and Donna returned to do her duty to the family business, controlling and bitter and miserly in her efforts to succeed.

Donna counted pennies as if constantly afraid one would roll away under the foundation, though the inn had never been in any true financial peril. Her husband, Daniel, was a good man and son-in-law, but he liked to say he married Donna, not her hotel, and the retired schoolteacher soon had enough reason to resent the hotel's demands.

Their daughter, Janet, had spent her life looking for a man to rescue her from the remoteness of her family and had three father-less children to show for it.

And Pearl pretended to be crazy . . . Why? It had seemed a good idea when she first set upon it. It was an expression of disappointment and grief for the way things had turned out. It was a cry for attention; the elderly were all neglected until they couldn't be. And it was the boldest claim she could make: she had nothing left to lose.

Until Kate gave away the household food. She was still an inno-cent. As much a Harrison as Pearl's father. The family name was all but lost, reduced to a sign at the bottom of a driveway, but Kate must not be.

On the blueprints Pearl could see each hiding place in the center of each cottage as clearly as the spine on a dog's back. She wondered if Donna remembered them, if Delilah had even known. They must have played in the closets as little girls, but Pearl couldn't quite remember now. At some point those who knew about them used them for storage. The last time she'd stepped inside one of those slim spaces herself was 1946. The day before their wedding, she and Kenneth stole one more kiss in the heart of the Nocturne, where they had stolen dozens. Then they surrendered it to the spiders.

But now murder had come to Evergreen, and a family might need to protect itself with secrets like these.

Pearl peeled back the thin dusty page of the blueprints, and then turned one more and saw something in one of the drawings that she had not thought of for fifty years. Something worth show-ing Kate, if no one else.

Something like joy rattled in the cavernous empty spot behind Pearl's ribs.

CHAPTER 22

He's been in the worst kind of mood since the sheriffs came to talk to him yesterday," Reece said of her brother as she filled her plate with sweets.

The girls stood in the dining room behind a table draped with a white cloth and covered with platters and towers of desserts. They held dishes heaped with one of everything. Gran wouldn't normally have allowed Kate to visit the buffet in the dining room, but Reece's parents were paying guests, so an exception was made.

Kate was less interested in the treats than in Austin. When she and Reece arrived in the dining room, Austin took his piece of pie outside. Holding the plate while shoveling in the pie took two hands, and an object under his sweatshirt poked out at a funny angle, like drumsticks jammed in a hip pocket. Kate never did see what it was. He wolfed down dessert, left the plate on the porch, and slinked off for parts unknown. Kate had watched him slouch-walk his way down to the creek, new snowflakes dotting his bright hair and gray sweatshirt. She was alternately itching to follow him and relieved he wasn't coming after her.

"What did the sheriff want with Austin?"

"They wouldn't let me listen, but grown-ups tell each other everything." Reece nodded to the corner of the dining room, where Mrs. Benson and Janet had their heads tipped toward each other over the small square table. "Bet she's telling your mom right now. Mom *did* say he pawned the Nintendo Saturday and they wanted to know if he might have seen anything suspicious." Reece popped a petit four in her mouth and talked around it. "Of course he didn't. If he did he'd just brag about helping solve a crime. But he's being a monster. Mom's pretty mad about the Nintendo. They could have returned it to the store for full price."

"But why is Austin worried about Grandy?"

"I *know*. Something is seriously wrong."

Kate agreed.

Across the room, Mr. Benson was frowning at Reece's overloaded plate of dessert.

"Time to go!" Reece piped, and she headed out of the dining room, carrying her goodies to safety on the terrace before her father could politely object. In spite of the trickling snowflakes, she plopped down into one of the outdoor chairs. Kate put her food on the table at Reece's elbow. She wondered how to take the loot to Charlie. If she wasted it, she'd get an earful of trouble from Gran.

"Did Austin tell you he stole a phone from Mr. Gorman?"

"He never tells me anything, but I believe it." Reece giggled. "Maybe he'll get arrested."

"Mr. Gorman punched him in the face to get it back. I saw it."

"You saw?" Crumbs fell out of Reece's mouth.

"Austin was pretty mad at me."

"At you? Why?"

Kate shrugged.

"He said a baseball hit him."

"Nope, it was Mr. Gorman."

"Did Austin cry?"

Kate shook her head, though she wasn't one hundred percent sure.

"Did your Grandy see it? Maybe that's why—"

"No. Let's find out why Austin's really here," Kate said. She left her plate and took the steps down the terrace onto the path that Austin had taken. Reece followed but brought her desserts along.

The path was paved with a fine layer of crushed gravel. It passed under Great-Grandma Pearl's bedroom window, then turned away from the inn. Here it led to one of the footbridges that crossed the creek, and then the path became a large loop with crooked branches that meandered to each of the cottages. Chairs arranged on the banks of the creek in the shelter of tall cottonwoods had been covered with tarps in anticipation of snow. Already, Austin had vanished.

Kate paused at the bottom of the footbridge to listen for footsteps or another giveaway. There was a hiking trail at the back of the property that led up over a foothill and down toward another creek, but hiking didn't seem like something Austin would have come to do.

Reece arrived next to her chewing a chocolate-covered strawberry. A hunk of chocolate coating fell to the ground.

A rapid tapping behind them caused Kate to turn around. Inside her bedroom, Great-Grandma Pearl had slipped behind the pretty rice-paper screen and was rapping her knuckle against the window. Kate waved uncertainly.

"Is your great-grandma really crazy?" Reece asked.

"I don't know. But shush. She hears just fine."

Having got the girls' attention, Great-Grandma Pearl started pointing to her right, looking excited and mouthing words that Kate couldn't make out.

"She looks crazy," Reece said. "And if we can't hear her she probably can't hear me, right?"

Beside Pearl's window was the terrace entrance marked Private Residence. Beyond this was a gigantic bay window covered with drawn curtains—Gran and Grandy's rooms. And beyond this, a path around the far side of the house took visitors through a small grove of aspen trees, naked since October, around Grandy's workshop, and back to the front of the lodge.

The girls followed that path and peeked around the corner of the building, but the rapping on the glass grew more vigorous. Kate returned. Great-Grandma Pearl was pointing to the right again, with both hands this time. Kate pointed at the private entrance, her expression a question mark. Pearl nodded vigorously.

Kate pulled the door open and entered the hall. She knocked on Great-Grandma Pearl's door and waited, but the woman never responded. When Kate peeked back outside again, the window was empty.

Crazy, Reece mouthed.

"Maybe she knows we're looking for Austin," Kate surmised.

"She's a mind reader too?"

"Why would he have come in here?"

"Because the sign says not to," Reece said, brushing her fingers against her jeans.

Or because Austin was looking for Grandy, Kate thought, but she was still confused by the possibility that Reece's brother was honestly worried. She turned away from Great-Grandma Pearl's door and stared at her grandparents' apartment. Gran was in the kitchen today. Grandy would be wherever Gran had sent him, to paint a scuffed wall or repair a broken screen or prune some shrubbery around the creek. Whenever the last beauty of autumn finally fell away from the yard, usually at the beginning of November, Gran could never be made happy with the way things worked until the following spring. One more reason why Grandy occasionally dared to suggest they close for the winter.

Unless Grandy was here, sad about the death of his friend. Impulsively, Kate reached out and grabbed their doorknob, which was usually locked. Today the knob turned in Kate's hand.

She wasn't sure who was more startled: her or Grandy, who sat in an armchair beside the curtained window. He had been dozing, an impression made greater by the way his entire body jerked to life at the sight of her.

"The door's unlocked," they both said at the same time. Kate was explaining her invasion but Grandy had asked a question edged with annoyance. His gaze stayed stern. A strange feeling washed over Kate, a sensation of having swallowed something too hot on a bitter cold day. It burned through her chest and her stomach. She couldn't remember Grandy ever being angry at her.

"I'm sorry, Grandy. I just wanted to see if you're okay. I heard about Mr. Gorman."

The sharpness in his eyes softened, then he tipped his head back against his chair and closed his eyes again. "Thanks, Agent K. Everything'll be all right."

"Did Austin come to see you?"

"Who?"

"My brother," Reece said from the hall.

"Who—? Never mind. No one's been here but you two. Go on now. I have a wicked headache."

Kate pulled the door closed and headed down the hall back toward the foyer, quickly to get herself on the other side of the red velvet privacy rope as swiftly as possible. She went under it, but Reece stepped over it, catching her shoe and nearly sprawling with her plate into the foyer. A cookie tumbled onto the dark carpet and Kate stooped to pick it up.

"Maybe he went back for more food," Reece said, seeming

disappointed about the contaminated cookie. "He's always hungry. I'm going to take my plate to the kitchen and I'll peek."

"I'll wait here," Kate said. Reece jogged off, and Kate stared at the paneled walls behind the potted tree, knowing that they contained a secret door where Great-Grandma Pearl might even now be spying on her.

"What was that all about?" Kate said loud enough for the old woman to hear.

"How am I supposed to know?" The low voice was Austin's, and the boy marched down the stairs on the other side of the reception desk.

"You shouldn't eavesdrop on people!"

"I wasn't. You just weren't paying attention."

Austin finished coming down, hands in the unipocket of the hoodie he wore every day. He made a beeline for the dining room. The bulge Kate had seen under his sweatshirt was gone now. She strode across the foyer to intercept him.

"What were you doing upstairs?" she asked.

Austin stopped, slowly turned around. "It's a public place."

"Not exactly. Reece said you came to check on Grandy."

"Your mom said he was resting. So I decided to stretch my legs."

"Reece told me the sheriffs visited you."

"Reece said. Reece said. Did she also mention they'll be visiting you too?"

"Me? Why?"

"You know as much as I do about what happened in the shop yesterday."

"You're just trying to scare me."

"Maybe. Snitch."

"Am not!" Kate cried. "Mr. Gorman's cameras can prove it."

Austin seemed to have forgotten the cameras. He looked stunned for half a second, then recovered. He took his hands out of his pockets.

"They'll prove I didn't snitch!" she said.

"They can't prove what you might have said!"

"Grandy will say—"

"Do you think he cares about that today? His best friend was slaughtered last night! Stabbed like a bazillion times. You know what I'm thinking? I'm thinking maybe he's the killer."

Kate couldn't think of a retort to that.

"S'what I told the sheriffs—that you were there yesterday, you and your grandpa, and that he and Gorman got into a fight."

"They didn't fight! They were just talking."

"You're so naïve, Kate."

"Oh, and you're so helpful. Bet you left out the part where you stole that phone!"

They faced off, nothing more than a few stairs between them. Austin's wild hair made him look especially scary. He jumped off the staircase and stuck a finger in her face. He leaned in, close enough for her to see flecks of bright-orange paint under one of his fingernails. Then he poked her on the shoulder and looked disgusted.

She set her jaw. "If they ask me maybe I'll tell them what you did to Mr. Gorman, and what he did back—" A horrible thought popped into her mind, and she stopped. "Did you?" she asked. "Did you kill Mr. Gorman for beating you up?"

He tilted his head and looked down on her out of the corner of his eye, thinking.

"Maybe it'd be good for you to think so," he whispered. "Even though my money's on your dear Grandy."

"You found him!" Reece declared, coming out of the dining room again with a cookie in each hand.

"No." Austin slipped a long arm around his sister's shoulders and put her in a goofy choke hold. "No, *I* found *her.*"

CHAPTER 23

The Fox moved quickly after he left Detective Warren. He didn't have much time.

Three Heavies waited in his Camaro in the parking lot, brothers who'd been with him long term and showed up to help before he had to think of who to ask. There was Hector, who acted first and only sometimes asked for forgiveness later; Brick, who almost never spoke and didn't have to be told what to do; and Jones, a wild hothead who liked to jack up his natural temper a few notches just for show. He wasn't the only Heavy who liked to be feared, but he was the best at toying with his audience.

Brick wore a new blade at his waist today. The Fox couldn't see the hilt, but the sheath was long enough to jut out from Brick's hip at an odd angle when he sat.

The Fox started the engine, and his brothers asked no questions as he pulled out and took the most direct route to the I-25 bridge over the South Platte River. In a city of more than one hundred fifty square miles, his destination was less than two miles away from the police headquarters. He would use this luck to his advantage, visit, and leave before Warren had the chance to track Antonio Demarco to the same location.

"Watch for a tail," he said to Hector, who rode shotgun.

The day was as gray as the dirty freeway, the chill of November sharpening the senses. To the west, snow was already falling in the highest elevations. It was the middle of the afternoon in a washed-out landscape of concrete and exhaust. The sun wasn't strong enough today to put color in anything, might never be strong enough again.

Deshawn Johnson gave one last thought to his son, then made the boy take a seat on the sidelines of this mental game.

The thing about people who lived under bridges: they may or may not be there at any given time of day. Antonio, of course, would not be there. But someone who knew him might be. Someone who also knew his companions. A ragtag family of teenagers, the Fox thought, recalling the one officer's remark about a street family. An easy group to outmuscle and outwit.

The green bridge, five pairs of girded iron arches that supported Interstate 25, vaulted the river between the Broncos' football stadium to the west and Six Flags Elitch Gardens to the east. Downtown Denver was just another mile east. Not a bad location for a tight group of homeless teens who might make their daily living panhandling, or hawking marijuana, or selling themselves.

The Fox found his way through the cloverleaf turns of the freeway exchange and the frontage roads that twisted underneath them, finally arriving at the two-lane road that passed directly under the bridge and alongside the South Platte. He pulled into the shadow of the overpass and scoped out the scene from the car. Concrete piles, rusting iron girders, sharp-edged river stones lining both banks. Overhead, the muffled hiss of freeway traffic zooming over the deck. On the other side of the river, a pretty little blond thing was having a smoke on the footpath that passed under the arch. Behind her, the stadium parking lot was a blank black slate, silent as space on this Sunday when the home team played away.

The girl saw him and exhaled a cloud of indifference. But she kept her eyes on his party.

The gun he'd used to shoot Antonio was still under his seat. He groped for it, wrapped his fingers around it, and climbed out of the car. Hector came next. He opened the trunk and retrieved a sledge-hammer. The girl ground her cigarette under her heel and, quick as a mouse, swung around one of the arches where it touched the ground and scurried up the rise, sure of her footing, disappearing into a chaos of girders and braces and plywood patches.

The Fox heaved his gun out into the South Platte. It splashed and sank and promised, if anyone ever found it, to support the idea that Antonio Demarco was killed by one of his own.

"Let's call them down for a word," the Fox said.

Hector swung the hammer into one of the girders, where it resounded until the very sky seemed to hum. Hector laughed and shook out his hand.

"Just let me climb up," Jones shouted, getting out of the car.

The Fox waved him off. Hector struck again.

"Lookin' for Charlie," the Fox boomed. "Charlie Fuse."

After a few seconds a bushy head appeared at the top of the arch, dirty brown and bearded. Big guy, almost the Fox's size, but younger.

"No Charlie here," he said.

"We'll just wait for him to get back then," the Fox said. "Maybe make ourselves at home while your people are out."

Brick had approached the foot of the arch and stood on the concrete base, showing off the knife at his hip and the muscles popping out under his sleeves. He tested the traction of his shoe on the sloping iron, then started ascending like a monkey on a rising tree branch, all arms and legs.

"Get off!" the bearded one shouted.

Already Brick was a third of the way to the apex.

"What's it you want with Charlie?"

"I want him to die," the Fox said.

At this the beard revealed a broad grin. "Then maybe we got something to talk about."

Brick's wide foot slipped, and he barely kept himself from tumbling into the slow river.

"But don't bother coming up. Save your strength for the real work."

The man sent the little blond bird, calling her Eve, which made Jones howl and do a crude dance up by the car.

"Come to Adam, baby girl, come give me sump'n good."

She ignored him, coming down the arch with a six-pack of cheap beer in one fist while Merridew, he said his name was, stayed up high in the nest. She didn't descend all the way. The rest of Merridew's people stayed tucked out of sight, flickers of hair and whispers behind their makeshift apartments.

Squatting on the beam, Eve tossed a can to each of them the way a soldier might throw grenades. Hector stood by the Fox's side, leaning on the hammer handle. He caught each can and hurled one up the bank to Jones. Brick stayed at the base of the farthest arch. The first can Eve threw at him split open when it struck the girder, spraying beer in wild arcs.

"Just take it to him," Merridew ordered.

There were two cans left. Eve popped one out of its plastic ring and let the other dangle from her wrist. Warily, she went the rest of the way down, eyes on the Fox, and walked the intact can to Brick, who didn't budge from his post.

"Charlie split yesterday," Merridew was saying to the Fox. "Stole my ride and took off."

"Where'd he go?"

"You think he'd tell me? Why d'ya want him dead?"

"Why do you?"

Merridew shrugged. "He's trouble. You're here poundin' on my door. What more proof do I need?"

Eve held the warm beer out to Brick. He took the can and then caught her slender arm in one fist before she could leap away.

"I'll take me some a that," Jones announced. "Don't use her up now."

The Fox craned his neck upward. "Maybe you can give my boys a tour of your digs. Make sure you're not hiding a killer up there."

"A killer. Wow. That's a shame. But Charlie? He was a real slacker. Don't know if he had murder in him. Wow. Who was it?"

"My son."

"No way. Dude. That's heavy."

"You mocking me?"

"Never."

"'Cause if Charlie's your man it makes no dif to me whether I take out him or you."

At the car, Jones withdrew a pistol from his waistband. He leveled it sideways, pointed up at Merridew, and locked his elbow. "Just say when," Jones said.

Eve swung the last beer on its plastic leash up at Brick's head. It struck his ear and came loose, fell to the rocks, and tumbled into the river.

"You should cut that out, baby," Merridew said. "Don't make them mad. Look, guys, Charlie was never my man. No more'n Eve's my woman." Eve yanked against Brick's fist and he poured his drink over her head. "Well, maybe you can do more with her than I could. Take her if you want her. And I care about Charlie even less. If he was here he'd be a body in the river, that's all."

"He had partners," the Fox said. "A blond boy and a dead one.

163

If you can't give me Charlie, tell me where the blond buddy is and I'll leave you be."

Eve stopped struggling and turned her face up toward Merridew. There was a challenge in her eyes that the Fox couldn't quite read. Maybe a plea. With Coz it had sometimes been hard to tell the difference. But he knew one thing for sure: when a man acted like he didn't care what happened to his woman, he usually cared too much. He nodded at Brick.

Brick twisted Eve's arms behind her back and held both wrists in one fist. Standing behind her, he yanked on her long-sleeved shirt and tore the knit top to bottom in one pull, revealing a clingy T-shirt layered beneath it. She kicked at Brick. He swept her feet out from under her and she came down on her knees on the jagged rocks, crying out, her arms pulled up high behind her.

"Don't know nothing about partners," Merridew said lazily. "But I can give you Charlie."

"Thought you didn't know where he was," the Fox said.

"Did I say that?"

In a lightning-swift move, a single tug, Brick hauled Eve's T-shirt up over her head and yanked it down her arms, pulling and twisting the fabric into a tight rope to secure her wrists. Only a grimy tank top covered her now.

"How many shirts does one girl need?" Jones complained.

"Talk fast," the Fox said to Merridew.

Merridew scratched some invisible itch under his beard and cast a careless glance at Eve's struggling form. The Fox wondered if he had misjudged.

"Well, I told you Charlie stole my ride. A sweet little vintage Honda CB77. Needed some work, but classic, you know? A Super Hawk. You ever see Al Pacino in *Serpico*?"

Jones fired a shot into the river. Merridew laughed. The Fox's patience came to an end.

With balance honed by years of street fighting, the Fox traversed the rocks and took Eve from Brick, tugging her by the T-shirt rope and hauling her to the water's edge. She stumbled and went in to her ankles, breathing hard, gasping. The cold water sent goose flesh rippling over her skinny arms. Her ribs and backbone heaved.

There was a scuffle on plywood overhead, a muffled argument.

Merridew twisted his neck to see what the Fox had planned for Eve.

"So of course I reported her stolen," he went on. "Wasn't ready to let her go, though a part of me was pretty sure I'd never see her again. It's been a sleepless night."

Still holding on to Eve's wrists, the Fox kicked the backs of her knees, forcing her to drop, and pushed her facedown into the dark waters. Now he was just mad.

"Anyway, it seems some stories get their happy endings. Just got a call—just a few minutes before you fellows showed up—from the Jefferson County Sheriff. Seems our friend Charlie crashed my fine bike up in Evergreen."

The Fox straightened at this news, and Eve came up coughing. Hector swung the hammer against the green arch one more time.

"Not enough," the Fox said. And down Eve went.

"No? You guys ask a lot of a man. Well, lucky for you the sheriff's people were full of information. They found it up at a place called Bear Creek Road. You know it?"

Brick went back to the arch and started scaling it. Jones leaped down from the car waving the gun and followed suit, coming up with more eagerness but less agility than Brick.

"C'mon now, I can't do everything for you," Merridew said.

His confidence faltered a bit under the metallic drumming of the Heavies' boots. "It's the best I got."

Eve's struggle against the Fox's grip slackened a bit. He yanked her up for a gasp, then pushed her down again.

Merridew started to unravel. "Seriously. Dawg! Charlie has nothing. No family, no money, no friends, no ride. He laid the bike down on some curve. Wrecked it. Where's he gonna go? He's up there somewhere."

"You give them Charlie's name?"

"What?"

"You tell the cops Charlie stole that bike?"

"No. No, just said it was gone!"

"Why not?"

Merridew didn't have a ready answer.

"Why didn't you point your finger?"

"Man . . ." Merridew cleared his throat. "I got my own issues with Charlie. Maybe I didn't want them to take him in just yet. Maybe I wanted him for myself. But you want him? Have him. Take him. He's all yours."

The Fox released the girl then and she went face forward into the water, then rolled over and scrambled for the other side of the river, kicking off the bottom and coughing hard, splashing. She freed her hands of the twisted shirt and covered herself, her face discolored by the cold, by fear, by fury.

"They impound the bike?" the Fox asked.

"Yeah."

"Where?"

"I don't know. Some tow lot."

"What *part* of Bear Creek Road?"

"How'm I supposed to know?"

"You want me to believe that you want this kid dead and you gonna track him down 'fore the cops find him themselves, and you don't think to ask the happy dude who calls you with such good news *exactly* where the boy might have died?"

Merridew backpedaled and complained but found the information quickly enough.

Eve reached the other side and staggered up the bank, aiming for the stadium lot.

"You might want to find yourself a better place to live," the Fox said to her back. "C'mon down now, Brick. Jones. We're going to Evergreen."

Jones spit on the road. "Evergreen? I hate that town."

CHAPTER 24

The pleasant smell of woodsmoke from the fire in the dining room's hearth scented the room. Austin and Reece were gone, and so was the brunch crowd, and only the skinny lady and the fat man who'd checked in last night remained in the dining room, sipping coffee and frowning as they complained about the forecasted snow and generally appeared to be miserable. Kate's family, too, seemed more distracted than usual. Olivia kept forgetting to bring the guests refills, though they were the only pair left in the room, and Alyssa forgot to gripe about the oppressive weather. Mr. Gorman's death had overshadowed it all. Kate herself was still shivering from her encounter with Austin.

She'd gone up to the second and third floors of the lodge to look for hints of what he might have done upstairs when no one was looking.

The event room at the top hadn't been used since the summertime, and it seemed as empty and unchanged as ever. On the second story were eight guest rooms, four on each side of a library that sat directly over the downstairs foyer. Towering windows at the front of the library overlooked the main entrance of the lodge, and groupings of high-backed chairs were arranged to maximize the view. At the back of the library, just across the short hall that connected the east side of the lodge with the west, a balcony railing looked down into the dining room.

From the balcony rail, it was easy to imagine that today's dining room had once been a grand salon. Its high ceiling was open to the second floor, and the huge fireplace on one side of the room warmed the coveted tables.

It was while Kate was in the library, looking for evidence of Austin and running her fingers over rows of old books, that she saw a single black SUV coasting up the swooping driveway. It parked at the curve right in front of the lodge.

The predicted visit from the sheriff's department came just as Kate realized, with a jolt, that she had forgotten to take a plate of hot food to Charlie.

She watched from a sheltered vantage behind a drapery as the two uniformed men approached. Olivia would like the one with the curly hair and dark glasses, Kate thought. He looked like he might like to go to parties and watch funny movies. The other one was harder to describe. He wasn't smiling, and his body and his uniform were both as stiff as if they'd come straight off an ironing board.

Gran's voice floated up from the reception desk. "I do wish they would've parked elsewhere."

Kate ran out of the library to the hall, where the balustrade under the second-to-third-floor stairway looked down onto the reception desk.

"Gran?"

It took her grandmother a moment to look up.

"Katherine? What are you doing up there? You'll disrupt the guests. Go on back to the cottage."

She knew the only guests were eating in the dining room, so she kept talking. "I saw the sheriff."

"So did I. Now scoot."

"Am I in trouble?"

Gran blinked. "What? No, child, of course not."

"Is Grandy?"

"Oh, he's in plenty of trouble with me, skulking down to that pawnshop with you in tow. Maybe this whole tragedy will finally get through his head *why*."

"I meant the sheriff. Is Grandy in trouble with the sheriff?"

"Why . . . why no, of course not. I'm sure they only have a few more questions about that . . . about that poor man. They were friends, you know."

"What about Alyssa?"

"Alyssa? Good grief, Katherine. Whatever for?"

"Well—"

"No, no. I'm sorry I asked. I have to take care of these officers now. You go do as I say. Questions later."

But Kate did not go back to her cottage. How could she? There were *police officers* at the lodge, two of them, and maybe they wanted to talk to her. She could not go back to a place where she could be found, because she worried about the questions they might ask: *Did your grandpa fight with Mr. Gorman? What about? What did they say, exactly? Where did your grandpa go last night?*

The men came in, and though Kate couldn't see them, one of them scraped his wet shoes on the mat before stepping through the door. A utility belt rattled with police things. A radio crackled.

"Deputies," Gran said, all formal and polite.

"Ma'am. I'm Deputy Sawyer. This is Deputy Krane."

"Donna Torrance."

"We're looking for Daniel Torrance."

"My husband. I believe he spoke with you this morning. At Bruce's shop."

"We have some additional questions to ask him."

Kate leaned out over the balustrade as far as she dared but couldn't see a bit of the foyer.

"Of course. I'll get him for you. Janet, please take these men back to the keeping room."

"The keeping room? It's such a mess," Kate's mother said.

"We'll have more privacy there."

Kate didn't think it was a mess. It was small and warm with old sofas that smelled like Great-Grandma Pearl's closet and soft quilts to burrow in. Kate did her homework there through the winter when the cottage was too cold and quiet. Its sliding glass door had a nice view of the creek and the two prettiest cottages, and Chef's bustling in the kitchen made her feel safe. The problem from Kate's point of view was that there would be no easy way for her to hear the conversation if they went in there.

But her mother disobeyed Gran's instructions as quickly as Kate had. As soon as Gran went to fetch Grandy, Janet said lightly, "Let's go to the dining room."

It was great news to Kate, who could spy from the library balcony more easily than anywhere else in the lodge. She ran on light feet to the rail and hid herself behind a potted tree.

The complaints of their only guests seemed loud now that the Sunday bustle had died out.

". . . no better in town than it is here," the man was saying into his coffee cup as the steam rose before his face. His chin tripled over his buttoned-up collar and tie. "And a pathetic wine list. Colorado isn't famous for its wine, so they really shouldn't bother with local pride and all that."

"I thought the Holy Cross Abbey was really quite nice." His companion took tiny sips and set the cup down between each one, clinking it on the saucer.

"Quite nice? Can a nice merlot overshadow a murder? I thought Evergreen had a low crime rate. But here we are, in the hands of a waitstaff that can't shut up about homicide. As if horrifying details will increase our appetites."

"That was in very poor taste, I agree."

"Did you hear that it might have been gang related? Here in this tiny town, *gangs*."

"Perhaps we should check out early."

"And lose a night's rate? No. Though I say for the price we paid, we should get more than views of the scrubby foothills—"

"We might have had a valley view from one of the cottages, they said. The topmost one, I think. The Full Moon?"

"And have to walk outdoors just to get to breakfast!" Kate watched the buttons of his vest. One of them might pop straight off at any moment. "I told you we should have booked the Aspen resort."

"I'm sorry you don't find that beautiful little creek out there more peaceful."

"It's going to freeze over tonight, just you watch."

They fell silent when Janet appeared, but they stared and craned their necks to see the deputies. Janet indicated that the men should sit at a table set for six directly beneath Kate's perch. It was as far as she could seat them from the pair at the front window.

"May I get you some coffee? Something to eat?" she offered when they were seated.

"That's hardly appropriate under the circumstances," Gran scolded, frowning as she came in and saw what Janet had done. Grandy trailed along behind her.

Janet lifted her chin and singled out the curly-headed deputy. Krane. "A slice of Hot Chocolate Cake, maybe?"

"Not tonight, thank you. But I've had it before." Krane was smiling. "Had to vow off sugar for a week after."

His starched partner put a small electronic tablet where his dinner plate should be and looked at Gran. She was glaring at her daughter as she yanked a chair out for herself. The pretty table would have to be cleared and reset afterward, even if no one ate anything.

"We'd like to speak to Mr. Torrance alone," Deputy Sawyer said.

"We've been married forty-four years. Nothing to hide from anyone." She sat and Grandy helped to scoot in her chair, and her posture dared the men to separate her from her husband.

"Janet, please get these officers some water," Gran said.

Kate's mother pressed her lips together and left the room.

Grandy lowered himself into the seat next to Gran. "So. How can I help you?"

The grown-ups dropped their voices to a level that was very difficult to hear. The volume went up and down, but mostly down. Kate closed her eyes, because shutting out the sights sometimes helped sharpen the sounds.

". . . that Mr. Gorman was involved in some illegal activity," she finally made out from one of the deputies.

"Illegal?" Grandy echoed.

Deputy Sawyer said more that Kate couldn't catch.

"He never told me anything about that." Grandy's voice was stronger this time.

"Oh, he didn't have to tell you," Gran boomed as Janet arrived bearing a tray with four water glasses. "That man was a fence—half of Evergreen knew it."

"A what?" Janet asked.

"A *fence*. He resold stolen goods. Don't look at me that way,

Daniel. Not everything in that store came in through the front door. I told you a million times why you shouldn't keep taking Katherine there."

"Kathy's been going?" Janet sounded alarmed. Grandy's water sloshed as his daughter set it in front of him.

"Now look, Donna. Rumors about that have been going around for years, but it's just talk. I swear Bruce never talked about it with me, and I never saw anything to make me think he was involved in something like that. Did you ever have proof of it? No. People just like to talk."

Deputy Krane said, "Now it seems there *was* some truth in it."

"Well, I wouldn't know."

Kate opened her eyes. Janet served the rest of the water and, seeming at a loss, sat down next to Deputy Sawyer with the tray still in her hands. The fat man and skinny lady were statues, their eyes on the window and their ears straining as hard as Kate's. She could see right down into their empty coffee cups.

". . . mentioned he was having trouble with anyone?" Sawyer was saying. "Someone angry with him? Any arguments that you might have overheard?"

"No." Grandy's white head shook firmly.

Deputy Sawyer sat so straight in his chair that his back didn't touch it. He tapped on the screen of his electronic tablet. "You were at the shop Saturday?"

Grandy nodded. The lawman must have asked what time, because her grandfather said, "As I said before, after lunchtime. Maybe around one."

The skinny lady leaned over her coffee cup and whispered to the man.

"We have a witness who says he heard you and Mr. Gorman arguing at that time," said Deputy Sawyer.

"Well, *sure*," Grandy said. "Bruce and I argue all the time. So often I can hardly remember every one. But when stuff like this happens, it's like you remember everything, don't you? Every last look, every last word . . ." He folded his hands on the table. "We were in a disagreement about how the Broncos were going to fare in Sunday's game."

The officers stared at him, expressionless. Kate was thinking of the men's phone call and couldn't remember anything about football. Gran looked down at her lap. Janet flashed a goofy smile at Deputy Krane.

"Did your disagreement cover money?" Sawyer asked.

Grandy shrugged. "We sometimes put a few Jacksons down on a game."

"Did either of you ever not pay up?"

"Course not. Even if that had happened once or twice, what's that worth? Nothing more than words. It was friendly, that's all."

Deputy Sawyer straightened his electronic tablet against the edge of the table. "Mr. Torrance, where were you last night?"

The guests were leaving the dining room now, Kate noticed, as slowly as Great-Grandma Pearl was prone to walk. They went out the side entrance, which would take them to the rear stairs.

"So now I'm a suspect, am I?" Grandy objected. "Because some kid says he heard us arguing about a ball game?"

"You know the witness?" Krane asked.

"For crying out loud, everyone here knows everyone else. He was Bruce's only customer while I was there. And may I just say that boy isn't exactly a star citizen?"

"The question is purely routine, sir."

"I was here. Right here. All night."

"He was," said Gran, still looking down at the table. "I can confirm it."

Except for when he drove off down the hill, before the man who couldn't pay arrived, Kate thought. He must have come back right after that. Kate wouldn't know as well as Gran would.

The old floorboard in front of guest room 3 creaked.

"Wait." The voice belonged to the guest lady. And in the silence that followed, Kate realized that these two had noticed the balcony view here and would come to do their own eavesdropping.

Swiftly, Kate flew into the library, leaving only a rustling of potted tree leaves behind.

She thought she heard someone at the dining room table speak her name but could not be sure. The busybody couple commanded all her attention as they tried to be sneaky about listening in, though they were at a disadvantage, being so large and conspicuous together. They remained in the hallway, where Kate suspected they couldn't hear much at all, which pleased her. Even if they were behaving exactly as she had, they had no business doing it.

Unable to hear any more juicy details from the hall, the woman walked boldly into the library. Kate heard her coming and had just enough time to fall between one of the fat chairs and its ottoman, where she made herself as small as possible. The woman stood at the bookcase closest to the balcony and stared at its book spines for the longest time, until finally she gave up on learning any more of the conversation below.

"Really, my dear," the man said from beyond the room, "I'm sure we don't need any further confirmation of our bad luck in picking this place."

"There's not even anything edifying to *read*," she said and then walked out.

When Kate heard the door to their room click shut, she exhaled her relief at not being noticed by the two unhappy people. In the tight space she placed her feet flat against the ottoman's side and shoved it away.

The footstool glided over the plush rug, her knees locked, and her legs came to rest on top of one of the twin knives from Mr. Gorman's pawnshop, the ones she wanted for Christmas, with the dragon hilt and the ruby-red eye and the red leather fire flaming down the sleek black sheath.

CHAPTER 25

It wasn't Bear Creek Road where Charlie Fuse laid down the bike, but Upper Bear Creek Road—*upper* standing for *uppity*, the Fox thought as they followed Hector's GPS to the location Merridew had given them.

It was possible that Merridew had lied. Possible, but more likely Merridew had decided to let the Fox have this round and was even now moving his people from that bridge. That's what he should be doing, anyway, because if the Fox came out of Evergreen empty-handed, he'd be headed straight back to the river.

Hector whistled at the sight of the huge homes.

Jones was unimpressed. "It ain't Beverly Hills."

The Fox held his tongue. His woman would have made a nice queen in a neighborhood like this.

"Never seen Beverly Hills," said Hector. "Don't care if I ever do. Place like this is sweet enough for me."

"You aim low. I hate Evergreen. Too small. Too tight."

Brick spoke rare words. "Hard to hate million-dollar real estate."

The road twisted under the lengthening shadows of the pine trees, which were faint under the low clouds. Snowflakes dotted the Fox's windshield and almost instantly evaporated. The neighborhood seemed designed to shut people out. On either side of the road were low stone walls, wrought-iron gates, old wealth and new architecture sometimes on the same parcel. Look but don't touch. Come no farther.

These people did a better job of guarding their stuff than he'd done protecting his boy. The thought became bile in the back of his throat. He shouldn't have left Coz to chase Charlie Fuse. He shouldn't have taken Coz to the job with him at all. What was he thinking?

Her voice came back then, screaming: *What were you thinking?*

Didn't matter now. Might not matter what he thought or didn't think ever again.

When the GPS announced their arrival, the Fox pulled his old Camaro off to the left side of the road. There was a shallow ditch on the right that he didn't want to get stuck in. Beside him was a fancy wall topped with decorative shards of something jagged and sharp. Ahead, a tight curve. And in the center of the road, a glitter of shattered glass caught up in the afternoon sun, and a large brown stain.

The Fox went directly to it and toed it with his shoe. The stickiness transferred to the sole.

His brothers spread out to poke around. Brick moved uphill, kicking at piles of leaves.

A sedan coming downhill took the curve without slowing much and braked hard when the Fox came into view. The Fox stepped aside and gave the annoyed driver a friendly wave.

"Anyone asks, we're looking for your girl's diamond earring," the Fox said to Hector.

His brother laughed. He had no girl and no diamonds and no reason to bring either up here.

"Shame if Charlie killed himself," the Fox said.

"Look here." It was Jones. He stood on the shoulder of the road fifty feet away, just at the outside of the sharp turn, and he was holding up a motorcycle helmet by the chin strap. Dead leaves spilled out of it and floated back into the pile at Brick's ankles. Fox came across the asphalt for a closer look, and by the time he arrived Jones had pulled something out of the soft bowl. A black knit cap with a narrow bill on the front.

"What fool wears a hat under his helmet?" Hector asked.

"The kind that can't get far," the Fox answered.

It was Brick who found the other smudges of blood, which were smaller than those in the middle of the road and not as dark against the dry ground. They were the same color as his name and uniformly crescent shaped, as if stamped by the rounded heel of a shoe.

"Track these," the Fox ordered. "'Fore the snow covers it all."

The four formed a loose line and, like a search party, began a slow march up the slope, following the marks. The tracks did not grow any fainter, which might have meant that Charlie Fuse continued to bleed as he climbed the hillside. Then, about a hundred feet from the road, the prints stopped.

"And here your man was struck down by a lightning bolt from the Big Guy," said Jones, "and punched straight down to where he belongs."

"Or he met some help," said the Fox, who saw, at the approximate spot where the next shoe print ought to have been, a disturbance in the landscape, a place that was flat and smooth, almost swept over. The random messiness of leaves and needles and dirt clods was missing here. The Fox pointed at it, and the men continued. More slowly now, because the clouds were thickening like spoiled milk and the light wasn't shining in their favor.

But within a short time the ground leveled off and the trees made way for a gathering of small houses. It had the landscaped look of a place people paid to visit. And sure enough, as the four men stepped out onto a footpath and followed it past the nearest cottage, they found themselves standing at the edge of a clearing that looked across a narrow creek to a huge three-story lodge. Each cottage had a wide porch and two doors, a low roof that was just starting to collect snow, leafless white aspens standing in every gap, and odd vertical siding that didn't match the main lodge, which seemed built of timbers meant to evoke a log cabin.

"Somethin' smells good," Hector said.

"I think our friend might have thought the same thing and checked himself in," said the Fox.

Hector pointed straight across the clearing. "Or he mighta just kept right on goin'."

"You and Brick go check that out. Jones, let's go get the car and drive on up for an official visit. I'm hungry. You hungry?"

"Course I'm hungry. We're followin' a blood trail."

While Brick and Hector crossed the property, the Fox turned around and headed back past the nearest cottage, the way they'd all come up. He slapped the little building with the flat of his hand, half worried that finding a blood trail so swiftly had been a little too easy, half fearful that Charlie and Merridew were blowing smoke in his eyes. He should've dealt with Merridew when he had the chance.

At the back of the cottage, a glint of silver caught his attention, and he followed it to a low rock wall. Bending over, he withdrew a slim instrument from between two smooth stones.

The name engraved on the top plate erased all doubt. He showed it to Jones.

"Charlie Fuse is here," he said, grinning.

"Or was," Jones said with a shrug.

"Let's go get us some dinner."

CHAPTER 26

Kate did not know what the dragon knife meant. She needed a minute to think about it, but one minute might take too long. There were sheriff's deputies downstairs who would probably like to know about this blade.

Mr. Gorman had two exactly like it. She had seen them both just yesterday.

Mr. Gorman had been stabbed.

Between yesterday afternoon and this morning, someone had hidden the knife up here under the ottoman. Maybe Austin. Maybe Grandy. Maybe anyone else who had been to the Kwik Kash and the Harrison Lodge in the past twenty-four hours.

In Kate's opinion, the hiding place wasn't a very good one. If a guest didn't find it right away, the housekeeping staff would soon enough. They vacuumed up here every other day unless they had reason to do it more often.

Maybe someone wanted it to be found. Which might have been the dumbest idea ever. Why would a person hide something they *wanted* found?

She didn't know the answer, but she believed with all her heart that if the sheriffs found it here where Grandy lived, and if they learned that he was gone last night, even for a little while, they might think he was the one who killed Mr. Gorman. Because it was what Kate herself was starting to believe. And if Grandy went to jail, who would be left to love her?

Kate had to find a better hiding spot for the knife.

The blade and hilt together were about as long as her forearm. She was glad it had a sheath. When she was sure the fat man and skinny lady were shut in their room, she quietly stood, listened for the grown-ups' voices downstairs, then stuck the sheathed blade down the back of her pants and covered the hilt with her blousy shirt and down vest. She walked straight as that Deputy Sawyer to the stairs and descended without using her hands to hold the knife in place.

Her worry about what to do if the weapon slipped straight down the back of her leg vanished when she got to the bottom, where a different problem awaited her: all of the adults were gathered right at the entrance to the dining room, smack in the middle of the foyer.

Deputy Krane and Deputy Sawyer both looked in her direction, while her family took no note. The officers showed no intention of interviewing her or of leaving right away, though Grandy kept inching toward the wide double doors. Kate unintentionally caught Deputy Krane's eye and he smiled at her, and she became so paralyzed by all the horrible things that could possibly happen right at that moment—at the top of the list being that the knife would jump out of her pants and she herself would be sent to jail, and Charlie would die of starvation—that she only stared back.

The fastest route from here to her cottage was to the left, down the hall past the kitchen and through the keeping room. But Gran and her mother were that way, locked in some low-toned argument, and Kate couldn't risk getting in the middle. After what seemed like a full hour of indecision, though it was probably only a minute, Kate stepped off the bottom stair and crossed the foyer like a tall, elegant African woman with a bucket of water on her head. She imagined she was a heroine she'd once read about named Mammy Kate. She took short, even steps and was very careful not to look at *anyone*. She went directly past the reception desk, right by the front doors, and slipped through the brass stands that held the velvet privacy rope. So focused was she on her efforts that the only bit of conversation she caught was the word *granddaughter*, and she thought Grandy had said it.

In the private hall, she huffed out the breath she was holding and put her hand on her back, found the knife still in place, and marched for the door to the terrace.

As she passed her Great-Grandma Pearl's door, it flew open and Kate yelped.

"It surely can't shock you that I'd be here," the old lady said. "Not with this weather about. You're not heading out in it, are you?"

Kate said in a voice that sounded much higher than normal, "I'm just going back to the Rising Sun."

"And here I thought you might be coming to visit me."

"You did?" Her gaze darted to the door.

Great-Grandma Pearl winked at her. "I won't stop you. But before you go, I want to show you something." She stepped out into the hallway.

"What?"

"It's in the kitchen."

Kate backed up toward Gran and Grandy's door. "I don't think we should."

"Why not?"

Kate put her hand on the knife at her back. It seemed to be slipping. She couldn't be sure.

"The sheriffs are here talking to Grandy, and Chef's getting ready for dinner. I'm not supposed to be in the kitchen. I was just going to go out this way." She pointed at the door she and Reece had passed through just a short time ago.

"Well, that's inconvenient. What I hoped to show you is in the pantry. I suppose it'll have to wait. Don't go that way at least." Great-Grandma Pearl waved Kate into her room. "Come in here first."

Her great-grandmother pulled the door wider and Kate stepped through. "Did that awful boy go home finally?"

"Who?"

"The one you and your friend were chasing. I've been keeping an eye on things since he slipped past here this morning."

"Austin."

"Very well. He's no friend of yours I hope?"

Kate shook her head.

"And is he gone?"

"Yes."

"Good. A body needs her rest. But look here." Pearl laid a light hand on Kate's shoulder and directed her between the rice-paper screen and the picture window that looked out on the creek and the semicircle of cottages. "Tell me what you see."

Kate did not have to be told that her great-grandmother was speaking of something out of the ordinary, something above and beyond the snow turning everything white and thickening the sky like flour in one of Chef's chowders. But that was all her eyes could see.

"Everything looks perfect," Kate said. "No one has even walked in it yet."

"And here you are, ready to rush outside and mess it up." But the woman's voice was gentle. "Actually, someone has passed over. Can you see? Look fast, before the proof is gone."

Kate strained her eyes but couldn't see any footprints anywhere.

The gravel paths were ribbons of powdered sugar and the ground cover was vanishing. The creek ran and bubbled like spilled Coke, black water against the white banks. It slipped quickly under the tiny footbridge and continued its run downhill toward town, and—

There, on the east side of the short wooden bridge, were two parallel rows of marks pressed down in the snow, no bigger than potato chips. Already they were filling in, but Kate could see the circle prints leading low along the water's edge; then, where a boulder obstructed the bank, they shifted upward and over the rise in the ground, crossed a narrow open space, and disappeared underneath the porch of the Morning Glory.

For a moment she forgot the officers in the foyer and the knife at her back. "Are they paw prints?"

"Good eyes, child. And what animal do they belong to?"

"They're bigger than a squirrel—a raccoon?"

"Bigger still."

"Is it a marmot?"

"Not down here. Those paw prints belong to a wildcat. A mountain lion not full grown."

"No way! Should we bring it inside? Maybe it'll get too cold out there."

Pearl put an exaggerated look of surprise on her face. "You think those beasts would live where they can't handle the temperatures? You're smarter than that, Kate. But look here, there are a few things I can't leave to your mother or grandmother to teach you. Heaven knows how the most basic things can escape their attention. Where a cub is, its mama is very close nearby. And you are small enough to make a hearty meal for a mountain lion mama and her babies."

"But what if its mama is dead?" she blurted.

Great-Grandma Pearl's playful surprise morphed to genuine alarm. "Why would you think that?"

"Because I saw . . . Because there was . . ." Everything seemed confusing in that moment, with her great-grandmother staring right through her eyes and into her head—which secrets might be okay to tell and which were definitely not. There was no way to explain the dead cougar being taken off the road without explaining why she was there to witness it in the first place. Charlie's voice was loud in her memory. She wasn't to tell *anyone* about him. And she never told secrets. And Gran wouldn't help Charlie, because he couldn't pay.

Kate blinked. "Because I saw this TV show, and they rescued animals, and, well . . ." It was as far as she could take a lie.

"Even if its mama is dead, cubs grow up and hunt just the same."

"I thought cougars only hunted dogs," Kate said. "Remember Mitzy?" According to Alyssa, the family beagle had been eaten by one of the big mountain lions.

Great-Grandma Pearl sighed. "Well, that's baloney," she finally answered, turning her face away. "So you stay away, hear?" Flakes were clustering together in the sky, thick and wet, before they hit the earth. Then she turned Kate back toward the door of the old study. "What's out there right now is far worse than that beast of a boy prowling around here like he owned the place. I want you to turn yourself around, young lady. Park yourself in the keeping room while this storm settles in. And if you need something at your cottage you wait until there's a grown-up to walk you there."

"Yes, ma'am."

"Good girl. Now get along. I'll have a rest and then I'll join you. You can read a book to me and we'll eat more chocolate cake."

The thought did not lift Kate's heart as she found herself back in the hallway with only one way to turn. Great-Grandma Pearl would probably keep an eye on that window of hers to make sure Kate obeyed.

The knife in her waistband had grown heavy, and the sheath was rubbing a bone on her spine. Very slowly, she walked back down the hall, dreading having to pass the gathered adults. So when she arrived at the rope and saw that the foyer was empty, Kate broke into a sprint, pressing her hand over the knife to hold it in place. She broke into the kitchen at top speed and nearly knocked over Olivia, who was dressed today in Gran-approved black slacks and a white blouse, though apparently no one had noticed the costume boots—knee-high buckle-ups hidden underneath the loose pant legs. But Kate recognized the clasp over the toes. Olivia's tray full of empty water glasses and champagne flutes nearly went over.

"Speed limit's twenty-five through here!"

Kate slowed to a speed walk. Still no sight of Gran, Grandy, or her mother. Or Alyssa.

"I like your boots," she said.

"Then you're forgiven."

Turning into the family dining room, she stopped to see what was in the warming trays. Grilled ham and cheese sandwiches that could have been plastic models. On Sundays, the guests always ate better than the family, unless there were leftovers.

Kate put three sandwiches on a plate and covered them with a second plate, making a sandwich sandwich. She tucked the flying-saucer bundle under her vest and held it tightly, then zoomed through the keeping room and out the back door. Here she made an abrupt left turn, staying close to the wall so Great-Grandma Pearl had no chance of spotting her.

In less than a minute Kate had returned to her own empty cottage. Quickly, she went to the kitchenette, separated the bread, and peeled the toughening ham off one of the sandwiches, then smashed the cheesy slices back together. Leaving the meat in the sink, she carried the sandwiches into her bedroom closet and shifted aside the clothes and the suitcase, having the sinking feeling that she'd forgotten to show this side panel to Charlie. It was locked from the inside, and when she knocked there was no sound of reply. Still, she had no time and couldn't leave footprints leading around the back of the house for everyone to see. She withdrew the knife from under her shirt, set it beside the plate, knocked again, then backed out, rearranging the dresses and shutting the closet door.

She fetched the meat and hurried back outside, swelling with pride and anticipation. All at once she had outwitted her family members, a knife thief, and the sheriff's department. Next up: an orphaned cougar cub.

Today was a good day to be a spy.

CHAPTER 27

Charlie felt feverish in spite of the pills he'd swallowed. His head ached from hating the world, and his swollen foot pushed against his shoe with so much force that his own toenails dug into the skin of their neighboring toes. He sat up, groaning, and reached down to loosen the laces. Every bone in his body ached. Even his fingertips felt peeled to the nerves as they brushed against the sticky blood that soaked his rank sock. The blood from his leg had started to dry up, and his pants stuck to the raw skin down the side of his thigh and calf. He feared the ankle was broken and he'd made it worse by dragging it up the hill in the dark. At least he'd kept his shoe on.

He was desperately thirsty, having drunk the Gatorade long ago.

As the hours passed it became clear that the girl would be no more helpful to him than anyone else he'd ever known. How much could an eleven-year-old do, really? Kids had short attention spans and no real concept of time, and their loyalty changed with the TV channels.

She would tell soon enough, if she hadn't already.

He had to get out before dark, before she came back with the dad she'd told or the cops the dad would call. He had to find a way to reach Uncle Jun.

Charlie took the kid's flashlight and stuffed it into his pocket, wrapped the blanket around his shoulders like a poncho, and stood on his good foot at the end of the cot. Again when he put his right foot on the ground pain exploded like a bomb and shot all the way up to his hip. He needed to splint it, and he didn't have too many ways to do that.

He sorted through the books in Kate's stack and found a hardback. He tore off the covers. Then he ripped up the bottom of his T-shirt and tied the covers to his ankles, unsure which was worse: walking on the injury or putting it in this vise. This was gonna be pretty, hopping out of this mess.

It took only two hops to reach the door, but long seconds to find the latch that opened it.

The door swung out silently onto a landscape already coated in a perfect layer of thin snow. It frosted the ground, the rocks, the tree branches, as fine and powdery as dust in an old house.

His luck could not possibly be any worse. Now if he went anywhere, he would leave tracks.

A low wall of stacked rocks sheltered the back of the cottage, and if he'd been healthier and the stones had not been wet, he might have tried to jump for them. At the end of the rock hedge, to Charlie's right, a cluster of recent footprints remained even though the falling snow was swiftly filling them in. They were large prints, as large as his own feet, and couldn't possibly belong to any little girl. There was more than one pair, he thought, and they had clomped around a bit before moving off.

Charlie craned his neck to the left, weighing his options and risks. His head pounded. There wasn't much to see past the end of this building. Some fir trees blocked the view, and it seemed that this closet sat at the very edge of the world.

Between the corner of the little house and the fir trees, a narrow gap of road was visible from where he stood in the doorway. Or it might have been a footpath, because what drew his attention to it was a flash of red and a mane of hair, a woman walking so briskly away from him that he wouldn't have been sure of seeing her, except he could hear the quick tapping of her heels on the pavement. And then, just seconds later and a few feet beyond where the woman had been, Charlie saw a blink of black-and-white, and the plastic lights atop the car though they were not lit, and he knew he was looking at an SUV that belonged to some kind of law enforcement.

He drew a sharp breath and started coughing on the dry air.

The heel clicking stopped.

He covered his mouth and choked silently until his eyes watered.

But nothing could have blinded him to what he saw next—passing through the gap, moving opposite the SUV, coming for Charlie rather than leaving him behind—the shiny low-riding black form of a classic sports car, an old-model Camaro.

It was there and then gone, having shown too little of itself for anyone to prove exactly what they'd seen. But Charlie would never forget that car or the man who drove it.

Quiet as the falling snow, Charlie withdrew back into the closet.

CHAPTER 28

As Kate stalked the cougar cub with several slices of ham, she was thinking of another great wildcat.

Katherine Whitby was born on a crisp night in October, just two hours after a heavyweight tiger named Montecore mauled and nearly killed his owner. At first it seemed that the events had nothing in common but blood. They took place more than seven hundred miles apart—Kate in Denver, Montecore in Las Vegas. Only the tiger made the late-night news.

She'd discovered the story by accident, when she was ten and had summer hours to kill on her mother's computer. She took that laptop to the little hideaway closet whenever possible, because it wasn't password protected. Her sisters', on the other hand, were bound in virtual chains with padlocks.

In Google's skinny search field she typed *October 3 2003* because she wanted to know if anything interesting besides her birth had happened in the world on the day she was born. "Tiger attack" was one of the more intriguing items on the list, and clicking the link led her to the story and the pictures, the amazing pictures, of tigers unlike any she had ever seen. White and majestic and twice as big in her mind as anything they had at the Denver Zoo.

That afternoon she pieced together a story that was both tantalizing and tragic at once, of two young men, Siegfried Fischbacher and Roy Horn, who rose from hard childhoods to become a world-famous entertainment enterprise. Fascinated by magic and spectacle, they eventually became fathers to a pride of wildcats, and their strange family—lions and tigers and almost everything but bears—soon took center stage. And then she found the story about a newborn white tiger cub that was rejected by its mother as soon as it was born. Roy Horn cautiously cut the cub's umbilical cord, revived the kitten with a weird version of mouth-to-mouth resuscitation, and named the tiny thing Montecore.

Montecore was seven years old and six hundred pounds when he took Roy by the throat and ended the men's careers. October 3, 2003. Kate's birthday. Roy Horn's birthday as well. His fifty-ninth.

It was said that Roy pleaded, "Don't shoot the tiger!" as he was rushed to the hospital, though the arteries in his neck had been slashed. He had two strokes and flatlined on the operating table three times. And when he finally awoke to a new life of chronic pain and disability, he and Siegfried united in their refusal to have the tiger put down. Roy insisted he had not been attacked. Over and over he said he had passed out. Montecore, worried for Roy's well-being, dragged him offstage to tend to him. This was his constant story.

"He saved my life," Roy kept repeating. "He is my brother. He is my brother."

THE COUGAR CUB'S FOOTPRINTS WRAPPED AROUND THE BACK of the Morning Glory cottage. Kate stooped to examine the ground where the cub's footprints had vanished onto dry ground. Here, the cottage sheltered the ground from the snow for just a little while longer. Her fingers dangled the shreds of ham, her shoes wobbled on uneven rocks that would not give up the cub's secret. But Kate thought it might have slipped under the crawl space right here, where a piece of the old wood latticework that wrapped around the base of the structure had rotted away.

She clicked her tongue and called out softly, "Here, kitty kitty."

She did not fear the dead mama mountain lion. She was much more frightened of finding a cub starved to death because his mama wasn't there to give him food, and because he didn't have his brothers to keep him warm.

He is my brother . . . He is my brother.

"Why does Alyssa hate me?" Kate had asked her mother last summer after Gran had grounded her for a smart mouth. Kate had, for once, trumped Alyssa's mean nicknames. Instead of retorting with Alyssa the Alligator and Uhlyssa-with-a-U, Kate had tried out a bad word from TV that happened to start with *A*. Gran took her dessert away, but that night her mother woke her in bed with a slice of pie.

By the yellow light of her bed lamp, Kate spooned some silky chocolate onto her tongue and left the crunchy crust on the plate to eat last.

"Alyssa doesn't hate you. Just ignore her and she'll stop."

"You could ask her to stop." The pie in her mouth made her words thick.

"No. No, that time has passed. Alyssa's a grown-up now. She does what she wants." Her mother toyed with the hem of the bedspread. "Someday . . ."

Janet Whitby never finished the sentences she began with *Someday*, just as Alyssa never stopped hating.

"We should have had you put down," she'd say when she was truly angry.

I'm not a wild animal, Kate would think. *And you're my sister.*

Kate posed the same question to her other sister one morning as Olivia applied false eyelashes at the bathroom mirror.

"Why does Alyssa hate me?"

Olivia opened her mouth wide as she put the bottom lashes in the glue.

"She was counting on your dad to pay her way out of Evergreen," Olivia finally said. "But he didn't want an extra kid, so he left. You were an accident, you know."

Kate was pretty sure at that moment that she didn't know anything. Her sister's explanation made less sense than their mother's.

"She calls me Kat the Killer. I never killed anything."

"Killed her dreams."

Kate couldn't understand how.

"Is Dad going to come back?"

"Doubt it."

"Then why is Mom waiting for him?"

Olivia shrugged.

"Why don't you hate me?"

"What's to hate? I like it here."

Now, in the snow, Kate tore off a piece of the thin ham and set it beneath a fir tree at the side of the small building. She backed away to a stump where she could sit and wait, placing ham bits in a line as she went.

"Here, Monty," she whispered. "Here, kitty kitty." She made herself as still as the snow on the ground.

The infamous tiger Montecore lived under Roy's protection for more than ten years after the incident that got so much public attention. The animal died at age seventeen at one of their estates, just this past spring, only a few months after Kate had first fallen in love with the strange story. By then she had read a lot of things about them, kind things and cruel things, praise from people who loved the men and spite from people who thought they were villains. Kate didn't understand everything she read, but she did understand one thing perfectly: this particular group of people, and maybe even the animals, believed in the power of protecting each other. It didn't matter that some eyewitnesses said Montecore had violently attacked Roy, or that Roy's brush with death had changed his life forever. What mattered was their belief: Montecore protected Roy and so Roy protected him—from the rumors, from the curious, from the fans who adored and the mobs who scorned, from anything that might bring them further pain.

Kate thought that's exactly what a family ought to do for each other.

"Here, kitty kitty."

She dangled what was left of the ham.

The girl waited patiently and did not feel the descending cold.

CHAPTER 29

Pearl had hoped to show Kate the tunnel recorded in the old blueprints, if it hadn't been filled in over the years, but that would have to wait. The day held more important diversions. A murder in the morning, a delinquent boy on the prowl, a visit from the law, and a cougar cub wandering about their property, bold as brass.

Pearl's son-in-law came into her room to light the fire after his visit with the sheriff's deputies. She wished she had been invited, but then she might have missed the cat and the child.

"I heard the British are coming too," she said earnestly to Daniel as he hung the poker back on the rack. The young firelight cast shadows that accentuated deep sacks under his eyes.

"Let's hope the snow holds them off. I'm ready for a quiet night, aren't you? I'll bring your supper when Chef puts it out."

Pearl felt sorry for him. "Make Donna bring it," she said firmly. "She likes excitement."

That won her a half smile as Daniel turned to go.

"I'm very sorry about the loss of your friend, my boy."

The remark turned his head, probably for being not only logical but clearly genuine. "Thank you."

He seemed to wait for her to say more. She decided to hold off on making any further remarks about his little business venture with the pawnbroker. "I know how precious it is to have some kind of life outside of these walls. We all need it. Anyone married to my daughter especially needs it."

Daniel left quickly with nothing more than a nod of acknowledgment.

When he was gone Pearl rose to replace the white screen in front of the window, both for privacy and to hold back some of the cold. It would take a little time for the fire to warm the large room. Then she went into her oversize closet in search of a blanket for her lap. She would read until supper—that old Bible story about the harlot who hid the spies in her room had been knocking on the door of Pearl's thoughts all day. Another story inappropriate for a child's ears. However did they edit the Bible for Sunday school?

But Pearl never did get to review the story, because as she reached up for the afghan folded and set on a high shelf, the bell at the reception desk rang and rang and rang as someone hit it repeatedly. An out-of-towner surprised by the snow, no doubt, all in a dither over the driving conditions—which wouldn't be truly interesting until sometime tonight—in *desperate* need of accommodations until the weather passed.

So she was surprised when she turned out the closet light and slid her father's little peep panel open to see four young men who appeared to be fit enough to cross the mountains in snowshoes without breaking a sweat. They were locals, Pearl surmised, because not only did they wear no coats, but their shirts had no sleeves. Their arms were heavily tattooed. Their necks, identically tattooed with bold-stroke lettering: MHH. Their feet, clad in the biggest, most neon, fresh-out-of-the-box athletic shoes Pearl had ever seen.

Not from Evergreen. Probably Denver.

It took Janet a moment to appear from behind the mailbox island, and she emerged as a quaking aspen among towering thick cottonwoods. Silly girl, overdressed for her part in scarlet sequins. Certainly these men were not of the type Janet hoped might romance her away from Evergreen someday, but neither were they here to eat her for lunch.

"How may I help you?" she said to the one who had been ringing the bell. His shoes were the same shocking orange as the vandalism on Mr. Gorman's windows.

"Name's Jones," he said, leaning on the counter. "Here to meet a friend o' ours that checked in this morning. Charlie Fuse."

Janet went to the computer. Hardly necessary, with their November dearth of visitors.

"I'm sorry, we have no guests by that name."

Jones turned and jacked up his elbows on the counter behind him. He faced the man Pearl presumed to be the leader, the most bizarrely appointed of the bunch, with red hair and eyebrows all the wrong color for his caramel skin tone, and a beard bleached white. No mustache. Horrid combination. He held a small silver object in his fist.

"Does he go by any other name?" Janet asked.

"What say you, Fox?" Jones said to the bearded one.

"If he's wantin' to mess with us, I suppose. He's about so high"—the one called Fox held out his hand at chest level—"black hair, twentyish. Asian guy." Then as an afterthought he withdrew a tight wad of paper from his pocket and unfolded it, smoothed it out on the desk. "Looks a little like this. Walkin' with a limp."

Slowly, as if afraid of giving the wrong answer, Janet shook her head. "I've been on the desk all day and haven't seen anyone like that, I'm afraid. In fact"—she tapped away on her keyboard—"we have only one check-in at this time. A couple."

The one standing beside Fox whispered over his shoulder. This one wore a black bandanna and had those ridiculous rings stretching out his earlobes. And were those *bullets* they encircled?

"Is it possible you've arrived before him?" Janet smiled. "Maybe the snow delayed—"

"Mind if we have a look around?" Fox asked.

The fourth member, who so far had not spoken a single world, wandered over to the red velvet rope and craned his neck down the private hall. This one was especially broad-shouldered and likely tipped the scales at over three hundred pounds. He wore a good-sized knife belted to his waist, the hilt covered by his big shirt.

Janet pretended not to notice the big man's intrusion. "Of course not." She withdrew a brochure and unfolded it. "Here's some information about our suites and cottages." She pointed. "These are our fall rates, if you decide to stay with your friend. You can exit to the cottages down that hall on the other side of the dining room. Just let me know if you'd like to see inside of one. There's a library upstairs that overlooks the entrance, where you're welcome to wait. The dining room will open for dinner in about an hour."

Fox took the brochure and folded it, tapped it against the palm of his hand, and looked around. His eyes passed straight over Pearl's spot but only registered the potted tree.

"Thank you, ma'am," he said, turning to cross the foyer. All four moved as one.

Janet called after them, "If I see your friend, who may I say is looking for him?"

Fox turned around. "Coz," he said. "He knows me as Coz."

Cause? Pearl frowned. What kind of a name was Cause?

The men passed out of Pearl's view, and for a moment she stood in the dim light of her closet, thinking, puzzling over the past and the present and the strangeness of the day, trying to piece together items that simply didn't fit. She fiddled with the strand of pearls still on her neck and hoped Kate had gone to the keeping room as she'd been told, where someone from the kitchen might keep half an eye on her.

Even as she thought it, Pearl knew Kate wouldn't have obeyed. Not on a day like today.

A few puzzle pieces snapped together. The dead cougar on the road. Kate's startling questions. A cub wandering alone so close to people. Kate would have gone searching and lured the orphan cub back to the cottage.

Instead of reaching high for the quilt, Pearl stooped for her boots.

CHAPTER 30

Charlie leaned heavily on his good leg, worried that if he lay down he'd never rise again. The walls were close in the dark, pressing in on the pain until he couldn't think straight. He couldn't remember how far it was to the road where he'd wrecked the bike. Couldn't be far, if a little girl—what was her name? Katie? Kate, like the princess in the tabloids—couldn't be far if Kate could walk there and back in the night. How hard would it be to slide down the hill to the road and hitch a ride away?

Impossible, if the first car that came upon him was a black Camaro.

He could barely walk. He needed transportation. He needed a car. Yes, a car. He could drive an automatic with his left foot. He could drive to Uncle Jun's house. If he could find it.

Charlie was less certain he could outrun Coz's father, who had found him with the speed of an avenging angel.

This closet was a sliver inside a bigger building, maybe a guest house. House or hotel, where there were guests there would be cars.

He withdrew Kate's flashlight and flicked its beams over the close walls, the low roof, the dirty floor. Almost directly in front of him, behind a stack of books, he saw a small cutout in the wall panel. It was about two feet square and hinged on this side. The hook-and-eye closure was latched.

Clumsy and aching, he moved the books aside, opened the door, and got to his knees.

It was dark on the other side, but his beam of light hit the most encouraging sign: a plate of grilled sandwiches and a pretty good-size knife. No harmonica.

"Kid came through after all," he muttered. "Almost." The sandwiches were cold and greasy, but he was hungry enough not to care.

Armed and fed, Charlie gained confidence. Knife in his right hand, light in his left, he pushed through hanging clothes and bumped against an accordion door, then entered a bedroom. It was a small house, and it appeared to be empty. No lights on, no noise or activity. The natural light coming in through the drawn curtains was dusky.

As quickly as he could, he half hopped, half dragged his injured foot along and ransacked the place. The closet was a waste of time: not a lick of men's clothing. In the bedroom he stripped a pillow of its case and began to fill it with anything that might be useful but not heavy.

An electronic tablet from the nightstand.

From the bathroom: a first-aid kit, an old elastic bandage, peroxide for his injury and maybe even his hair.

In the second bedroom he did better with clothing. Someone, some girl, had a thing for cosplay, and among her surprisingly high-quality garb was a brilliant black wool trench coat that fit his slim frame perfectly and fell almost to his ankles. Had he any money he would have left some to pay for it. His favorite knit cap with the bill had gone missing, so he took a black Stetson-style hat even though it was too tight on his crown. It would draw less attention than the turquoise wig on the shelf beside it.

He did find a very pretty roll of tens and twenties in a jewelry box on the dresser, but leaving this money behind as a gesture of thanks for the coat would probably be lost on its owner. He pushed the cash into one of the deep pockets and discovered a bag of weed, which he also decided to take. He could sell it if he had to.

Food from the kitchen.

Matches from the drawer.

In the living room: gold. He found a woman's purse, and in the purse, keys with a remote fob that would tell him which car they belonged to. There was no phone but he took the wallet, which held two credit cards.

The pain raised a sheen of sweat on his forehead, but he was ready to move. With one finger he pushed back the edge of a window curtain and looked out on the wide yard. To the right, a mansion-size house built like the king of all log cabins. To the left, a half-moon cluster of quaint cottages with porches and a creek that separated them from the main building.

Four men clad in black, immune to the white cold, stood on the footbridge that crossed the creek, taking in their surroundings like points on a compass.

The one who faced Charlie was Coz's father, the red-headed, white-bearded, howling wild man.

Charlie recoiled, and the curtain fluttered out of his hand. Though he'd seen the Camaro, the sight of the Fox put flesh on Charlie's fears. They could not have followed him here unless Merridew had a hand in it. If Kate had betrayed him, law enforcement, not the Mile High Heavies, would be storming the cottage. These men wouldn't leave before they tore the place apart.

As he saw it, Charlie could think of three ways this might go.

He could walk out that door two hops to his left and by exposing himself end the violence before it affected more people. In other words, he could die for a crime he didn't commit.

He could lure the Heavies away from the hotel, the way mama

birds lured predators away from their nests by pretending to have a broken wing, and then try to escape. Only his wing really was broken, and the Heavies were a murder of crows. And he'd die for a crime he didn't commit.

He could, maybe, find a phone and call the cops and try to explain. He'd probably be arrested. And might, after a long and public trial, be sentenced to death for a crime he didn't commit and then, while he waited, die at the hands of the Mile High Heavies' prison population.

Or he could return to the closet and hope—

Hope for what? That Kate wouldn't give him up in five seconds? That the crows would fly away?

Charlie shifted his vantage to the other side of the window and peeked again.

The Fox had turned around, his back now to the cottage. The gun he carried formed a lump under his shirt. All heads tilted toward center. Then two of the men, one big as a house and the other with neon orange shoes, turned to the lodge and went in through a door on a terrace. The Fox and his remaining friend looked toward the cottage that sat at the farthest point of the property. They walked to it together, away from the window where Charlie watched. Coz's father climbed the porch steps while his friend stayed outside.

In the walkway that ran under Charlie's window, dainty footprints pointed toward the lodge. The dot and triangle of a stiletto shoe. He thought of walking alongside them, but he'd be seen, and the prints left by his injured leg would be distinctive.

And Charlie didn't want to die. He just wanted to find a quiet place alone, to not bother anyone and not be bothered.

At the far cottage, the man who killed Drogo kicked through the front door and let himself inside.

Inside the lodge, Pearl donned her coat and her role as crazy old fool. Fully dressed for the outdoors, she watched the four rabble-rousers stand on the bridge and put their heads together to make some no-good plan. Then she left her room. She shuffled out past the reception desk, where Janet had her nose in a book, and headed for the kitchen, where Chef and her staff were prepping for the Sunday evening denouement. Diners preferred Sunday brunch, and Pearl predicted no one would come out in this storm.

As she expected, Pearl found the keeping room empty. She looked out through the sliding glass doors and saw Kate's footprints leading left, toward her little home. In the window of the Rising Sun, a curtain fluttered.

Across the clearing on the footbridge, the four men who did not seem genuinely interested in staying the night paired off. Two came this way toward the entry beside the dining room. The others aimed for the farthest cottage, the Full Moon. It was impossible to say what they wanted here, besides a man no one had heard of, but Pearl could only imagine that the timing of their visit was connected somehow to Bruce Gorman's death, and possibly to Daniel.

When the one with the odd hair coloring kicked in the door of the Full Moon and let himself in, Pearl resolved to let the men work this one out. She would stay out of sight and fetch Kate via the tunnel. If it still existed.

In the kitchen, the ruddy-faced cook looked up from a steaming pot and seemed worried that Pearl wasn't on her daughter's arm.

"What can I do for you this chilly night, Ms. Pearl?"

"I've come to cook up myself some Welsh rarebit."

"How about you take a seat at the family table and I'll bring you a bowl of hot butternut soup."

Pearl headed for the pantry. "You can't substitute melted cheese with orange squash and expect me to be happy about it, young lady."

"Well, I'm fresh out of Welsh rarebit!"

"Leave it to me," Pearl said, and she pushed through the swinging door of the dry goods pantry and seated herself on a stack of plastic crates. She sat there, waiting, and stared at the shelves packed with potatoes and spice bottles and canned tomatoes.

Chef's wide body darkened the door, hands on her hips. "Ms. Pearl, you can't stay in here."

"It seems you're out of porter," Pearl said, looking around.

"Don't keep beer in the pantry."

"Can't make Welsh rarebit right without a splash of porter."

Chef huffed and turned away. Gone to summon Donna, no doubt. Exactly as Pearl hoped.

Cursing her old creaky joints, Pearl rose from the crates and went to work.

CHAPTER 31

Deshawn Johnson pushed the cottage door closed, though its busted latch would not hold. He stood in the dim room. It smelled of furniture polish and carpet deodorizer. Even with the lights out and the curtains drawn it was obviously pretty and unaffordable, someplace he'd never be able to take Coz's mother. This angered him. She deserved a place like this. Charlie Fuse didn't.

The Fox believed the lady in red behind the front desk when she said she hadn't seen Charlie. But someone here had given the killer shelter or taken him to a hospital. That harmonica of his had been carelessly abandoned, not likely by the man who owned it.

If Charlie was somewhere at this lodge, he wouldn't stay long after he learned of their arrival. When the darkness covered him he'd bolt, even if he were injured, even if this snow turned into a blizzard. They had about an hour to find him before dark.

They would.

The cottage was winter quiet. Deathly silent. He went through the living room, kitchen, bathroom, and bedroom, then looked out the window to the back, which faced a forest of green trees getting flocked by Mother Nature. He did this without any real expectation of finding Charlie, but was surprised to find himself imagining what his life could have been if he'd just had a little more time and a little more luck.

He pulled his phone out and texted Coz's mother. Out makin it up 2 u. Sorry baby.

In the kitchen, a slim vase of summery silk flowers stood in the middle of the table. She'd pick something like that for Coz's casket. All white and yellow.

The Fox set the phone next to the vase. He did not, could not, wait for her reply. Her voice, even as a text, might derail his plans. She would pull his heart toward a home that no longer existed. Even if he lied she would drag the truth of his intentions out into the open, and she would argue with him, and he wouldn't be able to deny her anything.

Best act without permission. Later she would understand. Eventually she would forgive him.

He walked out into the snow and left his life behind.

A soft spotted muzzle with long whiskers was sniffing the air around the ham when the violent splintering of wood startled it back into the crawl space. Kate rose from her stump and went to see what might have caused the frightening sound. The snow was falling heavier now and tickled her nose. The rocks under her feet were merely wet and dark, still warm enough to melt the snow on contact, but the white stuff would gather soon enough.

Kate stepped out from behind the rear corner of the Morning Glory just as a man kicked in the Full Moon's front door. He had funny hair and was with another man who wore a black bandanna around his head. Were they robbers? She looked toward the lodge, hoping that Grandy had seen. He'd be the one to stop them or call the sheriffs to come back.

She could see the back of the lodge from here. The two-story windows that looked in on the dining room were golden and bright, flanked by terraces and doors that led inside. The sky was shifting from gray to iron, and the indoor light made the snow glitter. It was a pretty scene, something from a Christmas card but without the decorations. Without the people that made Christmas matter. There was not a soul in sight.

———

Hector had kicked his way into two more cottages and confirmed they were vacant. The pristine snow, thickening in the air now with big wet flakes, was their confirmation that no one but they had come or gone. They left the doors open as they plowed through the buildings, each empty.

The Fox waited for Hector at the bottom of the third porch. "You got it out here?" he asked as Hector descended.

"Where's he gonna go? He can't move quick and he'll leave tracks. You bet I got it."

"Shoot anything that moves," the Fox instructed.

"My specialty."

"I'll get the last one." The Fox pointed his own pistol toward the cottage where he'd found the harmonica. It was the largest one, and set apart from the others. "Think it's someone's personal pad."

"So you can read, can you? Impressive."

"We'll be done before dark."

The Fox turned away and walked a line of new tracks through the fresh snow.

Inside the lodge, a gun went off. Just one shot. Nothing Brick and Jones couldn't handle.

———

The old wood shelves of the pantry had been replaced by stainless racks at some point, and Pearl could only hope that the panel behind them hadn't been altered too. The shelving was fully loaded and too heavy for her to move, so she began the laborious process of rearranging the pantry items. She'd been at it for only a moment when a girl in the kitchen screamed and someone told her to shut up. With a jar of pickled banana peppers in one hand and a jar of gourmet olives in the other, Pearl stopped to listen.

"It's just a question," a man was saying. "This man is somewhere in this building." He rattled a piece of paper. "Tell me where."

Janet's daughter Alyssa raised her voice. "You can't just barge in—"

"Can and did, girl."

"If you don't put that gun away I'm going to call the sheriff."

"You ain't callin' no one *un-til* I put this gun away. Go on now, put that phone in the sink. I said, put it in the sink."

Pearl wished she could see what was happening on the other side of the thin door.

There was a gunshot, and she dropped the olives. They crashed onto the slab floor and the tiny black spheres rolled around in shards of glass. A pool of oil oozed outward, reaching for the door, and the old woman waited for another shot to punch right through the pantry and into her heart. She hoped to the high heavens that the girl hadn't been shot. Olivia, the one with the fabulous costumes, was crying. Something splashed down into water. Only silence followed, no shrieks of pain or fear or grief.

"Now, I count seven pair o' eyes in here 'sides mine," the man said. "I got me fourteen rounds and no time for interviews, so y'all just speak up now and tell me where this one is. Name's Charlie.

You do that an'—you just don' learn, do you? Throw that one in the water too. Go on now."

This time there was a splash and no gunshot. Salty olive oil stretched its fingers toward the pantry door, threatening to leak out.

"Look here, you wastin' my time. If I hear a siren I jess start shootin' y'all."

"Has *anyone* seen this guy?" Alyssa demanded. "Please. Just say so."

Chef said, "We don't see guests here in the kitchen. You ought to leave us be, mister."

The man snorted. "Not all o' you are on the cook line. You and you shore ain't."

He could only mean Alyssa and Olivia, dressed for the dining room.

"No one looking like that's eaten here *ever*," Olivia said.

"Didn't say nothin' 'bout eatin'." Silence again. "All right. In the freezer. Go on. No, not you two. Sit. You the chef, fat girl? Yeah, all right, take your people in the freezer."

"They'll die in there," Alyssa protested.

"Not s'quickly as they will out here," the man said.

Kate jumped when the gun went off. She dropped the ham and pressed her back against the Morning Glory, trembling. Someone was shot! What if it was Grandy or Chef, or Great-Grandma Pearl? What if it was her mother? What would happen to her? In the blink of an eye Kate imagined a funeral, imagined Alyssa saying she didn't want anything to do with her, imagined being escorted away in a government car by some lady who pretended to be her friend and delivered to the home of an evil foster mother who locked her in a basement and took the money that should have bought Kate food.

Her view was blurred by tears when she dared to peek around the side of the cottage again. The dining room remained empty. What if they'd killed everyone and she just hadn't heard? In front of her there was only the man with the black bandanna and the heavy earrings guarding the river like a soldier, gun on his hip. She moved, and a rock shifted under her foot. He turned toward the sound.

Kate tried not to cry as she tiptoed along the back of the cottage to the other corner, rattling rocks even though she tried to be quiet. She might be able to run back to her home, right next door. But when she looked, the man with the funny hair was standing on the porch of the Rising Sun, pressing his face to the window.

The feather whisper of feet passing through fresh snow alerted her. She spun to the sound and saw that the cub had come out from under the crawl space to eat the abandoned ham. But the footsteps persisted from the front of the house. The one with the bandanna and the gun was coming to investigate. Quickly Kate moved and the cat tensed, ears erect, tail flicking as it watched her. At the halfway point in the rear wall Kate pushed hard against the siding, and a tall door cut along a seam sprang open, exactly the same way the closet at the back of her cottage did. She crawled up onto the floorboard and twisted, trying to find the door catch in the darkness. Her fingers missed it. All she could do was grab the edge of the door with her fingers and pull it closed as far as possible. But it wasn't far enough.

Lying on her belly, she looked through the gap and held her

breath. She could see the cub, sniffing around for more ham. She could hear the man's clomping as he came nearer. She tugged the door tighter and it slipped off her fingertips. She grabbed at it again, and then went still.

His cheekbones came around the corner first as he scoped out the scene, his profile wary. At his feet the cub yowled.

"Dang cat," he muttered.

The cub was equally startled and leaped in the opposite direction, mimicking the sound of Kate's feet on the stones.

The man moved off.

Kate took a breath and let go of the door again. She scrambled to her feet, looking for the latch while the light was on it. She saw it right away.

As she leaned out to take hold of it, the cub jumped up into the closet and brushed against her leg. And as she pulled it closed and slipped the hook into the eyehole, the little cougar stood on its hind legs to sniff her fingers, looking for more meat.

The Fox took fresh stock of the private cottage before he entered it. Along the walkway between the little house and the massive lodge, footprints made by a pair of women's shoes were filling rapidly with snowflakes. An empty bird feeder swung from the porch eaves, and there were snow boots lined up under the bench, four pairs. Three adults and one child, side by side just as they were in the tiny four-by-four entryway of his apartment, three pairs, all adult. Coz had huge feet, even as a twelve-year-old.

The child's boots were purple.

The inhabited cottage stood closer to the lodge than any other, making it the worst place for a fugitive to hide. The structure was also closest to the road, which made it desirable for a man who might have trouble getting very far very fast. Charlie Fuse had been here; the motorcycle and the harmonica told the Fox that much. The question was whether he remained.

Fox put his foot through this door too.

The interior had a strange smell. Ladies' perfume and hair spray and stale coffee, and something else under all of it. Weed. And an odor like an unwashed shirt that didn't match the tidy and feminine space.

To his left, a living area. Neat except for the bookshelves in the corner of the room, overflowing with books and toys. Girl toys at a glance. Old Barbies and a pink CD player and some stuffed unicorns, coloring books and pen kits, art supplies. A desk and lamp for doing homework. A box labeled *Spy Kit* on top of the desk, open and empty.

A purse on the coffee table. The Fox went through it quickly. No wallet, no keys, no phone. No sense.

To the right, a kitchenette. A box of Cocoa Puffs left out on the counter, top open and wax bag sticking out. The trademark bird grinning at him stupidly. He stared back at it for a long time, then snapped back to the present.

Just beyond the kitchen was a bathroom. And off the living room, two unremarkable bedrooms, twin beds in each. The Fox gave everything only a cursory glance. There was no one here, and nothing odd except, in the closet that belonged to the little girl, next to her sparkling tennis shoes and summer flip-flops, sticking out from under a row of plastic-covered dresses, was a plate that bore half of a cold grilled cheese sandwich.

He turned around. It was time to get back to his brothers, to get this job done before it had time to slide out of control. But something held him here. Something he could not name.

On the nightstand, beside a plastic cup printed with red and white hearts, was a small iPod, its earbuds hanging over the side of the table. The Fox picked it up and turned it over. The device was chrome in a hot pink case, and on the back was a black skull and crossbones with a rhinestone bow on its head.

He put it in his pocket and left the girl's home.

CHAPTER 32

The Mile High Heavies' self-guided tour of the Harrison Lodge took the brothers approximately ten minutes. By the time the Fox returned to the lodge, Brick had collected the lady in red, two aging managers, and the inn's only guests, and corralled everyone in the dining room. These five sat at the fancy tables no one would have the pleasure of eating at tonight. Jones added two pretty girls from the kitchen and said he'd left five others in the walk-in freezer. The smaller girl in black and white cried and clung to the one who wore an expensive pantsuit and high heels. This one stared at the Fox without blinking, her arms crossed across her ribs. She was the only one who offered him eye contact, and he respected that.

"Who we missin'?" he said to her.

"The staff in the freezer," she said. "You should just let them go."

"This ain't gonna take long if you don' let it. Who else?"

"No one. What do you want?"

The Fox glanced at Brick, who blocked the passageway that opened onto the foyer, and at Jones, leaning against the frame where the dining room passed into the hallway and the kitchen beyond.

"Where's your housekeeping staff?"

"They go home at three. Seriously, why are you doing this?"

"Maintenance?"

A white-haired man lifted his face out of his hands and said, "I'm maintenance."

"I thought you're management."

"Jack-of-all-trades."

Deep lines on his face said the multiple roles were wearing him out. The woman next to him kept her hands folded on the table but cast him an apologetic glance. Old married couple, looked like. The only two in the room wearing wedding rings.

"Who else might show up?" the Fox asked.

"The night watchman comes at eleven thirty," said the pantsuit.

The woman who'd given them so much information at the front desk had twisted a white napkin into a linen rope. Her attention was on the outdoors, on Hector and his gun. Tears left black smudges under her eyes and smeared the heavy makeup that caked her cheeks. The Fox sat down at a table near Jones and picked up a table knife, then struck a wine glass with it. The crystal shattered and the woman jerked her head toward him. "Room reservations?" he asked her.

The red lady shook her head in a daze.

"Dinner reservations?" he asked the pantsuit.

"They're on the computer," she said.

"Jones, escort this young woman to the computer so she can call everyone with the bad news. There's been a fire in the kitchen and the restaurant gotta close for the night."

The pantsuit didn't move.

"Maybe I oughta set the fire first," Jones said to the Fox. "So she don' gotta lie t'anyone." He grinned.

The girl went then, out the dining room's main entry, passing by Brick without waiting for him to move out of her way. Jones followed her, passing the police sketch of Charlie Fuse into the Fox's hands.

"Post a notice on the driveway," the Fox said to Jones as he went out toward the reception desk.

"Or I'll just stand there and give notice." Jones aimed his gun at the pantsuit's back and pretended to fire it, then chortled as he went out.

The girl who'd been clutching her sank to a trembling crouch against the wall, snuffling into her crisp white sleeves.

"Who else?" the Fox asked again.

The woman with the folded hands took up the pantsuit's role as spokeswoman. "Look, this is a family-run business. All my family's here and my employees are slowly freezing to death. It's our duty to protect them."

"Well, my duty's to my family too."

"Please tell us what you want so we can send you on your way."

"I've already asked for what I want," the Fox said to the red lady.

The napkin rope in her hands was bending into twisted lumps. "And I told you the truth. I've never seen the man you're looking for."

"What man, Janet?" said the spokeswoman.

"Are you family too?" the Fox asked Janet.

"What?"

"Are you part of this *family*?"

"Yes, but what—"

The spokeswoman interrupted. "What *man*? Do you have a name? A picture? By all means, show us!"

"You, sir." The Fox stood and approached a table where a morbidly obese man scowled at the white tablecloth. "You mad you got nothin' to put in your mouth?" When the doughy face finally turned upward, all pink-cheeked, the Fox said, "I don't see the family resemblance."

"They're our guests," the spokeswoman said. "Please let the two of them go. Please."

"I don't think there's room in that freezer for this one," said the Fox. "And this one"—he nodded to the fat man's companion, who was making a study of the plate glass window—"she'll freeze faster than a drop o' water."

The white-haired man stood and motioned for his wife to sit down. Her mouth fell open but she obeyed. "I suppose you're here for me," he said. "So let's go, and you can leave the others out of it."

The Fox wasn't sure what to make of this one. The old man and Charlie Fuse had nothing in common but a slim build. Was he trying to be a hero?

The spokeswoman seemed to agree. "How on *earth* is this about you, Daniel?"

"I've just been thinking." Daniel balanced himself with one hand on the table and spoke to the Fox. "You figured out Bruce Gorman wasn't working alone. Whatever your beef was with him, you blame me too."

"What has this got to do with Bruce?" the spokeswoman demanded.

"Dad?" Janet said.

The Fox didn't know who Bruce Gorman was, but he didn't miss the smirk that crossed Brick's face. The two brothers caught each other's eyes. Brick shook his head. Fox let the family talk. They'd eventually say what he wanted to hear.

"What do you mean, working alone?" Janet whimpered.

"Bruce and I were running a penny auction scam. Online pay-to-bid, you know? I set up the website and programmed the software. He provided the merchandise."

"A *scam*?" Janet echoed.

The spokeswoman had closed her hands into fists. "I thought such auctions were legal."

"Bruce and I had fake accounts on our own site. Dozens of straw bidders. One of us won every time. We'd prolong the bids, collect the bidding fees, and keep the product—Bruce would sell it in the storefront or on another site after the online bidding closed."

"For land's sakes, *why*?" said the spokeswoman. "We are well-to-do! What possible need did you have for more money?"

"A man needs something just his own, Donna," Daniel said. He looked down at his wife's bowed head. "Something not controlled by anyone else."

"I don't know what you're talking about."

"You tell me what to eat! You tell me what to wear! You tell me where to go and how to spend my time!"

The girl in the corner had folded in on herself and covered her cheeks with her long-fingered hands, her eyes wide and cartoonish.

Janet said, "That poor man was murdered because you . . . you . . ."

Daniel's voice came down a notch. "Because I'm a fool. I didn't have a say in that money any more than I'm trusted to have a say in how it's spent here. He gambled away all of our profits."

At this news, Brick laughed aloud. Daniel glared at him.

"I guess someone must have figured it out," Daniel said to Brick. "Someone like you?"

Brick continued to laugh, but he shrugged and shook his head.

"You think we're here to score a double homicide," the Fox said, confirming Daniel's foolishness.

He cleared his throat. "You said you're looking for a man. My daughter would protect me—"

"They're not looking for *you*!" Janet yelled.

The Fox produced the sketch of Charlie and held it up for

everyone to see. He walked it around the room, starting with the fat man. "Charlie Fuse," the Fox announced. "Seen him around here?"

The man shook his head and his jowls.

His waiflike companion looked at the drawing, then at her lap. "If he's Japanese," she said softly, "the name might be pronounced Foo-*say*."

"Finally," the Fox said, "someone with useful information." He turned toward the others. "These two maybe got an excuse, not being *family*. But the rest of you . . ." He just wanted to shoot them all, for their privilege, their self-righteousness, their assumptions about right and wrong. "I know he's here. What I can't figure is why you'd put your family at risk to protect him."

Donna made a move to stand again. The Fox stopped her.

"Sit."

She was more annoying than the rest, every bit as outwardly controlled and controlling as her husband accused. She was a fit woman for her age, the sort who probably measured her food portions and had her clothes dry-cleaned every time she wore them. But she did sit.

"Sir, I promise you we do not know this man. We're not protecting anyone but ourselves. You've already searched the property, you know that—"

"I know that not everyone in your family is here," the Fox said.

From the reception desk, the professional voice of Ms. Pantsuit on the phone reached into their silence. Then the red lady Janet started to cry uncontrollably.

Donna spoke over the outburst. "Y-Yes. Yes, you're referring to my mother."

"Am I?"

"Do you know where she is?"

"No."

"Please, sir—"

"Please, sir," he mimicked. The lies grew more intolerable with their size.

She swallowed her words and looked down at her hands. No longer folded, but fidgety. "My mother is elderly and frail and not always . . . clear-minded. She'd be the last person to hide a . . ." Her hands stilled for a moment, and she blinked as if she didn't recognize her own fingers. Then she looked up at him and finished without stumbling. "She'd be the last person to hide a fugitive in this lodge. She wouldn't have the wherewithal to do it."

The Fox dropped the sketch of Charlie onto the table in front of her and walked to the window. The sun hadn't completely set, but the snow clouds made the world darker than it should be. Hector stood on the bridge and lifted his chin when he saw the Fox. *Everything's good here.*

The Fox pointed at the far cottage, and Hector jogged off toward it.

"I don't know anything about an old lady. I was talking about the girl," the Fox said. He withdrew Charlie's harmonica from his pants pocket and slapped it into his palm. "Where's the girl who lives here with your happy, truthful, law-abiding family, the one who wears purple boots?"

No one answered, and then everyone did:

"At a sleepover," said Daniel.

"At the cottage," said his wife.

"I don't know!" Janet burst. "Please let me go find her!"

The Fox laughed. "What kinda family don' know where its kids are? Or its old people?"

"She's at the cottage," Donna repeated firmly.

"Your mother or your grandbaby?"

"The child."

"Which cottage? You mean the one over this way"—the Fox pointed—"where she keeps her toys and eats her Cocoa Puffs? The cottage that stinks of weed?"

"What?" Janet said.

The girl squatting in the corner covered her mouth with her hand.

"You so used to the odor you don't even smell it anymore." He pointed at the girl. "Not even on your own kid?"

Donna tried to take over again. "If she's anywhere, she's at the cottage. She knows to go there on a Sunday night. It's there or the keeping room, and the one with those orange shoes cleared out that area when he blazed through here."

The Fox fished in his hip pocket and withdrew the iPod that looked so much like his son's.

"How old is she?" he asked. No one replied. He slammed the iPod down on the table, and as his arm came down, the man Daniel stood up. "How old is she?" the Fox yelled.

"If you've done anything to harm her—"

The Fox put a heavy hand on the old man's shoulder and shoved him back into the chair. He missed the seat and went all the way to the floor. "Don't you get high an' mighty an' act like you're the good man here. You got no idea where that child is and you gonna pin that on me. Just you try."

"Eleven," Janet whispered. "She's eleven."

"What's her name?"

"Kathy," Janet said at the same time Donna murmured, "Katherine."

"Seems to me you don' know her name, don' know where she is, you don' deserve to have a kid."

"She's always hiding," Janet began. "She knows all the nooks and crannies, she keeps herself busy. She—"

"You gonna blame your child for the fact you don' know where she is?"

"She's a good girl!" Janet said.

"An' my boy was better!" Fox roared. "An' I always, always know where he is! You wanna know where he is now? He's on a metal table, lady. A cold metal table in a freezer in the dark with a bullet through his brain. An' I know who did it!" He grabbed the sketch of Charlie, and it crumpled in his fist. "This one shot my boy even though he done nothin' to deserve it. Yeah, you got that much right. I'm here for a double homicide—my boy's, and this one's."

He was trembling, out of control.

"You say you don't know where Charlie is, or where your girl is. I'm gonna make you prove it. We're all gonna play a bit of hide an' seek now. I'm lookin' for your girl. You're lookin' for Charlie Foo-freakin'-say. And I'm gonna kill the one we find first."

CHAPTER 33

There was no cot in this black box, and no flashlight for Kate to see by. Dust made her sneeze, but she managed to do it without making a sound, even though Reece said that holding in a sneeze would make her eyes pop out of her head. It didn't. She clipped her shin on the corner of a box, then sat down on it. The cub was quiet while it licked Kate's fingers with its huge sandpaper tongue. When it nipped her with its teeth, she yelped and bopped it on the nose.

"You can't eat those," she whispered.

The baby mountain lion started to complain, and in the confines of the small closet Kate worried it would draw the thief's attention. She tried to stroke the cub's fur, but the big cat was restless and hungry and wouldn't tolerate being picked up. It was bigger than she expected, bigger than Reece's tabby cat and almost as big as Mitzy, the beagle who'd been eaten so long ago. Kate thought about putting the cougar back outside but feared that man with the gun would shoot it.

She squatted on the floor and began running her fingers over the surface of the walls, looking for the small interior panel that would allow her to pass into the Morning Glory's rooms. She found it, but the latch had rusted and no amount of jiggling or hitting it would make it budge.

"Now what?" she asked the cat.

Then Kate remembered that the hiding compartments in the other cottages were slightly different from the one in hers, because these duplexes had separate living areas, which meant the closets were accessible from both apartments. She checked the other wall and quickly, in a mirror location, found a latch that slid open easily. The panel creaked as she opened it. The passage was blocked by pillows stacked on a narrow shelf. She pushed these off into a pile and then lifted the shelf off of its brackets. The cub leaped out into the bedroom beyond and would not return when she called. She slipped through as well.

The disappearing sun had taken all the color from the room. Everything was cast in a range of grays from cement to charcoal. A bed, a dresser, two night tables, a reading chair.

A cold breeze skimmed over Kate's skin, but the window was closed. Kate crept out of the hiding place on all fours, listening for the robber, who might have broken in. She stayed on her hands and knees until she reached the bedroom door, where she could see that the cottage's front door was wide open and snow was falling at an angle that drifted onto the covered porch. The cub was prowling in the kitchen, sniffing the air.

As she crawled along the wall, the shadows of the cottage hid her. In the open doorway, the brass latch plate was dangling from one screw and splintered wood stuck out like an explosion. Across the yard, the lights from the lodge's dining room illuminated the picture behind the glass: Gran and Grandy and her mother at a table. Olivia crouching against the wall near the cold fireplace. A giant blocking the entrance to the hotel foyer. The man with the mismatched hair and beard—the one she'd seen kick down the door of the Full Moon—was standing, pacing, talking to someone she couldn't see, because the terrace pillars hid whoever it was. Outside, between Kate and her family, the robber with the black bandanna and the gun still walked back and forth over the footbridge.

She could not see Alyssa or Great-Grandma Pearl.

Right in front of her, big boot prints marched down the front steps and turned onto the path that curved around to the Rising Sun. The cottage where Charlie was hiding.

Charlie might know what to do.

As Kate decided how to get there, the man with the funny hair made hand motions to the bandanna man, who left the bridge and turned away from Kate, up toward the Full Moon at the top of a small rise. She watched him, craning her neck past the door until the dark cottage swallowed him up.

When he was gone she sprang from her crouch and leaped out onto the front porch, running on her toes and trying her best to put the balls of her feet right in the widest spot of each boot print. The steps were slippery. She almost went down but caught the rail and managed to save her neck. But she smudged the print.

At the bottom of the steps Kate could see that the door to her own home was yawning open. A sickening feeling filled her stomach: What if these bad men who were breaking down doors and bossing around her family were friends of Charlie's?

The sky was almost black now, stars hidden and city lights far away. Kate glanced toward Great-Grandma Pearl's rooms and wondered if she should go there instead. But to do that she'd have to walk straight across the clearing, in plain sight of everyone.

A warm weight pushed against her leg. The cougar cub mewled and flicked its tail against Kate's hip. She made a quick decision and ran for home, leaping from boot print to boot print, and the wildcat followed.

The cottage door was open, broken. Inside the rooms were still and cold. The half-eaten sandwich on the floor of the closet told Kate that Charlie had been out, might have even run away while she was chasing the cub. She picked up the hard crust and broke off a piece. The cat snatched it from her.

She pushed on the secret panel. Locked. She rapped on the surface.

"Charlie?" she whispered. Then louder, "Charlie, are you still here?"

If he had gone out the rear of the cottage, Kate would have to risk going outside.

"Charlie? I need your help. There's some guys with guns here. I think they're robbers. I don't know what to do."

A few seconds later the panel eased open.

"You alone?" he asked.

"Yeah."

Charlie pulled the panel open farther. They peered at each other, each of them propped on their elbows.

Kate said, "Everyone's in the dining room, except one guy just went over to the Full Moon."

"What's that?"

"The cottage way over on the other side. What are they doing, Charlie? What do they want?"

Charlie withdrew into the closet without answering. Kate crawled in after him.

"We should call the sheriff. I don't have a phone. Do you? There used to be a phone in our cottage, but when the line broke they never fixed it. Everyone but me has a cell phone. I just borrow Mom's if I need to call Reece, or I use Chef's phone in the kitchen."

She sat cross-legged on the floor as he eased back onto the cot. It was too dark to see his face, though the dimming light from the cottage caught the bottoms of his dirty sneakers.

"Is your leg better?" she asked.

"It's coming along."

Out in the closet, the cougar cub was held up by the bagged dresses, which rustled when it brushed against them. But it wanted to get to Kate badly enough that it finally leaped through the opening and into Kate's lap.

"Is that a dog?" Charlie said.

"A cougar."

"What the—?" The cat's tail flicked him in the face.

"It's an orphan," Kate said. "I think you killed its mom. I mean, your motorcycle killed her. The animal people took the other cubs and left this one by mistake."

Charlie didn't respond to that either.

"They have guns," Kate said. "Can you help us?"

The silence stretched out.

"What do you think we should do?" she asked.

"I don't have any idea."

"But grown-ups always know what to do."

"Did you tell anyone about me?"

"I promised not to."

"But *did* you?"

"No!"

He withdrew farther into the darkness before saying, "Then I say you should hide in here with me. Just until they leave."

"But what if they shoot my family?"

"They won't shoot your family."

"But what if they *do*?"

"Nothing I can do to stop them."

The cat yowled and began investigating the closet. It knocked the empty bottle of Gatorade onto the floorboards.

"If you don't keep that thing quiet they'll find us and shoot us too."

"We have to try to stop them, Charlie."

"It's not my family. And my ankle's busted."

She had not expected his refusal to help her. The surprise brought hot tears to her eyes. They just flared up, the way they did when one of the mean girls at school said something rude about her not having a dad. The jabs themselves were never as bad as letting the girls see her cry. She was glad Charlie could not see her.

"Would you just let them shoot *your* family?" she asked.

"I don't have a family to be shot."

Kate's throat was tight.

"Well," he said. "I had a dad. But then I grew up."

"Dads don't stop being dads when you grow up. My Grandy is still my mom's dad."

"Lucky her."

"I don't have a dad," she said. "He left when I was a baby."

Charlie didn't say anything.

"What if they kill my mom?"

He sighed the way grown-ups do when they're irritated, and Kate decided she would leave. She was a good spy. She could figure this out on her own.

"Do you know anyone who lives up here named Jun?" Charlie asked. "Jun Tsukino?"

Kate didn't. She copied his refusal to answer her questions.

"He might not live here anymore."

"I thought June was a girl's name."

"Not everywhere." The cot squeaked as Charlie's weight shifted in it. "In Japan there's a big group of people called Yakuza," he said. His voice was softer now, patient. "You ever heard of them?"

She shook her head even though he couldn't see. The word made her think of a kazoo.

"The word *yakuza* means 'outcast.' So the Yakuza is basically a family made up of people who have no family."

"Is the Yakuza your family?"

"No. The real Yakuza is like the Mafia. A crime gang. That kind of family. Do you know what I mean? Not my style."

Kate had heard about the Mafia. Olivia did a school report on the St. Valentine's Day Massacre when she was in high school, and Kate had sneaked one of her library books to look at the pictures. She didn't think the Mafia was actually a family.

"Most families are failures, Kate, so people like me have to make our own. I guess what I'm trying to say is that if you lose this family, you'll just find a way to make another one of your own. People do it all the time. Nothing wrong with that."

Charlie didn't understand anything.

"That's stupid," she said.

"No, it's just reality. It's every man for himself out there. Or every girl. The sooner you learn that, the better."

"I don't want to make a different family." Kate hated the way her voice sounded when she cried, all wobbly and stuffed up. She scooted aside so she could open the panel again. "I'm going to help them."

"They're not your responsibility."

The panel scraped the floor as she drew it back. "What do you mean?"

"They're the grown-ups. They're supposed to be taking care of you. There's nothing you can do for them, Kate."

Kate did not have a quick answer for Charlie. She hadn't had time to make a plan yet. In the gray light of the yawning panel she tried to come up with something, a strategy, which is what Mammy Kate must have done all those hundreds of years ago.

"Have you ever heard of Mammy Kate?" she asked Charlie.

"No."

He might not know as much as he thought about things after all. During her fifth-grade social studies unit about the Revolutionary War, Kate had to do a report about someone who had done something heroic. She had meant to write about a spy, someone like Anna Strong, but when she was doing research she happened on a strange tale about a slave woman from Georgia named Mammy Kate. At first Kate read the story just because they shared a name. Then she loved the story because of who Mammy Kate showed herself to be.

"Mammy Kate was a slave woman from Georgia," Kate said. "It was during the Revolutionary War. Her owner got captured by the British and they were going to hang him, so she made a plan to rescue him."

"You're not a slave and you're not a mammy."

"She was a super tall woman, really big and strong, and she said she was the daughter of some African king. She tricked the British guards by getting them to let her do their laundry. And when she went into the prison to get her owner's laundry, she put him in the basket and carried him out!"

"America's first urban myth," Charlie said.

"It's a true story!"

"He must've been a small man."

"Maybe small as you," Kate said.

"So are you gonna go offer to do their laundry? Maybe clean their knives and guns?"

Kate decided not to tell him any more after that, about how

Mammy Kate's master thanked her by freeing her and how she refused to leave. About how he eventually became the governor of Georgia and gave her property and wrote her into his will, and how Mammy Kate and her husband, Daddy Jack, wrote the governor's family into their will. How when she died, Mammy Kate gave each of her nine children to each of the governor's nine children, and their families became one.

Charlie wouldn't get why she liked that story.

"My teacher said Mammy Kate didn't have to help her owner that way. Most slaves wouldn't. But it sure worked out nice for everyone that she did."

Kate was crawling away from Charlie when he said, "Kate, stay here."

"I want to help."

"You could help *me*."

"I did already."

"I know. I mean, thank you. Don't go out there, Kate. They'll kill you."

She hesitated, half out of Charlie's black room. Dying wasn't something Kate could easily wrap her mind around. Old people died, and people in tragic news stories and sad movies. Killing was an even stranger idea, because why would anyone want to *make* another person die on purpose? In a war, she supposed, or if someone was really, really horrible and had to be punished. Bruce Gorman wasn't a soldier, and except for hitting Austin in the nose he wasn't a bad man, but because of him, dying and killing were unwelcome visitors knocking on the door of Kate's home. A killer had hidden a knife in the library, and men were holding her family prisoner with guns. And though she did want to be a good spy, she didn't want to be one who died in the line of duty.

"You said they wouldn't shoot my family."

"I hope they don't."

"Why would they kill me and not shoot my family?"

"Kate"—his voice cracked on her name and he cleared his throat—"you can't go."

Talking to Charlie was doing her no good. She left the room and then turned around on her knees to close the panel.

"If you're so worried, you should come with me."

He lay on the cot and didn't move.

The cub she'd named Monty followed her out.

She pulled the panel closed, put the shoes and suitcase back in place, and dragged the plastic-covered dresses back across the rod.

CHAPTER 34

The Fox waited for the cottage to become a ball of fire, which it did seconds after Hector emerged. If Charlie was here, they'd burn him out.

"We don't have a lot of time," the Fox said to the stunned gathering in the dining room. They'd rushed to the window, hands on the glass, on the tops of their heads, covering their mouths. In the dark, the display was quite theatrical. The candles on the tables had not been lit and the atmospheric lighting in the room was low. Only a few landscaping lights along the paths outdoors glowed through the snow. "This is gonna be a very short game. One of you is coming with me. We're lookin' for Charlie and hopin' we don't find your girl instead. Every three minutes we don't find him, my brother'll set fire to one o' them cute little houses. All but one of you gonna stay here with my brothers Jones and Brick. So that leaves"—he counted the six cottages—"eighteen minutes 'fore we set the lodge on fire."

The spokeswoman Donna opened her mouth, but it took several seconds for words to come out. "Sir, I promise you we've never seen the man you're looking for."

"That's not the same as him not being here, is it?"

The old man Daniel turned around. "I'll come with you. I know where a man can hide around here, if he's trespassing."

"You'll stay here," the Fox told him.

"What? Why—"

"I'm her mother," said the lady in red, Janet, who couldn't stop blubbering. "I should go. I have to find her."

"Katherine has to stay *hidden*," Donna said. "Don't you understand?"

"I have to protect her."

"Protect her! Now, after all these years, you finally want to do your job?"

Janet blinked. "I always—"

"You *never*!" Donna yelled. "You abandoned that baby to me! I named her! I fed her! I was the one who taught her how to walk! A girl knows when her mother doesn't love her."

The soap operas of rich people had never interested the Fox. He glanced around the room, looking for someone to go with him. The old man might try to be a hero. He passed over the fat man and the waif, who had no motivation to save this place or the people in it. He glossed over the girl in the pantsuit. Too much attitude. She'd be a hassle.

"I *love* Kathy," Janet said, glaring through red-rimmed eyes. "But a girl *does* know when her mother doesn't love her."

The Fox's gaze landed on the little waitress in black pants and white blouse. Young enough to handle the snow and actually be helpful. Timid enough to follow instructions. She saw him look and averted her eyes.

"When will you wake up and figure out no knight on a white horse can save you from yourself?" Donna said.

The Fox crammed Charlie's harmonica into his pocket and pointed at the waitress. "You," he said.

Janet snapped out of the argument with her mother. "Olivia? No."

"Olivia," said the Fox. "Let's go."

His guns made their protests moot. He directed Olivia past Brick to the front of the hotel. Behind it, the flames of the cottage crackled as they reached for the night sky.

CHAPTER 35

The underground passage between the kitchen pantry and the Rising Sun cottage was another one of Dr. Harrison's ideas, inspired by the tunnels built by World War I soldiers. Of course, he didn't have warfare in mind, but he believed in the importance of redundancy. If his Japanese guests were in the lodge at the moment they needed to hide, they couldn't very well run across the yard to their cottages, now could they? And so he forced a tunnel out of the difficult terrain, carving and digging and demolishing, and braced it with beams. He ventilated it with air shafts and filled it with water barrels and canned food.

Pearl remembered that her mother had objected to the expense. Already the Second World War had required them to spread their resources as thin as possible, and the cottages themselves were squeezing them beyond their means. But her husband insisted.

Can you put a price on a saved life? he had asked.

So far as Pearl knew, the tunnel, like the closets, had never been used for its intended purpose, or any other, except for the one Halloween when Donna and Delilah used it to spook the chef and housekeeper after they went to their cottages for the night.

The stainless steel pantry shelves were not the originals, of course, and when Pearl finally emptied the one of enough weight to pull it out of the way, its casters rolled smoothly across the floor and revealed a blank wall. She feared the passage might have been boarded up. The original shelving had been attached to a hinged door, and they moved together as one. But then she noticed the marks in the wood where the old shelving had been anchored, and when she ran her fingers over the nail holes she felt a draft passing through. When she finally found a notch at the edge large enough for her to tug on, the hinges on the false back didn't complain too much, and the panel yielded.

In front of her were a tiny landing and a set of unfinished wood steps that descended to a dirt floor. Surely they were not built with an eighty-seven-year-old woman in mind! But faced with a wooden staircase before her and crazy gangsters behind her, Pearl took her chances with the stairs. There was no electricity down here, no light except for the flashlight she had brought. She stepped through and pulled the panel closed behind her, but there was nothing she could do about the shelf.

Why was going downstairs so much more difficult than going up? These knees of hers! After spending too long envisioning herself falling headfirst down the flight, Pearl held the rail, lowered herself to her derriere, and scooted down the steps, thanking the good Lord for the Japanese attention to detail in sanding the planks smooth as river stones. She arrived with nary a splinter.

The door at the bottom was held tight by design and disuse. A bolt could lock it from the inside, but there was no keyhole in the knob—a safety feature to ensure no one could lock anyone inside. It was as hard to open as a pickle jar, and the smell that rushed out when she finally did it was worse. The tunnel still seemed to brim with the anxiety of war. She shone a flashlight into the cavern, and her beam of light didn't reach the end. The timbers that held up the ground were not as tall as she remembered and the tunnel not quite as wide, just big enough for a single-file line of grown men. The dry climate had saved the wood from rot, but it was impossible to know how stable the timbers were.

Well, if she died buried in rubble, the question of her mental state would be forever confirmed.

The dust in the passage was as thick as the snow on the ground and came up in puffs around her boots. She walked as she had to Daniel's door—was that just this morning?—with the expectation that she would get what she wanted when she arrived.

The tunnel took a corner turn and, after about twenty yards, came to its end, and Pearl's heart fell. There was no staircase here, nothing but an iron ladder anchored in the dirt. At the base of the ladder was an old army footlocker with chipped paint and buckling joints. The ladder was bolted to beams and ended at a row of tight wood planks ten feet over her head. Her knuckles and knees were no match for that gymnastic feat.

She might as well hope someone would show up right now with a plate of hot Welsh rarebit.

Pearl placed a shaky foot on the bottom rung.

～

Charlie tucked the sheathed knife that Kate had given him into the waistband of his pants. He clutched the car keys and the pillowcase full of loot and pushed the door open on the back of the house. The landscape was gunmetal gray, the sky too thick with snow to make any room for moonlight. The shelter behind him was a wedge of blackness. He hopped down out of the smothering room and crushed the snow under his sneaker. The cold and pain cut through him again, a double-edged dagger. But it was finally dark, finally the right time for a getaway.

He put one hand on the side of the house, balancing, preparing. He knew which way to head out, but he didn't move. He couldn't go.

And he couldn't think of any way to save the girl. All he could think of was the gunshot that hit his ears as he sped off on Merridew's stolen motorcycle and Coz's bloody body, alone on the ground. What if it happened again?

The tears he'd tried to hide from Kate froze on his cheeks. He wiped his nose with the pillowcase and stood in mounting snow on one foot, a flamingo without a flock. The keys in his palm were slick with his chilled sweat. His injury throbbed, refusing to go numb.

Behind him, a rousing thud rattled the floorboards and bounced the musty cot, and the clatter sent a flock of roosting crows squawking into the frigid air.

The silence settled again. Then another strike. Though he'd anticipated it he flinched.

"Kate?" The muffled sound of someone calling the kid's name came right from the spot where he'd rested his head.

"Kate? I sure hope you're up there. You and I have some serious plotting to do, young lady."

It was time to go, he told himself. Time. To. Go. Now or never. He reached up to tug on the bill of a knit cap that was no longer there.

Thunk. "Kate, child." The voice was strong and frail at the same time. "We must help each other out now."

They were words from Charlie's past. An echoing voice from the only real family Charlie had ever known. Uncle Jun.

If Charlie turned his back on that voice again—if he walked away from Eve's plea for help, if he turned his back on another child that he might have been able to save—Charlie would be even less of a man than the father last glimpsed in his rearview mirror as he drove out of Evergreen.

We must help each other out now.

Charlie dropped the pillowcase sack at the room's entrance and turned around, then climbed back into the room on his knees. He reached for the cot and tipped it on its side against the wall. With his light he spotted a ring in the floorboard and traced the line of the trapdoor to the hinge. Bracing his body, he yanked and jostled and strained, and when he hit upon the correct angle and the floor popped up easily he almost fell into the gap. A blinding light came out of the hole straight into his face. He threw an arm up over his eyes. The offensive beam faltered.

"Kenneth?" the light said.

CHAPTER 36

K ate went out the front door of her home, which was when she saw the Full Moon burning like a sun. Wood crackled and split while falling snow melted and hissed and evaporated, bouncing off the heat as if it were a trampoline. Steam rose from the wet landscape. The roof was beginning to cave.

Beside the house, a skinny flame licked the side of a Ponderosa pine. At Kate's feet, the cougar cub crouched low to the ground and shied away from the bright flames, then leaped off the porch. It headed down the path that led toward the front of the lodge, past the terrace at the rear and the kitchen at the side. Kate followed. In the kitchen, she could use Chef's phone to call 911. Then she might be able to find out what they were doing to her family.

The smell of braised beef rushed out when she opened the kitchen door, and the cub darted into the building before she could stop it. The kitchen was completely empty, and Kate relaxed until the cub spotted the slab of meat on the butcher block and leaped for it. Kate knocked a metal bowl onto the floor trying to stop the cat from jumping onto the table. The noise startled her as much as the cougar. It shot out into the family dining area and Kate darted for the pantry. The noise was sure to bring grown-ups running. Inside, someone had left the light on, and one of the portable shelf units was askew. Kate pulled the door behind her just as someone came inside to investigate the noise. His slow-stepping shadow cut the gap under the pantry door as he passed.

The cub mewled. The man chuckled. A muted shout came from the freezer, and the man yelled at whoever made it to shut up.

"Beggar in the house," he said. "Hunting fugitives works up an appetite, don't it?"

He threw some of the cooked meat onto the floor and the cub tore into it, chewing the wet mess and growling low in its throat.

Waiting for the man to leave the kitchen seemed to take hours, but when his shadow passed by the door again, Kate cautiously slipped out.

The cougar was crouched on one of the rubber mats, licking the crevices for every last smudge of juicy fat. A huge metal table had been wedged under the freezer door handle, but when she tried to move it, nothing budged. She ran into Chef's office and reached for the phone on the edge of the desk. The weight of it felt flimsy in her hand, not heavy enough. She couldn't get a dial tone. Turning it over, she saw the battery had been removed.

There was another phone upstairs, on a table in the hall just outside the library.

Kate went to the kitchen doors and stood on tiptoe to see through the small round windows. She couldn't quite see the foyer from here—it was around the corner—but it would be too dangerous to run across the wide-open area to get to the main staircase. Anyone in the dining room might see her. She opted to try the back stairs, which came down beside the family keeping room. She might also be seen there, but the risk wasn't quite so bad.

There was no door between the keeping room and the hall, just an arched passageway. She was in shadow as she looked out into the dining room access that the food servers used. The man with orange shoes stood in the access with his back to her, eating something. Everyone else that she could see was facing the windows, watching the Full Moon burn.

Kate crept to the staircase, passing close enough to the man to have touched him. But she was a stealthy mouse, and seconds later she found herself upstairs.

The battery had been removed from this phone too. She tried the doors of each room and found them locked.

There was one other phone that she knew of, up one more flight in the event center, the wide-open ballroom with a bar and a bathroom and a view of Kate's whole world.

As she climbed to the third floor, the phone behind the reception desk started to ring. It was a soft sound, meant to be pleasant. It reminded Kate of the Christmas bell choir Grandy had taken her to hear in Denver one year. Kate looked down over the banister. The phone down there was larger and more complicated than the other units—the brains of the operation, Grandy liked to call it. But there was no way for her to get to it. And no one came to answer the incoming call. Someone in the dining room gave instructions in a voice so low-pitched that Kate couldn't make out the words.

The event center was dark tonight. Grandy usually turned the lights on because it looked pretty from the driveway at night, but this evening he never had the chance. Kate crept up the stairs and across the parquet floor and was not surprised to find that phone as disabled as the others, but when she looked out through the panoramic windows onto the blazing cottage, flames in the window of the Nocturne, right next to the Full Moon, came as a shock.

Why were they burning down the cottages?

Kate tiptoed to the other side of the room and looked down on the front of the lodge. Olivia stepped out through the front doors, and Kate raised her hand to strike the window and get Olivia's attention. But the man with the weird hairdo, the orange crop and the white beard, stepped out behind Olivia before Kate made any noise. He held a large gun and used it to prod her along.

Again, the phone on the first floor rang and again, no one answered.

Standing on top of the lodge, completely alone, Kate saw that Charlie was right. She was no Mammy Kate, and she didn't have the brains to stop four men from burning down her home or hurting her family. She didn't even have a good plan. Her heart started beating so fast and so hard that she felt like all the bones in her body were rattling.

She returned to the second floor, crawled across the carpet, and lay down in the library behind the balcony rail where she might hear the conversations in the dining room.

No one was talking. There was only that horrible man noshing his meat with as much sloppy pleasure as the cub. The sound of it made Kate feel queasy.

A voice cut the silence downstairs. "There's no fugitive here, there's only Kathy," her mother said through a tight throat. "Would he really . . . ? Why would a man hurt a child?"

"He won't find her," said Grandy. "That girl is better at staying out of sight than any kid in the history of the world."

"But if she doesn't know— What if she's in one of those compartments between the duplexes. You know, the old storage rooms? What if the fires . . . ?" Janet's voice gave out and the most awful tears took over.

Kate's terror rose into her throat.

"Maybe if you'd paid more attention to her than to those trashy novels we'd have a better idea what was really going on here," Gran said.

"Donna, now's not the time," Grandy warned.

Gran raised her voice over Janet's sobbing.

"A woman has to make sacrifices for her family, Janet. Heaven knows I've made them for Mother and all of you. This lodge was Delilah's dream, not mine, but who else was there to keep it going? I knew my duty and thought I taught you to know yours. I never tried to stop you from leaving this town, leaving this business. You could have done whatever you wanted with my blessing. Anything but leave your children before they're grown. So don't think you can have my pity right now. You should have cried those tears of yours years ago."

"I came back," Janet defended.

"You came back because Katherine's father tired of you. You *knew* he wanted no children, not even the two you already had—"

"He loved those girls."

"He was going to ship them off to boarding school!"

"No—"

"And you thought you could hook him with a pregnancy, and when that didn't work you thought you could leave your life behind and become whatever fantasy he thought he wanted. Stupid girl. You're so stupid that you'd do it all again for the next man who promised you a vacation to South Dakota!"

"Donna, stop!"

"No, Daniel. I've wanted to say my piece for years, and if takes something like this for the chance to be heard, so be it. You wronged those children, Janet. *You.* Especially Katherine. I'm the one who should get to fall apart right now, but here we are again, you playing the tragic figure and me holding the world together."

Kate clutched her knees to her chest. She hated the fighting, wished for a way to make them all just be happy.

"If that man kills Katherine, Janet, I'm going to blame it on you."

From Kate's position on the floor her view skimmed the surface of the carpet and ran the length of the library. She could see the spot where she'd found the dragon knife just a few hours ago, and she realized that she'd forgotten to ask Charlie what he'd done with it.

She could see beyond the ottoman that had covered it and past the curtains that hung in the sidelight windows, through the french doors that guests could open if they wanted to read in the fresh air. Beyond those doors, another balcony and the main drive, and a set of flashing red and white lights blinking through the fir spruce trees as they rose from the main road.

Kate sat up.

A fire truck climbed the driveway. Someone had called the fire department. A neighbor? Didn't matter. The firefighters were as good as the sheriff's department.

Kate got to her feet and ran. Her feet hit the floor hard and made more noise than she thought possible. She ran past the locked guest rooms, pounded down the main stairs, raced past the dining room, and shot out the front entrance faster than the cries of "Kate!" and "There's the kid!" She ran out waving her arms and slipped on the snow-slicked ground, recovered her balance, and got to the top of the circular driveway before the fire truck had made the last curve. She kept running toward the flashing lights, shouting at the firefighters in the front of the truck. "They're burning it down! They have guns! They have my mom and grandma and—"

Two gunshots went off, one right after the other. They seemed to fire right beside her head, louder than anything she'd ever heard.

She grabbed her ears and ducked without knowing what she was dodging or where it was coming from. And when she did, her feet went out from under her and she went down, landing hard on her rump and smacking her head on the ground. The blow stunned her. For a time she couldn't see anything but a bright flashing light; she couldn't hear anything but a screaming buzz. She couldn't feel anything except the unyielding ground under her back. Pain brought her around, an ache that started in her tailbone and pulsated up her spine, and something like burning that licked at her elbows the way the fire licked the cottage walls.

When the world finished spinning she rolled onto her stomach and saw that the fire truck had stopped. Across the parking lot, behind two rows of lights, the man with Olivia had leveled his gun at the truck. A starburst crack marred the windshield. One of the headlights was out. The driver and his rider had ducked out of sight within the big rig. Kate couldn't see her sister.

A third shot cut the frigid air and struck the front of the truck, but this bullet came from the hotel. A huge man, big as a football player, was standing outside the glass doors, covering for his friend.

Kate tried to get up and run away. She tried to push herself off the snow-covered blacktop but her arms wouldn't work, and when she lifted her eyes and saw the man who had been with her sister running toward her, his hair red like fire, Kate didn't even have the strength to scream. He was surefooted on the slick ground, quick and strong, and he bent to scoop her up without missing a step. He tossed her as if she were nothing more than a fumbled football, caught her, and tucked her tightly against him. His arms were smooth and muscled and confident, and she knew as she bounced against his chest that he would not, could not, drop her.

The jarring hurt her head. Her teeth clacked together. She shut her eyes so hard her nose wrinkled. The even huff of his breathing and the wild-animal strength of his heartbeat surrounded her.

She wondered if the white tiger Montecore had actually saved his human brother Roy or tried to kill him, as many claimed.

Kate almost felt safe.

CHAPTER 37

The old woman couldn't come any farther up the ladder, and when Charlie informed her his name wasn't Kenneth, she almost wouldn't allow him to come down.

"I'll just hang here and block your way," she threatened, though he could see the trembling of exertion in her arms. She was an eccentric, he thought, wearing squat winter boots, an old coat, and a strand of pearls.

"If you break a leg or a hip, then who'll help Kate?"

At the sound of the little girl's name, the silver-haired lady dropped her tough-gal act and, over a long and painful minute, lowered her quaking self back to solid ground.

"What have you done with my great-grandchild?" she demanded as Charlie lowered his legs, rolled to his hips, and searched for a rung with his good foot.

"Nothing." He performed something like reverse pull-ups as he descended the ladder on just the one leg, one rung at a time. "She's done it all to herself."

"That's a ridiculous thing to say." Her light turned upward. "Oh, I see you're in fine shape. What's wrong with your foot?"

"Busted my ankle."

"Then what good can you possibly be? Oh, never mind. Where is she?"

"I don't know."

As Charlie made his painful and awkward descent down the

ladder, she struck him on the back of the knee with the bulky old flashlight.

"I tried to stop her, but she's got her own mind," Charlie said.

"Then you didn't try hard enough," she said as he reached the ground. The simple effort had raised an embarrassing sweat at his temples. He rested a moment at the bottom and she stepped away, keeping him in the center of the light.

"Might as well tell me now," she said. "Are you one of them?"

"One of who?"

"The thugs who put my staff in the freezer and are doing heaven knows what to my family."

"No."

"What's your name?"

"Charlie."

She frowned.

"Charlie. They said you're their friend. They came here to meet you. I heard them ask for you by— No, wait. You're Japanese."

Charlie was mildly surprised. In his experience people tended to hedge their bets and declare him Asian. Few were confident enough to distinguish Japanese from Chinese from Korean from Vietnamese at a glance.

"I am."

The tension left her shoulders and she closed the gap between them. "Can't be your friends, can they? They pronounced your name wrong."

"How would you know that?"

"Let me see the side of your neck," she ordered.

"What?"

She lifted her flashlight. "Come on now."

He turned his head away so she could see the skin under his ear.

"Hm. I guess that's as much as I can expect for now." She held out a paper-white hand toward him. "Pearl Nagasawa," she said. "Too early to say if it's a pleasure to meet you."

He frowned. This woman was as Japanese as Hillary Clinton.

She nodded. "Yes, you could pass for one of Kenneth's relatives. Then again, my eyes aren't what they were."

Charlie didn't especially care who Kenneth was except that the man might have saved him from being bludgeoned to death by a flashlight.

"So then." She aimed the light down the curving tunnel, which was how Charlie had always imagined an old mine might look, but smaller and without a mine cart rolling down a center track. A few feet away from where they stood, the tunnel curved to the left.

Pearl sighed. "The child rarely does what she is told, and I daresay that is her best quality. However, it's ruined my plans to hide her down here until your 'friends' went on their way. You are not the person I expected to find in that compartment up there."

"Their leader is a guy with copper-colored hair and a white beard."

"Truly, I don't understand your generation."

"Did you learn his name?"

"Cause, he said. Who names their child Cause?"

The name struck fresh fear in Charlie's stomach.

"Coz. C-O-Z. I think it's short for Cosimo."

"Oh yes. A nice Italian name." Pearl paused. "I don't think he's Italian. But these days one might—"

"Where did he—"

"And the others called him Fox. I hardly know which one is stranger."

"The others. I saw four of them. Are there more?"

"Not that I saw. Only four came into the lodge, anyway. For all I know they surrounded the—"

"Where are they now?"

"If you intend to be helpful you should know we're working blind, my boy."

Charlie started hop-limping down the corridor. "Do you have a phone?"

Pearl followed him. "In my room. That's no good. We'll have to use the one in the kitchen. But first, I would like to know how you came to be in a closet my husband built more than seventy years ago. Only the family know about it, and even some of them have forgotten."

"I don't think we've got time for that."

"Let's make time. I need to know who you are."

"I'm the guy who's going to help you save Kate."

"You're not too convincing, hopping around that way like a pogo stick."

"Kate found me, Mrs. Nagasawa. She found me, and she helped me, and she gave me a place to stay where no one would— Wait. Are you the one who tosses out the ones who can't pay?"

"I most certainly am not. She found you? When?"

Pearl was prone to shining the light in Charlie's face rather than down the passageway. He squinted against her probing and pointed straight ahead. "What's waiting for us down there?"

"A kitchen pantry. I suppose you're hungry. All the young men I ever knew were always hungry."

"We need a plan."

"I don't suppose you have one. Well, don't look at me. I make my plans and they're shredded to pieces when I open trapdoors and find vagabonds instead of granddaughters. Tell me what we're going to do, Charlie Fuse. I suppose you know better than I what we're up against, if it's your fault those men are here."

Charlie paused at one of the braces and held himself up. He was winded, and the door at the end of the passage was still twenty-five feet away.

"How many people are up there? I mean your people. Not the Fox and company."

"I'm sure I don't know. There are four or five decent souls in the freezer. I suppose we should get them out first."

"What else can you do?" he asked.

"What else can *I* do? Oh, this is a fine start. What are *you* going to do?"

"I know how to use a knife." He pulled a dragon-handled blade out of its sheath, and it glinted in Pearl's beam of light. She recoiled. "I can do street fighting."

"With that?" She pointed to his ankle, splinted by a library book.

"Think of it as a built-in baseball bat."

"I see. Well. I can crochet doilies. What can we do with that?"

He set his mouth in a grim line. "Not much."

"We must work on your sense of humor."

"Maybe when we're done."

Her light flickered off, and she whacked the bulb with the palm of her hand. It flared bright again.

"I can call the sheriff," she suggested.

"I'm not on really good terms with them right now."

"Is that so? What exactly did you plan to do with our phones? If you think your street fighting and my doilies are going to be enough—"

Charlie held up his hand. "Look, the Fox is an impatient guy." He recalled the alley, the black Camaro, Drogo driving into the greenhouse doors, and the Fox firing into the back of the Chevy before the sound of the crash died away. "Kate might need us to move faster than anyone else can get here. How brave are you?"

Pearl laughed at that. "I'm clawing my way through a seventy-year-old tunnel with a man who might challenge me to a street fight at any moment. I can hold my own."

Charlie wondered how many people were going to die before the morning dawned.

"Mrs. Nagasawa, you want to know the most important thing about me?"

"That you're a street rat who still knows his manners?"

"I'm the man the Fox came here to kill."

Her laugh faded and her smile turned sad. "And why does he want to kill you?"

"He thinks I murdered his kid."

"He thinks."

"But I didn't."

Her eyes remained on him, steady and patient, as if knowing he hadn't finished what was necessary for him to say. Her eyesight might not be what it was, but he believed this woman could see through his heaving ribs and into his black heart. He cleared his throat and looked away. "But I didn't save him either."

He expected anything but the aging hand on his shoulder, light as a feather and heavy with wisdom.

"I've waited seventy years for this lodge to become the place my father and husband built it to be. Kate was right to shelter you here. She knows more than any of us about saving people who need it. Speaking for myself."

"We can't let him kill her," Charlie said.

"We won't." Her eyes brightened in the shadows behind the

flashlight, then her mouth formed an O of surprise. "It's just come to me, Charlie—what I can do. In fact, what I do best."

Charlie shook his head. He didn't have a single guess.

"Young man, I can do crazy."

CHAPTER 38

The snowstorm might have masked the smoke and the blaze, but still the firefighters were here. A neighbor must have made the call. After the little shootout that had just gone down in the parking lot, the law would come too, which was as it should be. Maybe even as he had hoped. From here on out, the success of the Fox's plan would depend entirely on timing.

Without his signal to stop, Hector would continue to burn the cottages. Brick and Jones would use the hostages to hold off the authorities. He'd abandoned the shrieking girl Olivia as soon as he spotted Janet's youngest daughter. Olivia would explain that he had the child and what he'd promised to do to her. At some point, these stubborn people would give him what he wanted.

Cradling the child in his arms, the Fox hoofed it up the gently sloping hillside behind the cottages. He needed a lay of the land, a good vantage. He was looking for a spot protected from the uniforms about to descend upon the place, but it had to be a place with a broad view of the lodge. He was so pumped with adrenaline he might have carried the girl with his pinkie finger hooked into the shoulder of her pink jacket vest. She weighed next to nothing and she put up no fight. He'd seen her smack her head on the ground, and this worried him a bit.

"You Kathy?" he asked.

"Kate," she said. "Like Mammy Kate. Do you know about her?"

"No."

"Most people don't."

Great. A talker.

"Keep quiet now, hear?"

She obeyed immediately. A good girl too. This prompted the Fox to stoop and put her on the wet ground beside a tree trunk. He meant to show her the sketch of Charlie, but it seemed he'd dropped it during the shootout. So he squatted in front of her and got a good look at her face for the first time. Mussy black hair framed a perfectly round face and wide clear eyes. The Fox realized he had expected someone his son's age and stature, someone old enough to run to the corner store alone for an eighty-nine-cent fountain drink. This girl was a young eleven, without an ounce of street smarts.

"I'm lookin' for someone," the Fox said. "A man with hair like yours, skinny guy half my size. Looks Asian. You seen anyone like that around here lately?"

Kate stared at him but did not open her mouth. And she did not shake her head to deny it.

"I need to find him. It's real important. See, he murdered my boy, my son, Coz, who's just hardly older than you. He's a bad man, this one, and he's runnin' from what he done."

The soft skin beneath her chin puckered and pulled down the corners of her mouth. A tremble shook her shoulders, maybe the chill of the ground seeping into her clothes. He stared at her until she looked down at her hands.

"Charlie says you'll kill me," she whispered.

In the distance, the fire's crackling swelled as Hector lit up another cottage, the third. It matched the expansion in the Fox's chest, relief. Not only had the girl seen Charlie Fuse, but they had spoken to each other.

Tears spilled over and dripped onto her vest, raising purple spots in the pink.

"Charlie," the Fox said. "That's the one. Where is he?"

"Are you going to kill me?"

"Charlie's the killer here."

"What about my family? Did you shoot my sister? Olivia was—"

"All you have to do is tell me where Charlie is."

"Why are you burning the cottages?"

"Where *is* he?"

He hadn't meant to yell. She flinched and covered her face with her arms. His instinct was to strike her, and had this been the spineless, screeching Olivia he might have done it. But Kate cried silently.

Young as she was, the kid seemed to understand her predicament. If she had wanted to tell the Fox where Charlie was, she couldn't have done it for the crying, which held her mouth open and her throat closed. He had to calm her, and he had to stay calm. For Coz, he could not afford to lose Kate or his temper.

He dropped from his squat onto one knee and leaned toward the girl. How monstrous he must look to this child who lived so far from anything resembling a housing project. He cupped her cheeks in his hands and tilted her face up so she would look at him. Her hair was damp with snow.

"Kate." Calming, soothing, the way his woman had taught him to talk with Coz when the boy was a babe and his father needed the child's attention. It was a foreign way, nothing he'd ever learned in his growing-up home. But it always worked, and even now it amazed him.

She drew in stuttering breaths and looked at him through glassy eyes.

"I'm sorry I yelled, girl. The fires—sometimes you gotta smoke out the enemy. You're not the enemy, okay? I can tell you're a good girl. You gotta tell me where Charlie is. He needs to answer for his crimes."

He was surprised that she didn't avert her eyes this time. Her stare unnerved him to the core, the way she studied his face as if memorizing it. Her breathing evened out. Snow was collecting on her eyebrows and lashes.

"Where's Charlie?" he repeated.

"Your hair is funny," she whispered.

She reached up to touch his chin, her fingertips nearly as white as his beard. He forced down the anger that flared up in his throat. It wasn't a hard question he was asking.

Her gaze went to the copper hair on his head.

"It makes you look . . . It makes you look like a fox."

Kate closed her eyes and the full weight of her head sank into his hands. He felt her breath, lighter than the snowflakes, on the skin of his arms.

"Hey there. What you doin' now?"

"He's in the cubby," Kate murmured. "It's not their fault."

"What cubby? Where?"

"Don't kill my family."

The girl slipped out of his palms and sank against the tree. Playing possum was a wily trick, and his temper gained the upper hand. He slapped her across the face.

She didn't react. A wide smudge of blood transferred to her cheek. The Fox looked at his hands, then grabbed the child by the shoulders and pulled her away from the trunk. That wasn't snow that had wet her hair. Sticky blood from her own head made her black locks blacker. Now he saw the inky smears on his shirt where he'd hugged her to his chest as he ran.

The Fox pressed his wide hand to the injury and swore. He would have given his own life to get Coz back from the men who took him. He would have betrayed any of his Heavies, to say nothing of a murderous fugitive. He could only hope Kate's family felt the same way about her.

CHAPTER 39

The last thing Pearl expected to see when she and Charlie craned their necks around the pantry door was that lurking wildcat licking Chef's Dutch oven clean. Red-wine-braised short ribs, she guessed from the scent and the clean bones. Which was too bad, it being one of Chef's finer dishes. Far superior to the crab cakes.

"Is that a cougar?" Charlie whispered. The exertion of hopping up the stairs had wet the fringe of his hair.

"A fat and happy one," Pearl said. "I don't think he has room to eat your leg, if you're worried about that."

Seeing no one, Pearl stepped boldly into the kitchen, ignoring Charlie's wild pantomime that seemed to indicate she should stay put. For goodness' sake, this place had been her home since 1929, and she could come up with a million reasons to be wandering around in it. He might think she wasn't keeping an ear out for the fellow with the gun—there, she could see where a bullet had penetrated the oven door—but she was. This girl was still sharp as a tack.

And the shouts of protest coming from the freezer, the angry pounding, were loud enough to cover up any noise Pearl and Charlie might accidentally make. Its door was barred from the outside. A stainless steel worktable with a backsplash was propped against the door at an angle, its legs braced against the treads of a heavy rubber mat. The lip of the backsplash had been jammed under the door handle with force enough to bow the metal. Not even the safety releases inside the freezer, the ones required by law to prevent employees from getting locked in, could overcome this simple barricade.

Constantly glancing around the room, now toward this door, now toward that passageway, that exit, Charlie helped her drag the mat out of the way, then withdraw the table. He yanked on the handle and pulled the door wide. Instead of tumbling out, the people inside withdrew into the cold until Pearl ducked in with her finger pressed to her lips.

"Ms. Pearl!" Chef exclaimed. Her ruddy nose and cheeks were rosier than ever. "You're the last person I expected."

"Have you *any* idea what your employees keep stocked in that pantry?" Pearl said, raising an eyebrow in Charlie's direction.

"We heard more shots," said a tall woman in a white chef's coat, vigorously rubbing her arms.

"Then let's hope they've reduced their own number. Best get straight out." Pearl pointed in the direction of the exit on the opposite side of the kitchen, where delivery doors opened onto an asphalt lane that rounded the lodge and led out to the parking lot.

"Watch yourselves," Chef ordered as the small crew filed outside, giving curious looks at Charlie as they passed. In the light he was much grimier than Pearl had first noted. And the blood on his shredded pant leg was a terrible sight. The cougar cub, who had responded to the quiet invasion by leaping down onto the floor to clean himself, now came out to sniff at Charlie's injury. Charlie kicked at the animal and winced, though he missed it completely. The cub darted under the low shelf of a portable prep table.

"Call in the cavalry for us," Pearl murmured to Chef, who brought up the rear.

"You're coming too, Ms. Pearl," Chef insisted.

"Not without my family."

"You know they'd want you to come with me."

"If they were in any position to be telling me what to do, don't you think they'd be here doing it? Go on, Chef. Any minute now the one who locked you up is going to come see why you've quit raising a ruckus."

"Wait," said Charlie. "I have an idea."

IT DID NOT TAKE MUCH PRETENSE TO STOOP AND SHUFFLE LIKE an ailing woman through the family dining area. Fear for Kate, for all of them, and regret that her father's vision for the lodge might end as a tragic headline in the *Denver Post* pressed down heavily. Weariness rushed over Pearl. Her legs begged her to sit down, the way snow sirens called wanderers to take a short nap. If she sat she'd never rise again.

Pearl had never meant to become a cynical old crone who deceived her family. There was a time when she had believed she could motivate Donna to embrace a vision for the hotel that was greater than a pretty spread Martha Stewart might have dreamed up. She thought if she became the ideal patron—that is, one who needed more than she could offer in return—Donna might be inspired to true hospitality, as her sister Delilah had been. As their father and grandfather had been. Instead Pearl's second-born child carried her mother's needs like a martyr carried his cross.

Donna had carried so much grief over the years. Her attitude couldn't be entirely her fault.

Pearl passed under the arch and stepped into the hall, where the ghost of a memory from a November night long ago caught up with her. She was fifteen and anticipating the holidays with unusual excitement. The cottages were built. The grounds were ready for winter, and Kenneth had already helped her mark a fir tree to cut for Christmas. A light snow fell on the lodge, where their Japanese guests had gathered to conserve warmth and fuel. In the keeping room, under the supervision of their aging housekeeper, Kenneth was teaching Pearl simple Japanese, though there was nothing simple about it except her growing affection for her tutor. Already she loved the fine angles of his face and the smooth planes of his skin, the patience in his voice, his skillfulness in the garden with the hori-hori knife, and his knowledge of how to make things grow in these mountains' tough conditions. The kitchen buzzed with dinner preparations and the chatter of women as their female guests taught her mother and the cook how to steam rice and make miso soup with precious ingredients from Denver's Little Tokyo. In the grand parlor—which didn't become a formal dining room until after the war—her father sipped tea before the fire with the women's husbands. Seventeen content souls in a snug warm house.

Then the doorbell summoned her father, and their number increased to nineteen, but the chatter died away. As Dr. Harrison rose to greet the unscheduled visitors, the men in the parlor rose with their teacups and silently filed out, gathering in the kitchen. Kenneth joined them, the light gone from his eyes. It was necessary even here in Evergreen, this keeping out of sight.

Pearl carried a newspaper into the parlor and then ducked behind her father's beautiful waterfall console radio, which stood taller than her shoulders, so she could gather news of the visitors. Two men stomped the snow off their boots and removed their hats in the entry hall. She recognized Mr. Renquist, a bushy-faced businessman who had political aspirations and made the bulk of his money off summer tourists. The other, tall and angular, was a stranger.

"Dr. Harrison, may I introduce Carl Wilson."

"Gentlemen."

He politely accepted their hands but did not offer to take their hats and coats. By the glance they exchanged, Pearl guessed they'd expected his chilly welcome.

Mr. Renquist said, "We've spoken, Dr. Harrison, about my mounting concerns regarding the free Japanese who continue to arrive in our state."

"I believe it's more accurate to say that you have spoken."

"The impact of their race on this fine state can't be under-estimated."

"I'll agree with you there, sir."

"The Denver population is exploding due to those fleeing the West Coast."

"They are here of their own will, at the governor's invitation, and with the president's blessing."

"They are a rising flood."

"Of a few thousand souls?" Dr. Harrison said wryly. "Don your life vests, men. Our limited understanding of the world is about to be enriched by our own citizens."

Mr. Wilson leaned into the conversation. "Dr. Harrison, we are aware of your . . . er . . . appreciation for the Japanese culture, and yet I am compelled to point out that whatever these people may call themselves by law, they are Japanese by blood, and their loy-alty must be questioned for as long as this war endures. Indeed, the security of the nation remains at risk for as long as they move freely."

"President Roosevelt seems to think it enough to deny them

access to the West Coast. Oh yes—and to property, and the right to vote, and—"

"Mr. Wilson and I are drafting a petition for President Roosevelt to expand his executive order to include all Japanese within our borders."

"On what basis? No Japanese citizen of this country has ever been found guilty of treason."

"Not yet."

"And where on earth do you propose to put them?"

"There are only ten internment camps at present. Plenty of room for more."

Dr. Harrison shook his head. "I'm sorry. I must have missed your intent. Why do you bring this to me? Mr. Renquist knows that I think the executive order already in effect is incredibly ill-advised."

Mr. Renquist gave Mr. Wilson an I-told-you-so tilt of his head. Mr. Wilson said, "Because of your travels and business dealings with the Japanese, your knowledge of the people and their ways will be an invaluable aid to us. Whatever you may think of this effort, our desire, of course, is not to make merely a patriotic argument, but an informed—"

"I will not be the man to help you." Dr. Harrison stepped around them and briskly opened the door. "Good evening, sirs."

The fear Pearl felt when the men had gone returned to her now as she stood in the hall, ready to step off the brink into unknown dangers. "Will they question our loyalty, Father?"

"They will question it," he said. "But they will not be able to discredit it."

Seventy-two years later, for love of her family and loyalty to her father's heart, Pearl stepped into the dining room and faced the gunman who stood in the place of the old Zenith radio.

CHAPTER 40

This vantage wasn't ideal, but the Fox could see enough: below, the third cottage aflame. Snow gathering on the eaves of the lodge. Flakes melting in the heat and the creek. Trees like fast-burning birthday candles. Just two or three of them. Now four. Beyond the hotel, the dizzying red and white lights of the fire truck were joined by the blues and reds of law enforcement. No sign of his son's murderer. No sirens announcing the capture of a killer.

No sound but his own mumbled prayer that the girl wouldn't die before he found Charlie Fuse. He tore off the hem of his shirt and pressed it against the back of her head. He'd never intended to kill her, only motivate her family. He wasn't the monster Charlie was. Of course, if she died now, everyone would believe otherwise.

In the window of the dining room, backlit by weak gold light, the lady in red fell to her knees, palms and forehead tipped against the glass. She looked small from up here. A chigger instead of a cardinal. Squashable. Her mouth open like Coz's mother's when Detective Warren cut her so deep with the news of her son's murder that the Fox felt the wound himself. They were all bleeding to death right now, leaking that invisible red blood.

All because of Charlie. The whole world was collapsing, stabbed by events that never should happen, killed by their own kind. Before the night was out the Fox was going to kill that man.

He studied the structures, trying to picture a cubby big enough to hide an adult. What might something like that be, and where? A footlocker? A trunk? A cupboard? No, not practical for a man who was injured and would need to hide for a day or two. An attic? A cellar? A closet?

With the girl's head in one hand, the Fox flexed his other fist, feeling the small cuts where his knuckles had broken the glass covering Jesus' face. And he changed his prayer, hoping it wasn't too much to ask that she just wouldn't die.

A crack and a boom from one of the fiery cottages drew his attention. It might have been anything. Collapsing wood, a melting TV screen, a can of cleaning spray, a bottle of barbecue lighter fluid. He did not expect to see a panel in the back wall come flying off its hinges, burning from the inside as if sprayed with something flammable. The piece of siding lay among trees in the snow, steam rising at its edges. He looked back at the cottage. More than just siding had been sent flying by the fire. It was a skinny door. The missing piece created a gap like a child's missing tooth in the back of the house. Flames crept to the edge of the gap, testing the cold air.

The Fox swiveled his head to the east, where he'd found Charlie's harmonica tucked under a rock at the back of the private cottage closest to the lodge. That's where he would begin.

In the shadows of the night, Hector's form jogged from the third cabin to the fourth. The Fox whistled. Hector stopped and looked up.

Gently, the Fox lifted Kate, secured her gangly body in his arms, and began a cautious descent.

CHAPTER 41

Rule number one of playing the crazy: remove all filters from your mouth and mind.

"We don't see too many of you up here in Evergreen," Pearl said, pointing her finger at the violent tattoo that seemed to strangle the gangster's neck. She stared at it for as long as she dared, almost as long as it took for everyone, including him, to register her sudden arrival in the room. "Did you know there's a theory floating around here that your type is responsible for yesterday's murder of one of our citizens? Dreadful prejudice, but there it is." Pearl extended a hand, and though he didn't take it, she waggled her elbow as if he had. "Thank you for honoring us with your presence."

She turned away from the man in the ridiculous orange shoes and he cackled. Ghastly.

"Mother!" Pearl heard Donna's voice but didn't pay it any mind. She was taking inventory. A woman slim as a geisha and a man fat as a *rikishi* held hands at a table, looking shell-shocked. Pearl smiled at them. Daniel was seated at a table covering his face. Alyssa stood like a soldier next to the fireplace. No sign of Olivia. No Kate. Janet had collapsed before the glass with her head in her hands, her hair-sprayed hair mussed and stuck to itself in all the wrong places. Donna stood beside her daughter.

Then Pearl noticed the flaming cottages and felt the blood rush out of her head. Three of them: the Full Moon, the Nocturne, the Twilight, all in a blaze. She reached out for the nearest chair and sank.

"Daniel." He lifted his head and she flung her hand toward the burning buildings, unable to take her eyes off of them. "You foolish boy. What did you go and do that for?"

He did not reply. It would be impossible not to weep. Already she could barely see over the tops of her full eyes.

"I thought you were in your room," Donna said faintly.

"Someone had better call the fire department."

"Someone already has," Alyssa said. She pointed toward the foyer.

Pearl twisted in her seat and leaned so she could see out of the dining room, past the glass of the looming front doors. Outside, lights blinked like Christmas. Inside, the gang's token brute guarded the doors, a pistol in each hand.

"That was nice of him," she said, turning back around and settling into the seat. The knot deep in her throat made it almost impossible to keep her voice light. "Have we gathered to watch them work? Why aren't they on it already? Are they waiting for the lodge to catch?"

"No, Mother. I was just saying that maybe we should go outside."

Pearl put her hands on her knees as if to stand. "Yes, let's. The view is better from the terrace. I'll get some popcorn from the kitchen."

"Stay put, lady."

"What, you don't like popcorn? You can come with me. Pick out whatever you crave."

"Sit down."

She stood up. "No, truly, I can't allow it. I've been the hostess here since I was a girl. I simply won't tolerate the guests doing the serving."

The man in the orange shoes pointed his gun at her.

"Daniel, stop her," Donna said.

Pearl kept moving. "Let's not have any fuss."

"Lady, you can't leave."

She did stop moving and granted him the courtesy of her attention, though she tried not to look at the weapon.

"I most certainly can," she said. Behind her, Daniel stood from his chair and Alyssa stepped away from the cold fireplace. "I can leave through that door there and get out to the terrace. I can go back through the kitchen and through the delivery door, or Chef's office for that matter. There's also a way out through the keeping room, you know. I can leave through the front if your friend would be so kind as to hold the door for me. Oh, and there where the private residences are—have you given him the tour yet, Donna? No?—back near our rooms there's another exit to the back and also one out through Daniel's shop."

"*Mother.*"

She hoped the guest couple was listening. They might learn something useful. She hoped her own family did not truly think she was so batty that they wouldn't read between the lines—namely, that the Harrison Lodge had far more exits than it had hostage takers. Janet, making as much snuffling noise as an elephant, had also turned her attention to Pearl.

"Daniel is a fine woodworker," Pearl continued. "Those balusters lining the second and third floors? He turned those. Speaking of which, one might even go to the second floor and leap from the library balcony. In a desperate situation, that is."

"Shut up. And sit down."

"Oooh, I see, I see. Please do forgive my misunderstanding. You meant to say I *may not* leave. Then maybe we can reach a compromise, yes? I wonder if it would be possible to invite the firemen *in* for this event. It would be rude to leave them out of the action."

"Jones!" The call came from the giant.

"What?"

"We need to move these people."

"Why?"

"Law's here now. The waitress is with them. You can bet SWAT's on their way."

Pearl caught her daughter's attention and wished eyes could say everything hearts needed to tell.

"Where's the Fox?" Gun drawn and eyes on the room, Jones started stepping around tables toward Brick's location.

"Lost him. But he's got the kid."

Janet gasped. Donna broke gaze with her mother.

"He said the plan's to kill the kid," Jones said.

"Well, he didn't do it."

Alyssa went to her mother and took her hand.

"If he's got the girl we don't need these folks no more," Jones said. He lifted the pistol toward the fat man and closed one eye, sighting. "You're an easy target."

"Just move them to a small room," Brick ordered. "No windows." He backed away from the front doors.

"I know just the place!" Pearl exclaimed. "The pantry does not have windows, but there is popcorn in there. And plenty of food. We'll practically be self-sustaining."

"This one's not gonna fit in no small room," Jones said, drawing back the hammer.

"Sir," Pearl said. "If you treat my guests poorly I'm going to have to ask you to leave."

"Shut up, old hag."

"Mr. Jones," Donna said. Taking long elegant strides, she placed herself in front of the couple's table, shoulders back and chin up. Pearl saw her fingers clenching and releasing, though she kept her arms at her sides. "Your colleague says our granddaughter Olivia is talking with the sheriff. She is a smart girl, attentive to detail. She'll give them a full account of who is here—our number, our names, our ages. Mr. Jones, I don't know what the Fox has promised you for your help, but the authorities will be armed with information. It seems to me you're more likely to leave here with your life if you protect ours."

"Don't you know nothing about brothers, lady? He don't have to promise us a thing."

Daniel came to life. "So do your part to keep him alive," he said. "SWAT'll try to separate you. Pick you off one at a time."

"Better stick together," Pearl said.

"No more talk," Jones shouted.

"The freezer is bulletproof," said Pearl.

Alyssa brightened. She was slow to catch on, Pearl thought, but they were all starting to come along. Only Janet's face was still carved with confusion.

"And the safe in Chef's office," Alyssa said.

Pearl sighed. The safe *might* be large enough for Kate but was of no use for holding adults.

Then Alyssa said, "I know the combination. You and your brothers could take the weekend cash."

Jones frowned.

"Really," said Pearl. "Have you ever met such a cooperative bunch?"

"I hate this town," said Jones.

The big one swept his gun across the room. "Kitchen. Now."

CHAPTER 42

Charlie hid in the pantry but worried about the freezer, which he'd forgotten to barricade again after he and Pearl let the staff out. His nerves were knots. The Heavies would notice his mistake as soon as they came into the kitchen. If Pearl had played her part right the family's captors would try to contain them with the rest of the hostages.

Even if she had manipulated them to perfection, Charlie had already screwed up.

It was the cat that saved him. As the sounds of pattering and shuffling feet entered the kitchen, Charlie heard the cougar's cry, followed by someone's surprised laugh and a "Hey, would you look at that!" directly outside the pantry door. Through the crack he could see two of the intruders.

The cat's distraction lasted only two or three seconds, which was all Charlie needed. Holding the knife Kate had given him up and ready at the side of his face, he threw his shoulder against the pantry door and shoved the weight of it into the leading Heavy.

Charlie had no vision of having a standing fight—or of even having a true fight, despite his bravado with Pearl. His only goal was to disarm his opponent. The force of the door knocked the man in the shoulder and he toppled sideways. Although he put out his right arm to break his fall, he kept hold of the gun with his left. With only one reliable leg to hold him up, Charlie let himself fall into the gangster. He grabbed the neck of the man's shirt with his left hand and stabbed at the gun with his right, but their weapons were in opposite hands and his angle was all wrong. They fell and hit the ground as one, Charlie on top. He heard the man's jaw hit the concrete. The guy's teeth clacked together. Charlie's face smacked the man's rock-hard skull.

"Jones!"

For a slow-motion blink the pair was stunned.

The family members scattered, eyes on the gun. Behind him Charlie heard a fleshy crack and a grunt. A woman squealed. He hoped this was the work of Chef, surprising the big guy from behind with her huge marble rolling pin. The crash that followed as the man went down and toppled a rack of baking pans confirmed this hunch.

Charlie recovered first. Lighter and faster, he threw his knife hand back over his body in an arc, rolling onto his left side. He threw his right knee, gaining speed, and flipped himself on top of Jones's left arm, pinning it down. With the force of a full swing behind the knife now he plunged it into the guy's gun hand.

He almost missed. The blade caught the thick fleshy side of the palm beneath the pinkie finger and went all the way through, penetrating the black rubber mat underneath. The man screamed. The gun dropped. More blood than Charlie thought possible rushed out onto the mat.

Both men tried to recover the gun. Maybe—Charlie thought a hundred times afterward—maybe the smart thing to do would have been to let go of the knife, but he held on and pressed down. Without Charlie's weight on his back the Heavy rose to his knees, awkwardly favoring his injured side, and rolled Charlie off of him. Jones slapped at the gun and it spun away. Charlie dived for it and nicked it with his fingertips. The man put his mouth over the knife handle and bit down on Charlie's clutching fingers. Charlie jerked away, freeing Jones's bleeding hand from the blade and knocking him in the teeth. They scrambled. Charlie reached for the gun with his good leg.

On the other side of the kitchen Charlie saw an obese man holding a door open while a woman in a red dress rushed out the door in treacherously high heels. A white-haired man was coming toward Charlie, stooped as if to help them on the floor. Charlie kicked the gun toward him.

The gun discharged and the whole room cowered. A pot of red sauce on the stove top exploded, and everyone took a sharp breath. The fat spotted tail of the cougar cub shot out of the kitchen toward Chef's offices. The sight of the tomato base gave Charlie a queerly disembodied sense that something unthinkable had happened to him, until the sound of the pistol spinning across the hard floor grounded him again. His eyes spotted the weapon in time to watch it glide away under the ice maker.

From somewhere behind Charlie, Pearl yelled, "Daniel, here," and the man with the white hair jumped over Charlie without seeming to realize that Jones was winding up for another round of scrambling—this time for Charlie's knife. Charlie cursed and rolled. Jones caught Charlie's bad ankle with his wounded hand and slammed it into the ground. Charlie howled.

Jones started a belly crawl toward Charlie, eyes on the knife. Charlie corrected his grip and stopped rolling away. He swiftly twisted back toward Jones, knife outstretched. The Heavy's face came up short an inch away from the blade's tip, still slick with his own blood.

Someone shouted, "Stop there!"

Neither man turned toward the command, but both froze.

"Charlie, I've got him." It was the white-haired one who spoke. Charlie thought he was the one called Daniel.

Daniel was coming at Jones with the other Heavy's weapon, holding it with his elbows and wrists cocked like a novice. At the back of the kitchen, the big man was still down, his thick cheek squashed against the rough texture of the cold floor. Chef stood over him with her gray-and-white marble rolling pin. A pretty woman in a gray pantsuit was helping Pearl toward the fat man at the door.

Charlie didn't put a lot of confidence in Daniel. Besides his inexperienced hold on the gun, his eyes were on Charlie's knife, not on Jones's next move.

"Find something to hold him," Charlie said.

Chef stepped over the fallen man and stalked across the kitchen to a long roll of plastic wrap mounted on a spool. "This'll do just fine," she said. Still holding her rolling pin, she peeled off the edge of the wrap and hauled it in an unfurling sheet back to Jones.

"Plastic wrap?" Charlie asked.

"Twist it into a rope." She demonstrated. "Unbreakable."

While Daniel stood over Jones, Charlie and Chef fashioned strong strands of plastic rope, which Charlie cut with the dragon blade before binding Jones's feet and wrists.

"You go now," Daniel said to Chef while Jones lashed out with obscenities. "If Donna's got the sheriff here, tell them it's two down in here, two to go."

"Never thought I'd be so happy to leave my own kitchen," she said, cinching the knot behind the man's ankles. "Take the wrap flat around his legs a few times for good measure. Make me feel better."

"First I'm going to wrap his mouth," Charlie said.

Chef headed out the same door the others had used.

"Come back and tell me if they found Kate," Daniel called out. "I'll bring her to you myself."

"Kate?" Charlie asked, taking the wrap around Jones's head, making sure not to obstruct the man's nose. "What's happened to Kate?"

Daniel had not put down his gun. He stepped back from Jones but in response to Charlie's question shifted the pistol slightly, pulling both men into its range. "What do you know about Kate?"

Charlie let Jones's head drop not too gently to the kitchen floor. The relief at having bested the Heavies had made him stupid. He shouldn't have said anything about Kate. He winced at the pain in his leg and chose not to say more.

"Never seen you around here before," Daniel said. "Pearl said she knows you."

Charlie didn't meet his eyes. He could only assume this man was a manager or some big mucky-muck. "I'm a recent arrival."

"I know all the arrivals. Where'd you get that knife?"

Now that Charlie's adrenaline was returning to normal levels, his ankle was killing him. Seated on the hard floor, he leaned back against the short wall between the pantry and the freezer. He wiped the knife on his jeans, which were shredded and still sticky with dried blood from the motorcycle accident.

"I'm just borrowing it," Charlie said. "Is it yours? Here. You can have it."

"It's Bruce Gorman's. You borrow it from him?"

"I don't know a Bruce. Kate left it with—"

"You with these guys? Are you the one who killed my friend?"

Charlie closed his eyes and dropped the back of his head against the wall. A murder charge at every turn? What, did he have a sign on his back that said *Pin the murder on the scapegoat*?

"No," he said. "I've never killed any—"

His words were cut short by a yell and a crash. Charlie's eyes snapped open as Daniel was knocked over by the Heavy who was supposed to be unconscious. Charlie tried to spring to his feet, but his injury took him right back down. As he watched from the floor he found the man's towering physique so impressive that he wondered if the guy had faked his own blackout.

The giant barreled into Daniel and lifted the older man off his feet before pushing him over. As Daniel absorbed the hit, he fumbled the gun and lost his grip on it. The big man saw it fly and snatched it out of the air. With his other hand he unsheathed a knife at his hip and drew it back, then sliced at Daniel's face, catching the arm of the man's glasses and tearing them off his nose. The spectacles skittered across the stove top and then hit the wall. Daniel fell.

Charlie had recovered and found his knees. He crawled toward Jones with his only idea: to place his own blade over the man's vulnerable heart and create a standoff.

He wasn't quick enough. Even if he had been, Jones's friend had the upper hand. The Heavy pointed the pistol at Charlie and held his knife at Daniel's throat. The blade was a twin to the one in Charlie's sweaty palm. Both their hands choked dragonhead hilts.

"Cut him free," he ordered Charlie. "Cut Jones loose, Charlie."

Behind the plastic wrap covering his lips, Jones's victory grin was a grotesque distortion. Charlie tried to think of something clever. The Heavy applied pressure to his blade, and a drop of blood oozed out from Daniel's jaw. Charlie began to slice through the twisted plastic.

"You're all working together," Daniel said. "There's no other way you could have both of Bruce's knives."

Charlie cut the plastic on Jones's wrists. The man sprang out of them and struck Charlie at his temple. Charlie's vision became a tunnel of humming gray stars.

Jones pulled the plastic off his own mouth, then grabbed the knife from Charlie's slack fingers.

"We don't work with his kind," Jones said.

"That blade was hush money," Brick said, looking at the knife Jones had taken from Charlie. He was samurai steady, holding the gun on Charlie and the blade on Daniel. "Don't know how it ended up here. I don't like it, Jones. Kill blade followin' us around like bad luck."

Great, Charlie thought. The knife he'd used against Jones was the murder weapon in another case.

"Which one of you killed Bruce?" Daniel asked. The knife was still at his throat.

"Brick could tell you, but then he'd have to kill you," Jones said, cutting his way out of the plastic around his legs. He had a laugh at the old joke. "What you say, Brick? Give this one a taste of his own tactics?" Jones rose and went to the spool of plastic wrap and began to yank off long lengths.

"Just take them both out," Brick said.

"The Fox wants this one for hisself."

"The Fox ain't here, and this is going south."

Jones kicked Charlie so that he fell onto the floor, then flipped him over to tie his hands.

"Do what you want with the old man," Jones said. "Maybe show him what you did to his buddy? What—he was the guy with the pawnshop, yeah?"

With confirmation that the knife at his throat was held by the man who'd murdered Bruce Gorman, Daniel shrank against the cabinet at his back.

"Why?" he said.

"Man got greedy," said Brick. "Tried cheatin' us. The better the merchandise we brought him, the less he wanted to pay for it. He thinks we're stupid, but we know he's getting paid twice for all of it. Sell it online in a fake auction, then sell it again in his storefront."

Jones lashed Charlie's legs together with such speed and force that Charlie howled.

"People in this town are the stupid ones," said Jones. "Some kid showed up right in the middle of everything thinking to tag the man's store while we was there workin' on him. Can you *believe* it? Stupid kid. Stupid, greedy people."

Charlie put the facts together quickly: Brick had killed his fence with the stolen knives, and Jones gave one of the blades to some boy who had witnessed the crime. *Shut up or we'll cut you too.* Poor kid probably didn't know they'd passed the murder weapon to him. But how had it come to the lodge?

"This one's ready for the Fox." Jones stood and kicked Charlie in the ribs.

"I'm not waiting," Brick said. "We're sitting ducks."

"Do what you want," said Jones. "The Fox is my man, and I'll get something for caging this one." He grabbed Charlie's wrists and half dragged him, half frog-marched him across the floor. "Freezer didn't work out so well for us last time. Toss 'em in here."

He opened the pantry door.

CHAPTER 43

The longer he stood in the dark, the better he could see.

"No lights," the Fox said to Hector as they met. The flashing glow of the emergency response teams made the risk clear enough.

He caught Hector's disapproving glance at the girl.

"She fell," he said. He kept moving toward the cottage that stood apart from the others.

"She's no good to us dead."

"Girl ain't dead. Till I find Charlie, no one but Coz is dead."

Footsteps crushing snow was the only sound of the Fox's progress. The precipitation was wet and thick and shifted easily under his shoes, which did fine on the blacktop of a basketball court. This terrain challenged his surefootedness of body and mind, but there wasn't any room in his head for doubt now. He could sense Hector's itch to burn some more buildings, to dislodge those bullets from his ear gauges and spit them into someone's eye.

"You feelin' me, Hector? No one."

"I feel you."

Hector caught sight of the reds and blues and pulled up short.

The Fox kept going. "What'd you think the fires were for?"

"*What?*"

The Fox spoke over his shoulder, raising his voice to a loud whisper. "You didn't think anyone was gonna notice that?"

"Them in the house! *What?* You *wanted* the law here?"

The Fox paused and turned around. He tried to remember

what it was that had first brought him and Hector together, but standing there in the cold with someone's daughter rather than his son in his arms, all he could think of was the time Hector took Coz to get inked behind his back. There were some things his brother didn't understand, would probably never understand.

"Go make some tracks."

"What?"

"That the only word you know? Tracks. Go make some runaround out there so we're not leavin' a Hansel 'n' Gretel trail."

"We oughtta be makin' us a trail right back into that hotel, Fox. We'll get snared out here."

"Got something to check out first."

"Let's check it out and then get inside."

"Tracks, Hector. Go. Then meet me where we found the harmonica."

Hector held his tongue and took off jogging, each foot landing heavily with the possibility that he might not come back.

The Fox faced the private cottage. He was only ten yards away now, and it didn't take a flashlight to see the looming shape of the rock wall that had sheltered Charlie's instrument. In front of it the ground was as smooth as an iced cake. But at the back of the cottage, the snow had been disturbed in a small area not even two feet wide. The Fox arrived at the mess and watched the snowfall gradually filling in the depressions. Someone had stood here briefly and turned in an indecisive circle, neither coming nor going.

He stood in the middle of the prints and found himself standing uncomfortably close to the wall. Shifting the child in his arms so he could free one hand, he ran his fingers over the siding. The Fox searched for a crack or a hinge or a knob, something in the rough shape of the door exposed by fire at the back of the flaming bungalow. When he couldn't locate one he started knocking on the wall. Rapping lightly, listening for a change in the sound—something solid, something hollow. If there was a distinction here his ears weren't sharp enough to pick it up. For a long time he searched this way, back and forth, widening the arc of his reach. The nearby chatter of authorities and radios increased as people gathered. He might have wasted only a minute in this effort, but time became a knife at his throat, pressing in.

For all he knew the fiery door that had popped open had been the only one of its kind. Charlie might have been inside. He might be anywhere and nowhere. The Fox dropped his frustration into the side of the house with his fist, then spun away on his heel.

A panel popped open and tapped his shoulder as he turned. It opened onto a storage room, black and windowless.

The Fox felt for the gun in the back of his pants. He lowered the girl onto the floorboards a short step up off the ground, moving aside a white cloth sack that was in the way. The space was too small for her to lie down in. He sat her up against the wall and a stack of books. She stirred and murmured.

When he touched the sack his fingers brushed an object that might have been a weapon. He opened the bag and found a flashlight among several other items. Flashlight in hand, he eased himself inside the tight space. The handle he had been seeking was inside the door, and he pulled it shut with a click, then turned on the light. He spotted the hook-and-eye closure in the top of the door and hesitated, thinking of his prints in the snow, thinking of Hector. Thinking of the cops.

He latched the door and turned his flashlight into the space. Only a few feet away from his high-top shoe was a hole in the floor that plunged some ten feet down into the ground. A chill draft brushed against his bare arms and face, colder than it was outdoors. An old army cot had been tipped against the wall to the left, and the trapdoor leaned against the far side. An iron ladder descended from the lip of the hole, which he judged to be just wide enough for him and the girl together.

On his belly he leaned into the hole and had a look. The tunnel was only a little wider than the room and stretched out farther than the beam of light. But one thing was clear: the passage aimed directly for the hotel.

The Fox got to his knees, reached for the girl, and tugged her up onto his back so that her monkey arms hung over his shoulders. He held her wrists together with one hand, crammed the flashlight into his back pocket, and prepared to enter the hole.

Kate felt the cold against her cheek, but her body was warm. She wished for a light so she could see what was happening, but she wasn't afraid of the dark. Her head hurt.

Her father was carrying her to bed. It was past time. She had been out doing things she wasn't supposed to do, and she should have been in trouble, but she wasn't. Her mother called out from far away and asked if she wanted a piece of Chef's chocolate cake. She did want it, but her voice wasn't working. She hoped her mother would bring it anyway.

He set her down, but the bed was hard and he forgot to tuck her in. Where was her pillow? The cold crept over her shoulders and seeped in where his warmth had been. *Don't leave me*, she tried to say. *Don't go.* But he was already gone.

CHAPTER 44

The group that escaped the kitchen was quickly corralled by sheriff's deputies and led to the bottom of the parking lot. Someone had brought a chair and a blanket for Pearl. They placed it under a temporary shelter erected at some distance down the driveway behind a man-made barricade. The swirling lights of fire trucks and sheriff's vehicles were causing quite a stir behind her eyes and exacerbated her fatigue. But though she grew weary of the questions, she also understood that this was the very moment, more than any other in her life, that she needed to stay alert.

The others were with her, some sitting, some standing, some milling about, all in various stages of interview. Donna and Janet, Alyssa and Olivia, Chef and her sous-chefs and the busboy Tyler, the guests Mr. Green and Ms. White—two strangers made more human to Pearl simply for having been named and granted a shared experience with her. Mr. Green's sharp personality had been blunted by his brush with fear. Pearl noticed a burn scar rippling over his ear and wondered at that story. Ms. White looked paler and thinner than ever. All but Mr. Green and Olivia, who couldn't stop chewing her nails, were draped in blankets dotted with crystal snow. The neighbor who had first spotted the fire and called the fire department had gone home to brew coffee for everyone.

Behind the glimmering gold windows of the lodge, flames still licked at the falling snow with their long tongues. Now that Pearl and the others had identified how many hostage takers were involved—two accounted for in the kitchen, two at large—the fire chief and sheriff had dispatched a handful of guarded firefighters to the burning cottages to prevent the blaze from spreading.

A SWAT team had been dispatched from Denver and was just now arriving, a swarm of dark bats quietly flapping about someone else's cave.

Pearl's sharp ears overheard someone in the distance crack a joke about Mr. Green with the knife in the dining room. No one under the canopy laughed.

Daniel and the mysterious visitor Charlie were still inside the kitchen. Kate was still missing.

Janet sobbed into Olivia's hair. Alyssa sat stone-faced apart from everyone else.

In her soft camp chair, surrounded by warm wool, Pearl set her jaw for her great-granddaughter's sake and endured questions from every direction. It was her responsibility, having witnessed as much as she had. Everyone wanted to know everything, again and again. Deputy Sawyer from the Jefferson County Sheriff, who had been to the inn just that afternoon talking to Daniel about Mr. Gorman's death, introduced Pearl to Detective Warren of the Denver PD. Apparently he had a connection to the Fox and the young Charlie Fuse. Pearl was the only one who could positively identify Charlie.

"Why hasn't Daniel come out yet?" Donna asked. No one answered her. "And what about Katherine? Why isn't everyone out there looking for Katherine! You know that man has her. You know which way he went."

"We could use your help explaining the layout of the hotel to the team, Mrs. Torrance," Deputy Sawyer said.

"I've already explained it to you," Donna objected.

"Too bad I left the blueprints in my room," Pearl said.

"They keep that sort of thing on file at the city," Donna told her.

"Firsthand information is always best," said Sawyer.

Alyssa stepped forward. "Gran, you just sit. I can do it." To Deputy Sawyer she said, "Who should I talk to?"

"I'll introduce you." He stood and extended a hand in the direction he wanted her to go. They began to walk up the hill together.

"Alyssa," Pearl called out. Her great-granddaughter turned around. "They need to know about the hiding places. Are you aware of those?"

"What hiding places?"

"And do you know about the tunnel under the Rising Sun?"

"There's a tunnel under our cottage?"

"Better let me have a word with someone, then," Pearl said.

Deputy Sawyer said, "I'll send someone over."

The pair turned away once more and left the group of stunned witnesses.

Detective Warren continued his interrogation of Pearl. "You said you spoke to Charlie while you were looking for Kate?"

"I did," said Pearl.

He held out a photograph of Charlie, who looked much younger and far less world-weary than when she'd seen him. The pain of his injuries might have accounted for that. "Mrs. Nagasawa, what did he tell you about his relationship with the Fox?"

"He said the Fox thought Charlie killed his boy."

"Did he tell you what really happened?"

"He only said that he wasn't responsible for the child's death. Except that he didn't save him. Said it like a man condemned. Is it a crime, I wonder, not to stop someone from committing a crime?"

Detective Warren was a short man, even when sitting down,

and though young he had the hunched look of a man whose spine had already been pounded down by life. His square face bore the poker expression of a man trained to withhold information, but when she asked this question he broke eye contact with her and fell silent.

When he did not reply she said, "It was a rhetorical question."

"The boy's death was brutal."

"Charlie doesn't strike me as a brutal man. For that matter, neither does the other one. The Fox. Does he have a real name? I heard someone say it was Coz. Cosimo?"

"Deshawn Johnson. Coz was his son."

"Ah, you know this man."

Warren didn't confirm it, though Pearl thought the answer was plain as day.

"Detective, I've lost a husband and a daughter. My husband's death was a grisly affair, and we only had four years together. I know grief when I see it. It's fury's kissing cousin. I suspect Mr. Johnson just doesn't know what to do with either emotion."

"Maybe you should come be a part of our profiling team." His smile was wan.

"Don't tease an old woman."

The neighbor returned with a large coffee thermos and a friend to help pump the steaming brew into paper cups. Pearl and the detective both accepted. Though Pearl couldn't tolerate the bitter black it was still good for warming the hands. The neighbor moved on to Olivia and Janet, whose sobs had become hiccups.

"So if Charlie didn't kill the boy, who did?" Pearl asked.

"As it happens, we have someone in custody. Man by the name of Joe Bright. Goes by the street name Merridew."

"Does Mr. Johnson think you have the wrong man?"

"He doesn't know we have him at all. We just arrested the suspect this evening on the testimony of a witness."

"An accessory?"

"A young woman. It's too early to say whether she participated, though her testimony so far has been reliable."

Pearl lifted the cup and let the steam warm her chapped face.

"What unfortunate timing. I guess we should let Mr. Johnson know."

"Hopefully before he kills anyone."

A commotion up in the direction Alyssa and Deputy Sawyer had gone turned Detective Warren's head. He stood to investigate it.

"Detective," Pearl said, "in the months after my husband was murdered—"

"It was a homicide?"

"Well, I don't suppose one can legally pin such things on a wild animal, but in my heart that's exactly what I did. It was sixty-four years ago. The statute of limitations is probably long past."

She gave the detective credit for preserving a patient face.

"Anyway. In the months after he was gone I spent hours in the foothills with his rifle, shooting anything that moved. And when I realized the futility of that exercise, I started leaving the rifle at home. I wanted nothing more than for the beasts to take me too."

She had regained his attention now.

"I wanted to die, Detective."

"What stopped you?"

"My daughters. They were babes at the time. One day my mother brought them to me while I wandered. The infant was wailing, and I didn't want to take her. But that stubborn woman, she forced me."

From the corner of her eye she found Donna, who was kneeling in front of Janet. "The moment I held her in my arms she stopped crying, and I never went to the hills alone again."

Detective Warren was looking uphill. He said, "I think they have one of Deshawn's men. I should go."

"I wanted to die, Detective," Pearl repeated. The man had already taken two steps away from her. "And I wanted someone else to do it for me. Do you hear me, sir?"

He stopped and turned back, listening.

"If not for my children I would have found a way. You know Mr. Johnson. What do you think he wants right now, with it being his child that was taken from him?"

The lawman put his hands in the pockets of his wool coat and pursed his lips.

She said, "I'll bet you he wants more than Charlie Fuse."

CHAPTER 45

The pantry smelled earthy and strong, like root vegetables. Potatoes, beets, carrots. Charlie lay prone, racking his mind for a way to cut his plastic bonds loose. Daniel's breathing was loud, gliding along the gray floor straight into Charlie's ear.

"There's a tunnel behind that shelf," Charlie said, finally managing to roll onto his side. Jones had secured his hands behind his back. "Behind the wall. Pearl brought me up that way."

Charlie twisted his neck to see the man's face. He was staring at the ceiling, resigned. "At least we got everyone else out."

"We'll get out too. Tunnel's right there. Don't you know about it?"

"Donna tells me nothing. Did you see Donna get out? I didn't actually make sure she was . . . I was focused on the guns."

Charlie wasn't sure which one was Donna. He did a sideways sit-up and tried rolling to his knees, but the stabbing pain up and down his right leg was unbearable. He settled for inching across the floor on hands and hip in a funny sort of crab-meets-inchworm walk. On one of the shelves was a small tower of anchovy cans. He was able to knock it over with his chin. They clattered to the hard floor, and he selected one from behind. With just a little fumbling he popped the ring tab and peeled back the lid. Fishy oil slicked his fingertips.

"Donna your wife?"

"Yes. Pearl's daughter."

"Guess if they're cut from the same cloth she'll be fine."

Daniel lifted his head and nodded. "That's quite a stink you've let loose."

The sharp edge of the sardine lid was a fair knife, slightly dull. And though the oil made it hard for Charlie to hold on, he managed to worry the plastic around his wrists with short sawing motions.

"Kate asked me to help you guys," Charlie said.

Daniel grappled with his own can of little fish.

"I basically told her to get lost."

"Why?"

Charlie weighed his answer. "I wanted to save my own skin."

Daniel raised his eyes to Charlie but didn't reply. Charlie could feel the tough twisted plastic yielding under the sharp edge. A gap opened up between his hands. He pulled harder, frustrated, fighting more than his physical bonds now.

"I just wanted someone to know the truth," Charlie said.

"In case we don't get Kate back? You wanted us to know who to blame?"

The plastic finally weakened to the point where Charlie could withdraw his wrists even though it wasn't fully severed. He freed his hands and went to work on the ties at his feet.

"I wanted you to know that she saved me," he said. "That even if I die before this is over, she saved me. And I mean—"

"Better hope she doesn't die before this is over."

"—I mean, only a kid would love people who don't know how to love her back. I never figured it out. The older I got, the harder it got."

"Kate hardly knows you. She doesn't love you."

"I was talking about the way she loves you guys." Charlie put his anger into attacking the ankle ties.

"You're right," Daniel said. "I just wish you weren't. If anything happens to that girl—"

"She'll outlive us all." The last of Charlie's bonds finally fell away. "I know a few things about the types that can survive."

"Do you? And how old are you? Have you even hit twenty yet? What do you know about survival? Have you ever had to fight for anything that matters?"

Anger and shame burned Charlie's ears. He cast the plastic away. "I was talking about Kate."

Charlie grabbed the foot of the empty shelf just above its casters and drew it back into the room. It rolled smoothly across the floor. Daniel's hands were free now. He took the rack from Charlie and pushed it all the way against its twin on the adjoining wall.

Balancing on one leg, Charlie pulled himself up, wiped his greasy hands across his pants, and reached for the false panel at the back of the wall.

It moved before he laid his fingers on it. The base scraped the floor of its own accord and Charlie helped, thinking that Pearl had told their allies about the cottage closet and the passage, and they'd come in to ambush the Heavies.

Instead the Fox stood between the men and freedom, and little Kate lay still on the cold slab at his feet.

CHAPTER 46

The sight of Charlie standing there waiting for him, all but welcoming him, so stunned the Fox that for a second all thought left his head. Over the past twelve hours the fires of his mind had consumed all of his sense until it seemed his skull was an empty chamber. For some time now he'd been numb to real anger, sensing only a smoldering, smoky heat. And then *whoosh*—the door opened and the fresh oxygen that was Charlie Fuse rushed in, and the Fox's mind combusted.

He raised the arm holding his gun and strode into the room, pressing the weapon into Charlie's forehead. The kid stumbled backward on a bad leg and hit a shelf. It shifted under his weight and rolled sideways a few inches before hitting the wall and knocking several food items off the ledge. A jar exploded on the concrete louder than a gunshot, followed by the pungent scent of brine. The Fox leaned in against the weapon and the boy's head went back, resting on the shelf. With his thumb he cocked the hammer.

The Fox would have shot Charlie without a conscious thought or word except that two things happened right before he squeezed the trigger. The first was an awareness that bloomed in his mind hotter than the fire: Charlie was the last man to see his boy alive. This punk had heard Coz's last words, seen his last expressions, watched him take his last breath, and as much as the Fox didn't want to know that account, he also wanted to experience it as a firsthand witness. He wanted to feed on every last detail of his son's death. He wanted to be with Coz, even in this way. His son's pain would be his last meal.

The second distraction was a movement in the room. A human movement behind him. The Fox ducked to avoid a blow that did not come, because the movement was not directed toward him. He spun as an aging man lunged for the open wall panel. Some grandpa was aiming for Kate, who was the Fox's only means of control over the unfolding events.

He swiveled his gun and fired at the old man. The hit took him in the leg and he collapsed, shouting. Charlie started shouting too, doubled over with his hands clutching at his ears.

"She's mine," the Fox said. Or he thought he said it. His own voice was nothing more than a vibration in his throat. The tiny room was swelling with a high-pitched, reverberating hum.

There was a door opposite the one he had entered, the kind that swings in both directions. It shook with some disturbance on the other side. A blockade was being moved.

Charlie was saying something, but the Fox couldn't hear the words.

When the obstacle on the other side of the door fell away, the faces of Jones and Brick peered in. Their guns were drawn. Jones's hand was wrapped in a dish towel. The open door seemed to give the humming a vent, and slowly the noise died down and the Fox's hearing returned. The old man was yelling.

". . . do to her? What did you do?"

It didn't matter anymore, the Fox thought. The dark world consumed goodness all the time. He went to Charlie, who was still doubled over, elbows braced against his knees, hands wrapped around the back of his neck.

"You were with my boy," the Fox said.

"I didn't kill him."

"You took him to—"

"Ender was the one who—" Charlie interrupted himself. He didn't finish his excuse. Slowly, he straightened and balanced himself on the rack at his waist. He put his injured foot on the floor and then let go of the shelf, standing on his own. The only sign of his pain was a nerve in the side of his face that flickered. He looked the Fox in the eye.

"I was with Coz," he said.

"Don't speak his name."

Charlie looked away. "I know what happened to him."

"You think I care what you know?"

The kid nodded with no way of knowing just how right he was. The Fox spoke to Jones. "What's the word out there?"

"All under control. We're just waitin' on you."

"Don't wait on me anymore. I got what I came for. You seen Hector?"

"No."

Brick said, "We seen SWAT. They're creepin' around the back."

"Phone's been ringin' out front," Jones offered.

On the floor, the old man was losing blood, but his leg wound wasn't grave yet. "Patch him up," the Fox ordered. "He's your ticket out."

"Shoot Charlie and be done with it," Brick said. "I'm not turning myself in. Whatever way you came in, we'll go out the same."

"Who said anything 'bout turning yourself in?"

Brick shook his head. "No way, Fox. The old man knows about the broker."

"What broker?"

"Pawnshop guy. Our fence."

The man on the floor moaned, "I swear I won't tell. I won't say a thing."

"What pawnshop? What'd you do?"

Jones and Brick looked at each other. Jones shrugged. "We put him out of business."

The Fox had not prepared for this contingency. In different circumstances he would have had these two brained for their stupidity, murdering a man when they could have just found another business partner. But it seemed they didn't have any brains.

"Forget it," the Fox said. "I don't care. You're on your own."

"I promise . . . ," the man muttered.

Charlie was sweating, eyes measuring the amount of blood on the floor. Jones stepped between him and the Fox. "We're your brothers, man. We never turned our backs on you. Don't you walk away from us."

"I can't walk away from anything now. Don't you get it, Jones? You the one's got to do the hard thing. Patch this man up. Answer the phone. Disarm yourselves and get this man out."

Brick said, "Leave grandpa here. I ain't riskin' it for him. Blood's on your hands, Fox. You called this down on us."

"SWAT'll shoot you on sight, second you step outside without a hostage."

Charlie cleared his throat and held out his hand toward Brick. "The knife you used to kill your fence—find some bleach and wash it up. Give it to me. I'll put my prints all over it if you promise to take this man back to his family."

Brick spit on the floor.

The kid spoke in earnest. "If he doesn't keep his word, like—if he says you're the killers, the evidence will contradict him."

Jones said, "Why?"

"I'm a dead man," Charlie said. "Why not? And you"—he turned to the old man—"you're not going to say anything about it, are you? Because these two have a hundred brothers who will hunt you down if you do."

"Of course. Of course."

The Fox could not make heads or tails of Charlie's behavior. "You're a negotiator now? You think you'll save them and I'll save you?"

"No—"

The Fox swung the butt of his pistol at Charlie's chin and opened a red cleft in it.

Charlie's head snapped back and hit the rim of the shelf behind his neck. As he recovered, he touched his fingers to the cut and looked at the blood. "I'm just trying to get everyone out alive."

"You think you stand a chance."

"No. No I don't. Not anymore."

CHAPTER 47

Charlie was surprised that they agreed to his plan, and then anxious that it would take far too long to execute. He was lightheaded, but thoughts of his next task—getting Kate out—kept him on his feet. He had no idea what he was going to do. The Fox's intention was clear. He would put a bullet in Charlie's head. When his son's life was avenged, he'd go out to face authorities with Kate as a shield. She would buy the Fox time to give a public account of his son's life and death.

Charlie could see the goose egg on the back of her head, rising up under her coarse and unruly hair. He could see his stupid harmonica sticking up out of the Fox's back pocket.

Kate stirred on the floor, in and out of sense, mumbling. Jones and Brick cleaned the dragon dagger and then let Charlie handle it, three guns trained on his head. They wrapped the knife in a towel and gave it to the Fox to plant on Charlie's body. Daniel lay still in the corner, waiting, his eyes only on Kate. Charlie realized he had no way of controlling whether Jones and Brick kept their end of the deal.

"This happens the way I say it will," the Fox said to his brothers. "I want ten minutes."

"Please," Daniel said. "Kate needs a doctor as soon as possible."

"Few minutes won't make no difference to that."

"Please."

ERIN HEALY

Fox ignored him. "SWAT's out there, you best stay in here where they've got no windows. Who has the phone?"

Jones pulled a mobile out of his pants.

The Fox backed out of the pantry onto the landing, where Kate still lay at the top of the wood stairs. He picked her up by one arm. Her head flopped around.

"No—" Daniel whispered.

"Charlie comes with me. You finish this, Brick. Do it right. Ten minutes, then make your call, tell them you're comin' out. I'll follow when I'm ready."

Charlie limped to the gaping passageway. Brick moved to close the panel behind them. The Fox put a hand on it. "You're my brothers," he said. "You know what I say is true."

"It's true, Fox," Jones said from across the room. "You're the man."

Brick nodded. The Fox withdrew, and darkness swallowed the tunnel before Charlie had taken the first step downward. He needn't have taken any at all. As soon as the last sliver of light passed out of the space, the Fox put his shoe squarely on Charlie's spine and kicked him to the bottom.

He wasn't certain whether he blacked out, but when Charlie blinked, his body had come to rest in a heap on the packed dirt. He pulled his arms out from under him and a pain shot through his shoulder. A petty hassle compared to the fire in his leg.

A light blinked on, danced around the close walls. He squinted and absorbed another kick, this time to his ribs.

"Walk," the Fox said. "Crawl if you have to."

Charlie crawled. The grit of earth stung the cut in his chin, in all the cuts that had sliced him in the last twenty-four hours.

306

"Mine's the only voice that's gonna speak my boy's name, hear?" the Fox said. "His name is—his name was Cosmos. His mama's idea. You don't deserve to know why, but there it is. I liked it well enough. Cosmos. And you? You were my boy's black hole."

Charlie put one hand in front of the other, one knee in front of the other, which dragged the dirt, and followed the bobbing yellow-sun flashlight on his horizon. The tunnel had surely lengthened since he and Pearl walked through.

"Black Hole, you are going to tell me about my son's final hours."

"I don't know how—"

"You told me you know! Do you know or not?"

"I was with him until—"

Another kick in the ribs. Charlie collapsed on his side. He wasn't sure how far along the tunnel they'd come, but he sensed they'd turned the corner. The Fox's shoes crushed clods of dirt as he pivoted in the small space. He lowered Kate and propped her up on the wall opposite Charlie. Her feet touched his outstretched arm. Then he crouched over Charlie, shining the light directly into his eyes.

"I want you to consider what you took from me. When I get back I want you to confess how you swallowed my son's light." He straightened and reached behind him, withdrew Charlie's harmonica, and dropped it on his face, striking Charlie's nose.

Kate's breath dragged along the tunnel walls, slow and heavy, measuring time and finding it short. Charlie dropped his head onto his arm. His fingers closed around the lost instrument. The present Uncle Jun and Aunt Makiko gave him when he turned eleven.

"Stay here." The Fox left Charlie and walked to the end of the passage with his light. It bounced on his stride.

Charlie scrambled to Kate's side in the dark. He cupped the child's head in his hands and whispered, "Kate? Are you awake?" She didn't give him any response. His fingers found the sticky swell in her skull. He traced the line of her round cheek and followed her bony shoulder down the length of her arm. He took her hand, listened for her heartbeat, tried to measure the warmth of her skin. He peeled off the black coat he was still wearing and draped it over her body.

A clattering echoed around the far end of the tunnel, sounds of the Fox knocking around inside of that box at the base of the ladder. Then he made a shuffling return. Charlie sandwiched Kate's chilly hands between his palms and dared not speak. The old instrument became a gift to her. He bent her weak fingers around the chrome and tucked her arm across her stomach.

"Now," the Fox said. Light on Charlie's face plunged the rest of the world into blackness. "Tell me everything you know."

Charlie started with the facts. They had taken Coz to the getaway car, then to the bridge, and then Merridew's disapproval had sent them east, toward the airport.

"None of that. I don't give a rip. I want to know how my son was. What he said, what he did. I'll get to your part later."

It wouldn't do to mention the tears, the wet pants. "Your son was . . . brave. And grown up. For his age. He . . ." Why, oh why couldn't he find words? "He told us he was twelve. He told us his name."

"Did he ask for me?"

"Yes." Charlie tried to remember if the boy had actually done it. But yes was the only right answer. "He knew you would find him. He said it."

The Fox threw something against the wall and yelled from

the bottom of his belly. A light shower of dirt rained down onto Charlie's skin. He held his tongue until the Fox said, "More."

"He tried to get out of the car, but his hands were tied. And I buckled him in."

The light jiggled as the Fox bounced it against his knee.

Charlie said, "The girl here. Kate."

"We're talking about Coz."

"Kate and Co—your son. They have a lot in common."

"This privileged doll holds no candle to him."

"They're both strong—"

"Cosmos. We're not talking about anyone else now. Hear me?"

Charlie took a deep breath. "They, he, was strong. Respectful. Courageous to . . . to the very end. Don't let two kids die like this."

"An eye for an eye," the Fox said. "Good Lord says that don't work, but I tell you, I've tried other ways and look where I am now. Girl means nothing to me."

Charlie couldn't see a way out of this.

The Fox said, "Did Coz put up a fight?"

Charlie hesitated. "It took two of us to best him."

"Why didn't you let him go? Twelve-year-old kid."

"Merridew thought he'd snitch, bring you back to our bridge."

"Merridew's your partner. The blond kid."

"No, that was—" Best not to say Ender's name, Charlie thought. "Merridew's like the head of the family. Big guy. Viking."

"I went to your bridge. Just this afternoon. Didn't need no snitch to get me there."

How? Charlie wanted to know. "Your son must've got his smarts from you."

"How would you know?" The light turned on Charlie, accusing. The passageway seemed to narrow. The scent of dirt became something frightening. "You got no idea how smart that kid was. Smart enough to talk his way out of a grave if you'd only let him try."

"Merridew wasn't interested—"

"Stop with the Merridew dude! We're talkin' about you, Black Hole, you and my Cosmos."

The Fox's voice was disembodied, his form cloaked by the blackness at the light's edges. "Tell me how Coz died," the Fox said. "Tell me everything."

"I don't know—"

"You know!" the Fox screamed.

"I ran away! I was a coward, a coward for your son. I wasn't the one who—"

"You did! You were the one! You know!"

"I can tell you what I—"

"Don't lie to me!" The Fox's voice became crazed. "Take responsibility for once in your life. Just one single time before you die! You will confess it! The whole world will know that I was right to take your life tonight! Look here! Look here!"

The Fox took his light out of Charlie's eyes, and it took long seconds of urgent straining for Charlie's sight to adjust and find what the Fox wanted him to see.

The Fox stood over Kate, his gun pointed straight down into the top of her head.

"No no, no, no no no . . ."

And more: Kate's eyes had opened. They were alert, bright and watery and catching the horrible reflection of the Fox's beam. Her fist was white, gripping the harmonica. She stared at Charlie like a trapped bird, too afraid to flutter a feather.

"Don't kill her. Don't do it. Please don't."

"Did anyone beg like that for Coz?"

The Fox was trembling. His flashlight vibrated and his voice was unsteady. "Her blood's on your hands too. Unless you confess."

Charlie held up both hands in front of him. "Dear God, man, why would you—?"

The Fox cocked the hammer.

"Okay! Okay!" Charlie locked eyes with Kate. Nerves rocked his voice. "You knew I came down here for this. You don't have to use her. I did it! Your boy is dead because I've never cared about anyone's life but my own!" He was shouting, every word screaming, *Don't kill her*. "Your son was brave. And he did exactly what I told him to. I think he thought I was going to drive away and just leave him there, you know. I didn't even cover his face, and he knelt there in that huge vast field and he looked so small . . . But . . . But . . ." It was how Charlie had imagined it so many times in the hours since he heard the gunshot. Merridew, cold. Ender and Eve, shocked. And himself, driving away, his back turned, his eyes averted. Without even so much as a *Don't kill him. Don't do it. Please don't.*

Kate blinked once, slowly, and Charlie thought the terror faded from her eyes a bit.

Something hit the dirt in front of Charlie. A spray of dust alighted on his hands.

"Take it," the Fox ordered, and he tipped the light downward to shine on the dog-eared, curling pages of an old spiral-bound notebook.

A ballpoint had been attached to the cover. Charlie reached for it. "Where did you—"

"Write it. Write down every word of your confession. I want them to know what you did to my boy."

He recentered the barrel of his gun on the crown of Kate's head.

"You have three minutes."

Charlie gathered the book to him like a hungry man hoarding food and he began to write. And as he put the pen to paper, the answer came.

CHAPTER 48

The cold was going to freeze Pearl's hip joints in place. The snow was falling more swiftly now. At least two inches had accumulated, and the skies showed no sign of letting up. One of the cottages was a total loss. The others were still smoldering. They had apprehended one of the ruffians, the one with bullets in his earlobes. Better there than in someone's body.

Donna appeared at Pearl's side and extended her hand. "Want to stretch your legs?"

"Don't you think tonight that's a bit like saying, 'Want to break your hip?'"

"Then let me rub your feet."

Donna dragged a chair close to her mother's and lifted Pearl's slender boot onto her lap. "When did you have time to put on a pair of boots?"

Pearl only gave her an enigmatic smile. She had not noticed how the recent years had lined her daughter's face. Of course, the light wasn't especially flattering right at the moment. And the light-hearted entry to the conversation quickly passed.

"You lied to me," Donna said.

"About what, the condition of my mind? Maybe a little."

"Why?"

"Have any of us been entirely honest with each other about anything, Donna?"

"For goodness' sake, what's that supposed to mean?"

"Oh, your husband pretends he doesn't need room to breathe, some fresh air outside of these walls. Your daughter pretends she's still a maiden who will be rescued by a knight. And your granddaughters act like their roles here are worthless compared to what they could be doing anywhere else in the world. That Olivia puts costume play above her responsibilities."

"It's harmless fun," Donna said.

"Her drug habit isn't."

Donna sighed. "And what is it that *I'm* guilty of pretending?"

"You never wanted the responsibility of this place." Up on the hill, the lodge glowed brighter with every fallen snowflake. "It was your father's vision. And your sister's. Never yours."

"I couldn't let it die, could I?"

"Yes, you could have."

Tonight it seemed possible to see individual flakes landing atop each other, creating delicate glassy piles of something broken.

"Your sister never really needed to *feel* needed," Pearl said. "Delilah came by hospitality naturally. It was a gift. But you, you'll pardon my saying it, Donna, but your gifts are a little more . . . administrative."

Donna's touch on her foot was perfectly firm and gentle. Warm. She didn't deny the facts.

"I thought, in your efforts to make sure the dream didn't die, you lost sight of the dream itself. Such as welcoming those who need shelter, especially those who are in desperate need of it."

"Mother, we can't just—"

"Ah. Ah. Stop. You asked me a question. Why did I lie to you? I did a little pretending because . . . I thought that if you had someone in your life who could only take from you, and never give back, maybe it would remind you of what this lodge has always been about. I thought you needed to be reminded."

Pearl watched her daughter's strong fingers knead the soft ball of her foot.

"Maybe I did," Donna said. "I still think you could have come up with a better way."

He watched Charlie tear the paper out of the book and fold it, then fold it, then fold it.

"Read it aloud," the Fox ordered.

Charlie stilled and looked up at him, squinting into the light the Fox held on his face. The rest of the world was in darkness, out of the reach of the light. The man on the ground would pay his price, finally. He stank like a gym sock and looked like the beaten man that he was—injured, dirty, sweaty, cornered. Guilty. Charlie held the paper up to the Fox, who had the gun in one hand and the flashlight in the other. He refused to budge.

"Read it now."

"The blood of Cosmos is on my hands," Charlie said without looking at the paper. "I killed him by failing to keep him alive."

A voice spoke over his in the darkness. "Deshawn."

The Fox cursed his brothers, who could be the only reason that Detective Warren had found a way down here. But he held the light steady on Charlie. No one would keep him from his aim.

"It ain't your time yet, Warren. Stand down, you'll get your turn."

"Deshawn, I just want to know if everyone's okay."

"Shut up now. Charlie and I are having a talk."

"The girl's all right?" Stubborn pig. He was going to ruin it all. "We heard she hit her head. I'm sure you're taking care of her, but if she needs a doctor I'd like to help with that."

"I'm all right," Kate said. Her announcement startled the Fox, who thought she had slipped back into unconsciousness. He cursed that too. He didn't want to hurt the kid, but it was impossible for a man to get what he needed without threatening what mattered to people. And this girl mattered, because these were self-righteous scum who thought they were better than him, who thought he didn't care about his family and didn't love his son, who would blame every bad thing in the world on his failures as if they had none of their own. He would shoot her if he had to. But it would be a whole lot easier if she didn't see it coming.

"See? She's all right."

The Fox let the light flicker over her for a brief second to pacify the detective. No need to show that the gun was trained on her. She had curled into a tight, quiet ball under a jacket, clutching her shins. Then he put the spotlight on Charlie again.

"Deshawn, thanks to an eyewitness we've arrested the man we believe shot your son. He's in custody right now."

"I got the man killed my boy in my custody. Didn't you hear him?"

"I did. But you know, I've been doing this job a long time, and in my experience a guy will say anything if you tighten the screws enough. I know you, Deshawn. I understand why you're here. Any dad would want justice for his son, and we're so close to getting it for Coz. But right now we have to make sure no one else gets hurt. You're a good man, and I need your help to make sure we don't punish the wrong guy."

"Read the rest," the Fox ordered Charlie. "Read it all so our friendly neighborhood detective can hear what you got to say."

"Maybe we could all go out so everyone can hear—"

"*Shut up!*"

His furious shout bounced off the walls but silenced the detective.

Charlie responded by putting his hands on the ground and pushing himself up with excruciating slowness. The folded confession stayed tucked between his fingers. But the Fox was surprised when Charlie took an unsteady step toward him. More surprised to feel his own pulse spike.

"Open the paper and read it," the Fox said.

"I know it by heart," said Charlie. Then he tucked the folded note into the pocket of the Fox's shirt. The Fox didn't stop him, couldn't without having to juggle the light and the gun. So he let Charlie have his way. Charlie said, "The blood of Cosmos is on my hands. I killed him by failing to keep him alive."

The words had tricks in them. They twisted and turned like a stubborn knot.

"Just say it straight. You killed my son."

Charlie closed the gap between them and leaned in close enough that when he whispered, not even the little girl at their feet could have heard what Charlie said. "I wish I could have had a father who loved me so much."

"Deshawn," the detective called out.

"We're cool," Charlie said. He pushed the flashlight aside so that blackness swallowed them both, and with his other hand he guided the Fox's gun into the bony bed of his ribs. Charlie leaned into the weapon.

"Kate's not the one who killed your boy. So if you're serious about justice, you'd better kill me instead."

The Fox didn't even have to think. He pulled the trigger.

And just as he had hoped, he heard the report of two separate shots.

MONDAY

CHAPTER 49

The pillow was not her pillow. The scratchy gown did not belong to her. The room didn't smell like the one she shared with her mother. Kate woke lost and crying. Her head really hurt.

"Shh, shh, Kathy, sweetie, I'm here."

The voice was her mother's, right beside the bed.

"She doesn't like that, you know." Alyssa's voice, but different from the way Kate remembered it. Different in a nice way.

"Doesn't like what."

"Kathy. She likes Kate."

"She does?"

"We should start calling her Kate."

"Why didn't she ever tell me?"

If Alyssa answered she didn't use words.

"Honey, are you cold?"

Kate nodded, or thought she did. Her neck was stiff. Her ears still seemed to ring with the sounds of explosions.

A blanket was drawn up around Kate's shoulders, the soft green one from home that she wrapped herself in when she watched TV alone in the evenings. This time her mother's hand held it down on her back, rubbing in small gentle circles.

Kate opened her eyes, squinting.

"Alyssa, turn down that light."

Immediately the glare became less painful.

Kate's mother sat on a stool pulled right up next to the big white bed in the big white room. A pale curtain hung behind her. Her hair was brushed away from her face in a simple ponytail. She wore no makeup. Instead of a sparkly dress she wore jeans and a sweatshirt and she smelled like . . . well, like herself. Without the hair spray and perfume.

"Hi, Mom."

Her mother smiled the prettiest smile she had ever seen.

"We've been worried about you."

A tube had been stuck in the back of her hand. A machine beside her bed beeped. "Am I in the hospital?"

"You cracked your head pretty good. They want to keep you under observation for a while."

"Is everyone okay?"

Her mother's smile faltered. "We're all good. Great-Grandma Pearl, and Gran and Grandy, your sisters . . ."

"Grandy got shot in the leg." Alyssa sat on the foot of the bed. She still wore her gray pantsuit but had shucked the jacket, and her pretty green blouse matched her eyes. Below the collar was the Siegfried and Roy souvenir pin that Kate thought Alyssa had thrown away. The white tiger's eyes glinted under the fluorescent lights. "How many candy bars do you think he'll sweet-talk Gran into for that one?"

"But Grandy's *fine*, isn't he, Alyssa?" Mom said firmly.

"He'll be walking soon enough."

Kate's mind was puzzling, trying to remember all the details and put the various pieces together, even though she also wanted to go right back to sleep. Then she remembered, and she started to cry again: "Did Grandy kill Mr. Gorman? I found his knife and was so scared."

"Kathy—Kate! No! No, he didn't do any of that!"

"Fortunately his crimes are limited to stealing."

"Alyssa, really." Their mother sighed and reached for a tissue to give to Kate.

"What? At least now I know where I get it from."

"Enough. Things are going to be different here from now on, starting with the way we treat each other and talk about each other. Am I clear?" Her eyes were on Alyssa, who glanced down at her lap.

"I only meant it's nice to think that Grandy understands. Understands me. What it's like to want something more."

"And I'm sure he'll have plenty to say to you about that, now that everything's out in the open." She shook her head. "I don't expect to escape such a conversation myself. It's been a long time since he's lectured me. I suppose we're past due."

Kate's eyelids were heavy, pulling on her mind.

Alyssa called her back. "I got you something, baby sister." Twisting around to the bed table, she picked up a magazine with a photograph of a beautiful lion on the cover and gave it to Kate.

The Wild Animal Sanctuary, Kate read.

"It's a place way out on the other side of Denver. They've adopted all kinds of wild animals, including big cats. I thought we'd go see them. When you're better."

It might be a joke. Kate didn't take the magazine at first.

"Apparently Alyssa needs a little education on the subject of wildcats, and she thinks you'd make a good teacher."

Kate bit her lip, not at all sure that a day trip with Alyssa sounded like much fun. But the wild animals were exciting. "Can everyone come?"

"Yeah. Sure. I'm not very good at saying I'm sorry, Kate. But I'd like to try."

"Frankly," their mom said, "we're both just glad to have the chance."

Kate took the magazine and opened it. The pages parted on an article about how the sanctuary had helped rescue some displaced animals after a large wildfire.

"The cottages were on fire," she said, and she closed the magazine on the photo. Her mother glanced at Alyssa.

"The firemen put those out. We only lost three. Thank God, the blaze didn't spread far, and those can be rebuilt. But you . . ." Her mother's eyes got watery. "Well. They'll let you get back home to us just as soon as you're out of the woods. Until then, I'll be right here with you." She squeezed Kate's hand.

"Where's Charlie?"

Alyssa frowned. "Don't waste your time worrying about—"

"Alyssa. He saved her life."

"Or jeopardized it, depending on how you tell the story! If he makes it out of this alive I'll do us all the favor—"

"You can hold your tongue in here or flap your lips out in the hall." She pointed toward the door. Alyssa blinked, then fell silent.

Their mother turned to Kate. "The bad man who took you is dead, Kate."

"The one with the funny hair?"

"Yes. He hurt you and he hurt Charlie."

The news made the spot right in the center of Kate's ribs ache. "He didn't hurt me. I fell. He was a little scary, but I don't think he was a bad man."

Her mother brushed Kate's hair off her forehead. "Kate, honey. What he and his gang did was wrong, no matter what the reason. He might have started hurting everyone."

"Charlie was nice. I just wanted to help him."

"I know you did. The doctors are helping Charlie now."

"Is he going to die? I don't want him to die—"

"We'll make sure to find out how he's doing."

"Is he alone? Charlie shouldn't be alone."

"Actually, your Great-Grandma Pearl said the same thing. Isn't that strange?"

TEN DAYS LATER

CHAPTER 50

Charlie was not allowed to have a phone, but Detective Warren made it possible for him to place a call. At the appointed time he brought a cell phone into the ICU and hooked the earbuds into Charlie's ears. That much was exhausting. The Fox's bullet had passed straight through Charlie's chest, shattering a front rib, penetrating his lung, and nicking a back rib on its way out. Every breath was like having his arm sawn off.

"She's in protective custody," Warren explained.

"That a fancy way of saying . . . she's in jail?"

"Besides the fact that she's got no one to bail her out, it's the safest place for her, at least until the trials are over. Hard to say how long Merridew's reach is. You know what I mean? Anyway, say what you want, but the call's recorded. Got it?"

"Yeah." Already Charlie was out of breath.

The call connected and after a short series of transfers from one secure operator to another, a timid female voice came on the line.

"Charlie?"

"Hey, Eve."

She exhaled as if she'd been holding her breath. "They told me what happened to you. You gonna be okay?"

"I ever not been?"

She laughed, a nice sound that made him smile.

"Had to call," he said. Charlie took the deepest breath his injured lung allowed. "Had to say thank you."

"For what?"

"Detective . . . Warren told me."

"I didn't do you much good, did I? I'm sorry, Charlie. Maybe if I'd said something sooner."

"You did lots of good. Merridew's . . . where he should be."

The oxygen in Charlie's nose tickled. His ears itched from the tubing and the earbuds. Every fiber in his sheets was uncomfortable.

"What made you . . . snitch?" he asked Eve. "Snitches . . ."

"Get stitches. I know. But I was on a one-way road to getting killed, Charlie, whether I snitched or not. That poor kid. He'll be in my head forever. It could have been any of us."

"Yeah."

"The guy who shot you? The Fox? He paid a visit to our bridge first."

"I heard . . ."

"Merridew all but sold me to them. And Ender—I know you two were friends, but he knew the Fox would recognize him, and he wouldn't come down to help me. The two of them would have just sat there and watched me die. Or worse."

"So . . . sorry."

"They found the Fox's gun, Charlie. The one he used to kill Drogo. He threw it in our river!"

"Yeah?"

"And they found Merridew's gun, too, the one he used to shoot the kid. They found it just twenty feet away from his body."

"It had my prints on it."

"Merridew's too—"

"No . . . He had gloves. How can they . . . prove I didn't fire it?"

"Well, because I saw it." That one stayed suspended in the air for a moment. "And you can ask Detective Warren, but when I went in I gave them the shirt Merridew was wearing. He gave it to me to wash for him, but I didn't. I think they found gunpowder on it. What do they call that stuff?"

"Gunshot . . . residue."

"Yeah, that. And the kid's blood."

"Smart girl."

Eve was quiet for a moment, and Charlie realized he missed her. He missed most of the old family, however messed up they were.

"Where is everyone . . . now?"

"No idea. Ender took off after the gang dropped by. Took off and just left me there. I got a beating for that. Merridew thought that I was covering for him."

Charlie closed his eyes.

"The others, I don't know. I went straight to the police and they took Merridew after that, and I guess everyone just split. Giggles, Star, Scratch—"

"Didn't even know their real names."

That laugh again. Like a steaming hot meal on a cold night.

"We knew yours at least."

Charlie tried to laugh too. It sounded like a wheeze.

"Man, you sound like a sorry sight."

"Sorrier than . . . you've ever seen . . . Eve."

"Dottie."

"What?"

"My real name is Dottie. Dottie Wingate. It was my grandma's name, I guess. Never knew her, but here I am. Lame, huh, to get someone's name and never know a thing about them?"

"Nice to meet you . . . Dottie."

"You too, Charlie."

"Thank you . . . again." He didn't know what else to say. Mostly he wanted to sleep.

"Guess I'll see you in court then," she said. "Though you've got a longer list of charges than I do. Show-off."

Charlie grinned. "See you in court."

CHAPTER 51

S he hated to wake him up, but it had to be done. She was too old to have to wait for anything anymore, and these people with their uniforms and loaded guns told her she could only have a few minutes. Land sakes! They guarded his room, as if the kid stood a chance of escaping them with his pinned ankle and punctured lung.

Pearl Nagasawa took a few seconds next to Charlie's bed and shook her head. The most glaring thing wrong with this picture was that the poor boy had suffered so long alone. Well, that would end today. She took a seat.

"Charlie," she ordered. She rattled the guardrail at the side of the bed. "Charlie, wake up."

He mumbled something that sounded like *make me*.

"Last time I saw you, you threatened to break my leg or my hip or some such ridiculousness. Wake up, young man, or I might add that to the long list of charges against you."

She was joking, of course. But a man who couldn't exercise his body could still exercise his sense of humor, and he *said* he'd be willing to work on that when the drama was over. So maybe it wasn't quite over yet. Pearl didn't see the point of putting it off.

"Lemme alone," he groaned.

"Can't. I've got a lot to cover in just a few minutes. Are they letting you have coffee yet?"

At the mention of coffee Charlie's heavy eyelids opened to slits, then widened slightly when they saw Pearl. His whole body put itself into the effort of helping him take a breath. "Mrs. . . . I can't remember your name."

"Pearl Nagasawa, and it can be forgiven this once."

Charlie was patting the mattress, fingers searching for the bed controls. Pearl handed him the remote.

"How's Kate?" he asked as he slowly elevated his head.

"She's coming along wonderfully. Kept her home from school this past week, got a whole roost of clucking hens fluttering about her, just the way it ought to be."

"Her head . . ."

"The girl does concussions with style. That's Kate for you. But she's more than a week in the clear now. It seems she's out of the woods."

Charlie closed his eyes and sank into the pillow.

"She has been going on about you, you know. Begging to come see you."

He protested weakly, holding up one hand. "No."

"You must prepare yourself. Because eventually we'll give in, you see. She wears us down that way. But don't worry. We'll wait until you're strong enough to stand up when she tackles you."

"The last time she and I talked . . . I didn't do what I should have."

"Clearly she doesn't hold it against you."

"I didn't know . . . I wasn't sure . . . if my life would be enough for him."

"It wasn't, of course. But I don't believe the Fox ever wanted Kate. Those SWAT fellows dropped him as fast as he dropped you. Faster even. All that newfangled night-vision technology. It only took one shot." She shook her head. "After they found the Fox's right-hand man, Hector, they unraveled the rest pretty quickly. I wish they'd been able to spare you this"—Pearl waved a hand over Charlie's chest—"but Detective Warren tells me that a shootout like that's always their last resort. I think that was what the poor man really wanted, Charlie. Revenge, yes. But mainly an end to the pain."

The young man nodded.

"You're looking a tad worse than when I last saw you, though the physicians assure me you'll be just fine."

He frowned at her. "Thought that information was confidential."

"Confidential? Charlie Fuse, you are Colorado's reigning bad boy. Nothing about you will be confidential for a very long time. Starting with the fact that it seems you are a distant relative of the Nagasawa family."

"What?"

"The media loves that sort of thing. Adds great pathos to the stories, don't you see?"

"I'm related? To who?"

"To *whom*, Charlie. To me, of course—well, not by blood but by marriage. As for Kate, though, as it turns out, the two of you have some common DNA. What? You don't believe me? Well, how else did you think I convinced your doctors to tell me how you're coming along?"

Charlie just stared at her. Poor, poor boy. He probably suspected the pain-killers.

"It seems you have an uncle," Pearl explained. "Jun Tsukino."

"What?"

"Yes, Jun Tsukino, your mother's brother. Did you forget you wrote a note to him before Mr. Johnson shot you?"

"You have the . . . note?"

Pearl looked at her watch. This was taking much longer than she intended. She really needed to get down to business.

"Your note is evidence, Charlie. The Jefferson County Sheriff has it. At least I think they're the ones . . . Never mind that. Detective Warren did provide me with a copy of it, but I've given it away."

Charlie continued to stare, more alert than coffee could have accomplished. Good.

"It gets a little complicated. Next time I come I'll bring a chart. Come to think of it, that would have been helpful now. But there it is. Your paternal grandmother married my husband's first cousin's son. Do I have that right? Yes, I do believe. Back in the late sixties sometime. See?"

"No."

"Right. It took me a little while. But you would not *believe* what can be done on the Internet these days. Olivia—you haven't met her yet but you did steal her favorite coat, so I suspect you'll find you have some common interests . . . not the drugs, I hope—well, she has been helping me with this project."

"Olivia?"

"Yes. Kate's half sister. We are indeed the right kind of family for such a one as you. Let me try again, as it can be stated a few different ways. You are my first cousin three generations removed. Wait, I mean to say that you are my late *husband's* first cousin three times removed."

"You're making this up."

"Why would I do that?"

"I don't know."

Pearl crossed her hands over the purse on her lap and weighed her response. "Fine, then. I'm making this all up. If that makes it easier for you it's of no consequence to me."

"Makes what easier?"

"At last. Down to the reason for my visit: it seems the city has filed quite a few charges against you."

He nodded.

"I didn't write them all down, never did have a head for the legalese. By the way, you should know the family has decided not to file any charges against you for the things you took from the cottage. I mean, after all, you didn't actually *leave* with any of it. Other than Olivia's coat, which is ruined, it's all recovered. Even Alyssa agreed. You have no idea what that was like."

Charlie's face was stone.

"But there's the attempted robbery of the marijuana dispensary, the destruction of property. You are likely most culpable in the kidnapping, though as I'm sure you know, your role in the homicide of the young man is still being investigated."

She didn't blame him for not looking her in the eye.

He said, "And the man in town, the pawnshop guy? Is his death on my list too?"

"Of course not. Daniel cleared that all up, and the two brutes who did it confessed."

"Why? They put my prints on the knife—"

"Idiots had you put your prints on the wrong knife. The one that had Mr. Gorman's blood on it seemed to have been handled by everyone. And apparently the sheriff has recovered some video footage of the crime."

Charlie exhaled and tipped his head back against his pillows again. He looked exhausted.

"Charlie, even with that great bit of news, you need an attorney."

He nodded again. He was a bobblehead doll by now. "Uh, last time there was a public defender."

"I'm sure they're fine people, fine and overworked. We intend to find someone for you who can give you their undivided attention." Pearl opened the purse on her lap and withdrew several sheets of paper. "Olivia helped me with this too. Look, we like these three and they're willing to talk with you. I want to know what you think."

He took the pages but now, finally, looked at her rather than at them.

"I don't understand."

"You're going to go to jail, Charlie. Do you understand that much?"

"Yes."

"We just want you to spend as little time there as possible, so that—"

"Not that part. The part about . . . why you'd help me."

"You're family."

"You just said you made it up."

"No, I think I said that it makes no difference to me whether you're actually related to us or not. The point isn't what you believe, but what we're going to do."

"This is not . . . what most families . . . people . . . would do."

"True, even of us. However, I say that taking on a murder charge in exchange for an old man's life, and a bullet for a little girl you don't even know, also fits into that category."

"I'm a terrible person. You have no idea."

"That may be, but it's time you get to know the Harrisons. We're not too holy ourselves, but we've been helping people who aren't even related to us for more than four generations. It's just that, for a little while, we forgot." Pearl stood and collected her bag. "You take a look at those attorneys' profiles and let me know which ones you'd like to speak to."

"When you first saw me . . . you thought I was someone else."

She felt momentarily embarrassed. "I didn't exactly *think* you were Kenneth. Family resemblances do show up in the oddest places. You have the structure of his cheeks and brow. But listen, if memory serves, that cousin—her name was Emi Momoi, by the way. She might have had a Western name, as Kenneth did. I don't remember. His family called him Kiyoshi. Anyway—that cousin stayed with us during the war for a while. I found her in one of the old ledgers. I'll show you sometime. She moved away a few years later, when she married. She would be your great-grandmother, as I am Kate's."

"Kate and I . . . are related?"

"Young man! Have you been listening? Yes. In its simplest translation, you and Kate are fourth cousins. Whoever hears of that kind of thing anymore these days? We just say, 'He's my relative' or 'She's my cousin,' as if that's helpful. We forget who we are, how we fit."

Charlie had covered his eyes with one hand and rubbed his brow, but he'd failed to hide his mouth, which was pressed together in an unsteady line over his chin.

"I wasn't sure how receptive you'd be to the news," Pearl said quietly.

"Mrs. Nagasawa, thank you."

"That's Grandma Pearl to you. Even though technically we're cousins. The alternatives are atrocious."

"Not Great-Grandma?"

"I'm hardly that great. You'll learn that soon enough."

Pearl made her way to the door and put her hand on the knob.

"Mrs. Na—Grandma Pearl?"

"Yes?"

"Is it possible . . . I mean . . . I wonder if I could work out . . .

some help paying for . . . all this." He indicated his broken body. "I'll work. Pay it back. Somehow."

"Hospital bills? No. I'm afraid my generosity stops with the attorney, Charlie."

He blushed. "Uh, okay. I'm sorry."

"Land sakes, boy. I do believe that I'm going to have to repeat everything we've just discussed when you regain your hearing! You wrote a note to your uncle. You remember that?"

Charlie nodded in a way that made her doubtful.

"It said, 'Uncle Jun, I'm sorry I didn't understand the value of what you offered me until it was too late.' That one—short and sweet."

"Yeah."

"Well, you can guess what he said when we finally put two and two together and tracked him down."

Charlie's laugh was nothing more than a puff of air. "Am I . . . supposed to guess?"

"No, I'll let him tell you. He's here, at the hospital right now, taking care of paperwork. We had to take turns, you see. So much red tape and unnecessary complications in your case. You really should get an address."

She couldn't resist that last bit, and she winked at him.

"You will take Jun's address this time, won't you? He's got such a lovely place. I used to pay him and his wife visits now and then, up until the last few years when I lost my own way." She opened the door wide and smiled. "Evergreen's not so small as you might remember. The family keeps expanding."

CHAPTER 52

Snow fell again after Thanksgiving, but no one complained. Most nights Kate woke to the *boom boom* of memory and a painful throbbing in her ears. The quiet of snow comforted her. It meant a day indoors, sitting in the keeping room by the fire while Chef made a stew and her mother sat next to her under the old afghans, reading a book aloud. Turned out Janet had decided she was a fan of Cornelia Funke.

But this morning Gran had said there would be time for that later. Great-Grandma Pearl wanted their help bringing in some boxes from one of the old storage rooms. Kate got there first. She stood at the back of the High Noon and faced west, liking the way the snow covered the charred ruins of the three burned cottages, muffling the disaster of it. She framed the scene with one eye closed and her fingers stretched out before her, wishing she'd brought the camera Grandy gave to her. All the white covered most of the black and turned the tragic view into something almost pretty.

Great-Grandma Pearl held Gran's arm as they came over the footbridge and onto the pea gravel path together, snow yielding to their sturdy boots. Kate wasn't truly spying, but they hadn't noticed her yet.

"We'll stay closed until spring," Great-Grandma Pearl was saying. "We can start rebuilding then. In the meantime we need a

Christmas together, really together. Because there's a good chance that afterward—I mean, who knows how much time we have? If Daniel has to go to jail . . ."

The women let the thought float away on the smoke coming out of the chimney connected to Great-Grandma Pearl's room.

Gran said, "Did you know that for a while I feared he'd actually killed Bruce? When he disappeared Saturday night and didn't tell me where he'd gone . . . Which is worse? That I lied for him or that I believed he was capable of murder?"

"I guess we're all capable of that. On some level. But he didn't kill, so where was he?"

"Fetching Olivia. Apparently she got herself into some trouble at that party and needed bailing out."

"So he stayed silent to cover for her."

"What a mess we are."

Kate's great-grandmother said, "Aren't the lawyers saying they might keep his sentence to under a year?"

"Even a year," Gran said. "What will we do without him?"

"We'll probably learn that we can get by. And that he shouldn't be imprisoned here at the lodge any more than in a cell. There's help for hire."

"I just never understood how he felt." They paused at the front of the cottage and turned to look at the trio of burned structures. "You know, yesterday Daniel took a call from Mr. Benson—the father of that boy who tried to get rid of Mr. Gorman's murder weapon here? Austin."

Great-Grandma Pearl shook her head. "I still don't understand why he did it."

"Is it so hard? Fifteen-year-olds can be brilliant idiots. He was pretty sure he had the murder weapon. With so many reasons for the sheriff to put him under the microscope, why not plant the knife on another equally likely suspect? He couldn't exactly point to the real killers."

"I heard he's been assigned some community service time for the vandalism."

"Yes, and his father wants to know if he might do some of it here."

"Here? Do you trust the boy?"

Gran shrugged. "Can Mr. Benson trust Daniel? We're all just doing our best to make things right, aren't we?"

"I'll do my part and lock my door," Kate's great-grandmother said. "So did you agree to it?"

"Daniel agreed to it. Didn't ask me."

"Ah."

"But it seems like the right thing to do. Maybe Daniel can teach him a few things."

"That is his gift, isn't it? Young people," Pearl said. "And the day is also young. We still have the Rising Sun, the Morning Glory, and the High Noon."

"Now there's a hopeful thought."

They proceeded around the side of the cottage to the back of the High Noon.

A flash of gold and gray through the trees turned Kate's head. There in the ground, just behind the thick trees, a familiar set of prints marked the fresh snow.

"The cub!" Kate called out. "It's here! The one I told you about."

"The one who ate Chef's roast?" Gran replied, appearing at the corner of the building. "I would have liked to see that animal."

"You would have had a fit to see it on the kitchen counters," said Great-Grandma Pearl.

Gran laughed. "You know it won't be able to stay here, Kate. We're going to have to call someone."

"Like a zoo?"

"More likely a preserve of some sort," said Pearl. "There's one that specializes in big cats, isn't there, Donna? South of here?"

"Alyssa is going to take me to the Wild Animal Sanctuary," Kate announced. "They have tigers!"

"A different one. Something Springs."

"Serenity Springs, I think."

"That's right. Olivia can help me look them up when we get back. We'll see what they recommend."

Kate blew into her cupped hands to warm them. "Why can't we just feed it and watch it grow?"

"It needs to be with its own kind," said Great-Grandma Pearl, resting her hand on Kate's strong shoulder. "It won't survive the winter otherwise."

Gran fished a key out of her pocket and went to the panel in the back of the cottage.

"How come this one's locked and the others aren't?" Kate asked as she waited for the compartment to open.

"This was the only one that had anything valuable in it."

"Like old treasures from the war?" Kate asked. "Jewelry and money?"

"Not quite." Gran stepped up inside. "Maybe you should have stayed at the lodge, Mother. I don't want you falling."

"Not a chance. Give me something small to carry."

Gran blew dust off the top of a large box. "It's a shame to think these hiding places were never used for their original purpose."

"A shame?" said Great-Grandma Pearl. "I think it's wonderful that no one ever had to hide from their fellow man in here. The internment camps were bad enough. What would have been a real shame is a genocide right here in Colorado. Besides—just think. Without these closets we might never have met Charlie."

Gran only raised her eyebrows at that.

"When you rebuild the burned cottages, will you put the closets back in?" Kate asked.

Gran pursed her lips and studied the stacks of boxes without seeing them. "Yes, I suppose I will. For the historic value, you know."

Over the next hour Kate, Gran, and Great-Grandma Pearl emptied the High Noon's long, narrow closet of its cardboard boxes and stiff paper tubes. They carried armloads of these back to the lodge, where they unloaded their loot into the empty dining room. Grandy and Olivia came to help while Alyssa and Janet worked together at the reception desk, canceling winter reservations, paying bills, and making appointments with heating contractors and plumbers, landscapers, and other service providers to prepare the lodge for its first closure. Chef made spiced cider and steaming potpies from the leftover Thanksgiving turkey, then promised to teach Kate how to make them the next time school was called off for a snow day.

The boxes hardly contained the treasures Kate might have dreamed up. Most of them held pictures, photographs of the lodge and the people who had visited or lived there, dating from the 1920s when Great-Great-Grandpa Harrison traveled abroad and married Ethel in New York and summered in Evergreen. Here the house was being built, with wagons of lumber being pulled up the narrow mountain road. Here was the first Christmas in the same room where they all now gathered. Here was the very first housekeeper, whose name might have been lost to time if not for Ethel Harrison's tiny, precise lettering on the back. Greta Wainwright. Here were the men who dug the tunnel, men who had dug many tunnels to save lives and swallow others in World War I. The land had changed over the years, trees standing down to the arrival of new neighbors. Here was Evergreen then and now: the lake's boathouse, the warming house, the ice skaters, the loggers, the celebrities.

The family spread the photographs out on the tables, which still wore their white tablecloths but little else, and those who knew the stories—mostly Great-Grandma Pearl but occasionally Gran and Grandy and even Janet—stopped whatever they were doing at the time to tell them.

Kate sank into the history and had no desire to rise out of it. "Did Siegfried and Roy ever visit here?" she asked no one in particular.

Grandy laughed and Gran slapped him on the arm. Great-Grandma Pearl said, "That's doubtful. I think I would have remembered them."

Kate picked up a picture of Great-Grandma Pearl and Great-Grandpa Kenneth planting roses at the front of the house.

"Watch your fingerprints, Kate," said Gran. "These things are the originals."

"We should have copies made," Grandy suggested.

"Oh! Look at this!" Great-Grandma Pearl lifted a print into the air. "I do believe this is Emi Momoi—Kenneth's cousin. Yes, someone wrote her name on the back. Wonderful. We'll set it aside for Charlie. That boy's a doubter."

"We should write down the stories so everyone can read them," said Kate. "We could put them on our website."

"Now there's a fine idea," Pearl said.

Gran wiped smudges off a gilded frame with a soft cloth. "I'm sorry I ever took these down," she said. She held a family portrait.

Kate pushed Gran's arm down so she could see for herself. By now she easily recognized Great-Grandpa Kenneth, frozen in time, almost the same in this photograph as he was in the frame Great-Grandma Pearl kept in her room. A young woman stood next to him, holding a swaddled infant. A little girl stood between them, holding Kenneth's hand.

"That's me." Gran pointed to the baby. "And your great-aunt, Delilah. My word, I never realized until this moment how much you two look alike."

Pearl was taking the lid off of a deteriorating file box. "Oh yes, I've seen that forever."

"What makes memories unbearable one day and life-giving the next?" Gran asked, staring at the image.

No one answered that.

"Look here," Pearl said. Grandy stooped over her shoulder and looked into the box. "Old newspapers. I wonder if Charlie would be interested in these?"

"Why would he be?" asked Gran.

Grandy picked up a newspaper and held it up. The brittle pages were filled with columns of Japanese characters.

"The *Rocky Nippon*," Pearl explained. "And here, the *Colorado Times*. These were issued bilingually for years. Kenneth collected them for his family to read. He was a huge fan of Jimmie Omura's articles. A fine journalist by any standard."

They were interrupted by Janet, who came in from the reception desk holding an unfolded letter and its sliced envelope. "Mother, a letter from Mr. Reginald Green."

Gran groaned. "Our most unfortunate guest ever. Along with that wisp of a woman. What was her name?"

"White," everyone chimed in.

"Mr. Green is still unhappy about his visit," said Janet.

"I think that poor man will be unhappy for the rest of his life," Gran said.

"He writes, 'I hope your continued neglect won't force me to spread negative reviews about the criminal goings-on in Evergreen and, in particular, at the Harrison Lodge.'"

"Continued neglect?"

"He's asking what we are going to do to make their 'disastrous stay' right for him and Ms. White."

After a pained silence, Great-Grandma Pearl started to laugh, and everyone in the room soon joined her. Gran laughed harder than anyone.

"I guess we're going to have to give them a full refund," she said. Gran cast a sidelong look at Kate. "And throw in a free night if they'd like to come try us again. How does that sound, my wise child?"

"I don't think they should stay here for free," said Kate. "If I were you I'd pay for them to go somewhere else."

CHAPTER 53

That night as Janet tucked Kate into bed she sat atop the blankets and gave her daughter a photograph.

"That's you," said Kate. "You always look so pretty. Who are the others?"

Her mother pointed. "These are your sisters."

"They're so little!"

"Alyssa was as old as you are now in this shot. Olivia was nine. And that's you. You were only a month old."

"And that—" Kate pointed to the man beside her mother, handsome but unsmiling.

"That's your father. His name is Bill Roland. Gran had it put away with the others."

Kate stared at him and felt nothing. No connection to the father she had never known. The empty feeling came as a disappointment.

"I am sorry, Kate. I'm sorry for leaving you when you were so little. I thought you'd be better off here without me—one of many mistakes I will spend the rest of my life trying to correct."

"It's okay."

"You can keep this, all right? It's yours. Do whatever you want with it. And whenever you have questions, you can ask me anything, okay?"

"Okay."

Janet looked at her expectantly. "I'm sure you must have questions."

"When will I get to see Charlie again?"

Her mother smiled and her shoulders relaxed. "Probably not for a while. But you will see him again. I promise. Lights out in ten minutes, all right?"

"Yeah."

"I'll be out here watching some TV. Tell me if it's too loud."

Kate thought it would be impossible for her mother's presence ever to be too loud.

"Good night, Kate."

"Good night, Mom."

When her mother's form left the doorway, Kate rolled off her bed and pulled her footlocker of treasures out from underneath it. Grandy had brought it up for her before nailing down the trapdoor in the secret closet. She had no desire ever to go into the tunnel again.

Kate placed the picture of her family and Bill Roland inside, then withdrew the shiny harmonica that Charlie had pressed into her hand the night he was shot. The chrome surface smudged easily, and she rubbed her prints away with the cuff of her bedsheet. Then she closed the locker's lid and pushed it back under the bed frame.

Out in the Rising Sun's tiny living room, she heard her mother having a conversation with Olivia, who had broken up with her boyfriend and was having a lot of drama about it.

Kate put her lips to the instrument's edge and blew the softest note she could imagine. A single note that managed to sound like three notes perfectly matched. Not a harmony. Just a happy coexistence.

She turned off the light and pushed the harmonica under her pillow, and sleep came quickly, lullabied by the voices of her family.

Sometime in the night her mother covered her with an extra blanket.

ACKNOWLEDGMENTS

This book, like each one before it, was brought to light by my own family of pros and sages (who are nothing like the dysfunctional relations of this particular tale). "I thank my God every time I remember you."

- Agent Meredith Smith and the staff at Creative Trust
- Publisher Daisy Hutton
- Editors Ami McConnell and L. B. Norton
- The entire Thomas Nelson Fiction and HarperCollins Christian Publishing teams
- My beloved husband, children, parents, siblings, aunts, uncles, cuzzies . . . and niece
- Readers extraordinaire, especially those of you who keep checking in with me. Yeah, brothers and sisters, you know who you are.

DISCUSSION QUESTIONS

1. *Hiding Places* is a story about families—some related by genes, some brought together by circumstances or values. What longings cause people to gravitate toward family structures even if they've experienced pain or betrayal?

2. Charlie tells himself he doesn't need anyone and claims he joined Merridew's street family for practical reasons—a place to sleep, help buying food. What do you think the real reason was?

3. Kate's childlike instinct is to protect her family even though they don't protect her. What informs families' assumptions about the "right" or "wrong" ways to care for each other? What factors make families vulnerable to breakdown?

4. Why do family members hide personal truths from each other?

5. What makes young children such a powerful force in a family unit? Consider Coz's role in changing the Fox's life, and Kate's relationship with Pearl.

6. Pearl's grief over the deaths of her father and husband eventually became a wedge between her and her children. Do you blame her for her poor relationship with Donna, Daniel, and Janet? At what age do children become equally responsible for their part in the relationship with their parents?

7. What's your opinion of Pearl "playing crazy" as a way of teaching Donna the value of serving someone else's needs?

8. Pearl understands the Fox's behavior because she sees herself in him. Is it possible to experience grief without harming the people closest to us?

9. What is the glue that holds families together? Loyalty? Blood? Purpose? In *Hiding Places*, which "family" has the strongest glue?

10. Charlie is transformed from a man who shirks responsibility for others into a man willing to intervene for strangers. What transformed him?

11. Was Kate's love for her family naïve or exemplary? How would you characterize it?

12. Is the human desire to belong to a family unit selfish or selfless?

GUILT MIGHT BE THE MOST DANGEROUS MOTIVE OF ALL.

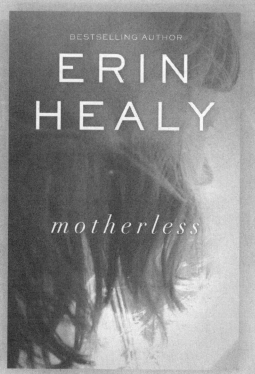

BESTSELLING AUTHOR

ERIN HEALY

motherless

"*Motherless* by Erin Healy is a mesmerizing story about secrets and the lies we tell ourselves. If you loved *Gone Girl*, you will gobble this one up. Highly recommended!"

—COLLEEN COBLE, *USA TODAY* BESTSELLING AUTHOR OF
THE INN AT OCEAN'S EDGE AND THE HOPE BEACH SERIES

DON'T MISS THESE OTHER NOVELS BY BESTSELLING AUTHOR

ERIN HEALY

"DEKKER AND HEALY FORM A POWERFUL TEAM IN CRAFTING REDEMPTIVE SUSPENSE."

—LISA T. BERGREN, AUTHOR OF *THE BLESSED*

AVAILABLE IN PRINT AND E-BOOK

ABOUT THE AUTHOR

PHOTO BY MICHAEL HEATH

Erin Healy is the bestselling coauthor of *Burn* and *Kiss* (with Ted Dekker) and an award-winning editor for numerous bestselling authors. She has received wide acclaim for her novels *Never Let You Go*, *The Promises She Keeps*, *The Baker's Wife*, *House of Mercy*, *Afloat*, *Stranger Things*, and *Motherless*. She and her family live in Colorado.